RICHLAND STREET

RICHLAND
STREET

A NOVEL BY

Kevin O'Kelly

Miami · Florida

Library of Congress Catalog Card Number: 96-61466

O'Kelly, Kevin
   Richland street : a novel by / Kevin O'Kelly
   283 p. ; 21 cm
   ISBN 0-9653864-5-7
   I. Title
813'.54—dc-20   96-61466

Designer: Tom Brady

Printed in the United States of America
10 9 8 7 6 5 4 2 1

This book is fiction—it's made up. If some of the characters seem familiar, or some of the events seem like things that really happened, it's because, as the Preacher said, there's nothing new under the sun.

ISBN 0-9653864-5-7

SONG CREDITS

To N.P.

1

I STARTED OFF this week in my own bed. When I woke up Monday morning the old Westclock on the dresser said 7:15, but I knew that wasn't right; that clock hadn't been wound up since school was out two months ago. I figured it was between nine and ten o'clock. It was getting hot. My room's the coolest one in the upstairs of the house—it's on the northwest corner—but it can still get pretty damn hot in the summertime. I've got this little old oscillating fan on the dresser that blows air back and forth across my bed. It does a pretty good job of cooling, but nothing like those big pedestal floor fans they have down at the Jacksonville Naval Air Station. My room does have a real high ceiling that's supposed to make it cooler than it would be otherwise. All the rooms in the house have high ceilings, because the house is old and that's the way they built them back then before they had electric fans to keep people cool. Our house is one of the oldest in Columbia, built in 1796.

I dozed off again for a couple of minutes. Then I came to, thinking about what a big disappointment, when you get right down to it, that trip to Jacksonville was. I didn't want to think about it. So I got up and pulled on a pair of bluejeans—no shirt, no shoes—and traipsed on downstairs to the kitchen.

"Well, well, look who is here." That's the welcome I got from Agnes, who was sitting at the kitchen table, her back to the screen door, shelling field peas. She had a big pile of greenish brown pea pods on the table in front of her and a colander in her lap. As she talked she would run her fingers up and down the husks, splitting them open so the peas would fall into the colander, and drop the empty pods into the trashcan on the floor beside her chair. "It sho was nice while you was in Jacksonville."

I picked up the newspaper that Momma had left folded on the table across from where Agnes was sitting and glanced at the headlines. Agnes's mouth kept on running.

"I guess we has just got to put up with you now. I sho am sorry your momma ain't gonna send you off to Jesus School like she was talking about."

"Christ School," I corrected her.

"B-29s Pound Korea Reds," *The State* headline said. I turned to the sports page. The Columbia Reds got pounded too: the Greenville Spinners beat them seven to one. Now they were eleven games out of first place in the Sally League.

"She ought to send you to one of them military schools, like The Citadel down in Charleston."

"That's a college. You gotta finish high school first." I put the paper down and lifted the top off the double boiler on the stove.

"Well you ain't never gonna finish high school at the rate you is going. That hominy's warm and the bacon in the frying pan's cold. You know what time it is? I ain't gonna put down everything I'm doing and cook you no egg. If you want a egg, you gotta cook it yourself."

I didn't want an egg. I helped myself to the grits and crumbled up three strips of cold bacon and stirred them into the hominy along with a glob of warm butter I scooped up from the dish on the table. Then I went to the Frigidaire and took out an Edisto Farms Dairy bottle and poured myself a glass of milk. I sat down at the table upwind from the fan blowing on Agnes. I couldn't stand the smell of nigger sweat.

"It's a blessing your poor poppa can't see you now. With you getting expelled from school and all."

"Aw go on, Agnes. They let me back in the next day."

"They sho did. But your poor momma had to take off from work so she could go to Wardlaw school and ax them to take you back. You oughta be ashamed of yourself, causing Miz Palmerston all that trouble. You is just shiftless, lazy and no 'count."

I have to admit that I caused Momma some trouble last year. Last year was not too hot for me academically. Ninth grade was tough, but I *did* pass, just barely. Agnes doesn't know anything about academics. She just doesn't like me. Back in the eighth grade when I was making almost all A's and was in the Junior Honor Society she used to say I was fat and lazy and good for nothing. At least she can't call me fat now. I weigh the same now that I weighed in the eighth grade and I'm six inches taller: nearly six feet tall and around 135 pounds. Kind of skinny, actually.

What Agnes can't stand about me is that I don't work. I just don't like to work, even though my best friends work: Browder has a paper route and Snake cleans out the Lance peanut-butter cracker company office three times a week. Browder has to work but Snake doesn't: his old man can afford to give him an allowance. Momma doesn't have to work, but she does. She's the assistant director of the Richland County Health Department. She used to be a nurse; that's how she met Poppa, when he was working in a hospital in Atlanta right after he finished medical school. Poppa left Momma enough money—insurance and all—that she didn't have to work.

Poppa got killed in the war; a German rocket bomb hit the hospital he was working in in England. I was nine then; I'm 15 now. Anyway, Momma's got money in the bank and she's got this house, free and clear since my grandmother Palmerston died three years ago. Agnes came with the house. She's been working for the Palmerstons since the Confederate War. She doesn't live here though; she lives right down the hill on Pulaski street and walks to work every day—unless it's raining, when somebody has to go pick her up. I'm supposed to drive her home every day at

5:15 if I'm around. I've been doing that for a year and a half now, since I got my driver's license the day I turned 14. Chauffeuring old Agnes and running errands for Momma's about the only work I do. I like to drive and I don't mind Agnes's bitching; I'm used to it. I ought to be.

Anyway, Momma and I have been living here since the war—with Grandmomma Palmerston until she died three years ago. Grandmomma Palmerston and Momma didn't have a whole lot in common, I don't think. Grandmomma Palmerston was a high-church Episcopalian and Momma came from this little town in north Georgia, Jalapa, where she was raised a Methodist. I mean Momma says her people were Methodists but from what I've seen of them they really don't put much stock in churches and religion and stuff. Religion was a big deal with Grand-momma Palmerston—religion and social standing. You see, this neighborhood was high class before the Confederate War; it's been going down hill ever since—except that the governor of South Carolina still lives here, across Richland street, about half a block from us. I could throw a rock and hit the governor's mansion from my bedroom window, if I could throw worth a damn.

Grandmomma Palmerston had to quit going to church when her arthritis got real bad during the war, but Momma and I used to go a few times a year just to please her—to the Good Shepherd Episcopal Church on Blanding street. One thing Grandmomma Palmerston did, the summer before she died, was send me to Kanuga, the Episcopal camp up in the mountains of North Carolina. It was o.k.—not too religious—and I really liked riding the horses up there. That's where I got to know Snake, only they called him Zack back then: Zachary Taylor McBain, Jr. Snake lives in Shandon where the cream of Columbia society lives today, only Snake's not real wealthy: his old man's in the insurance business.

Well like I said, Kanuga's where I met Snake. (Actually I *met* him on the train going up to Kanuga, in the railroad car at the end of the train where all the Columbia boys that are going to

Kanuga ride.) He's a year older than me and I guess he outgrew Kanuga that summer. He never went back and I didn't either. Momma said she'd send me back if I wanted to go, but I said I wasn't interested. After Grandmomma Palmerston died we just kind of quit going to church too—Momma and me. Although Momma did start up again for awhile last year when I was in the ninth grade and having all that trouble in school. She got to talking to the pastor at Good Shepherd and he was the one who gave her the brilliant idea of sending me off to Christ School, which is also up in the North Carolina mountains somewhere near Kanuga. But she really didn't want to do it—send me off to school—and I promised her I'd behave myself and work real hard at Columbia High next year.

I'm telling you that was a relief: being assigned to Columbia High and knowing I'd be getting the hell out of Wardlaw Junior High School. Junior high's o.k. for the seventh and eighth grades—like it used to be—but there was no call for them putting the ninth grade at Wardlaw which they did for the last two years. A real stupid move. But this year they went back to putting the ninth grade in high school where it belongs. Until the dramatic events of this week began to unfold, it looked like I'd be going to Columbia High next month and so would my buddies who flunked the ninth grade at Wardlaw—like Browder.

Just as I finished breakfast and finished reading the funny papers, I heard Browder hollering for me outside.

"Cap! Clarence Algernon Palmerston, Jr.! Come out here!"

"Keep your shirt on, Browder, goddammit! I'm coming." I glanced at Agnes as I got up from the table. It drove her loco for me to cuss like that. She didn't even look up but just mumbled something and kept on shelling those field peas.

I opened the kitchen screen door and waved for Browder to come on in. He was halfway up the driveway leaning on his bike. "So how was Jacksonville, old buddy?" he asked as he parked the bike on the grass.

"Real interesting. Come on up to the room and I'll tell you about it." As we passed through the kitchen old Agnes was still mumbling and shelling those peas. She was talking to herself; she talks to herself a lot.

"Hello Agnes," Browder said, but she didn't pay him any mind, just kept mumbling to herself. She doesn't like Browder or any of my friends—except Snake. She thinks he's high class.

Browder went ahead of me up the stairs taking them two at a time. He's kind of nervous. I don't mean like he's scared but like he's got a lot of nervous energy. When he walked into my room he picked up my catcher's mitt off the dresser and began pounding his fist in it. Whop! Whop! Whop!

"Hey Browder, you got some fags?" I asked as I closed the door. "I smoked my last teege last night on the bus back from Jacksonville."

"I got a couple." He pulled a smushed pack of Luckies out of the front pocket of his bluejeans. The two cigarettes in it were practically flat. I took the one he offered me and reached into the top drawer of the dresser and pulled out my Ritepoint lighter and Wade Hampton Hotel ashtray. Momma knows I smoke but I don't smoke in front of her and I don't leave cigarettes and ashtrays and things out in the open in my room.

Browder sat down on the edge of the bed and I handed him the ashtray. Then I gave him a light. He inhaled a big gulp of smoke; he was excited. "Hey Cap, I saw Daniel Sellers last night. He can get Sandburg."

"I've heard that before." I settled into the straight chair and tilted it back against the window sill.

"Naw, no shit." He threw his head back and blew a stream of smoke at the ceiling. "Her old lady's letting her go out again. She can go to Wednesday night prayer meeting. Can you get your car?"

"Maybe. How do you know she won't be on the rag?"

"She won't because she was last Wednesday. Calhoun and the Eau Claire crew picked her up in his station wagon. She jacked them off. Old Calhoun shot off all over his new tailor-mades —that he bought from Lackey's right before school was out."

That put me in stitches. "Old Calhoun," I said, laughing my
fool head off, "he's the only boy I know who'd wear tailors to a
gangbang."

Browder thought it was funny too. "Maybe he *had to* dress up,
to make his old lady think he had a respectable date. So he could
get his car."

I knew I could get my car Wednesday night. Momma doesn't
mind me going out on weeknights when school's out and she
hardly ever needs the car at night herself. I could tell her I was
going to the Columbia Reds game. I hoped like hell Sellers wasn't
lying and he really could get Sandburg. If anybody could get her,
I thought, Sellers could. He lived just a couple of blocks from her
and didn't mind going up to her house in broad daylight and
sitting on her porch and talking to her or her old lady. He's the
same age as she is—Shirley Sandburg, not her mother. Sellers is 14
but he doesn't have his driver's license. Even if he did he
probably couldn't ever get his car because his old man is always
going out in it at night. Sellers's old man is a real whorehopper
—talks about it all the time, Sellers says—and his old lady doesn't
seem to mind. Sellers's old man's got some dirty Victrola records
that Sellers played for me and Browder one time. One song was
about a woodpecker pecking in my backyard and how the hell he
keeps his pecker hard.

I got real excited thinking about picking up Sandburg. The
reason I did was because here I was, 15 years old, and I'd had my
driver's license for almost a year and a half and I'd never had a
piece of ass. Browder hadn't either.

"Well I can get my car Wednesday night; I'm sure of it. Sellers
just better be sure he can get Sandburg."

"He is," Browder said real serious, and then started grinning.
"But if something happens and he can't get her, we'll just go
screw Grandma Caldonia."

"Like hell we will. You know who Grandma Caldonia
reminds me of? Miz Sumter, the math teacher."

"Well she does favor her some," Browder agreed. They both were about 65 years old with short gray hair and both built like professional wrestlers.

"Hey you remember that time in the seventh grade when old lady Sumter almost hit Alvin Garfield over the head with that desk chair?" We both got to giggling like girls.

"Old Alvin said something Miz Sumter thought was sassy," Browder remembered, "and she grabbed that big old desk chair —must've weighed 40 pounds—and swung it up over her head like she was gonna bring it down on *his* head."

"Old Alvin threw up his hands," I chimed in, "and hollered: 'I'm sorry! I'm sorry! I apologize! I apologize!' The whole class was bug-eyed and scared shitless. That's one mean white woman, Miz Sumter. And Grandma Caldonia reminds me of Miz Sumter. I wouldn't no more want to fuck Grandma Caldonia than old lady Sumter. Besides, it costs money to fuck Grandma Caldonia. Hey, how much does she really charge?"

"Weelll...I usually gets five dollars for my dates." Browder did one of his best female impersonations; it was hilarious. "You can jew her down, though," he added, half serious. "But you don't need to, Cap. Your momma'll give you five dollars. I'll just go along and watch."

"Like hell you will." We were both guffawing like maniacs. I almost fell out of the chair I was leaning back in.

"O.k. I'll just run over to the State House and roll me a queer and get the larsh to screw Grandma Caldonia." The State House—the state capitol—is only a couple of blocks from where Grandma Caldonia hangs out, at the Soda Arcade on Main street. All these queers congregate on the south side of the State House around the steps facing Lower Main street after sundown every day.

"Why don't you just let one of them suck you off for five dollars?"

"Because they only give 50 cents to suck you off. You have to suck *them* off to get five dollars."

"Bullshit. I heard there's this nigger queer who'll give *ten* dollars to suck a white dick." Funny thing about the queers at the State House: that's about the only place in South Carolina that's not segregated. They really *do* have interracial mingling at the State House.

"Naw," Browder said, "not ten dollars. You know what Harry Wald does, and he'll only give you five dollars."

"Ach! I giff you five-ff dollars." I did my German impersonation; Harry Wald's this old German fellow who hangs out at Breedin's drugstore across from the Jefferson Hotel. "I giff you five-ff dollars und I brown you three times."

Browder about doubled over laughing. "Cap that's great! You oughta be in Hollywood. I can't believe they kicked you out of the Wardlaw Junior Theater..." Then he remembered: "Hey, you haven't told me about Jacksonville."

"O.k., I will. But let's get outta here. Let's go somewhere."

"Where you wanna go?"

"I don't know."

"Well, how about the green hole? Let's go to the green hole."

"Sounds good to me. You wanna bike it?"

"Naw, let's hoof it across the trestle."

2

I LIKED GOING to the green hole with Browder. Browder and I have been good buddies since the fourth grade at Logan Elementary School. That's when he saved my ass when three boys ganged up on me. He's a natural-born fighter, old Browder. (They called him Billy at Logan; his real name is Robert William Brown.) Browder's a little shorter than I am but he weighs more, and it's all muscle. He didn't shoot up six inches in one year like me, but grew a little each year and filled out gradually. He's strong as hell and fast. To be a good fighter you've got to be strong and fast. Me, I'm neither one. But I've got endurance and I can take a lot of punishment. Nobody's ever knocked me out in a fair fight or made me holler for mercy—not since grammar school anyway. I haven't won many fights but I haven't lost many either. Old Browder's never lost a fight and nobody's ever even fought him to a draw—that I know of.

Browder gave one of his best performances just before I left for Jacksonville. We were cruising up Main street in Momma's '49 Plymouth—Browder was riding shotgun and Radar and Sellers were in the back seat—and we picked up a drag race with this '49 Pontiac six. It had a Blue Devil sticker on the back window so we knew they were from Dreher High; there were four boys in the Pontiac. Well the old Plymouth ate up that

Pontiac on the get-off, as you'd expect. When they caught up with us at the next light, Browder stuck his head out the window and hollered: "That Pontiac sure is a sorry piece of shit—just right for a bunch of Dreher queers!"

This boy in the back seat leaned out and yelled back, "Who the hell you calling a queer?"

"I'm calling you a queer, Dreher queer," Browder answered, real mean like.

"I'm gonna beat your ass," the Dreher boy hollered back. Just then the light changed to green and the Pontiac hooked a quick right onto Hampton street. I was in the left lane, but I cut across anyway and swung in behind them. (There wasn't any traffic; it was around midnight.) I put on my bright lights and started riding their bumper. We kept yelling at them and giving them the finger. After a few blocks the Pontiac pulled into an alley off Pickens street and stopped. That boy in the back was out of the door before they quit rolling. I pulled up behind them and Browder jumped out.

That Dreher boy came out in a crouch, posing like he was Marcel Cerdan or somebody. Old Browder just tore into him like a wild man, swinging those big fist of his so fast you could hardly see them. You couldn't see too much anyway since the light was pretty dim, just what was given off by a street light on Pickens street. Anyway, that Dreher boy never got a chance to size Browder up; he came under this barrage of fists a split second after Browder jumped out of the car—Browder moved that fast. The other fellow never even had a chance to fight back; the only thing that kept him on his feet for about ten seconds was Browder hitting him. Really. Browder's left would send him reeling in one direction, then his right would straighten him up and send him in the other direction. That's what it would've looked like in slow motion; mostly what we saw was a blur, but we could tell that Browder was working him over like a punching bag. Not that all of Browder's punches hit home: you could tell that some just glanced off that cat's shoulders or forearms—which he managed to hold up in front of his chest and face for a pretty good while. But with all the punches that Browder threw there were enough good ones to pulverize the poor bastard. When he finally crumpled to the ground, Browder backed off. He tried to get up but he could only get up on one knee. You could tell he was so dazed he didn't know where he was at. So Browder looked at the other Dreher boys and said, "Y'all pick up your buddy and go on home." And they did.

Dreher boys generally don't know much about fighting. They think fights are like they are in the movies or like the boxing matches you see in the newsreels. They don't see too many real fights. Out in Shandon when two boys get into a fight it's more like a cussing and shoving match, like little children. If they ever get around to throwing any real punches, they act like they're in some kind of athletic contest. One cat swings and the other cat either takes the blow or dodges or blocks it; then it's his turn to throw a punch. It's like a damned tennis match: the ball's in your court, old chap. Those Dreher boys just don't seem to have the instinct to haul off and beat the living shit out of somebody. You develop that instinct watching real fighters in action—boys like Marvin Grange or Greek Karras or Jimmy Barnes or Willard Smoak—north Columbia boys. Out in Shandon they don't have boys like that to set the example. They just don't know much about fighting at Dreher High.

Take Snake for example; he goes to Dreher. He's a good old boy but he doesn't know the first thing about fighting. He can do other things though. He's one of the best pool players in Columbia for his age (16) and he's got to be one of the best drivers in Columbia no matter what age. I can't tell you how many cops he's outrun. What he does is shake 'em, because that '47 Mercury he drives is not fast by any means. Old Snake's got great reflexes and great concentration; and he notices things; he always knows where he's at. He can outfox anybody; he'll cut across a lawn or drive that Mercury through somebody's backyard to lose somebody that's chasing him. He can slither out of anything; that's why they call him Snake. If a cop ever *did* catch him, Snake would talk him out of giving him a ticket, because that boy can make up the damnedest lies you ever heard and tell them with such a straight face and act so sincere that you'll believe him. Like I said, Snake's got a lot of talents, but he's no fighter.

I don't know why I was thinking about fighting when Browder and I started out for the green hole. The last thing I wanted to do that day was get into a fight. Actually, the mess I was about to get into would be a lot worse than any fight I'd been in up to that time.

I put on some Keds and a T-shirt and we went back down to the kitchen where I grabbed a half loaf of bread and a couple of cans of vienna sausages, over Agnes's objections, and stuffed them into my Boy Scout knapsack along with an army-surplus canteen full of cold water and two bathing suits. Browder didn't want to go back to his house and pick up his suit so he borrowed one of mine. Sometimes we just swim in our shorts at the green hole—or go naked—but you never can tell who might show up. Mrs. Grant, the truant officer at Columbia High, went out there one day before school was out and caught some boys who were playing hooky—and were naked as jaybirds. You never can tell what might happen. If it's convenient to wear a bathing suit I always wear one.

First we headed for W. W. Fogel's store on Calhoun street to buy a couple of Pepsis and some fags. We went there because old man Fogel will break a pack and sell you cigarettes for a penny apiece. Browder and I decided to buy ten Pall Malls—even though we both usually smoke Luckies—because Pall Malls are longer and you get more for your money when you only have a dime to spend for fags. We had 60 cents between us but the Pepsis cost seven cents apiece plus two cents deposit on each bottle and we wanted to save some money for cakes and more bellywash later in the day.

We walked along Calhoun and Wayne streets under the shade of big willow oaks to Elmwood avenue where we turned left and crossed the Seaboard railroad tracks and trudged up the hill past the main entrance to Elmwood cemetery and then descended towards the river walking in the hot sun along the edge of the cemetery. The grass had just been mowed and the humid air was heavy with its sweet fragrance. The cemetery's wrought-iron fence ended with Elmwood avenue's pavement as we neared the Southern Railway tracks. Grass gave way to weeds and when we'd crossed the tracks we were on the edge of Potter's Field.

Two colored men were digging a grave. One was leaning on a shovel and the other was in the hole chopping with a mattock. "They must be fixing to electrocute some nigger down at the penitentiary," Browder observed. We passed on by. The unpaved extension of Elmwood avenue and the city of Columbia ended at the C. N. & L. (Columbia, Newberry & Laurens) railroad tracks which angled off to the right.

As we walked along I told Browder that only two other boys from Columbia had gone on the Scout trip to Jacksonville. Both belonged to the Explorer post at St. Peter's Catholic church; one was from Eau Claire and one from St. Andrews. Browder didn't know either one; he's never been in the Scouts. I belonged to the Senior Scout outfit at Covenant Presbyterian church, which Snake had talked me into joining last winter; before that I was a member of the regular Scout troop at Epiphany Lutheran church. When our scoutmaster at Covenant Presbyterian announced that we were eligible to send a certain number of boys to this Senior Scout Regional Rendezvous at the Jacksonville Naval Air Station, I was the only one interested in going.

"I tell you Browder, it was more like a week of Navy boot camp than any Boy Scout outing I've ever been on. You'd think they were trying to shape us up to send us to Korea. As soon as we registered, the first morning we were there, they made us all stand out in the sun with our hands behind our backs—they called it parade rest—for over an hour while this Navy officer made a speech telling us how lucky we were to be Sea Scouts and Air Scouts in a free country. It must have been over a hundred degrees. Boys were dropping like flies, fainting from the heat. They just let 'em lay there until that cat stopped talking—until he finished telling us how tough it was to be in the Navy air corps.

He said that in our future plans we should consider the challenge of trying to become a Navy aviator."

"Did they take y'all up in an airplane?"

"They sho did. In a C-47, one of those twin-engine jobs that paratroopers jump out of. That was some fun: riding in that airplane and looking down on the city of Jacksonville and the ocean." Browder had never been up in an airplane and neither had I until last week in Jacksonville.

"Did you go to the beach?" Browder asked. He'd never seen the ocean.

"Sho nuff. They took us there in a Navy bus." I was telling Browder how easy it was to float in the salt water when we reached the C. N. & L. tracks. We got in between the rails and began stepping off toward the canal, skipping the sticky ties and crunching the gravel under our Keds. The vertical sun was really beating down on us out there in the open on the tracks. It was hot as hinges. You could see the heat rising from the gravel road bed; the tops of the rails were shining like mirrors; creosote was bubbling up from the wooden ties.

"One thing I really liked was the television. They got a television station in Jacksonville and it looks just like a movie it's so damn clear. You tune in to Hopalong Cassidy and it comes in like it was on a movie screen—not like at Wilson Radio." Browder and I had watched the Charles-Walcott fight on the television set in the window at Wilson Radio Company on Main street. We didn't see much; it looked like a couple of ghosts shuffling around in a snow storm. There's no television station in Columbia; they have to use this big antenna to try to pick up Atlanta at Wilson Radio.

When we got to the beginning of the trestle over the canal we decided to climb down and sit in the shade by the water and drink a Pepsi. The water in the canal ran fast and deep and thick and muddy. We sat down under a willow tree next to the water and I opened one of the Pepsis with my Boy Scout pocket knife. The drink was still cold and made a fizzy sting in my nostrils as I took a swig before passing the bottle to Browder.

"I'm about ready to plunge in here," he said; "I'm so hot."
"Naw man. It's too nasty. Let's go on to the green hole." Both
of us had jumped off the trestle into the canal many times—on
bets or dares or just to impress other boys because it's about a
30-foot jump—but I never enjoyed swimming in the canal.
"It's not as nasty here as up there at the dam." Browder started
laughing. "You sure was hot to dive in up there. Remember last
Christmas?"

I remembered and I had to agree that it was nastier up there
just above the dam—where Broad river backs up so still and
khaki colored and where all that slimy gray water pours in from
Smith branch which carries off all the sewage of the town of Eau
Claire. Browder and I were fooling around up there the day after
Christmas—it was real warm for that time of year, in the
seventies—and we saw this pair of real nice-looking girls walking
across the locks. They were sisters about 14 and 15, good-looking
and real friendly. You don't usually see girls like that at the dam;
you don't usually see *any* girls at the dam, unless it's at night and
they're parked in a car with a boy. I asked them where they were
from and they said Parr Shoals, this hick town about 25 miles up
the river. But they didn't talk country at all and they were well
dressed, wearing nice shirts and girl's bluejeans rolled up neatly
at the ankles and bobbysocks and loafers. Not trashy at all. I
mean these were girls you wouldn't be ashamed to be seen with
at Sox's drive-in.

Browder asked them what they were doing there at the dam
and they said they were visiting their uncle, Mr. Baldwin. I
couldn't believe it. Mr. Baldwin is this old fellow who lives with
his wife in a shack by the Southern Railway that's got no
plumbing or electricity. He catches rockfish in a bunch of traps
he built on the rocks out in the river below the dam and he fishes
for mudcats above the dam. He raises collards and okra and stuff
in a garden he's got around his house next to the tracks. Also he
goes up and down the railroad picking up coal that falls off the
trains. That's what he does for a living. And these nice-looking
girls were his nieces. I couldn't believe it.

One of them asked us what *we* were doing there and I said we'd come there for a swim. They watched as we took off our shirts and shoes and dove into that nasty water above the dam with our jeans on. We paddled around and told them to come on in, the water's fine—though actually it was cold as a witch's tit. They giggled a lot and seemed to get a big whip out of watching us. But when I started to get out the oldest one said that it was time for them to go and they hightailed it off to old man Baldwin's house. We never saw them again.

"Wonder what ever happened to those girls," Browder said as we lounged on the bank of the canal. "Speaking of girls, you haven't finished telling me about Jacksonville. Did you get to see her?"

"Who? Juanita Gunter?"

"Why hell yes. Did you think I was talking about Esther Williams?"

"Naw. I called her but she wasn't home." The truth was, I called her three or four times every day I was there but nobody ever answered the phone. I'd gotten her phone number and address from Anita Hunsecker. While I was at the Jacksonville bus station waiting for the bus to go back to Columbia I wrote her a letter telling her that I just happened to be in town that week and I was sorry that I'd missed her.

3

JUANITA GUNTER was a girl in my eighth-grade class at Wardlaw.
That was Miss Amick's homeroom section. Miss Amick was also
our social studies teacher. Browder was in that section so he
knew Juanita, though he didn't pay much attention to her—not
as much as I did anyway. That was where Browder—Billy
Brown—got that name, in Miss Amick's class. He and a couple
other boys came in late from recess one day just as she started
talking about the Bill of Rights. Miss Amick told them to write
their names on the blackboard and go take their seats; she'd deal
with them later. She turned away from them and went back to
talking about the First Amendment just as my old buddy had
finished writing B-i-l-l-y B-r-o-w on the board. When she looked
away he added, real quick, d-e-r and headed for his desk. The
whole class was watching him and practically went into hysterics.
Miss Amick about cracked up too, when she looked at old Billy
who was grinning from ear to ear. "O.k., Billy Browder," she said
as soon as she could get herself together, "you can plan to spend
a half hour in detention hall after school today." She almost
broke out laughing again.

Miss Amick was a great teacher. She was fresh out of college
but she knew what she was doing. Real confident. And you could
tell she really liked us. She always seemed to know what was

going on. She'd even tease us sometimes; like when I'd get excited arguing politics and my voice would register a new high on the squeaky scale. But I didn't mind her teasing me. I didn't even mind her being for Truman in the election. To tell you the truth I had a crush on her. And I wasn't the only one. But it was Juanita who *really* got on my mind.

Juanita was new to our class in the eighth grade. I mean almost all of us had been in the same seventh-grade section and some of us had been together since grammar school. Juanita joined our class at the beginning of the school year and left at the end; she was what they called an "army brat"—her old man was a lieutenant colonel at Fort Jackson. There were usually a couple dozen or so army brats at Wardlaw, who rode in on a schoolbus and generally stuck to themselves at recess and in the cafeteria and went back to the fort after school and everybody forgot about them. There were a few exceptions though—a few girls from the fort who latched on to local boyfriends. These girls were pretty mature: in the seventh and eighth grades they'd go after Columbia boys in the ninth grade. That didn't exactly endear them to the local girls who'd say they were trashy but were really jealous of them. Anyway, for one reason or another, Columbia girls and fort girls didn't much get along—except in the case of Juanita, who was the only army girl in our section. Juanita was different. She made friends with the most popular girls in the class—went home with them, stayed overnight for pajama parties—and became one of them, one of the most popular girls in Miss Amick's homeroom, if not *the* most popular.

In the crew she ran around with there was Kerry Higgins, the smartest girl in the class, the secretary of the Wardlaw chapter of the National Junior Honor Society. There was Jane Slade, also in the honor society, who was undoubtedly the silliest smart girl in the class, but not bad looking. Then there was Carla Dalton, another honor society member, a cute freckle-faced girl. Mandy Jackson was considered the best-looking girl in the class, even though she was a little on the skinny side; she was in that crew. And so was Anita Hunsecker, who was neither a brain nor good looking but was just a real nice girl. Juanita made better grades than Anita and Mandy did—though not quite good enough for the honor society—and in my opinion she was prettier than Mandy; she sure had a better figure.

I hung around a good bit with those girls at Wardlaw. Right after I got my driver's license Momma sometimes would take the bus to work and let me have the car for the day and I'd take the girls and one or two compatible boys for a spin after school. Once we drove Juanita home to Fort Jackson—actually we let her off at the first gate to the fort on Forest Drive. Although I'd sort of liked Jane Slade at one time, Juanita was the one I really became attracted to.

I had a good view of Juanita in homeroom and social studies class, because my desk was two rows over and one seat behind hers and the row between us was vacant. I stared at her a lot and sometimes drew pictures of her, because I like to draw and look at art books and she reminded me of that famous painting "Whistler's Mother." Not that she looked like an old granny but because she was so calm and poised and wore these full, pleated skirts that draped so gracefully over her legs when she was sitting down. All the popular girls wore long skirts by then, in the eighth grade; the year before, in the seventh grade, most of them were still in little-girl dresses with skirts than ended about where their knobby knees began. But I didn't know Juanita in the seventh grade and I couldn't imagine her looking like that, dressed like that, not wearing lipstick.

Juanita had luscious lips. Her lower lip drooped just a little, which sometimes made her look kind of pouty when she wasn't paying attention to whoever was looking at her. Usually, though, she paid attention—if she knew you were looking at her—and smiled and acted real friendly. Not stuck-up at all. She had a nice bright smile; her mouth was wide and she had good regular teeth—not dazzling pearls as I recall. Anyway, with those soft rosy lips out front her teeth didn't make much of an impression. Her eyes were more interesting: they were warm and dark but would light up when she smiled, with flecks of green sparkling in the brown. Her hair was rich lustrous brown, slightly wavy, and cut medium long just off the shoulders.

But to be honest, what I admired most about her was her tits. They were her most salient feature, you might say. They were prominent all right, but perfectly proportioned, just right for her. In wintertime they stood out proudly beneath her pullover sweater like the headlights of some expensive European sports car. In warm weather she often wore a loose-fitting silk blouse and if you looked sideways under the collar you could get a glimpse of the brassiere that restrained those magnificent knockers.

Juanita also had a good mind, as I've said; she made pretty good grades. I often wondered what she was thinking when she sat there at her desk and wasn't thinking about schoolwork. Sometimes she seemed preoccupied, kind of sad. She was a mystery to me. I hadn't watched her develop like the other girls. She just materialized, fully formed, three seats from me in the eighth grade like she'd come from outer space. Well, she wasn't *that* strange. She said she was born in New Jersey, but she didn't talk like a Yankee—though occasionally she'd use a Yankeeism like "guys." You could tell she'd spent most of her life in the South—in Jacksonville, Florida she said. I wondered if she had some problem I could solve. I wondered if I could ever get my hands on those tits. I became obsessed with that girl. Even now, 14 months after she'd moved back to Jacksonville—when her old man was transferred out of Fort Jackson—14 months after I'd last seen her, I was still obsessed with her.

"Come on, Cap," Browder said as he handed the Pepsi back to me for the last swig, "you can't daydream about that girl for the rest of your life. Let's move on to the green hole."

Browder and I each lit up a Pall Mall before we climbed back onto the trestle. We smoked as we crossed the canal and headed on out across Broad river. The surface of the river was 25 or 30 feet below the level of the canal, so once you passed the west bank of the canal the trestle became about 60 feet high. Huge gray steel beams spanned the river on top of stone pillars that rose up from the rocks in the river bed at 30-yard intervals; wooden crossties overhung the beams and anchored the single pair of rails to the trestle. The big stone blocks that formed the pillars varied from sandy colored to pink to gray to light blue—just like the rocks in the river. The greenish brown river water was real shallow—not like the canal—and flowed lazily around the rocks, which were mostly big smooth boulders or slabs, though you could see some smaller jagged ones along the main channels. If you jumped you'd have a hard landing; you'd get killed for sure. It was better to look straight ahead and not down; then what you'd see was a procession of black crossties linked like a belt of machine-gun ammunition by a pair of silver rails marching straight and level through the air and shrinking in the distance until the tracks and ties dissolved into one little speck on the other side of the river half a mile away.

Walking across the trestle really wasn't dangerous because there were these platforms with water barrels on them that were spaced out on the trestle about every 100 yards. Whenever you heard or saw a train you always had time to get to a barrel platform where you could stand while the train went by. The barrels had been put there to hold water in case it was needed to put out a fire—in case a cinder from a locomotive set fire to the ties. But there was no chance of that now that the C. N. & L. had switched from coal burners to diesels.

A slight breeze from the west stirred the air as Browder and I stepped out on the trestle over the river. There was no sign of rain; flocks of fleecy white clouds drifted across the bright blue sky. We were about a quarter of the way across the river when we heard the honk of a diesel up the track coming towards us. We couldn't see the train yet because the railroad curves into the woods at the other side of the trestle. We'd just passed one barrel and Browder wanted to go ahead to the next one. We had plenty of time and I told him to go on ahead, but I was going back to the barrel we'd just passed. To tell the truth I'm afraid of heights and I didn't want to be on the same barrel platform with Browder who liked to clown around. I wasn't one to cut the fool 60 feet up in the air; I didn't even want to look down. I wanted to be by myself when that train roared past, where I could look off into the distance or up into the sky and think about something else. So I stayed back and Browder went ahead to the next barrel. As the train came around the bend I looked across the tracks and a little ways downstream to where the Saluda flows into the Broad to form the Congaree river. The Saluda river comes off the bottom of Lake Murray and is always cold and usually clear like a mountain stream. A dozen or so buzzards glided aimlessly high above the mouth of the Saluda. As the train came on and passed the barrel where Browder was, I turned around and looked upstream. I could see the Highway 176 (Broad River road) bridge about a mile and a quarter away. I couldn't see the dam, which is half a mile farther up the river. That's where the canal begins, at the dam. Water is drawn off by locks at the east end of the dam into the canal to supply drinking water for the city of Columbia. There were goats on the grassy bank that separates the canal from Broad river. I remembered the day last summer when Browder and I put my rubber life raft into the canal at the locks and floated down to the trestle popping off goats with our B-B guns.

As the train thundered by boxcar after boxcar and the rails shuddered and buckled under their iron wheels and the platform trembled beneath my feet, my thoughts turned again to Juanita. Browder said I'd been daydreaming about her. That's not the half of it. For the last 14 months I'd been fantasizing about running into her almost everywhere I went. I'd be going to the Piggly Wiggly with a list of groceries to buy for Momma and I'd imagine that I'd see her there—in the paper products aisle. Juanita, what are you doing here?... Well, you see, we just moved back here, Pops got transferred back to Fort Jackson, but they've run out of toilet paper at the fort... Naturally when I'd get to the Piggly Wiggly she wouldn't be there. She wouldn't be at Ed Robinson's dry cleaners either; I'd imagined that her old man had been promoted to general and sent back as commanding officer of Fort Jackson and Juanita would be at Ed Robinson's picking up his uniform because the cleaners at the fort didn't do a good enough job. No, she wouldn't be at Ed Robinson's and she wouldn't be at Oliver Motors on Elmwood shopping for a new car, or at Cromer's on Assembly street buying boiled peanuts, or at any of those other places I'd half convinced myself she might be—hoping against hope that I'd ever see her again.

The idea that her old man might be transferred back to Fort Jackson wasn't too realistic; most people believed that the government was going to shut the fort down, especially after Governor Thurmond ran against Truman for president and South Carolina went for Strom. Things have changed some since then, though. Truman must've got a lot of satisfaction out of Strom getting beat running for the senate against Olin D. Johnston. (Strom tried to out-nigger Olin D.; it was hopeless.) So maybe Truman wasn't so pissed off at us now. And with the war in Korea it didn't make much sense to close down the fort. So the chances of Juanita's old man getting transferred back to Fort Jackson might've improved a little, but looking at it realistically—taking into account all the possible U. S. Army assignments in the world—you'd have to say that the odds were still a couple hundred to one against. Still, I kept fantasizing about her reappearing in Columbia.

There was no end to the long-shot possibilities. I'd take a seat in the grandstand at a Columbia Reds game and look down to the boxes and there she'd be. Of course! The Reds were playing the Jacksonville Tars: Juanita's uncle had just bought the team and she'd come up with him to watch the Tars play.

Stranger things have happened I thought as I stood clutching the flimsy rail of that violently vibrating platform 60 dizzying feet above the rocky shoals of Broad river. Better to occupy my mind with visions of Juanita than equally improbable but less pleasant ones of tumbling into the airy void or being sucked under the wheels of the passing freight train. When the caboose had rattled past I looked up the tracks and saw Browder waving for me to come on. Farther up the tracks, on the other side of the trestle, I imagined seeing two figures coming out of the woods on the left side of the railroad. They would be wearing dungarees and pretty shirts. Juanita and her sister! What are you girls doing here?... Why we came to visit our uncle, Mr. Lanham, who's got a whiskey still over there on the Saluda river.

But when I got to the end of the trestle only Browder was there. We took a path to the right of the tracks that winds through a stand of pines and hickory and along the fairway of the abandoned St. Andrews golf course before it hooks back into the woods and then begins a steep climb to the little green hole, or the blue hole as it's sometimes called. The blue hole is much smaller than the green hole and more open to the sky; it reflects the sky's color. The blue hole is surrounded by a lot of red clay that washes in when it rains; it's never as clear as the water in the green hole. The water in the green hole is clearer than what you'll find in any pond or stream around Columbia. It's not really green; it just looks that way from the reflection of all the trees and vines and the moss on the rocks and the ferns that grow in the crevices of the granite cliffs around the green hole. Sometimes when there's pine pollen on the surface the water seems to have a yellowish-green tinge when you look at it from above, but most of the time it's a deep emerald green. When you get down into it the water's clear like it came out of a faucet—not like the water of Lake Murray which actually *is* kind of olive green, especially in the shallow parts where mud gets stirred up from the bottom. You can't stir up mud from the bottom of the green hole because it's so deep that nobody has ever touched bottom that I know of.

Everybody likes Lake Murray but some parents will go into conniptions just at the mention of the words "green hole." You'd think there was some whirlpool or undertow in the green hole that grabs little children and drags them down to its bottomless depths. Sure, some people have drowned at the green hole, but what do you expect when college boys come out from the university at night and jump off the high cliff drunk? Some are bound to go down and not come up. They didn't drown because the green hole's so deep. When you're in water over your head it doesn't matter whether it's seven or 700 feet deep. There's a lot

more water that's over your head in Lake Murray than in the
green hole but Lake Murray's just fine as far as most people are
concerned. It was just fine for our eighth-grade class picnic. That
day at Lake Murray in the eighth grade pretty well screwed up
my life.

The picnic was at Johnny Dixon's lake house which wasn't
too easy to find, on a dirt road off a paved road that came off
Highway 176. We all met outside Wardlaw school at the Park
street gate on this Saturday morning in May—May 14 to be exact.
Most of the class was there and so was Miss Amick, our homeroom teacher. Before we left for the lake Miss Amick checked to
see who had brought written permission from their parents to go
swimming. Three or four girls didn't have swimming permits and
said they didn't plan to go in the water. Preacher, a boy who's
father is the pastor at Epiphany Lutheran church, brought a note
from his mother saying that she really thought it was too early in
the year to go swimming but since everyone else had agreed on
that date she'd suspend her better judgment and give her child
permission to go in.

Johnny Dixon—who was the only other boy in the class
besides me who had a driver's license at that time—led the way
driving his Chevy Bel Air with his mother riding shotgun. Miss
Amick was driving her Chevrolet coupe, I was in our Plymouth,
and there were three other cars driven by parent volunteers. Most
of the boys wanted to ride with me. Four boys piled into my car
and so did the two prettiest girls in the class, Juanita and Mandy
Jackson. Juanita was staying with Mandy; she had spent the night
before at Mandy's house which was only a couple of blocks from
the school. Unfortunately they both got into the back seat. In the
trunk I had my government-surplus inflatable rubber life raft that
my Uncle Lewie had given me the Christmas before.

It was about 20 miles from the school to the Dixon place on
Lake Murray. About halfway there Mrs. Dixon signaled for
everyone to pull in at the filling station at the turn-off to Irmo.
She and Miss Amick wanted to redistribute the passengers more
evenly among the cars. I was informed that there were two

people too many in my car but nobody volunteered to leave—at first. Eventually, with our gracious hostess and beloved teacher putting on the pressure, Juanita and Mandy—being good girls—moved out of my car and into Mrs. Dixon's. But before they left they said that they'd like to ride back from the lake with me. So right there on the spot I picked out two of the boys in the car, Stringbean and Ackbo, and told them that they'd have to go back with somebody else; I had to make room for Juanita and Mandy. They—Stringbean and Ackbo—didn't like that one bit; they accused me of having excessive honey britches for Juanita. That surprised me because both Stringbean and Ackbo were practically going steady with girls who weren't in our home-room. I thought that they were the most mature boys in the eighth grade and would understand my predicament. Sure, I admitted I liked Juanita and I wanted her in my car; since she was staying with Mandy, I had to make room for the two of them. The grumbling soon turned to joking and by the time we reached the Dixons' cove on Lake Murray we were all friends again.

At the Dixons' place while other swimmers were playing around near the shore, Ackbo and I showed off by swimming all the way across the cove, a distance of about 200 yards. We got out of the water on the other side and waved to our fans and then plunged in and headed back, not racing but each trying to outdo the other in the professionalism of his Australian crawl. As I approached the shallow water I lifted my head to see two swimmers starting out for the other side: it was Juanita and Jane Slade. No, I wasn't tired; Ackbo went on in to shore but I turned around and joined Juanita and Jane to make their crossing a threesome.

Juanita glided through the water doing an easy crawl with her face out of the water. Her hair was wet, laid back and glistening in the sun, streaming water as she stroked. I churned my way in between Juanita and Jane and turned toward Juanita and went into the side stroke. She gave me a big wide-mouthed smile and kept on going—speeded up a little actually; I couldn't keep up with her doing the side stroke. She got a good ways ahead of me and Jane who I figured I'd better stick with since she wasn't all that strong a swimmer. When Juanita saw how far she was ahead of us she stopped and started floating on her back; then she flipped over and dove under like a porpoise and popped out of the water in front of us doing the breast stroke. Jane as usual thought it was funny and started giggling like a ninny; I was afraid she was going to swallow half the water in the lake. When she finally calmed down the three of us swam close together to the other side.

Juanita was the first to touch bottom and wade out onto the shore. She was wearing a satiny green one-piece bathing suit that was a few shades darker than the green-tinged water of Lake Murray and showed off nicely her smooth skin-colored skin (nobody had a tan that early in the season). And her figure also stood out nicely in that bathing suit. There wasn't another one like it—Juanita's figure—in the eighth grade. Straight shoulders, gorgeous nobs, tight tummy, delicious buns, sleek thighs: that girl had it all.

We rested for a few minutes sitting on an old pine log. The bark was long gone off the log which was probably the trunk of a tree that died from drowned roots when the area was flooded to form Lake Murray 20 years before. The beach, if you could call it that, was clay—more orange than red—with little pebbles all over. Jane got real giddy stepping over the pebbles which hurt her tender feet. She got to dancing around laughing and giving us a good show as she made her way over to the log where Juanita and I were sitting. As I said, Jane wasn't bad looking—just silly. Actually she looked real good in the black-and-white one-piece suit she was wearing. She was kind of petite, not near as tall as Juanita, who was only a couple inches shorter than I was back then.

When Jane said she was ready to go the three of us started back, sticking closer together this time. We were about halfway across the cove when Johnny Dixon came sloshing up in his outboard runabout. He said that Miss Amick didn't want us swimming way out there and that we were to get in the boat and Johnny would take us back to where the others were.

Juanita was the first up into the boat. She put her hands on the gunwale, gave a kick and tumbled easily into the runabout. Jane couldn't do that. Juanita tried to pull her in but couldn't get her up the side of the boat; all the giggling Jane was doing didn't help. I had to boost her up from the water. There I was treading water, that cute little ass wiggling and squirming in my face. Ordinarily I would've taken advantage of the situation, but I didn't want Jane to tell Juanita that I'd been feeling her up. So I boosted Jane up to the boat as properly and gentlemanly as I could.

Johnny delivered us to the swimming area in front of his house. Miss Amick was standing on the grass at the edge of the water and motioned for us to come over. She was wearing a halter top and knee-length shorts and was smoking a cigarette. She scolded us a little and said that our parents had entrusted us to her care and that as long as she was responsible for us she didn't want us out of her reach—meaning we had to stay on this side of the lake and close to shore. She wasn't mad at us though: she gave us a crooked smile, smiling with one side of her mouth and exhaling smoke from the other. Miss Amick must've known that I'd been eyeballing Juanita since the beginning of the school year and now maybe she was glad that we finally seemed to be getting together. I hoped she was glad because I wanted her approval.

I asked Miss Amick if she'd mind if I drove up to the Esso station at the intersection of the paved road about a mile from the Dixons' place to fill up my inflatable life raft. We'd just use the life raft as a float, to sunbathe on in the water close to shore. That was o.k. with Miss Amick so off we went: Juanita and Mandy in the front seat and Browder and Shine in the back. Shine was a boy, not too big, who was always smiling and kidding around in an innocent sort of way. He had a good personality I guess; all the girls liked him—as a friend I mean. Browder was cheerful too, and he also liked to kid around, but the popular girls crew didn't like him the way they liked Shine. Browder was too powerful, too earthy; they thought he was wild. They didn't consider him part of their gang.

Juanita was sitting next to me and as soon as we got out of sight of the Dixon house I put my arm around her bare shoulders. She didn't seem to mind. I explained to the others: if I didn't drive with one hand people might think I was a safe driver; I had to uphold my wild reputation. Big joke. Remember, this is the eighth grade.

The air pump at the Esso station was broken so we weren't able to inflate the life raft. I bought a bag of Chee-tos at the station and handed them to Juanita. Together we ate a few and then passed the bag to the witnesses. Then we went back and joined the crowd at the picnic.

We had the same seating arrangements on the return trip to Columbia except that Mandy sat in the back with Browder and Shine. Miss Amick checked us out in the cars before we left the lake, about an hour before sundown, making sure that everybody was accounted for and we hadn't left anything. I drove real carefully back to Columbia—didn't try to put my arm around Juanita—because Miss Amick's Chevrolet was right behind us most of the way. We had a lot of laughs on the ride back. It amazes me, to think of it now, how eighth graders can keep up such a chatter.

I took Shine and Browder home first—even though it was out of the way in Browder's case—before dropping Juanita and Mandy off at Mandy's house. It was a little before eight o'clock when I got home; I told Momma I didn't want anything to eat and went right up to my room and turned on the radio. Usually when I was home on Saturday night back then I'd listen to "Gangbusters," but that night I tuned in to the "Hit Parade." I flopped down on the bed on my back and didn't do anything—didn't read, didn't draw pictures. My hands and arms and legs felt useless, practically disconnected like on a Raggedy Anne doll. My throat and chest were nice and numb like right after the burning stops when you'd swallowed a mouthful of whiskey. My stomach was light like it was filled with helium; I felt like I might just float up out of that bed, levitate. The radio was on but I didn't listen to it: I can't tell you what songs were tops on the Hit Parade. My mind just dissolved that night; I lost my powers of concentration and it'd be a long time before I'd recover them —which meant disaster in the ninth grade.

I couldn't even concentrate on Juanita as I lay in bed that night, although she was all that I thought about. She drifted back and forth and round and round in my head, changing images every second but always in fuzzy focus. I was dopey like in a trance and kind of feverish: I did have a slight sunburn. I could feel Juanita—in my delirium—better than I could see her—feel her cool smooth skin. But I didn't feel sexy; I didn't have the concentration or the energy for anything that night, even sex. I don't know when it was I finally got to sleep but it was way past midnight.

After Juanita moved to Jacksonville 14 months ago the images of her in my mind became much sharper. Those fantasies I had of her were probably good mental exercises, probably helped me clear up my head. She was this ghost haunting my brain: if I could give her form and a reason for being there maybe she'd materialize and come back into my real life. Either that or she'd go away completely and leave me alone.

My last fantasy of her was at the green hole.

4

BROWDER AND I approached the green hole on the path from the blue hole that winds through the woods next to the abandoned golf course. The coppery gray mat of decayed leaves and pine straw that padded the trail was dappled by early afternoon sunlight filtered through the overhead foliage. At the top of the lower cliff we looked out through a tangle of catbriar and muscadine vines across the green hole's shimmering surface to the rocky point and beyond that to the sheer granite wall of the high cliff; nobody else was there.

We descended from the lower cliff toward the rocky point on a path flanked by hog plum and wild cherry shrubs; morning glory vines laced the bushes and young pines and sweetgums with their cordate leaves. Other green valentines—lizard's tail pads —lined the soggy bottom of a gully we had to cross to get to the base of the promontory that ends up at the rocky point. There we left the shaded path—which continues on around the rim of the quarry to the high cliff—and climbed down over a pile of sun-washed boulders to the water's edge. A pair of chameleons scampered over the rocks out of our way while dragonflies skidded on the water and a school of minnows wheeled about in formation just below the surface.

Before diving in off the point we each took a couple of swigs of water from the canteen and I got out our last Pepsi, which was pretty warm by then, and tied it onto the end of a nylon cord that I carry in my knapsack and lowered it about five feet into the green hole where the water is real cold. The Pepsi was well chilled when we retrieved it after swimming around for about half an hour.

Browder had been up since four o'clock that morning with his paper route and he felt like sacking out after we finished off the bread and vienna sausages and drank the Pepsi. He stretched out in his trunks on a smooth sunny rock with his jeans balled up under his head for a pillow and his T-shirt over his face. I sat down on a pitted blue boulder at the edge of the water and dangled my legs in. I lit up a Pall Mall and stared at the high cliff. It wasn't long before I could see Juanita standing there on the high cliff with Anita Hunsecker at her side.

Howdy boys, Juanita would wave and smile. Her dark eyes would be flashing and her brown hair gleaming like gold in the afternoon sun... She was visiting Anita for a few days and they just had to come out and see where all the boys liked to swim... I'd just be so happy to show them around and I'd lead them along the path to the rocky point... Juanita would have on her green satiny bathing suit; she and I would dive in and start swimming towards the other side, over by the lower cliff, about 120 yards away.

I'd save her life. It wouldn't be a cottonmouth because there're no moccasins at the green hole; it'd be a rattlesnake. We'd climb up on this granite ledge at the base of the lower cliff and be so busy talking we wouldn't notice this big diamondback all coiled up and ready to strike Juanita. I'd hear the rattles; she'd see him and scream; I'd push her aside and grab that snake behind the head the way Scotty Irvine does and fling him out into the water, saving her life. She'd be so scared and grateful; she'd grab me and hug me... But wait a minute... That snake bit *me*! The fang marks were on my right wrist; it was beginning to swell. I could feel the poison entering my system... There wasn't a second to lose. Here, Juanita, take my pocket knife (being prepared like a good Scout I had it in my bathing suit pocket) and cut an X across each fang mark—use the little blade, it's the sharpest... Oh I can't... You've got to! But first tie a tourniquet around my arm; we've got to stop that poison going to my heart... Yes, use your bathing suit straps. Right, don't waste time untying them; cut them off at the shoulder... Tie the tourniquet tight. That's it, good girl; now make those cuts, make 'em deep—a quarter inch deep. I'll lie here as quiet as I can to slow down my pulse while you suck out that poison.

What a soldier that girl would be! After only the slightest hesitation she would get right with the official Boy Scout treatment for poisonous snakebites. There she'd be, kneeling over me on that narrow granite ledge her juicy red lips planted around my swollen wound gently but firmly sucking, drawing out the venom that threatened to kill me. She'd be so concerned with saving my life—the life that I without hesitation offered up for hers—that she'd hardly notice when the unsecured front of her bathing suit fell down and those lovely white breasts rolled out almost onto my chest. Two succulent pink nipples danced before my glazed and delirious eyes! She wouldn't care; she was so grateful to me—forever grateful. She'd move back to Columbia. She'd teach me to shag. I'd get in the Les Truands. I'd take her to formal dances...

That vision of the future evaporated as Tommy and two sixth or seventh grade boys from Camp Fornance appeared on the high cliff. "Hello there," Tommy called out, tipping his straw boater hat to Browder and me.

Tommy was this old fellow who'd been gassed in World War I. He got a 100% disability pension and made himself useful by taking care of children—young boys mostly. But he wasn't a pervert like Harry Wald; Tommy was a real good old fellow. Some people said he was retarded but he wasn't. At one time he'd been fully developed but then that gas washed away part of his brain and there were some things he just couldn't handle anymore. He didn't do or say stupid things; you could tell by the way he acted and looked that he was no moron. He was right dignified actually. He didn't talk much but he always said hello to people when he saw them. And he'd always answer you if you asked him a question. Otherwise he'd just stand there with this dreamy look on his face.

People in Camp Fornance trusted Tommy with their children; he'd do what the parents told him to do and wouldn't let the children do anything dangerous. He'd take young boys on hikes, but usually he didn't bring them to the green hole because most parents didn't want their children swimming in the green hole. Most of the time he'd take them to the meadow to go swimming. The meadow is a sandy-bottomed pool in Smith branch up near Sunset drive, way above where the Eau Claire sewage is dumped into the branch. You really can't do much swimming at the meadow because it's so small and the water's so shallow, not even over your head. They call it the meadow because it's next to a big hay field. A couple of years ago a boy set fire to the hay field and the Eau Claire fire department had to come and put it out. The boy's name was Kirk Finlay but he wasn't one that Tommy was taking care of.

At the green hole Tommy and the two young boys climbed down onto the rocky point where we were and Browder greeted them with "Dammit! You clowns woke me up just as I was dreaming I was about to get a piece of ass."

The boys giggled and looked at Tommy who was starting to take off his pants and put on his bathing suit which he carried neatly rolled in a towel. From the blank look on his face you'd think that he hadn't heard anything. The biggest boy—named Rick—wanted a reaction so he asked him directly: "Hey Tommy, what do you think about fucking?"

"Naw, that fucking's no good," Tommy answered in his slow drawl; "it makes you too weak."

That subject was dropped as Browder lit up a Pall Mall. "Hey, let me have a drag," Rick begged.

Browder passed him the cigarette. "Don't nigger-lip it."

The youngster sucked a lot of smoke into his mouth but only inhaled a little. He handed the fag back to Browder without any wet spots on it and announced, "We've just been to see where the fire burned down the Mirador Club."

"What you talking about," I demanded; "when did the Mirador Club burn down?"

"Last night," the youngest boy broke in.

"You're crazy. There wasn't anything about it in the paper this morning."

"That's because it just happened this morning," Rick tried to explain, "before sun-up. No kidding, it burned plumb down to the ground. Looks like they sprayed a lot of water on it but it didn't do no good. It's real wet up there and still smoking a little. The fire trucks must've left just before we got there."

"I think we better check into this, Browder," I said.

"Yep, I reckon we better. Wonder what caused it to burn down?"

"I bet they set it on fire to collect the insurance," I suggested, "like on 'Johnny Dollar' a couple weeks ago."

"Maybe we can solve the mystery," Browder said with a grin. A few minutes later we were on our way to inspect the ruins of the Mirador Club.

We left the green hole by the path that winds around behind the high cliff to Skyland drive. We took the fork to the right before you get to the Bates house and came out on Highway 176 right at the Broad river bridge. To our left the highway cut deep into the bluff, leaving steep banks on each side that were now covered by a blanket of virulent kudzu that concealed all evidence of the underlying red clay and smothered the few pine or oak saplings that had poked up from the banks, turning them into ghostly green humps. We went the other way, onto the concrete bridge that spanned the river with two wide lanes for motor traffic and raised sidewalks for pedestrians and cyclists and sturdy cement railings on each side. As we walked across the bridge I thought about driving Momma's car across it with Juanita and those others in the eighth grade coming back from that class picnic at Lake Murray. And I remembered how six days after the picnic I had Juanita in that car all to myself.

It wasn't easy. I was daffy after that day at the lake: couldn't think straight but knew I had to do something—had to go after Juanita and get close to her, make her like me, make her my girlfriend—just mine. I couldn't sit back any more just gawking at her in school. The trouble was I'd lost my senses but not my inhibitions; it wasn't like I was drunk or hopped up on cocaine. I was scared shitless. I didn't know what to say to her, was afraid of what she might say to me, afraid of the teasing I'd get from people like Preacher and Shine. If I started acting mature—asked Juanita for a date—Preacher and Shine would rag me without mercy. They'd be jealous really—not because they had the hots for Juanita too, but because I'd be getting out of this crummy Our Gang behavior pattern that they were stuck in. I was jealous too, not of them but of this ninth-grade boy who had been hanging around Juanita. So on top of everything else and with my brain absolutely muddled I had to contend with this ninth-grade oaf named Earl Tann.

Earl Tann was in the Wardlaw Junior Theater and so was I until a few weeks before I lost my head over Juanita. Earl Tann couldn't act worth a damn but he got a bit part in the Junior Theater's spring play that year, *The Secret of Pat Pending*. I had a falling out with the Junior Theater director, Miss Bono, over that—over her giving all these parts to ninth graders like Earl Tann who couldn't act worth a damn. Miss Bono said that this would be their last chance to perform with the group and that they should be given preference for some parts. Now Miss Bono was a good director; she'd been around a long time and she was famous—used to get written up in the newspaper. She was so stuck on her directing ability that she thought she could take clods like Earl Tann and put them in minor roles and not screw up the play. I disagreed vigorously—so vigorously that she got pissed off and said I could forget about appearing in the play myself; she wouldn't direct me. I could join the scenery crew if I wanted to. No thanks, I said, I quit.

Well the play was scheduled to open at the school auditorium for a four-night run on Tuesday, the week after our class picnic at the lake. On Monday I asked Juanita if she was going to the play and she said she supposed she was. For the next three days I tried to get up the courage to ask her to go to the play with me. A poet or somebody once said that simultaneous urgency and languor is the essential quality of youth. That was me all right: boy was I languid. On Wednesday I saw Juanita talking to Earl Tann. She wouldn't go to the play with him, I tried to tell myself, because he was in it and couldn't sit with her—at least not for the whole play; his bit part was in the third act. On Thursday afternoon as Juanita was heading for the schoolbus I asked her again if she was going to the play and this time she said yes she was, and before I could say a word she asked if I would come out to Fort Jackson and get her Friday night. She wound up asking *me!*

"All the way out there? Well I guess I can." I still couldn't help trying to act nonchalant, playing the old eighth-grade game. Juanita knew how surprised and overjoyed I was; she must have. Thinking about it afterwards I was afraid I'd seemed too eager and might have scared her. She smiled but looked a little worried as she got on the bus.

The next morning before school Juanita met me at the door to our homeroom and confessed that earlier in the week she had told Earl Tann that she would sit with him at the play but now that she was going with me she would have to tell him that she'd be sitting with me... By all means, I agreed, she should find Earl Tann and tell him that.

I don't know what happened but later between classes Juanita came to me and said that she couldn't go out with me that night unless some other girl went with us... O.k., I said, invite somebody... At recess I asked her if she'd found another girl to go with us and she said no... What about Anita Hunsecker?... Anita can't go she said.

By this time everybody in the class knew about our date and we were catching some pretty heavy teasing from some of the boys—especially from Preacher and Shine, as I knew we would. We both tried to play the game, not get mad, but I could tell it was wearing Juanita down. God I felt sorry for her. Growing up is hell, especially when you've got friends like Preacher and Shine. If you're going to date in the eighth grade it's better to date somebody your friends don't really know and can't tease —like Stringbean and Ackbo did.

When school was over Juanita walked out of the room without saying a word to me and I ran after her... Can you go tonight?... No I can't... If you change your mind and find out you can go, call me. 5-1314... What's that number again?... It's in the phone book under Mrs. C. A. Palmerston.

I turned away as she walked toward the school bus. Shine yelled at her... Cap wants to know what time to pick you up... She called back so everybody could hear: I can't go.

Preacher seemed sincerely sorry to hear that... Too bad, Cap. But since your girlfriend can't go, how about giving me a ride?... Me too, said Anita Hunsecker, I need a ride (Strange: hadn't Juanita said Anita couldn't go?)... Both Preacher and Anita lived in Camp Fornance, a good ways from the school, and so did Shine. Shine didn't ask me for a ride; he didn't know if he was going to the play or not. I'd have liked to have told them all to go to hell but even in the befuddled state my mind was in I could see the advantage of promising rides to Preacher and Anita—especially Anita, since she could be the other girl if Juanita called me later that afternoon and said that she could go if there was another girl along. But I really didn't much expect that Juanita would call. I told Preacher and Anita that I'd pick them up around a quarter to eight.

I felt pretty bad as I walked home from school that afternoon. In the kitchen Agnes handed me a shopping list that Momma had left for me. Look Agnes, I said, trying to be as nice to her as I could, I'm expecting this important phone call and would you please listen out for the phone while I go to get this stuff... She allowed as how she reckoned she might and I left on my bike for

McKeon's grocery with little hope that Juanita would call or, if she did, that Agnes would get the message straight.

When I walked in from the store Agnes hit me with the news. "Somebody called you all right. It was a white girl name of One Eater. Was that who you was expecting to call you? From out at Fort Jackson? I wrote her phone number down on the tablet next to the phone." I mumbled thanks and slammed the groceries down on the kitchen table and raced for the phone in the living room. Sure enough, there it was in Agnes's childish scrawl "ft jacksn 27211 xtend 53M."

Right after I saw the number I was almost paralyzed by fear. I'd never talked with Juanita on the phone before. I'd never called any girl before. I didn't like calling people on the phone. I was afraid—but I went ahead anyway. I dialed the number at the fort and asked the operator there for extension fifty-three M. A female voice answered and I asked to speak to Juanita please. Moments later Juanita was on the line... Hello Juanita, you wanted me to call you?... Yes Cap. You know where you let me off when you took me home that time... She began giving me directions on how to get to her house just as if everything that had happened that day hadn't happened—the teasing, the other girl crap, the I-can't-go declaration—like nothing had changed from when we made the date the day before. It threw me for a loop, short-circuited my already feeble brain: I couldn't get her directions straight. Finally she said O.k., I'll just meet you at the gate. Call me from the guardpost when you get there... What time?... I'll be there between 7:15 and 7:30, I said.

I was there at 7:10. I parked the Plymouth outside the gate and walked up to the sentry and asked if I could use the phone to call extension fifty-three M. He said O.k. and pointed to the phone inside the guardhouse. I picked up the receiver and asked for fifty-three M... The operator wanted to know if I meant five--three M or six-three M... The army does things differently. Anyway I was a little flustered—nervous as hell in fact—by the time I got Juanita on the line... Hello Juanita this is Cap... Oh Cap... I'm not early am I?... No just a few minutes. I'll be out there in two minutes... O.k. I'm parked just outside the gate. I'll see you.

The sentry was real interested... Got a date? ... Yes sir, sort of... I walked over to the car and leaned against the right front fender for about five minutes, until I saw two girls coming down the road behind the guardhouse. It was getting dark but the lights around the guardhouse were bright; I waved and one girl turned back as the other said something to the sentry and continued on towards me. It was Juanita in glorious motion: hips gently rolling, the skirt of her cotton dress reaching mid calf, billowing and swirling as she walked. Her broad smile practically incapacitated me and I almost fell over myself opening the car door for her.

When we were both inside I didn't want to move. I didn't want to disturb anything—her shiny hair, her freshness, the sweet smell of her powder hanging in the air—I just wanted to sit there and enjoy it forever. But we had to go and I didn't delay; off we went down Forest drive toward Taylor street. Conversation was easy thanks to Juanita. The girl I'd seen walking with her, she said, was her sister, aged 15. At the guardhouse the sentry had told her to Hurry up hazel, you've kept that poor boy waiting long enough. We talked about Boy Scouts; we talked about Girl Scouts. We discussed the advantages and disadvantages of having a big sister. We talked about our teachers. When I mentioned that we had to pick up Anita and Preacher she didn't seem surprised.

We went to Anita's house first. We were there for about five minutes because Anita wanted to introduce Juanita to her mother. Anita was proud to have Juanita for a friend and I could understand why. I'd have liked to have introduced Juanita to *my* mother. After the little visit I opened the car door and both girls got into the front seat, Juanita in the middle next to me and Anita next to the door. Perfect! We'd put Preacher in the back seat.

Preacher thought that Juanita wasn't coming so the girls decided to play a joke on him. They both ducked down in the front seat so nobody could see them when we pulled up to the

Lutheran parsonage. I went in to get Preacher and told him he'd have to ride in the back because I had some "things" on the front seat. As he got into the back Juanita and Anita popped up in front. Surprise! Lots of laughs.

Preacher was glad that Juanita could come and—guess what?—Shine could go too. He'd called Preacher and wanted us to pick him up. Swell, I thought to myself, we'll have an Our Gang quorum in my car; we could transact official business. But I had no choice but to go and pick up Shine. I figured I could dump him and the other two witnesses after the play before driving Juanita home. But it didn't work out that way. Things started going wrong the minute we stepped inside the Wardlaw auditorium.

Earl Tann met us at the door. He'd saved some seats for us in the balcony. Anita and Juanita thought that was nice but Preacher and Shine noticed that there were still a few single seats downstairs and said that they would sit down there. Naturally I went up to the balcony with the girls and that shitass Earl Tann. He acted like an usher showing us to our row of seats. I filed in first with Juanita behind me and then that bastard jumped in ahead of Anita and wound up sitting next to Juanita with me on her other side. When the lights dimmed and the play began, ninth-grade Earl Tann made the first move and put his arm around Juanita. She didn't seem to like it but she didn't do anything to make him stop that I could tell.

I didn't know what to do. I hated that son-of-a-bitch Earl Tann but he was a lot bigger than me—four or five inches taller and heavier too (I was kind of chubby in the eighth grade.) He had big hips like a girl and looked like he could've been Victor Mature's deformed ugly brother. If I picked a fight with him and made a big scene and then got the shit stomped out of me—I didn't see how that would win me any points with Juanita. Still I thought about going to get Browder—he was probably down at Dowling's drugstore playing the pinball machine—and the two of us would beat his ass to a pulp. But I didn't do it.

During intermission we all went downstairs—the girls and I to talk with our friends and Earl Tann to smoke in the boys' room. (That was before I started smoking; none of the eighth-grade boys who hung around the popular girls crew smoked.) When we went back to our seats before the third act Earl Tann maneuvered in front of Juanita—took the seat she had been sitting in and cut me off entirely from her. I glanced at her and this time she really seemed annoyed with that slimy bastard; after all, she'd promised to sit with me. When he put his arm around her again she looked truly unhappy; the shithead had really gone too far now. But that situation didn't last long because Earl Tann soon had to leave to make his appearance in the play. When he got up out of his seat he had the gall to ask me to wait a few minutes before we left after the play because he had to tell Juanita something. Yeah, sure, I said sarcastically.

I moved over next to Juanita and put my arm around her. She didn't respond the way I'd hoped she would; it wasn't like up at Lake Murray. She gave me the same frigid treatment she'd given Earl Tann, who soon materialized on the stage making an ass of himself as a member of the Wishington, D. C. Fire Department.

When the play was over and we'd rounded up Preacher and Shine, I told Juanita that I'd wait at the auditorium door exactly five seconds for Earl Tann to show up and deliver his urgent message. But we didn't have to wait at all; the clod was there before we were, still dressed in his stupid fireman's costume. I stuck close to Juanita; anything he said to her was going to be said in my presence. Well, uh... I'll call you Juanita... That's all he said. I got a big whip out of watching him squirm. When I was back at the wheel of the Plymouth with Juanita at my side I actually started to feel good again, for the first time in two hours.

It was either Preacher or Shine who suggested we go by the Zesto on North Main street and get some ice cream, and that's where I headed. On the way I got instructions from the back seat, from Shine: Put your arm around her... O.k., I said... No, Cap, said Juanita... Yes... No... Yes... No... O.k., I've got to turn up here anyway (those were the days before I'd learned to steer and shift gears with one hand).

I downshifted to second and swung easily into the gravel parking lot of the Zesto Sure-Is-Good-chocolate-dipped-air-filled-ice-cream place. I volunteered to go fetch the stuff and took everybody's order. I told Juanita I'd buy her anything her heart desired... No thanks she said sweetly, I don't eat ice cream... (Why? You afraid it'll make you fat? More than those Chee-tos I bought you up a Lake Murray? I didn't ask why; I'd made enough blunders already that night.)

From the Zesto I drove to Anita's house and dropped her off. When Anita got out Juanita moved over and hugged the door. Next we went to Shine's house, but he wouldn't get out. He didn't have to be home that early; he wanted to ride out to the fort with me... Go on, Shine, get out... Aw Come on Cap... He wouldn't budge. Preacher and Juanita got to laughing. What could I do? The joke was on me; I had to take it. So after five minutes in front of Shine's place we drove on to Preacher's with Shine still in the back seat. At least Preacher got out and went home.

The trip back to the fort wasn't too bad. Juanita assumed the position of the classic dashboard date: feet curled under her on the seat, upper body wedged between the dashboard and the door, facing backward so she could chat with whoever was in the back seat—in this case, Shine. We made a real jolly threesome. I thought I put up a damned good front.

The sentry waved us through the gate and Juanita directed me to her house. It was one of those flimsy looking wooden army buildings from World War II that were converted into duplexes and used as temporary officers' quarters; there were a couple dozen of those duplexes in the area, which they called Splinterville. Juanita opened the door and was out of the car as soon as we rolled up to her place. She wasn't going to give me the chance to walk her to her door... Goodnight Cap. Goodnight Shine... Night Juanita. See you.

It turned out that Juanita had asked Shine to ride back to the fort with us when I was out of the car buying ice cream at the Zesto. She'd asked Preacher too, but he'd said that it was too close to eleven o'clock when he had to be home. Juanita had told them that she was afraid I wanted to neck and she didn't want to. God, I wouldn't have done anything she didn't want me to do. I was no sex fiend. O.k., I have to admit that I could get a hard on watching her in homeroom or social studies class—often did in fact—but I never did after that day at the lake. The way I thought about her changed completely. What made her afraid of me? Did Jane Slade tell her I tried to feel her up in the water at the lake? Did Juanita think I was wild because Browder was my best friend? Hell, he's as timid as I am when it comes to respectable girls. Maybe she didn't want to be alone with me because she just didn't like me. If that was it my deranged mind wouldn't let me accept it.

Monday morning after the play Juanita was sitting at her desk in homeroom reading something while I was trying to figure out what to say to her. Miss Amick stepped out of the room and Preacher sneaked up behind Juanita and snatched the note she was reading out of her hands. The note was from Earl Tann and Preacher read it aloud to the class. The Wishington Fireman said he was sorry he put his arm around Juanita; he just wanted to find out if she was a nice girl; he knew a nice girl wouldn't want to be treated like that, and she didn't... What entertainment! Howls of laughter. I felt sorry for Juanita but I hoped the class's reaction would help her see what a dumb shit that Earl Tann was.

I'd apologize to Juanita the right way, on the telephone after school. When the time came to call her I was really scared—didn't think I could go through with it. But after stalling for half an hour I finally got the nerve to dial the Fort Jackson number and ask for Juanita's extension. A female voice answered—Juanita's sister I presumed. I asked for Juanita and moments later she was on the line.

"Juanita, this is Cap."

"Oh hello Cap..."

"Juanita I'm awful sorry about the way I acted Friday night."

"That's all right Cap."

"The reason I wanted Shine to get out before I took you home was that I wanted to tell you I was sorry about the way I acted. You know Shine knows all and Shine tells all. He told me about you asking him to ride with us when I took you home. I'm sorry I made you feel that way."

"Well..."

"You forgive me don't you?"

"Yes, I forgive you."

"Good. I'll see you. Goodbye."

And what was that all about? Somebody putting his arm around a girl's shoulder—not even trying to touch her boobs. You see, in the eighth grade nice girls weren't supposed to let you put your arm around them on the first date. In the ninth grade nice girls wouldn't let you kiss them on the first date. After they're promoted to the tenth grade, I learned a couple of weeks ago, nice girls won't let you tongue them on the first date. I could hardly wait for the eleventh grade.

5

BROWDER WANTED to stop and get a cold drink at Mrs. Dawkins store after we'd crossed the Broad River road bridge on our way from the green hole to the Mirador Club. Dawkins store was this little old dilapidated clapboard building right on Highway 176. At one time it might've had a gas pump in front of it but didn't any more. The store was up on stacked brick pillars and leaned a little on the side towards the river. Virginia creepers wrapped around the pillars and dog fennel grew up from under the sagging porch. An oval Grapette sign was tacked up over the door and next to it was a crinkled poster of Eddy Arnold advertising Prince Albert smoking tobacco. On the right side of the door was a sign that said "White Only."

Old lady Dawkins meant it; she didn't like colored people. One day this farmer from White Rock and his nigger stopped by there for something and must not've seen the sign and both of them went inside. Mrs. Dawkins ran them back outside hollering and whacking at them with a broom. My Uncle Lewie saw it; he told me about it. Funny thing is, Dawkins store is located right next to this lumberyard that's owned by a rich nigger. Everybody who works at that lumberyard is colored: stackers, saw operators, office help, truck drivers, even the foreman. Mrs. Dawkins wouldn't have any of them trading at her store. She was true to her principles.

Browder and I walked around the warped screen door which was stuck half open and stepped into Dawkins store. It seemed dark in there coming in out of the afternoon sun, and hot—there weren't any fans going. Strips of dirty fly paper dangled from the rafters undisturbed by any breeze. This skinny mean-looking old lady was standing behind a marbletop counter. It was hard to make her out at first in the dim light, but it was Mrs. Dawkins all right: she was ugly as homemade sin.

"You got any Pepsis, ma'am?" I asked.

"All I got's R. C. Cola and Nehi orange and Nehi strawberry."

"You got any of them five-cent cakes?" Browder asked.

"Just got some Moon Pies over there." She nodded her head in the direction of the countertop rack next to where I was standing. I lifted one off the rack; it felt hard and crusty like it was a year old; I put it back.

"Let's just get an R. C., Browder."

"You want two?" Mrs. Dawkins broke in.

"No ma'am," Browder answered, "just one. We'll split it."

That R. C. wasn't even cool. Old lady Dawkins took it out of the drink box but it was as warm as if it'd come right out of a crate. I figured the electric company must've shut her power off. I was glad we still had some cool water in my canteen. We finished that off when we got to the Mirador Club, which was only a couple blocks from Dawkins store, up the hill on the other side of the Lafayette tourist cabins.

We could see from the highway that those boys at the green hole hadn't been lying: the Mirador Club had burned clear down to the ground. It used to be a big white two-story frame building; all that you could make out up there now was a bunch of charred timbers and rubble lying all over the ground. The pine trees that had been next to the club had burned too, although some were still standing, sticking up into the sky like big black toothpicks. The road leading up to the club was pretty torn up and rutted, from all the fire trucks I supposed.

I'd never been on that hill before and as Browder and I walked up I checked out the scenery. The view was pretty good though it wasn't too inspiring—at least not if you looked directly across Highway 176. What you saw was the Dreher Packing Company slaughterhouse—you could smell it too—and beyond that the nigger shacks of Black Bottom. Over to the right was the Armour Fertilizer Works. If you looked toward the river you couldn't see it (not from the ground anyway; maybe you could've seen it from the top floor of the club), but you could see the other side. In the other direction, behind the club, was this big open field that had been planted in watermelons but by then was pretty well picked over and grown up in weeds. Just as we got to the top of the hill and started surveying the remains of the building, Browder pointed to two horses and riders coming across the watermelon field with a big white-and-black-spotted dog trailing along behind them. "Hey, that's old Calhoun and that yellow nigger he runs around with."

We both waved to them. Then I remembered: "Hey Browder, don't say anything to Calhoun about us having Sandburg lined up for Wednesday night. He might wanna go with us."

"Damn right. Him and the Eau Claire crew might even try to cut us out. We gonna keep her to ourselves—me and you and Sellers. Three's enough."

"Well if it ain't the Bobbsie twins, Cap 'n' Browder," said Calhoun as he reined in his big bay Tennessee walker.

"Howdy Red Ryder," Browder replied, "or are you Little Beaver?"

"Ho boys," said Gordon the mulatto, whose smaller wild-eyed bay was breathing hard.

"Looks like y'all had a big fire in the neighborhood," I said. Calhoun's English setter, named Mutt, came up to me panting and wagging his tail. I patted him on the head. He reminded me of a dog I had once, a collie that got run over by a car on Laurel street. Like Momma always said, the city's no place to have a dog—unless you keep him in the house like Yankees and some people out in Shandon do. Calhoun was lucky to live in this

farming area between Eau Claire and Camp Fornance where his
old man owned about 100 acres. Old Doc MacNab's a veterinarian and they've got lots of animals: dogs, horses, cows, pigs,
sheep, goats—and niggers to take care of them.

"I didn't even know about the fire," Calhoun said, "until
Gordon told me about it. His grandpaw was milking the cows
this morning when he heard the sirens and saw the flames
lighting up the sky."

Calhoun and Gordon dismounted and tied their horses to a
couple of dogwood trees and the four of us began rummaging
through the ruins. Old Mutt was sniffing all around wagging his
tail like he was hunting dead.

"Makes you wonder what all went on here," Calhoun said.

"My Uncle Lewie used to deal cards here," I volunteered, "in
the back room."

"Where you reckon that was?" Browder said.

"I don't know; he never brought me here."

"This here must've been the kitchen," Gordon observed;
"look at that old stove. And the hot water heater. Ain't much left
of it. And the refrigerator. Looks like somebody got here before
us and ripped out all the copper tubing."

"Hey man, look at all this silver!" Browder exclaimed.

"Hunh?"

"I mean knives forks and spoons. Look, all over the ground."

"Hey I'm gonna take some of these home to my grandmomma." Gordon began picking up eating utensils and stuffing
them into the pockets of his khaki pants.

"Me too," said Browder. "I'm gonna take some home too.
How about you, Cap?"

"Naw. My old lady's got plenty of that stuff. But I'll help you
carry some if you want. Put 'em in my knapsack."

"And would you looka here," Calhoun called out. "Look at all
these pictures."

Calhoun had found a batch of black-and-white photographs
under a slab of wet sheetrock. They were big glossy pictures,
almost the size of notebook paper, of people sitting at tables in

the Mirador Club—men wearing suits and ties and women in lowcut party dresses and whiskey bottles and Seven-ups and champagne glasses on tables with white tablecloths on them like in the movies. Some were of couples smiling directly into the camera; in other pictures there'd be a whole bunch of people either posing or acting natural or clowning like at a party. The people were all pretty old—middle aged—although some of the women might've been in their twenties. Some of the photos were wet along the edges and a few of them stuck together, but most were dry and shiny and in pretty good condition.

We all went over and sat down under the dogwood trees where the horses were tied and studied the photographs. They were souvenir pictures taken the night before the place burned down, Calhoun figured. But why didn't the people take them home with them, I wondered. Maybe they didn't like the way they came out, or maybe they left before the pictures were developed. None of us recognized anybody in the photos. After we'd gone over all of them I asked Calhoun if he wanted them. He said he didn't and I said I'd take them if nobody had any objections, which they didn't. I thought maybe I'd show them to Uncle Lewie; he probably knew some of the people.

"Man I'm thirsty," Browder said as I was putting the pictures into my knapsack; "that R. C. didn't do me a bit of good."

I handed him the canteen and he took a couple of big glugs and passed it back to me. I took a swig and looked at Calhoun who was sitting on the other side of Gordon and said, "Y'all want some water?"

Both said they did and Gordon took the canteen when I held it out. He took a swig and passed the canteen to Calhoun who drained it. Old Calhoun didn't seem to mind drinking after a nigger.

Calhoun took out a pack of cork-tipped Tareytons—that boy smokes the strangest cigarettes—and I brought out our last two Pall Malls. Since Calhoun didn't offer Gordon a fag, I thought I would. He waved it away with his hand and Calhoun answered for him. "Gordon ain't smoking; he's in training—gonna play football for C. A. Johnson High this fall."

"If I don't join the army," Gordon added. "I'll be 17 in October."

"You wanna go over to Korea and get you ass shot off?" Browder asked.

"We'll see." Gordon smiled like somebody who knew what he was doing.

"Hey, why don't we get us a watermelon," I suggested. You could see a few small ones lying out in that weedy field.

"Naw," Gordon said, "them watermelons passed. Besides they're hot; been laying out in the sun all day. And a hot watermelon's only good for one thing."

Browder started giggling. "I always heard colored boys fucked watermelons."

"You heard right," Gordon said. "Up in Oconee county where I come from all the colored boys fuck watermelons. What they do is sneak out in the watermelon fields right after sundown when the watermelons still warm. They cut a plug out o'em and they fuck 'em without messing up the vines or anything. And when they through they put the plug back in and it grows back so you can't tell it."

"You lying Gordon," Calhoun said.

"I ain't lying. It's the Lord's truth. Practically all the watermelons that come from Oconee county been fucked by colored boys. And that's all they got down at the market now—watermelons from Oconee county. These down here done passed; them up there come in late, still coming in now. You go down to Assembly street and ax them where they watermelons come from and they gonna tell you Oconee county. And just about every one o' them watermelons been fucked by a colored boy. And you can't tell it. If a white girl eats one o' them watermelons and swallows a seed she'll get pregnant."

"Gordon, you know that's bullshit," Calhoun said.

"Naw it ain't, Bud. It's the truth and everybody knows it." Bud, or Buddy, is the name Calhoun goes by at home. At school the teachers call him Angus. His full name is Angus Calhoun MacNab, Jr.

"Well I know I don't fuck watermelons," Calhoun said and tried to blow a smoke ring but there was too much breeze, "not when I can get a real piece of ass every now and then."

I was about to say something about Sandburg when Browder kicked my foot. We let Calhoun carry on about watermelons.

"I don't even much care about eating watermelons, but I do like to swipe 'em. It's like dove shooting: I'd rather shoot doves than eat 'em. Nothing much I like better than raiding a watermelon patch and carrying off a couple of big ones—for the sport of it. Now this field here's no challenge. Anybody can walk in here and take all the watermelons he wants. But the fellow that planted this field—colored fellow who lives over there on the other side of that stand of pines, Mr. Miles—he's got this other patch of watermelons planted close up to his house, practically under his back porch. Well one night last month I snuck in there and almost got myself killed. His old dog started to barking and old man Miles came out on the porch with his shotgun. But he didn't see me; I hid behind this big oak stump and when he went back in the house I crawled off with this juicy Dixie Queen—crawled off under his barbed wire fence and down to the hollow where I ate the heart out of that watermelon and threw the rest away."

"Hold on a minute there, Calhoun the Lawyer." Gordon was talking like Kingfish on Amos 'n' Andy. "You wanna know why Mr. Miles didn't pepper your ass with birdshot? Wasn't cause he didn't see you; was because your poppa told him not to. Mr. Miles knowed you was stealing his watermelons and told your poppa about it. Mr. Doc thought it was funny; he told Mr. Miles just to let him know whenever you took any o' his watermelons and he'd pay for 'em."

"You lying again, Gordon."

"Naw I ain't Bud. You ax your poppa."

"You crazy as hell. You think I'm gonna go to my poppa and ask him Poppa you been paying for the watermelons I been swiping?"

"If you don't you'll never know."

"Well I know for sure he didn't pay for the watermelons me and Stringbean and Dude Adolphus swiped off that truck on Highway 21 back in June."

"Tell us about it Buddy." Gordon winked at me and Browder.

"Brewster wheeled us out there in his gray ghost"—Calhoun began the story using Eau Claire crew lingo: ghost means Ford—"out past Moore's Pond to this steep hill where the watermelon trucks going up slow down almost to a walk and have to grab low gear. During the season there's a lot of watermelon trucks on that road; they load up in the morning down in Colleton county and try to make it to Charlotte before too late at night. Around nine o'clock they start coming up that hill, about one every 15 minutes. Well, Brewster stayed with the ghost, parked it on a side road that comes in about a quarter of the ways up the hill. Dude Adolphus stationed himself a little more'n halfway up the hill; Stringbean was about three quarters of the way up and I was a little bit further up.

"Well it wasn't long before this big Reo stakebody came along. It was really loaded but it was still moaning too fast for Dude Adolphus to catch it when it went past him. The wheeler downshifted a couple of times before he got to Stringbean but he was still moaning pretty fast. But that scutter can run—Stringbean, I mean—and he grabbed the tailgate of that Reo and hauled himself up and climbed up on top of those watermelons and started throwing them off into the ditch. I ran along behind and Stringbean tossed three watermelons to me but I could only catch one. By that time the truck had just about reached the top of the hill and Stringbean had to get off fast. He skinned his knee jumping off but he was o.k. We walked back down along the ditch scooping the hearts out of all the busted watermelons and eating them. We gave the only one that wasn't busted, the one I caught, to Brewster."

"I bet I know what Brewster said," Browder broke in...

"Aawwkk," Calhoun imitated Brewster's famous bird squawk, "y'all only bagged one! I wheeled you opes all the way out here in moot country and y'all only bagged me one!"

Gordon was chuckling as he got up and untied his horse and threw the reins over his neck. "Well boys, me and old Red gotta get back to the house now. Bud, I'll tell Grampa not to feed the horses till you bring old Prince in."

Gordon was standing flatfooted on the ground with his hand on the saddle pommel. All of a sudden he vaulted up on that horse's back without even touching the stirrups until he was in the saddle. Old Red reared up on his hind legs and then lunged forward, hitting the ground at a gallop. I'd never seen anything like it—not even in the movies.

"That's some nigger," I said as he galloped across the watermelon field.

"At least he ain't uppity," Browder said.

"He ain't uppity," Calhoun agreed. "Sometimes he just don't realize he's a nigger. Thinks he's just a boy. He used to listen to 'Captain Midnight' and all that stuff on the radio just like a white boy. Now he's gone back to his house to listen to 'In the Groove.'"

"Oh my god!" I exclaimed. "Is it that late?"

"Well it's past five. Gordon always can tell what time it is—within five or ten minutes."

"Browder we gotta go. I gotta get home before six or my old lady'll kill me. We got enough money left to catch the bus; let's do that."

"You got time," Calhoun pointed up Broad River road; "see that bus is just coming into Hinnant's filling station now. He'll be there for five minutes before he turns around and heads back to town.

"Hey tell me something, Cap: Stringbean said you went to Jacksonville to try and find that girl that was in our eighth-grade class, Juanita Gunter. Did you see her?"

"Naw, Calhoun, I didn't see her. I haven't seen her since that night at your place."

The day after I apologized to Juanita for getting fresh with her on the night of the play, Preacher walked into our homeroom and announced that he had another note to her from Earl Tann. He'd just given it to him to deliver to her, Preacher claimed, but he said he'd decided to read it first and let everybody read it. Juanita tried to grab the piece of paper out of his hand but Preacher was too fast for her. When I reached for it Juanita said to me No, don't look at it; it's none of your business... She didn't sound mean, just flustered. I drew back while the other boys begged to see the note. Then Juanita said to Preacher so everybody could hear, "Go ahead and read it. Let all the boys in the class read it—except one. I can't tell you who it is..."

Preacher cut her off by revealing that it was all a joke: there was no note from Earl Tann. Boy was I confused. My brain was already on its last leg and that incident about finished me off mentally. It was a good thing school was almost over and I had a good average in all my subjects going into those last two weeks; otherwise I might not've passed the eighth grade. Anyway, after all that had happened I was clobbered by the realization that Juanita still had something going with Earl Tann, still actually liked that turd. What to do now? Before my feverish imagination could come up with a solution, probably violent, Anita told me that Juanita was leaving: moving back to Jacksonville as soon as school was out, going away—permanently—leaving me and Earl Tann and the popular girls crew and Preacher and Shine... everybody! So what was the use? I might as well start trying to forget her; in a couple of weeks she'd be gone out of my reach and, I thought, out of the reach of that bastard Earl Tann.

But I was wrong. In the next two weeks the worst things that could've happened happened. Juanita didn't seem to care that I wasn't hanging around her any more. Earl Tann was, more and more, walking with her, talking with her—at recess, after school, before school. Yes, Juanita liked him, Anita Hunsecker informed me, and he was going to go down to Jacksonville with her family to help them move!

I couldn't believe it. How could her family tolerate that jerk? What could Juanita possibly see in him? O.k., he was a year older than me and taller; but I was going to get older and taller (my mother was tall, my father had been tall); I wasn't going to be like Preacher—five foot four and 13 years old forever I thought. So what if I was a little chubby? Earl Tann had an ass that would've looked good on Rita Hayworth if she'd been six feet tall. I pointed it out to Browder and he agreed. That misshapen bastard walking with Juanita! It offended my artistic sensitivity. His big round buns looked like they were going to bust out of his store-bought gabardines. He didn't even know how to dress. How could Juanita prefer that oaf to me? I was smart; I was rich (for Wardlaw anyway); I was articulate—I wrote articles for the school newspaper *The Magnolian*.

Now I could've understood if she'd dropped me for somebody like Stringbean—Ron Stark. Stringbean was tall and well built —not skinny, despite his nickname—good looking. And he was smart too, the only boy besides me in our homeroom who was in the honor society. Stringbean had many talents: he played the trumpet (I had absolutely no musical ability) and he was chosen the most valuable player in intramural basketball and he played first base for the Eau Claire American Legion baseball team (my only athletic achievements were winning a couple of swimming races and one boxing match at YMCA camp). Sure, I could've understood if Juanita had been attracted to somebody like Stringbean—but not somebody like Earl Tann who was just an ordinary shit.

I had to save her from that son-of-a-bitch. I had to talk with her privately before she left for Jacksonville. I thought I might get the opportunity the night after the last day of school, when Calhoun was having the class out to his place for a wiener roast. Besides Miss Amick and everyone in her homeroom, Calhoun had invited three boys he'd gone to grammar school with and two other girls: Stringbean's and Ackbo's girlfriends.

On Wednesday the last day of school, just after the final bell, a lot of people were standing around talking to Miss Amick, including Juanita and Kerry Higgins, the intellectual chief of the popular girls crew. When Juanita and Kerry walked away together I ran after them and asked them if they were going to Calhoun's wiener roast the following night. Kerry said she was going and Juanita said she supposed she was. I asked Juanita if she had a way to get out there and she said she hadn't. Just then Miss Amick called me over: Calhoun had left without telling our beloved teacher how to get out to his place, so she asked me for directions. After I'd explained the way to her—take the dirt road behind Hinnant's Shell station, go about half a mile and turn left after the white board fence—Kerry and Juanita had disappeared. That was o.k.; I'd call Juanita at home and ask her to go to Calhoun's party with me. I wasn't so scared anymore. What did I have to lose? I'd probably never see her again after Thursday night.

The trouble was, extension 53M was constantly busy Wednesday afternoon after school. I gave up that night and decided to try again the next morning, the day of the wiener roast. I got through that morning but the lady who answered the phone said Juanita didn't live there anymore; they'd moved! Already gone to Jacksonville? No, no, just to other quarters in Splinterville. Their phone number was now 738M. So I tried that number—again and again and again. All I got was a busy signal. Then as I was about to make another attempt, *my* phone rang.

It was Anita Hunsecker calling from Jane Slade's house where she and Kerry and Carla Dalton had spent the night before. That night, the night of the wiener roast, all of them except Kerry would be sleeping at Anita's; they wanted me to pick them up there and take them out to Calhoun's. Oh boy, my first full day as a ninth grader and I was still the official chauffeur of the popular girls crew. I didn't have to take Kerry because her father—Dr. Higgins of the staff at State Park, the tuberculosis sanitorium—was going to deliver her to the party. And oh yes, they'd been talking on the phone with Juanita all morning; she needed a ride. I was to pick up the crew at Anita's house first; then we'd all motor out to Fort Jackson and get Juanita. Those were my instructions. Oh well, at least it would be all girls; thank God they hadn't signed up Preacher or Shine to ride with me.

As it turned out Jane Slade wasn't able to go. Apparently the girls at her house got carried away talking about what fun it was to ride around with me, which registered negative with Jane's momma who decided she'd better stay home that night. So it was only Anita and Carla that I picked up at Anita's house, a little after seven o'clock.

I drove to the fort in a state of total confusion: why had Juanita switched houses? What was it with these military people, moving from one place to another on the same army post right before they were going to move to another state? Anita and Carla didn't know. Well did they know where Juanita's new house was? As a matter of fact, they didn't. Then how in the heck were we going to find her and pick her up? My brain clicked on (a rare occurrence in those days) and I answered my own question: I'd ask the sentry at the guardpost to tell me where Colonel Gunter lived. No I wouldn't, Anita said, because Juanita Gunter's father wasn't named Gunter—and he wasn't her father anyway; he was her stepfather. Neither Anita nor Carla could remember exactly what his name was—something like Boola. Juanita didn't have a father? For some reason that surprised me. I wouldn't have been surprised at all if they'd told me she didn't have a mother. I couldn't remember her ever mentioning her mother.

The sentry waved us through the gate and so we figured we'd go on to Juanita's old house and ask the people there where her new one was. Trouble was, when we got there none of us wanted to go up to the door and ask. I just didn't like the idea of knocking on the door of strange people and Anita and Carla were self conscious about the way they were dressed: they were wearing bluejeans and old shirts, which was the uniform that the popular girls crew had decided on for handling Calhoun's roasted and boiled wieners and mustard catsup and relish and drippy marshmallows and dogs jumping up all over you. After much discussion Anita and Carla agreed to get out of the car and scout around.

As they walked towards Juanita's old place somebody called to them from the door of the other half of the duplex. It was Juanita; she'd only moved next door. When I saw Anita and Carla going inside I got out of the car and went after them. This was probably going to be the last time I'd ever see Juanita and I guessed I'd might as well find out all I could about her. I marched boldly up the wooden steps and across the front porch and as I opened the screen door somebody ran from the front room into another room and slammed the door. I couldn't tell who it was—just caught the motion out of the corner of my eye. There was an overhead light on in the front room—which must've been the living room although it came directly off the porch, with no hall or anything—and a floor lamp was on beside a big stuffed chair next to where Juanita was standing with Anita and Carla. Who was that? I demanded.

Nobody would tell me. They all stood around with blank looks on their faces; must not've expected me to bust in like that. Well I was pretty sure who it was: it was that goddam Earl Tann and he had been necking with Juanita right there in the living room of her house. I'd been studying that son-of-a-bitch for two weeks; I knew how I was going to handle him. I might be afraid of girls but I've never been scared of boys—even when they were twice my size like that lardass Earl Tann. Now that this was the last day in my life that I'd ever see Juanita I wasn't afraid anymore of what she might think. I was going to do what I had to do. They could call the MPs and throw me in the stockade; I didn't give a shit. I was going in after that bastard.

As I grabbed for the doorknob the girls got excited. Stop! Wait! Don't go in there!... I paused just for a second and asked Why not?... Because, Anita said calmly, we don't want to see you blush ... It was only Juanita's sister who'd dashed into that room when she'd seen me coming up on the porch; she was in her underwear.

Juanita's sister called out from behind the door and asked Juanita what time she'd be back. Juanita said About 1:30... Well if you're not coming back till 1:30 you can't go... Juanita turned to me and asked what time we'd be back... Around 10:30 I said... She relayed that acceptable time to her big sister.

Juanita led the way out to the car and reached for the back door. She and Carla sat in the back and Anita rode up front with me. As we crossed Main street onto River drive we spotted Miss Amick's Chevrolet just ahead of us. She was alone in the car. That's good, I thought; she could take Anita and Carla home if I could detach them from Juanita. I really didn't have much hope of doing that but I was going to give it a try.

Stringbean and Ackbo and their girlfriends—Louise and Deneen, who both lived in Andrew Jackson Homes, the enlisted area at the fort—got a ride to Calhoun's place with Johnny Dixon. Johnny didn't have a girlfriend and he had to be home at eleven o'clock. Stringbean and Ackbo wanted to stay out later and, as usual, I didn't have a curfew; they wanted me to take them and their girls home after the party. I promised I would, knowing I could ditch Anita and Carla and hoping Juanita wouldn't jump ship. It was only logical that all the girls from the fort should go back in the same car. Three north Columbia-Eau Claire boys and three girl army brats: a perfect six-some, a mature situation—that's what I wanted for my last night with Juanita.

It was a bright night with a full moon, cool for early June, breezy with big steel-gray clouds racing across the sky. Calhoun took some of us over to the pasture on the hill in front of his house and let us take turns riding bareback on his horse Prince. Browder and Johnny Dixon rode him, and so did Anita and Carla and Kerry Higgins and Juanita (Mandy Jackson didn't want to; I think she had her period). My plans for taking Juanita home that night fell through, but I got an image of her printed on my brain that I wouldn't be able to get rid of—of her gorgeous dungareed ass planted on that horse's bare back, those sleek thighs caressing his ribs, her snatch nestled against his withers. I couldn't look at old Prince again without thinking about her.

The party broke up around 10:30. Johnny Dixon left then and so did Miss Amick, taking Anita and Carla with her. Stringbean and Ackbo and their girlfriends, Juanita and I, and Kerry Higgins stayed a while longer. Actually, we were waiting for Kerry's family to come and pick her up; her parents and little brother had gone to a movie in town and were going to pick her up after the flick was over. It was the decent thing to do—keeping Kerry company—but it turned out to be a big mistake.

Dr. Higgins' Buick pulled into Calhoun's driveway a little before eleven. Kerry's old man got out and shook Calhoun's hand and said how nice it was of him to invite all the kids out there. He said hello to Juanita but didn't recognize the rest of us. Calhoun introduced us. Hey, Dr. Higgins said, all you girls live out at the fort. We go right near the fort on our way home to State Park. No need for somebody to go out of their way and make a special trip to take you all home when we've got plenty of room and we're going right by there... The old doc had decided that he was going to take those three girls home and people just don't say no to doctors; they got into his car. Stringbean and Ackbo were really burned up; they waved goodbye to Louise and Deneen. I got a wave from Juanita. I hadn't been within three feet of her that night. That was the last time I saw her.

I didn't forget her though. She was on my mind for the next 14 months—until I came home that day from the green hole and the Mirador Club and things started happening that changed everything.

6

I LET BROWDER take my knapsack with him when he got off the bus at Elmwood avenue. All that silverware that he'd picked up at the Mirador Club was in it and he said he'd bring it back to my house the next day. Also he said he was going to check with Daniel Sellers as soon as he got off work at the Piggly Wiggly and make sure everything was set for picking up Sandburg Wednesday night. Browder said he'd call and let me know how it was after supper.

I got off the bus in front of the Governor's Mansion and stepped off catty-cornered across Richland Street towards our place. A long shadow preceded me into the deep shade of the magnolias on the other side of the street. Down the sidewalk our house, with a boxwood hedge and a solitary fig tree in the front yard, stood out: the white two-story columns on the porch had turned pale yellow in the late afternoon sun. When I got to our yard I slipped through a break in the hedge and cut across under the fig tree and headed toward the porch and the front door. Funny thing: the car wasn't in the driveway or under the portico where Momma usually parks it in the summertime. She wouldn't have put it in the garage; I figured she must've been late getting off work and hadn't gotten back yet from taking Agnes home.

We usually eat supper at six o'clock, Momma and me. She gets off at the County Health Department at five and it takes her ten or 15 minutes to get home in the five o'clock rush. Agnes has supper cooking or warming in the oven when Momma gets home. If I'm around when Momma comes in with the car, I drive Agnes home. If not, Momma takes her home. After she rests up a little and reads the mail she puts supper on; sometimes she'll add something to whatever Agnes fixed—like making us each a salad of lettuce and tomatoes or cucumbers or canned asparagus.

When I walked in the door the grandfather's clock in the front hall said five of six. I certainly didn't expect to find Agnes there, but there she was—in a clean gray uniform with white starched collar and cuffs and a frilly white apron—getting serving dishes out of the sideboard in the dining room. She'd heard me coming through the front door but didn't look up or say anything until I walked into the dining room. "One thing we can always count on: whenever your momma needs you you won't be nowhere to be found."

"We having company tonight?"

"Y'all sho is. And you ain't no help a'tall. Your momma had to go down to the grocery store to get some steaks." That sounded good to me because Agnes really knew how to cook steaks and I sure was hungry—hadn't eaten anything since breakfast except for those vienna sausages and bread at the green hole. Agnes had set three places at the table.

"Who's the company, Agnes?"

"Doctor somebody who knowed your poppa. You better go get yourself cleaned up. I ain't ironed them shirts you brought back from Jacksonville all dirty and messed up: two buttons off one o'em. You got plenty others in your drawer..."

I heard the car door slam as I was walking out on Agnes, on my way to the kitchen to get a cold drink of water. Instead of going to the Frigidaire I went to the kitchen door to meet Momma. I held the screen door open as she came in with a bag of groceries.

"I'm sorry I wasn't around to help you, Momma."

"That's o.k., sugar. How you been?"

"Fine. Me and Billy Brown went swimming. Didn't mean to get back so late."

"Maybe you ought to wear your watch," she said as she started taking things out of the bag and arranging them on the kitchen table—a head of lettuce, a half dozen tomatoes, a can of mushrooms, meat wrapped in butcher paper—"is it working o.k.?"

"Yes ma'am. But I'm always afraid of leaving it somewhere. You know, when you go swimming and have to take it off. Might even forget to take it off and jump in with it on and ruin it." Momma took the package of steaks over to the sink and opened it.

"Dr. Summerville is having supper with us tonight. He knew your father in England. He's passing through Columbia on his way back up north from Florida. Called here this morning from the Wade Hampton Hotel where he's staying. Agnes gave him the number at the Health Department. Sounds like a real nice gentleman. Was devoted to your father. Especially wanted to see you. These steaks look real good," she was talking to Agnes now: "you sure you got everything you need?"

"Yes ma'am. What time you wanna have everything ready?"

"Let's see. I invited him for 6:30... and we'll want to talk a little in the library first... Not before seven o'clock. I'll let you know when to serve, but it won't be before seven. Now I better go take a shower and change these clothes."

"You want me to put on a coat and tie?" I asked.

"No, that won't be necessary sugar; just put on a nice short-sleeved shirt. We'll try to make the doctor as comfortable as possible in this heat and humidity." As she picked up her purse from the kitchen table she remembered: "My goodness, Clarence, I haven't given you any money since you came back from Jacksonville. Here's five dollars. Do you need more?"

"No ma'am. Thank you." I could see Agnes looking on with disapproval.

"I hope you hadn't planned to go out tonight."

"No ma'am. Ah... but I *would* like to use the car Wednesday night, if that's o.k."

"As far as I know..." She caught herself being vague. "Well sure it is; you can count on it. Would you like to have the car during the day too?"

"No ma'am. Just that night—after supper." I poured a half glass of water from the coldwater bottle in the Frigidaire and drank it down. "Well I'm going on up to my room and get dressed. I'll be ready when you call me."

The slanting rays of the setting sun were streaming in through the open windows when I walked into my room. Agnes had forgotten to close the shutters. Either that or she just hadn't felt like doing it. Anyway, the room wasn't all that hot. I switched on the fan and turned on the radio. They were just starting to give the local news on WCOS.

God I wanted a cigarette. I had money now; I could run down to Fogel's and buy a pack of Luckies before old doc whatsisname got here—could fag one in my room before supper. But Momma'd see me and she'd know what I went after: cigarettes. I'd seem weak—a nicotine fiend, just couldn't do without a teege. Momma and I have these arrangements—unspoken agreements I guess you'd say—and one of them is that neither one of us will do anything that makes us look weak in front of the other. So I just had to suffer in situations like this. Momma didn't smoke so I couldn't steal fags from her when I was out, like Snake did from his old man and Browder did from his grandfather.

There was no shower in my bathroom and I didn't feel like taking a bath—not without anything to smoke lying in the tub. I'd just smear a little Arid on under my arms. And shave; hadn't shaved since Jacksonville. Before school was out I was shaving two or three times during the week and whenever I'd be going on a date. I had enough whiskers on my chin to shave every day but didn't because it irritated my skin and seemed to cause pimples—especially on the lower jaw below the corners of my mouth. I almost always had a pimple there on one side or the other.

After shaving I scooped up some water in my hands and rubbed it into my hair. It combed out fine; didn't need any Wildroot Cream Oil. Before I went to Jacksonville old Pete the barber gave me a pretty good square cut across the back but he took too much off the sides; ducktail still didn't come together right. I decided I'd let it grow and just get a neck trim right before school started.

I put on a short-sleeved sports shirt—a white one with pink vertical stripes—and stepped into the gray tailor-made pants I got from Len Harper back in June. Momma shelled out $14 for those fabrics so she might as well see me wearing them I thought. I was tying the laces on my white bucks when somebody rapped the brass knocker at the front door. I turned down the radio and opened the door to my room so I could hear what was going on.

I heard Agnes padding across the bare wooden floor in the hall in her rubber-soled shoes and opening the front door. I couldn't make out what she and the doctor were saying—didn't try to; it wasn't important. The two of them went down the hall to the library where Momma was. I could just barely hear their voices; the Persian rug on the floor and all the books in the library absorbed a lot of sound. Agnes's footsteps echoed across the hall again, going to and from the kitchen. I could visualize her holding a big silver tray in both hands waist high with a silver bucket of ice cubes, a seltzer bottle, a silver pitcher of water, one short and two tall glasses, linen napkins, and two fifths of whiskey—one bourbon and one scotch.

Momma only drank at home when she had company—which wasn't too often. Most of the time it'd be family—Uncle Lewie or relatives from Georgia—and they wouldn't get the silver-ice-bucket treatment. She did break out the fancy stuff for relatives from the other side of the family—any of the Montforts from Charleston. Grandmomma Palmerston was a Montfort before she got married. There aren't any more Palmerstons around anywhere that I know of; Momma and I are the last ones. Anyway, we didn't often see anybody from Poppa's side of the family—maybe a Montfort cousin every year or two, and to tell

the truth we didn't see Momma's people—the Evanses—all that
often except for Uncle Lewie who lives here in Columbia. We'd
go over to Georgia once a year to visit Grandma Evans and my
uncles and aunts and cousins who live in Jalapa. We'd go for a
week in the summer during Momma's vacation, usually the third
week in August.

Anyway, relatives would visit us here every now and then.
And once in a while we'd have some doctor and his wife for
supper, or some hospital administrator and his wife—people in
Momma's business. And occasionally Momma'd invite a single
fellow to have supper with us here. People would tell me that my
momma was nice looking and they were right: she wasn't bad
looking at all for a lady almost 40 years old. But Momma didn't
seem much interested in getting married again. I don't think any
of the single men she invited for supper—before Dr. Summerville—ever came back again. She'd always make sure I was here
when these old fellows came and she'd tell them all about me and
how much I meant to her. (Her sun rises and sets on my ass,
Uncle Lewie liked to say.) I was always polite to Momma's
friends, even to those I didn't much care for.

Most of Momma's friends were other ladies who worked
—mostly married but a few widows like her. Either they didn't
have children or they were grown. Sometimes the ladies would
come here to play canasta or bridge after supper on weekdays or
on Saturday afternoons. More likely Momma'd go to one of their
houses to play cards. And there was this one married couple that
had a house on a pond downcountry near Pelion; sometimes
she'd spend the weekend with them. I never minded staying here
by myself, especially not when she'd leave me the car. Agnes'd be
off after dinner Saturday and all day Sunday, so I'd have to fix
my own meals but that was o.k. with me.

Now when Momma's lady friends would come here to play
cards they'd sit in the living room, around the oak table. When
we had more important visitors she'd take them into the library.
That was Grandmomma Palmerston's favorite room, where she
had her writing desk, and all the books the Palmerstons had

collected for hundreds of years were lined up on three walls in mahogany bookcases with glass doors. My Grandmomma was big on reading and I read a couple of books to please her—*Two Little Confederates* and *Treasure Island*. Since she died the only books I've read were for school—if you don't count pocket novels which I usually only read the sexy parts of that other boys had marked. Except for that stuff I just didn't read books that weren't assigned in school; I didn't do extra reading even when I was making A's in English back in the eighth grade. Why should I? I was making A's in algebra too, but I wasn't about to go to the school library and check out some book of simultaneous linear equations to take home and work on in my spare time. That would've made more sense to me than wasting time reading something that wasn't true, reading fiction. I'd rather do real things than read about things that never happened.

Sure, there's supposed to be a moral to every story, but reading make-believe didn't seem to me to be a very good way to get morals. Take those books I read for my grandmother: what was the point? That people you hated and feared—Yankees and pirates in those books—weren't totally bad? Hell you could figure that out just looking at real people you didn't like or didn't used to like. Baptists for instance: some of them were o.k. as individuals and even when they were acting like Baptists they had a few good points. Instead of worrying about make-believe pirates, I'd rather concentrate on real-life Baptists: they were the people that could cause you trouble. And you couldn't study Baptists in books; you had to get out among them.

History books in my opinion weren't much better than fiction. There were certain historical facts you had to know—like the South lost the Confederate War. But you sure didn't have to read a book to know that. History books were supposed to tell you why certain things happened; but why should you give a shit? They'd already happened and there was nothing you could do about it. It was what was *going* to happen that mattered. And you couldn't figure that out unless you knew what was going on around you. And you learned that by getting out and doing things not reading books. If I was going to read something it'd be the newspaper or magazines like *Life* and *Time*—even though I hated those bastards for running down the South.

This crap about history repeating itself I thought was just that: pure horse hockey. If it was true, people who knew history would know what was going to happen and they sure as hell didn't—no more than people who studied the Bible knew when the world was coming to an end. Except for a lot of outdated and useless facts, you didn't learn anything from reading history books that you couldn't learn just by living. I remembered this book I read for social studies: we each had to read a book about a famous figure in history and I picked Genghis Khan. (Don't remember why; probably because there wasn't much left to choose from when I got to the biography shelf in the school library.) So what could you learn from that book? That if you were going to be a success—conquer the world or whatever—you had to be smart and you had to be willing and able to kick ass, or chop off heads in the case of old Genghis. Nobody should have to read a book to find that out.

But at least books like *Genghis Khan* by Harold Lamb couldn't do you any harm, I thought; they didn't distort things the way movies did. In the movies if you were decent and honest and did what was right you'd come out on top in the end. Everybody wanted to believe that and some poor souls actually did, but not many. Most people realized the movies were make-believe and they went to be entertained and to be with other people. I certainly liked going to the flicks; it was fun and it didn't put you under any mental strain like books did. My brain was so overloaded last year with Latin declensions and botanical genera and geometrical theorems and other such stuff that I couldn't have done any outside reading even if I'd wanted to—couldn't have made any sense of it.

Last year it got so bad that I even had trouble reading the newspaper. Back in the eighth grade I could read the editorials in *The State* and they made perfect sense to me; in the ninth grade I couldn't follow them at all. I definitely suffered an intellectual decline during that period. I started to recover when Dr. Gregory Ashton Summerville came for supper at our house.

I left my room when I heard Agnes starting up the stairs to get me. After she saw me she turned around and went back to the kitchen and I went on into the library. Dr. Summerville got up from the easy chair next to the window and stuck out his hand. Momma was sitting on the settee.

"Dr. Summerville, this is my son Clarence."

He was about as tall as I was, medium build, in his shirtsleeves and wearing a bow tie. He wore rimless eyeglasses and his dark hair was slicked back and parted off center, slightly over to the left side. He looked like somebody you might see in *Life* magazine in a picture of a Wallace rally. Maybe he's a Communist I thought. His handshake was firm though.

"Clarence, this is indeed a pleasure. I guess I don't have to tell you that you're the spitting image of your father."

"Yes sir... I mean no... Thank you sir." He was one of those people who said things in a way that got you all mixed up.

"Mrs. Palmerston, it's uncanny how much he looks like Al." He pronounced Mrs. the way Yankees do—not Miz but drawing it out: Miz-ziz. But he didn't have a deep Yankee accent; he sounded like he could've been from the South originally—talked a little like Wayne Poucher the radio announcer for the Columbia Reds games.

"He's a fine boy, Dr. Summerville. Al would've been proud of him."

The doctor sat back down and reached for a pack of Camels and a Ronson lighter on the coffee table next to the liquor. He must've taken them out of his coat pocket and put them there before Momma took his coat and hung it up in the hall closet. I guessed he was one of those 113,597 doctors they asked What cigarette do you smoke doctor and the brand named most was Camels. They're so mild they suit you to a T. He's one of those people who're afraid of getting a sore throat or TB I thought. People who're scared smoke Camels. Most girls who smoke

smoke Camels. They're so mild! Just like most girls who drink
beer drink Miller High Life. It's so light!

I sat down next to Momma on the settee. I figured she was
working on her second scotch and soda. The old doc was
drinking bourbon and water in a tall glass but the drink was so
weak it looked like scotch and water. That was good bourbon
Momma gave him: Old Fitzgerald bottled in bond. Nobody
offered me a drink and I didn't expect them to. If they had I'd
have taken scotch because I'd had a real bad experience with
bourbon one night last spring out at Camp Barstow with the
Scouts. Snake and I killed this bottle of rotgut that he bought
—Bourbon Deluxe—and I spent most of the next morning puking
my guts out. Old Snake thought it was hilarious and about
laughed his fool head off; he's got this real deep voice: Ho Ho
Ho... The slithery creature had been mixing my drinks —bourbon and Seven-Up—and had made them triple strength. Anyway,
it about killed my taste for bourbon.

"Clarence just got back yesterday from a Scout encampment
in Jacksonville," Momma announced: "He's a Senior Scout now."
The way she said it you'd think that being a Senior Scout was a
big achievement, like being an Eagle. The fact was, the only thing
you had to pass to become a Senior Scout was your fourteenth
birthday; actually you were supposed to be 15 but you could get
in at 14 and a half. I'd joined the Boy Scouts when I was
twelve—joined the troop at Preacher's church, Epiphany
Lutheran. I'd passed my Tenderfoot and Second Class and was
working on my First Class by the time I was 14. I was a patrol
leader and was supposed to be helping younger boys while
working on my own merit badges. They were big on advancement in that troop. Well it just got to be too much for me last
year when I was struggling to pass the ninth grade; I just couldn't
handle all that Scout stuff and the schoolwork too. So last
December I switched from the Epiphany troop to the outfit
Snake belonged to at Covenant Presbyterian, which was exclu-
sively Senior Scouts—nobody under 14—and not gung ho about
advancement. The Covenant Pres Scouts had a lot of advantages:

a motor boat up at Lake Murray and their own cabin at Camp
Barstow—called the "House of It"—an old nigger house that
must've belonged to some sharecropper before they sold the land
to the Scouts. Older boys like Snake could take out the boat—a
22-footer that used to be a lifeboat on some ship—and we'd cruise
around Lake Murray on Saturdays drinking beer. When we went
to the House of It on weekends we'd stay up most of the night
drinking and playing poker. Regular meetings were on Thursday
night and they were mostly bull sessions; afterwards a bunch of
us would go down to Nick the Greek's at Five Points and shoot
pool.

"The Scouts are a marvelous organization," Dr. Summerville
observed. "Unfortunately when I was a boy I didn't have the
opportunity to join. I hope my son will take an interest in
Scouting. He's ten now and lives with his mother on the Jersey
shore."

I caught Momma's eye and let her know I understood: he's
divorced. You can't get divorced in South Carolina for any
reason whatsoever. And the Episcopal church is totally opposed
to divorce: they'll excommunicate you if you get divorced.
They're as fanatical as Catholics when it comes to divorce; won't
tolerate it. Grandmomma Palmerston, I thought, would've just
as soon have a nigger sitting there in her chair as a divorced
person.

"Dr. Summerville lives in New Jersey, Clarence, but he grew
up in Richmond, Virginia." Then she turned to him and said,
"Clarence has so many interests and activities that it's hard for
me to keep up with them. Besides the Scouts he plays on the
neighborhood baseball team..."

"Oh yeah?" the doc broke in. "I've always loved baseball.
What position do you play Clarence?"

"Uh... third base... and catcher." Actually I never played
catcher in a game because my throwing wasn't accurate enough.
I'd let somebody else use the catcher's mitt Momma gave me for
my birthday and I'd play third base. I didn't have enough
throwing range to play outfield and everybody figured third base

was where I'd do the least damage. They had to let me play if they wanted to use my catcher's mitt which was the only one in the neighborhood.

"How often does your team play?" the doctor asked.

"Whenever we can get up a game with another team." The fact was we hadn't played more than a half dozen games all year. Last time was the week before I went to Jacksonville when we played the Rinky Dinks from Camp Fornance and they clobbered us 16 to 2.

"Oh you don't play a regular schedule?"

"No sir."

"One advantage my son has where he lives is that he can play in an organized league—the Little League they call it—with scheduled games and practices and uniforms—all the trimmings—and with adult coaches. They really learn the game."

"We can go out for American Legion baseball if we're good enough."

"That's the trouble: not everybody who wants to play is good enough for Legion ball. The Little League expands to take everybody in, lets everybody play at least a little. Now when I was a boy I didn't even have the opportunity to play sandlot baseball. Played softball in Phys Ed class at school; that's about all. Loved the game though. Devoured the sports pages; could spout off the batting average of virtually every player in the major leagues. Used to listen to major league games on a crystal set I built; picked up broadcasts from Washington and Philadelphia. And sometimes my father would take me to see the Richmond Colts play."

Oh boy I thought, did I know the type: the intellectual baseball fan. Went to ball games with Daddy. You'd see 'em in the grandstand at Capital City Park. Couldn't smoke, couldn't drink beer, couldn't cuss, couldn't horse around; all they could do was sit there with their old man and concentrate on the finer points of the game.

"Baseball and reading were my two passions." Dr. Summerville paused about a second to change the subject: "I read all Galsworthy's novels when I was a boy..."

Ohmygod I thought, he's going to ask me what books I read, but he didn't.

"Of course I was also interested in science—liked to fiddle around with my chemistry set; my mother always knew I'd be a doctor. I had a rock collection and an insect collection too. I'm afraid I disappointed Mother though when it came to music. I took piano lessons for ten years but attained no proficiency at all."

"Oh I'm sure you're just being modest Dr. Summerville," Momma chimed in at last. "I'd ask you to play for us but I'm afraid the Steinway in the living room is completely out of tune. Hasn't been played since before Mrs. Palmerston—Al's mother, Miss Clarice—since Miss Clarice's arthritis got so bad she couldn't play anymore. I never learned to play the piano and Clarence took lessons on the drums."

"Yes sir," I added, "but I never really learned to play them. I just don't have any rhythm." That was an understatement. After two lessons my drum teacher—this old fellow who had been in the German navy on a U-boat in World War I—threw up his hands and called me a Dumbkopf and said I'd never be a "dummer." I couldn't even play momma-poppa on a drum. I just didn't have any sense of rhythm. And when Grandmomma Palmerston sent me to Mrs. Sloan's ballroom dancing school to learn to dance it was a total disaster. At least I knew for sure I didn't have any nigger blood in me.

"Unfortunately nobody on my side of the family has any musical talent," Momma explained, "and I'm afraid Clarence takes after us in that respect. But in everything else he's like Al was—smart as a whip. When he was in junior high he was in the National Honor Society."

"Good for you Clarence," said the old doc. "What subject do you like best?"

I told the truth: "I like art."

Momma must've wished I'd said something else but she took the hand-off and ran with the ball. "Clarence just spends hours and hours down here in the library studying Miss Clarice's picture books." She flipped her hand in the direction of the shelf that held the twelve volumes of *A Treasury of European Painting*. On other shelves nearby were umpteen volumes of *Great American Painters and their Works*, *The Sculpture of the Renaissance*, *Great Art: Ancient and Modern*, and a lot of others.

"That's quite a collection you have."

"Yes. Miss Clarice loved art. She visited all the galleries of Europe."

"No, not just those—all the books."

"Why yes, I do suppose we have a lot. Almost all come from Al's family."

No doubt about it: the Palmerstons bought books—*The Library of Southern Literature*, *The Waverly Novels*, *The Complete Works of Dickens*, *The Works of Thackery*, *Simms' Works*... You could name any famous author and we probably had everything he ever wrote. But nobody here had read those books because if you'd take them off the shelf and open them up you'd see that the pages hadn't even been cut. Well, there were a few that Grandmomma Palmerston had read, mostly religious books.

"I wish I had more time to read," Momma said. "It's about all I can do to get through the *Reader's Digest* each month." Actually she usually managed to get through *Redbook* too, and *Colliers* and the *Saturday Evening Post* every week.

"Oh," something on the shelf behind Dr. Summerville's head caught Momma's eye. "Did you know that Al's mother wrote a book? And there's a picture of Al in it. Clarence, please get down your grandmother's book."

I walked around where Dr. Summerville was sitting and pushed up the glass door on the fourth shelf of the bookcase and pulled out *The Palmerstons of South Carolina* by Clarice DeClerk Montfort Palmerston, published by the R. L. Bryan Company of Columbia, S. C. in 1922. It told about the Palmerstons after they came over here from somewhere in England in the seventeen hundreds—listed everybody and said when they were born, when they got married and when they died and told about what the family did in the Revolution and in the War Between the States. Among the Palmerstons and their close relatives were some judges and governors and senators and generals—nobody that you'd ever study about in school but Grandmomma said they were important. On page four there was a picture of Poppa when he was 13 years old.

I handed the book to Momma and she opened it to the picture of Poppa and passed it to Dr. Summerville. In the picture Poppa was wearing knickers and dark knee socks and a four-button tweed jacket with a belt and a white shirt and a tie. He was standing with his arms hanging down by his side and his feet slightly apart. He didn't seem too self conscious about getting his picture taken; he was smiling just a little bit.

"My my. Isn't that interesting. That's Al all right. I had a suit just like that when I was a boy."

"He was his mother's pride and joy," Momma said. "Her only child. His father died when he was a toddler; died of TB—consumption they called it in those days. So Miss Clarice had to raise Al all alone—I mean she got no help from relatives; she could afford servants because through Al's father she inherited all the Palmerston money. Her own family, the Montforts of Charleston, were once prominent in the lowcountry, but they'd lost all their money. Miss Clarice didn't seem to pay much attention to them: her life was dedicated to Al and to preserving the Palmerston heritage for him."

And for me, she should've said. The truth is, though, Grand-momma Palmerston didn't make much distinction between me and Poppa. We were the same to her: lots of times she'd call me "Algernon."

"As Al told you, Dr. Summerville, he married me in Atlanta when he was an intern at Central Hospital. You can imagine what a disappointment that must've been for Miss Clarice—Al eloping with me, a cracker from north Georgia. But she made the best of it. She was a great lady, Dr. Summerville. We moved in here with her before the war when Al was setting up his practice in Columbia, and Miss Clarice did what she could to show me how to raise Clarence properly and tried to make a lady out of me. She took me to the Episcopal church, got me into the Junior League—wanted to get me into the Daughters of the American Revolution and the Daughters of the American Colonists and the Colonial Dames. Trouble was, I didn't have any ancestors that I knew of who would qualify me for things like the DAR."

Momma ran her finger between the two strands of pearls that rested easily along the top of her collarless blouse, and touched her neck behind the ear below a starburst earring.

"You see, my people were Welsh and Scotch-Irish and just sort of wandered into the hills of north Georgia sometime before the Civil War. I guess they were illiterate or maybe they just didn't see any need to keep written records. And the first ones couldn't even speak English much less read and write it. The story was that my great-great grandfather was over a hundred when he died, outlived all of this children, and for the last ten years of his life nobody could understand a word he said because he only spoke Welsh. Nobody in my family knew anything about the Revolution. There was no way Miss Clarice could get me in the DAR."

Momma took a sip from her drink and Dr. Summerville snuffed out his Camel. He was all ears.

"She did get me into the UDC though—the United Daughters of the Confederacy. That was sort of funny because from what I've heard most of the menfolk in my family hid out in the hills during the Civil War to keep out of the Confederate army. And a couple of my great-uncles actually joined the Union army —their money was worth a lot more than Confederate money. But one of my great-grandfathers did serve in the Confederate army and on account of him they let me in the UDC. And that was funny too, because after the war my great-grandfather joined the Republican party and was elected county treasurer during Reconstruction. In no time at all he had enough money to build himself a big house in town and buy up timber land in the hills and bottom land along the Tugaloo river. He was the one who got our family started in the feed and drygoods business, started the Evans & Sons general store in Jalapa. He always treated people right—gave them credit when they needed it—and when Reconstruction was overturned he just got out of politics and nobody bothered him."

Boy, I thought, give Momma a couple of drinks and she'll recite the whole family history. I didn't mind though. I liked to hear her tell it; she told it a little different each time. Old doc was really paying attention; he sat still and didn't move a lick; didn't even take a sip out of his drink while she was talking.

"Anyway, Dr. Summerville, when I came to Columbia with Al and baby Clarence, my mother-in-law wouldn't hear of me going back to work as a nurse. She had my time all planned out for me: UDC, Junior League, the New Century Club, the Book Club, Women of the Church, functions at Forest Lake Country Club... Well, to tell you the truth, Dr. Summerville, I just didn't fit in. Nobody was mean to me: that wasn't it. On the contrary, everybody was just as nice as they could be. It was just me; I just didn't feel I belonged with those ladies doing those things. Then when the war came along and Al volunteered for the Medical Corps, Miss Clarice couldn't object too much when I went back to work to help in the war effort. They needed nurses at Columbia Hospital to replace the ones who were called into the service."

Momma took another sip from her drink. Dr. Summerville touched the bridge of his glasses with his forefinger and pushed them back up on his nose as he waited for her to continue.

"After Al died Miss Clarice tried to get me to quit work, but I needed to keep busy to take my mind off what had happened. Just looking after Clarence wouldn't be enough—Miss Clarice was doing that anyway—and the UDC and the Junior League would only depress me even more. So I kept on working; got into administration; went with the County Health Department; got as high up as a woman can go. That's where I am now: as high up as a woman in my business can go in South Carolina—probably in all the South. I tell you, Dr. Summerville, sometimes I think that as soon as Clarence finishes high school and goes off to college I'll just pull up stakes and head on out to California..."

Just then the phone rang in the living room. "I'll get it," I said. "I think it's for me."

Browder was surprised when I answered the phone and told him that we hadn't finished supper yet—hadn't even started. He said he was thinking about shooting some pool that night and I told him to go ahead but I wouldn't be able to make it. Had he talked with Sellers? Yes and Sellers was glad to hear I could get my car Wednesday night and said he'd guarantee that he'd get Sandburg. Browder said he had to collect on his paper route in the morning and would drop off my knapsack when he was in our area. I reminded him that my canteen and two bathing suits were supposed to be in the knapsack. And all those pictures, he added. Yeah, don't forget my pictures. I didn't ask and he didn't say whether or not his old lady liked the silverware he brought her from the Mirador Club.

As soon as I walked back into the library after hanging up the phone Momma got up and said she was going to check with Agnes to see if supper was ready. Dr. Summerville scrambled to his feet and then fell back into the easy chair as she left the room. I sat down again on the settee. Across the room above the mantlepiece over the fireplace General Lee and Stonewall Jackson were looking over some battlefield in a colored lithograph in a gilt frame. General Lee was on his gray horse Traveller, who was behaving himself, and Stonewall was on his sorrel horse —whatever his name was—who was giving him a hard time tugging against the reins with his head down and over to the side like he was trying to shake off a fly or take a bite of grass.

"I was just remarking to your mother," Dr. Summerville said, "how tough it must have been for you growing up without a father. Especially since you were old enough when he left for the war to have some recollections of him—to know what a fine man he was, to have some idea of what you were missing."

"Yes sir."

"Now my son Tod is only a year or two older than you were when you last saw your dad. He came to visit me for a week in June. We went hiking in the Poconos and went to New York to see a Giants game—and the Bronx zoo. And we built a model airplane together and flew it in Middle Park in Plattville, the city where I live. When Tod's older I hope we can do a lot of things together."

Poor old Tod, I thought to myself, what could be worse than getting stuck with some old fart who wants to be your buddy? Who'd ever want to run around with some cat 40 years old? Even if he *was* your old man. *Especially* if he was your old man.

The doc looked like he was about to come right out and ask me for an opinion when Momma appeared in the doorway and announced that supper was ready. She led us into the dining room and told me to sit at the head of the table; all three places were set at the end of the table near the door to the kitchen. Dr. Summerville helped Momma into her chair and she asked me to say grace.

"Lord make us thankful for what we are about to receive," I enunciated clearly and distinctly with head bowed, "for Christ's sake, amen."

"Thank you Clarence. Now Dr. Summerville we have iced tea and iced coffee or hot coffee if you like..."

Everybody wanted iced tea and Agnes soon appeared with a pitcher of it to fill our glasses. I reached for the platter of steaks and passed it to Dr. Summerville. Momma helped herself to corn pudding while I grabbed a couple of biscuits and buttered them. Dr. Summerville handed the steaks to Momma and she told me to pass him the salad dressing. It was in a silver dish and looked like mayonnaise; I never could tell the difference between salad dressing and mayonnaise. The doctor slapped a glob of the pale yellow stuff on his salad plate—on top of the tomatoes that were red as blood and sliced like cartwheels and arranged neatly on a bed of lettuce leaves. After I'd helped myself to rice and gravy I speared the last steak. It was cooked in mushrooms and done to perfection: juicy and so tender you could cut it with a fork.

"Agnes was going to fix field peas with snaps for tonight," Momma said to Dr. Summerville, "but with today being wash day she found she just didn't have time to prepare them and cook them properly. It takes a long time you know. And she'd have had to fix cornbread too; we'd have needed cornbread to go with all that pot liquor."

"Well we don't need another thing, Mrs. Palmerston. This is all perfectly delicious. Anything more would be superfluous—even good Southern field peas which I enjoyed as a boy and still relish. I think the thing I miss most living up North is Southern cooking. You know they don't really cook their vegetables up there, serve them to you half raw—even stringbeans —can you imagine?"

"Yes I can. I remember the trip Al and I took to New York right after we were married. The half-cooked vegetables struck me right off, and the salad—what they *call* salad," Momma said with a giggle. "We were at this restaurant and the waiter asked me what kind of salad I wanted and I said mustard greens..."

Dr. Summerville was laughing. "I know what you mean; I know exactly what you mean..."

"Well I should have known better, having lived in Atlanta for two years. But in that restaurant in New York when the waiter said 'salad' all I could think of was what it meant back home in Jalapa—greens that you cooked. We didn't have the other kind of salad when I was a girl. There wasn't any lettuce and almost nobody ate tomatoes. A lot of people thought they were poisonous..."

"Or an aphrodisiac," Dr. Summerville interjected.

"Yes," Momma laughed. "They called them 'love apples.'"

"So you see, Clarence," Dr. Summerville said just as I was stuffing a big bite of steak into my mouth, "the world has changed a great deal since your parents were your age."

I nodded agreement.

"He is indeed a splendid lad," the doc said to Momma. "Just seeing the way he has developed reassures me—gives me hope that my own son will do as well in the absence of a fatherly presence."

"You must believe that, Dr. Summerville. I'm sure your son looks up to you, respects you. That's what's really important. You don't have to be with him all the time. You know, sometimes I think parents—mothers as well as fathers—involve themselves too much in their children's lives nowadays. Maybe it's because of the depression and the war: some people feel they got short-changed on their own childhood and now they're trying to relive it through their children. We're seeing a lot of childish adults who—in my opinion—are setting a bad example for their kids, giving them the idea that growing up is terrible and you don't have to do it: you can feel like a kid and play kids' games and act childish forever. If things keep going the way they are I wouldn't be surprised if in ten or 20 years we find ourselves with a generation of young people who refuse to grow up—or don't know how to grow up."

Momma was getting serious now. She put down her fork and took a sip of iced tea. "When we involve ourselves directly in kids' things we short-circuit the growing-up process. Children learn things best by stages, and some things they learn best from other children. Parents who aren't able to get involved in all their children's activities shouldn't feel guilty. They might be doing their kids a favor."

"That's a comforting thought, Mrs. Palmerston. And looking back on my own childhood I can see how I was perhaps oversupervised. When I went away to college at William and Mary I was well prepared academically but I didn't know how to drive a car. And there were a lot of other things I had to learn at the advanced age of 17. I had a lot of catching up to do—and maybe I overdid it." He smiled like he thought he'd said something funny.

"Nobody in my family went to college," Momma said, "but we all managed to grow up—except maybe my baby brother

Lewie. And even he's halfway settled down now; he's a partner in an army-navy surplus store here in Columbia. The other boys are still in Jalapa; two of them run the family feed and drygoods business and the other does some farming and has a cider mill. My sister is married to an accountant in California."

Momma took a bite of corn pudding before continuing with her family saga. The way Dr. Summerville was chewing his steak you could tell he was concentrating real hard on what she was saying.

"We all had to work when we were children—in the store, in the warehouse, on the farm. Those were hard times as you remember, Dr. Summerville—except that for farming people the depression started ten years earlier, not long after the First World War. My father worked hard and we kids had to work too, to keep the family business going—schoolwork was not that important. That's certainly not the way it is with us today—with Clarence and me—I'm happy to say. I don't have any business he has to help me with and I don't want him to waste his time working for somebody else. His schoolwork's his work; that's what's important."

Momma took another sip of tea and smiled mischievously. "Of course having fun's important too. We had fun in my family even during the worst of the depression. The children had fun; the adults had fun; and sometimes we had fun together. The adults didn't intrude in children's games; it was the kids who wanted to join the grown-ups and do grown-up things. The boys would beg the men to let them go with them on rabbit hunts or deer drives. My poppa would always say to them No, you're too little, until one day when one of the boys would be eleven or twelve and he'd say O.k., get your gun and come on.

"Poppa never taught any of my brothers to shoot. They learned from older brothers or from cousins or friends. They'd learn to shoot somebody else's .22 or .410 before they'd ask for one of their own for Christmas or their birthday. The boys would go out shooting squirrels or doves on their own before they were allowed to go with the big people. And they had their

ball games and horse riding and swimming and fishing—and
sometimes they'd let us girls go along if we wanted to, which
usually we didn't."

Momma smiled and batted her eyes. "My goodness, Dr.
Summerville, I'm talking a lot. You must think it's terribly
unladylike."

"No, no, Mrs. Palmerston. Please go on. Your experiences
were so different from mine. Tell me, when did you learn to
drive a car?"

"A car? I don't rightfully remember. But I was twelve when
I learned to drive Poppa's delivery truck. A cousin—a boy—who
was working in the warehouse taught me. Most of us children—boys *and* girls—learned to drive as soon as we were big
enough to see over the top of the steering wheel. Of course, there
were no driver's licenses back in those days. Life in the country—or in a country town—was a lot different from life in a big
city like Richmond or Atlanta or even Columbia. But no matter
where you live you're going to have problems growing up.
Brothers and sisters can help, but they can cause trouble too. And
the same can be said for mothers and fathers.

"Now Clarence has some fine young friends here in Columbia
from all kinds of home situations. His friend Billy Brown is like
him in that he doesn't have a father but he has a younger brother
and sister. They don't have a maid and his mother keeps house
for the children and her father, Billy's grandfather, who lives
with them but travels a lot because he's an inspector for the state
highway department. He's a fine gentleman—Mr. Hamilton,
Billy's grandfather—so conscientious and hard-working. He has
other family and some property upstate that he has to go look
after most weekends. So Billy doesn't see much of his grandfather. They live a few blocks away on Elmwood avenue.

"And Clarence has friends on the other side of Columbia—in
Shandon, the more prosperous part of town. His friend Zack
McBain lives out there. Poor old Mr. McBain—Zack's father—has
such a bad case of emphysema that he can just barely make it
from his car to his easy chair when he comes home from work

every day. The poor man has so much trouble breathing he can hardly eat—he's thin as a rail—but he'll smoke two packs of cigarettes a day—"

Momma stopped suddenly like she thought she'd offended the doctor.

"That's a shame," Dr. Summerville said quickly with a funny laugh. "It's not just people with emphysema who should stop smoking. We all should. There's no question that smoking is generally harmful to the broncho-pulmonary system. I'm going to quit myself—as soon as I can get up the will power." He laughed again and looked at me. "Clarence, listen to your mother and don't let yourself get hooked on those coffin nails. Once you start smoking it's not easy to stop, I'll guarantee you. Follow your mother's example, not mine."

He didn't have to worry about me following his example on anything. Momma now seemed concerned about making me uneasy and switched the subject. "Well we all need to do what we can to stay healthy. One thing we can be thankful for is that people are a whole lot healthier now than they used to be. You mentioned pulmonary disorders Dr. Summerville; I'll never cease to be amazed at the progress we've made in the last ten years. Pneumonia is no longer a threat to people's lives—at least not to young people's lives—and we seem to be on the road to eliminating tuberculosis altogether. Already they've started closing down State Park, the tuberculosis sanitorium here."

I knew about that. Dr. Higgins—Kerry's old man—was leaving State Park, moving on, taking Kerry and the family to North Carolina or somewhere. That was some girl, Kerry Higgins; made straight A's in the ninth grade just like in the eighth grade. Showed it could be done if you didn't let your head get all messed up—talk about setting a good example! I was going to miss old Kerry.

"They're doing that all over the country," Dr. Summerville said, "closing down TB sanitoria. We've got the wartime development of streptomycin to thank for that."

"Yes, and now we can control so many infections that used to run rampant among school children, like impetigo. Antibiotics have been a godsend to us in the public health field. With penicillin we're able to prevent the awful damage that syphilis and gonorrhea can do."

"But isn't there a problem getting people to come in for treatment? Most of the people who contract and spread venereal diseases aren't accustomed to medical treatment—don't have a personal physician—and they're usually too embarrassed or too ignorant to do anything about their condition."

"That's where *we* come in, Dr. Summerville—the county health department. I must say we have just about solved those problems here in Richland county." Momma rang for Agnes to come and clear the table for dessert.

"We've pursued an aggressive program of tracking down VD contacts and bringing them to the office for treatment. My assistant Mr. Peterson does most of the field work and he's wonderfully persuasive. Of course, the sheriff's department is ready to back us up but so far we haven't had to call on them. Anyway, we find the people and get them into the office and give them their shots.

"We observe strict confidentiality, Dr. Summerville. And that applies to minors as well as to adults. Any person who comes in—or is brought in—for treatment in my office can rest assured that we will tell no one—except their sexual contacts, of course, and we'll approach *them* as delicately as possible. When we have an infected married man, we'll sometimes let a family physician handle the matter. But we always follow up to make sure that both husband and wife received the prescribed treatment. With teenagers we treat them in the office and we never tell their parents."

Agnes brought out individual dishes of vanilla ice cream and a big bowl of sliced peaches.

"Those peaches look delicious," Dr. Summerville said; "it's been a long time since I've had fresh peaches." He piled about a dozen wedges on top of his ice cream. "But tell me, Mrs. Palmerston, wasn't there any resistance to your policy of confidentiality in regard to minors—giving them medical treatment and not telling their parents?"

"Well there was concern in the office that we'd get into trouble with the church people if we publicly announced our policy, so we never announced it. We just told every boy and girl we picked up that that was the way it was: we wouldn't tell their parents. And they came to believe us because we always kept our promise. I don't mean to brag, Dr. Summerville, but I was the one who persuaded our director, Dr. Carrington, to do this, and it was a big success. Boys began coming in on their own, right after the first discharge. They came in droves: word got around. They'd identify their contact and Mr. Peterson would go after her. We found that these girls responded much better to Mr. Peterson than they did to me or some other female health worker. They didn't feel threatened by him I guess—didn't feel he was being judgmental, as they thought we'd be."

I'd known that Momma was the head of the Richland county VD squad, though she didn't usually talk to me about her work. I'd heard about boys who'd gone to her office with a dose of clap; I knew they'd gotten free shots of penicillin and nobody told their parents. What I didn't know much about was how Momma handled the girls.

"Some of these girls—I'm talking about white girls, Dr. Summerville, twelve years old and up—would have dozens of contacts in one week. They might not even know the names of some of the boys they had relations with. So sometimes we'd have to do a lot of detective work—snooping around, talking to third parties—to identify or track down boys who hadn't come in voluntarily. We had to find the boys and give them the shots; in these cases we wouldn't have to worry about protecting a girl's reputation. The girl's activities would be well known."

Momma turned to me. "Clarence, do you know a girl named Abbie Joubert? Lives over by the university... "

"Uh... No ma'am. I don't know her—but I know *of* her."

"You see what I mean, Dr. Summerville? Well this young lady—she's 14—is centrally located in Columbia and has infected close to 100 boys from one end of town to the other, from Eau Claire to Rosewood."

Momma asked the doctor if he'd like some more peaches or ice cream and he said No, thank you, and she continued: "Yes, I've seen some fine young men come into my office with gonorrhea. Some I knew—sons of friends. And about as many were from Shandon as from the poorer residential areas. I always chuckle to myself when some well-meaning friend or acquaintance tells me I should move out to Shandon for Clarence's sake—or at least pull some strings and get him into Dreher High School, where he'd be exposed to higher-type people, and be in a safer and more proper environment. I laugh to myself because I know what their boys are doing and they don't.

"When it comes to VD, boys from north Columbia do tend to be younger when they contract it—14 or 15—while the boys from Shandon who come to my office are more likely to be 16 or 17. But from my days at Columbia Hospital I know that Dreher boys get into more automobile accidents at younger ages than Columbia High boys. That's probably because they have more cars—most families have more than one and some boys have their own car. So they're out riding around more. It breaks your heart to see these boys when they bring them into the emergency room. A lot of them will never walk again—and, of course, some are fatalities. But I just can't worry about such things, Dr. Summerville."

"No you can't, Mrs. Palmerston." The doc looked so sincere.

"But of course I do. Really, though, what I worry about most is Clarence getting polio. That's something that can't be treated or prevented. I'm glad Clarence doesn't care to swim in the pool at Maxcy Gregg park, but I'm not so sure that crowded swimming pools are an important factor in the transmission of polio. There's no evident correlation in the cases we've had here. We've only had five cases in Richland county so far this year."

"I agree there's little that can be done to prevent polio," Dr. Summerville said, "except to push ahead with research on a vaccine. We know it's a viral disease, like smallpox, and we can hope that someday we'll come up with some kind of inoculation for it."

"That will be a happy day for all the mothers of the world." Momma rang for Agnes to come and clear away the dessert dishes.

"Mrs. Palmerston," the doctor spoke suddenly, like there was something he had to bring up before we left the table, "were you serious when you said that you were thinking about leaving Columbia—moving to California?"

"Why yes, after Clarence finishes high school. There wouldn't be much to hold me here then. I have a sister in Santa Monica; she's always writing me about the marvelous opportunities out there. I'm afraid I'm kind of a foot-loose person, Dr. Summerville."

"Well let me ask you to consider central New Jersey. We don't have the balmy climate they have in California, but we've got equal or better career opportunities for a woman with your professional background." The doctor seemed excited; he paused like he was trying to catch his breath.

"Then when the time comes, when Clarence is ready to go off to college..."

"No, Mrs. Palmerston, I mean now. Let me explain. There's an opening for assistant administrator at the hospital where I'm head of the medical staff—the biggest hospital in Plattville, 350 beds. The chief administrator is a close associate and friend of mine, a wonderful person. We were reviewing applications for the position before I left on vacation last week; none of the applicants had your qualifications. Unless they've received an application in the last few days from someone more qualified than you—which is highly unlikely—you could have that job, Mrs. Palmerston, if you wanted it. The salary is open, but it would be much more than you're making now; probably twice as much. This is a municipal hospital; it's autonomous but it's technically part of the city public health service. We need someone in the hospital administration who understands public health. After awhile you could move completely into that area if you liked, with no loss of seniority or civil service status. We're quite advanced in those matters in New Jersey. You could even go with the state health service, where some of the top positions are held by women; it's not a disadvantage being a woman up there. Of course, to advance you'd probably have to take some extension courses at the university..."

"Oh I wouldn't mind doing that; in fact I'd like to. But really Dr.Summerville, this is all very nice but I'm afraid it's out of the question. Clarence is all set to go to Columbia High this fall..."

"But we have excellent schools in Plattville. And a boy as intelligent and good looking as Clarence wouldn't have any trouble at all adjusting. He'd be a big hit up there."

I felt like Sunset Carson just after he'd been ambushed. It happened so fast and the bullets were coming from all directions. I knew right off I was in a bad predicament; I'd just find me a big rock to get behind and keep quiet and figure out how to save my ass. The danger actually was concentrating my mind. The fog was lifting in my head and I was able to make out more things.

"Look, Mrs. Palmerston, I'll lay it out for you: all you'd have to have to get the job would be decent letters of recommendation from Columbia Hospital and from your present supervisor."

"Oh I could get those. Dr. Carrington at the health department has already offered to write me one. He thinks I'm wasting my time in Columbia and he's going to retire at the end of the year anyway—so it wouldn't be like I was running out on him."

"Excellent. And you'd have to go up to Plattville for an interview. With your credentials that would just be a formality, but you'd have to make an appearance before the hospital board before they could give you a contract."

"Well, I have a week's vacation coming to me that I can take anytime between now and Labor Day." Momma glanced at her wristwatch. "My goodness, it's getting late. Clarence, I suspect

Agnes has finished the dishes by now. Would you please drive her home?"

"Yes ma'am." I acted real nonchalant, like what they'd been talking about didn't affect me at all.

"Doctor, did Al ever tell you what the governor of South Carolina said to the governor of North Carolina?"

"Why yes, he did. At the officers' club, several times. He said the drinks are..."

Momma straightened him out. "What the governor of South Carolina said to the governor of North Carolina was: 'It's a long time between drinks.' So let's just go into the library for a little nightcap and finish discussing this matter."

7

AGNES ALWAYS got into the back seat of the car when Momma or I drove her home. I couldn't say for certain whether she did it because she wanted to or because she thought she had to —"Colored Take Seats From Back • Whites Take Seats From Front • South Carolina Law": that's what the sign said over the fare box on every city bus—but I was pretty sure she knew the difference between our Plymouth and a damned city bus. No, she didn't think she was on a bus; more likely she was making believe she was riding in Governor Thurmond's Cadillac limousine, sitting fancy on the back seat and being chauffeured around by a white trusty in a snappy uniform.

Grandmomma Palmerston never could understand why niggers were supposed to ride in the back. I guess that was because she never rode the bus. She rode streetcars when she was a girl, but that was before segregation. Back in slavery times colored men used to drive the horses and white people sat on the back seat of the carriage. Grandmomma thought that was where white people belonged when they were traveling, in the back. She had this saying:

Niggers up front
Carrying the trunk,

White folks behind
Taking their time.

That arrangement was all right for horse-and-buggy days when it
was the nigger's place to drive. They could handle horses—no
doubt about it. But then motor vehicles came along and they
figured niggers weren't smart enough to handle machinery. So
they gave all the driving jobs to whites. Naturally when they
wrote up the segregation laws they weren't about to put the colored section up front with the white driver.

Agnes was taking advantage of the law, I thought, riding in the
back like she was Madam Queen. As usual she didn't say a word
to me. I watched her in the rearview mirror; she wasn't even
mumbling to herself. I knew she'd listened to every word that
was said at the supper table, but it didn't seem to phase her at all.
Just as I was pulling up to Agnes's house I said, "Looks like
Momma's gonna move us up to New Jersey."

The front of Agnes's house sat up so high on pillars of stacked
bricks that it looked like it was on stilts. You could've driven a
car underneath the front porch if it hadn't been for all the fuel
drums and scrap lumber and other junk that was stored there.
The back of the house was closer to the ground because the
house was built on the slope of a hill. Wooden steps led up to the
front porch, which as I said was pretty high off the ground.
There was a big chinaberry tree that spread over most of the
front yard, which was no more than a patch of bare red clay that
merged with the dirt sidewalk of Pulaski street, also unpaved. A
light was on in the front room, which meant that Agnes's
daughter Flora was home. Flora's husband had run off and left
her about 20 years ago, like Agnes's husband had run off and left
her about 20 years before that.

"Your momma ain't moving to no New Jersey," Agnes said as
the car came to a stop in front of her house. "All she aims to do
is get them folks in New Jersey to write a letter and say We sho
do want you to come work for us and we gonna give you all this
money if you do. Then all she do is take that letter down to the

health department and show it to 'em and tell 'em about it. And they gonna say Miz Palmerston we sho don't want you leaving us and going off to no New Jersey. We gonna give you jest as much money as they is."

Agnes opened the back door. "Your momma's a smart lady. Hit's a shame you don't take after her."

"Night Agnes."

"Hmmph," she snorted as she slammed the door and stalked off toward her front steps.

I swung by Elmwood Pharmacy to buy a pack of Luckies after I let Agnes off. There was nobody in the drugstore—no customers, that is—only Andy the sodajerk and Doc Shealey the druggist who was shuffling some papers in the back. It was getting to be their closing time. I lit up a fag and flipped through the August issue of *Motor Trend* at the magazine rack before I headed home. I slipped the pack of Luckies into the right front pocket of my pants; it wouldn't get smushed—those were tailor-made drapes with 24-inch knees and plenty of room in the pockets.

The car radio came on when I turned the key. I'd left it on WNOK; the "Dance Party" was on and they were playing the summer's biggest hit, "Mona Lisa" by Nat King Cole. I was getting tired of that damned song but didn't bother changing the station; I'd be home before the song was over. I flipped my cigarette butt out the window as I turned onto Richland street and looked in the rearview mirror and watched the crimson sparks skip and dance across the pavement. Up ahead Dr. Summerville's 1950 Cadillac Coupe de Ville was still parked in front of our house. That was some jet. I had to admire the doc's choice of cars—but I wondered if he really knew what he had, if he knew what it'd do, or if he just had it because that was what doctors were supposed to have, Cadillacs.

I parked the Plymouth under the portico and slammed the car door as I got out and went around to the front door and let it slam too, as I walked into the hall, to make sure that Momma and Dr. Summerville knew I was back. They met me at the door to the library.

"Well, Clarence, it's certainly been a pleasure," Dr. Summerville said as he stuck out his hand at me, and Momma reached into the hall closet to get his coat.

"Yes sir," I said as I shook his hand.

"Remember, Mrs. Palmerston," he said as Momma handed him his coat, "I'll call you tomorrow before I leave town—around eleven o'clock if all goes according to plan."

"I certainly thank you for all you're doing, Dr. Summerville."

"My pleasure, Mrs. Palmerston. I really hope this works out —and I see no reason why it shouldn't. In the meantime, thank you for a delightful evening."

I opened the front door as they shook hands and said good night. Dr. Summerville told me good night and touched me on the shoulder as he walked out the front door. Momma stepped out on the porch with me and we watched him drive away. The night was quiet and we could hear the beautiful flutter of the Caddy's twin pipes as Dr. Summerville made the turn at Lincoln street.

"Sugar, I guess we've got a lot to talk about."

"Yes ma'am."

"But it can wait till tomorrow. You'll be here for supper won't you?"

"Yes ma'am."

"We'll talk about it then. Goodnight sugar."

"Goodnight Momma."

The first change in our lives—if Momma was really serious about that job in New Jersey—would be that we wouldn't be making our annual pilgrimage to Jalapa, Georgia this summer. That wouldn't be so bad, especially if Momma took the train up to New Jersey for the interview and left the car here with me. Maybe I'd throw a party. Agnes would be gone on her vacation so she wouldn't be in my hair. Maybe we'd have an orgy—invite all the whores in Columbia—screw upstairs and downstairs and *on* the stairs. That'd be fitting because if Momma actually did

leave Columbia the clap would take over the town—and where'd
be a better place to kick off the epidemic than right here at the
Palmerston mansion?

I wasn't focusing too well on the problem. I was lying on the
bed in my room smoking my second teege of the night. The disk-
jockey on WNOK put on a new recording of that French song
"La Vie en Rose" by Edith Piaf, Marcel Cerdan's girlfriend.
Cerdan was my favorite boxer; I hated it when he got killed last
year. I got out my sketchbook and began drawing a picture of
Cerdan knocking Tony Zale out of the ring. At eleven o'clock I
switched to WLAC in Nashville. CBS news was on; after that
Hoss Allen came on with all nigger music—rhythm and blues. I
wondered if you could get WLAC in New Jersey.

WLAC came in loud and clear in Jalapa, Georgia, but nobody
listened to it over there. They were all big hillbilly fans and when
they stayed up late at night they tuned in to WCKY in Cincinatti
so they could hear Ernest Tubb and Johnny and Jack and Little
Jimmie Dickens. They ate up that stuff. When I was in Jalapa last
summer I picked up WLAC on my cousin Rusty's radio—Rusty
was 14 then, my age—and they were playing Stick McGhee's big
hit "Drinking Wine Spo-Dee-O-Dee." Rusty said that was the
trouble with rhythm and blues: it didn't make sense; the words
didn't make sense; the title didn't make sense—not like hillbilly
music, where the words told a real story, like Roy Acuff's
"Precious Jewel." In rhythm and blues, according to Rusty, what
you had was a bunch of niggers howling out gibberish.

It was gibberish to him because he didn't understand the
nigger language. I had to explain to Rusty what it meant to drink
wine spo-dee-o-dee: you took a swig of sweet wine—blackberry
or elderberry wine or Imperial Reserve Port that sold for 70 cents
a bottle—then you took a swig of whiskey and then you chased
it with another swig of wine. That's drinking wine spo-dee-o-dee.
Calhoun MacNab explained it to me; his brass-ankle buddy
Gordon told him. Rusty couldn't have known because there
were almost no colored people in Jalapa, Georgia. And they
didn't have any wine there either, not even in the A & P; they

didn't even have beer; and they didn't have any government liquor. Hadacol was the only alcoholic beverage you could buy legally in Jalapa. The whole area was dry; the Baptists were in complete control. You could get white lightning of course —because the Baptists were the ones who made that stuff. But if you wanted anything else to drink you'd have to go across the river to South Carolina to get it.

But Rusty said they could get cider to drink. What do you mean—apple juice? Hell no, hard cider, he said; cider that's aged awhile, that's fermented, that's developed a kick. He had a jug of hard cider stashed away in the barn. He also had a jar of white lightning. We drank some of both the next day. We called it drinking cider spo-dee-o-dee.

Old Rusty was all right. He couldn't help it if he talked country. Everybody talked that way in north Georgia. It wasn't the grammar that was different; we made the same grammatical mistakes they did—except that we'd make mistakes on purpose and they'd do it because they didn't know any better or couldn't help themselves. They'd say "ain't" or "he don't" even if they were talking to their schoolteacher. But that didn't bother me; it was their pronunciation that drove me crazy, especially the way they made two syllables out of every long "i": nye-us for nice, rye-ut for right, why-ut for white. And the way they changed short "e" to broad "a": thar for there, whar for where, bar for bear. And the way they put "h" in front of every initial "it" —Hit don't matter—and dropped the "th" when a sentence started with "that": At's rye-ut. It was bad enough for a boy to talk that way, but I couldn't stand to hear those sounds coming out of a girl's mouth. Of course, to another country hick it was just fine.

Rusty didn't have a girlfriend last summer. If he'd had one he wouldn't 've had any place to take her, except maybe to an indoor movie. They didn't have any drive-ins around Jalapa. And even if they did Rusty couldn't drive on the highway to get there because you had to be 15 to get a driver's license in Georgia and the highway patrol kept a close watch on the main roads. And they didn't have anything in Jalapa like the Rat Club in Columbia. The Rat Club—actually the Mickey Mouse Club at the Palmetto theater—was where the junior high-school crowd went on Saturday morning to neck and raise hell. They had a Saturday morning matinee at the theater in Jalapa but it wasn't just for kids. Old farmers would come in there with their old wives to watch the horse opera and the serial. Everybody had to behave. The adults in that area were as retarded as the kids.

Old Rusty couldn't believe what I told him about the Rat Club. Of course I did tell him a few lies, but I told him the truth too. The first time a girl ever French-kissed me was at the Rat Club—a girl from Hand Junior High. Cousin Rusty thought that was disgusting; he said he wouldn't want any girl sticking her tongue in his mouth. That was a year ago; he'd probably changed his mind since then. I wondered if he'd started smoking. Well, I thought, it might be a long time before I'd find out—if Momma was going to go along with Dr. Summerville's scheme.

I could stand not spending a week with my hick relatives over in Jalapa, Georgia. What I knew I couldn't endure was spending whole years up there among all those unrelated loud-mouthed Yankees in Shitville, New Jersey. I belonged in Columbia, South Carolina and by God that was where I was going to stay. That was all there was to it, I told myself.

Wynonie Harris was singing "All She Wants To Do Is Rock."

"My baby don't go for fancy clothes,
High-class dinners and picture shows,
All she wants to do is stay at home
And hucklebuck with Daddy all night long,
All she wants to do is rock...
Rock and roll all night long..."

I turned off the radio and went to sleep.

8

ON THE MORNING AFTER Dr. Summerville came to supper I
decided to wait at home until Browder came by with my
knapsack. He was out collecting on his paper route. He usually
collected from most of his customers on Saturday but there were
some people he couldn't get ahold of until Monday or Tuesday.
Momma always left money with Agnes to pay him on Saturday
morning. Governor Thurmond did the same: left money with a
maid to pay the paperboy on Saturday. But sometimes old Strom
himself would come to the backdoor, Browder said, and pay him
in person—or Mrs. Thurmond would. She was a lot younger than
Strom and real good looking, a beauty queen, Miss South
Carolina of 1947. One time she asked Browder if he'd like a
dope—meaning a Coca-Cola—and invited him into the kitchen of
the Governor's Mansion to drink it.

That was the strongest stuff Strom ever drank, Coca-Cola. He
was a hard-shelled Baptist but I liked him anyway. I always
waved at him when he rode by in his Cadillac limousine and he'd
wave back if he saw me. I only met him personally—shook hands
with him—one time: at his inauguration reception in 1947.
Grandmomma and Momma were invited and they took me with
them. Grandmomma was surprised that none of the punch was
spiked. Some definitely would be at the next inauguration when

111

the new governor would be a "whiskey-palian"—Jimmy Byrnes. Too bad Grandmomma wouldn't be around to enjoy it.

People who liked to take a drink would breathe easier with Jimmy Byrnes in the Governor's Mansion. Strom had wanted to make prohibition a local option in South Carolina like it was in Georgia, but the legislature had the good sense to vote it down. Local option wouldn't stop anybody from drinking, I thought; it'd just make liquor cost more and give more money to the bootleggers. Actually, the sale of liquor was already illegal statewide most of the time: prohibition was already in effect all day Sunday and from sundown to sunrise every other day of the week. But you still could get good liquor anytime you wanted it if you were willing to pay a dollar or two extra a bottle.

I wondered what old Strom would do if he knew about all the liquor that was sold after hours right behind the Governor's Mansion at Tuck Booker's place on Blanding street. Tuck's house was next to his liquor store and if you wanted liquor after sundown you went around to the back door of the house and told him what you wanted and he'd go into the house and get it for you. He'd charge you $3 a pint for cheap whiskey or gin. If you were a young boy he wouldn't sell you liquor during the day; you'd have to come back at night and pay the bootleg price. Most liquor stores in Columbia wouldn't sell to young-looking boys. I guess they thought the Baptists were watching them and would call the police if they did. That was why the law said liquor stores could only stay open during daylight: so the Baptists could spy on them and see who they were selling the stuff to. Because at night the Baptists stayed home—except on Wednesday night when they went to prayer meeting—and the police had more important things to do than bother teenagers who just wanted to have a little fun and weren't causing anybody any trouble.

The law said you were supposed to be 21 years old even to buy a beer, but as long as you had a quarter you could get one at almost any drive-in restaurant in Columbia except Sox's on any night of the week except Sunday—when beer was only sold in places like the American Legion Hall. You had to look like you were old enough to go to college to get in the American Legion Hall. I'd never been in there. And most honky-tonks—like the Brass Rail on Main street—wouldn't let high-school boys in, though they didn't mind high-school girls coming in. Respectable girls of course didn't go to places like that. It was o.k. for them to go to the drive-ins, though, with dates or with other girls. Most of the drive-ins would go broke without the teenage trade.

What in the hell would boys and girls do, I wondered, if we couldn't cruise the drive-ins? In New Jersey you probably had to be 18—16 at least—to drive a car. They probably didn't even have drive-ins up there. It'd be worse than Georgia. If Momma insisted on moving to New Jersey I'd just have to flat out tell her that I wasn't going. I'd move in with Uncle Lewie. I'd tell her that I was too attached to the Southern way of life to survive up North; that I'd just pine away up there, separated from my friends and everything I held dear. I'd tell Momma that I was dating this respectable girl from St. Andrews; that I really liked her; that we were making all sorts of social plans; that I was getting into the Les Truands.

Actually, it was too late to get into the Les Truands for this year. The Les Truands is a social club for boys who go to Columbia High or Eau Claire High. At Dreher High they have a club called the Horsemen. The Horsemen and the Les Truands put on formal dances with live bands at places like the Jefferson Hotel; there were some good boys in each club. But there were also some good boys who didn't belong to either. For example, Ackbo belonged to the Les Truands but Stringbean didn't; Snake didn't belong to the Horsemen. Boys could belong or not; it didn't make that much difference. It wasn't like it was with girls, where you almost had to belong to a girls' club by the time you were a junior in high school. I figured 90% of the popular and respectable girls in Columbia belonged to FGO or Les Coquettes or LJF or one of the other high-school sororities. Each girl would invite a boy to be her date whenever they had a dance and the club would invite a whole bunch of stags. So if you were a boy and wanted to go to one of those dances it wasn't hard to get an invitation.

But if you wanted to be the one doing the inviting you had to belong to the Les Truands (or the Horsemen if you went to Dreher). There was this boy who hung out at Varn's drugstore who was a year older than me and was real proud of being a member of the Les Truands. He kept telling me that he could get me in. He wanted to put up my name but I told him I wasn't interested. And I wasn't at the time. But the main reason was that I didn't want to go through the Les Truands initiation.

The Les Truands would have their initiation at some house up at Lake Murray and it'd last all night long. They'd make all the new members strip naked and they'd beat them with paddles. One thing they'd make you do was pick up an olive with your ass and drop it into a Coke bottle. If you missed you'd have to eat the olive and they'd beat you and you'd have to keep trying with a new olive until you got one in. Another thing they'd do is make you lie on your stomach on a big sheet of canvas out in the yard; they'd cut a hole in the canvas and dig a little hole in the dirt underneath it; then they'd tell you to fuck mother earth. If you didn't seem to be doing it right they'd beat you with those paddles. Anyway, that's what I heard they did at Les Truands initiations. Everything was supposed to be a secret. Maybe it really wasn't that bad.

I was surprised by a couple of boys who got in the Les Truands this year. One was Preacher. I didn't think his mother would let him join. The other was this boy named Randy Wagner. Brewster Gannett nicknamed him "Wagblow" because he was always going around grabbing other boys' peckers. I couldn't understand why somebody in the Les Truands didn't blackball him for being queer. Brewster said that was the reason they wanted Wagblow in the Les Truands—because he was queer —so he'd suck them off.

Anyway, I was surprised when I heard they'd let Wagblow into the Les Truands. But that wasn't a surprise at all compared with the jolt I got when Browder gave me back my knapsack.

• • •

We were up in my room smoking cigarettes and I'd told him what had happened with Dr. Summerville the night before. I was stretched out on the bed and Browder was leaning back in the straight chair and fooling with the straps of my knapsack which was on his lap. He said he didn't think Momma would ever leave the health department because she was too important down there. But if she did and tried to take me up to New Jersey I'd just have to run away, Browder said; I'd have to pack up my knapsack and grab my guns and fishing gear and hike on up Broad river and live off the fat of the land. He flung the knapsack at me and I grabbed it with my left hand. Then I sat up on the bed and started taking thing out of the knapsack: the bathing suits, the empty canteen, the photos from the Mirador Club ...

It was like I'd been kicked by a mule. "My God Browder!" I yelled. "It's him!" The first picture—the one on top—was of Dr. Summerville sitting at a table at the Mirador Club with some blond-headed woman. There was no doubt about it. He didn't have on his glasses and he wasn't wearing a bow tie—but it was him all right. "This is the cat I was talking about. This is Dr. Summerville."

Browder examined the picture carefully. "That's a fine looking woman he's with."

Yes she was. Her hair was long and blond—looked white in the photo—and came down over one side of her face like Veronica Lake. But I wasn't studying her. I was thinking about the fact that Dr. Summerville was in Columbia before the Mirador Club burned down and what this would mean to Momma. When he called her he said he'd just arrived in town—at least I thought that was what she said he told her—but that could've meant the afternoon or night before. He could've gone out to the Mirador Club then, but where'd he get that blond bombshell from? Did he pick her up out there? Was she from Columbia? Or was she traveling with him? Whatever it was, I was sure Momma didn't know anything about her—pretty sure anyway. There was definitely something fishy here. Maybe they

were a couple of con artists traveling around the country and
swindling war widows.

If I showed Momma the picture that'd put an end to all this
New Jersey jive real quick, I thought. But then I thought again:
maybe not. Suppose Momma knew all about Dr. Summerville
and this dame? I didn't know what they talked about when I
wasn't around, or what they talked about on the phone. Maybe
Momma was the one who recommended the Mirador Club to
Dr. Summerville. She didn't go out at night too often herself, but
when she did, maybe that's where she went: to the Mirador Club.
Maybe it was her favorite hangout; after all, her brother Lewie
used to work there.

I really didn't know too much about Momma's social life. I
knew it probably wasn't all playing cards with her lady friends.
She had secrets from me just like I had secrets from her. That was
o.k.; neither one of us was nosy. But that was when things were
normal, and they sure weren't normal now. It wasn't just that I
was in danger of being ripped from my Southern roots and
dragged off to wither away in Northern exile; the worst danger
was that a pair of carpetbagger crooks might make off with the
fortune and honor of the Palmerston family. I needed to do some
investigating and get the evidence to squash this New Jersey
caper.

"Browder, let's go down to the surplus store and show this
picture to my uncle Lewie. Maybe he knows who this woman
is."

"O.k. I got my bike outside."

"Oh shit," I remembered that I'd had a flat the day before I
left for Jacksonville; "my front tire's flat and I don't have any
cold patches left."

"We can double-head on my bike."

"Naw, let's walk. It ain't that far."

Browder agreed and I put the photo into the manila envelope
that my last report card came in and stuffed it inside my shirt.
We went down to the kitchen and I cut two big squares out of
the crackling bread that Agnes had just finished making. We

headed out the kitchen door while she was squawking about us tracking crumbs all over the house.

We walked past the Arsenal Hill Community Center and around the rim of Seaboard Park. Some park. It was really just a big grubby hole in the ground with railroad tracks running into it and a big pile of coal on the bottom next to an ice house and some warehouses and a bunch of boxcars and hoppercars standing around and trucks going in and out.

My brain was really stimulated by all that had happened since the night before. For the first time in over a year I could feel it running on all cylinders. But if I tried to accelerate too fast on that New Jersey turnpike it'd start pinging again. My mind still wasn't completely in tune, but it was getting there. In the meantime it didn't hurt to think about other things. As we walked by St. Peter's Catholic church I thought about John Bernardin, the delivery boy at Varn's drugstore, who was a Catholic. His big brother was going to be a priest.

"Did John Bernardin's brother ever get to be a priest?" I asked Browder when we were in front of the Ursuline Convent.

"Old Joe? Probably. It's been four or five years since he went away to Baltimore to the Catholic seminary. You know he didn't flunk out. That's one smart fellow. I bet he's gonna be the pope someday."

"Naw, Browder. You gotta be Italian to be the pope."

"He's Aye-talian."

"Naw, I mean Italian from Italy," I said as we started across to the other side of Assembly street where most of the pawnshops were. We both liked to look at the stuff in the windows: guns, switchblade knives, brass knuckles, blackjacks. The businesses on Assembly street were run by white people but they catered to niggers. Of course a lot of white people shopped there too. Besides the pawnshops there were dime stores, liquor stores, surplus stores, shoe stores, clothing stores—where the prices were a lot cheaper than on Main street. For the colored people it wasn't just a matter of prices: they weren't allowed in the big department stores on Main street but they were welcomed in the stores on Assembly street where they even let niggers try on hats or shoes or clothes before they bought them. Assembly street was a mixed shopping district.

But once you stepped off Assembly street it was either all black or all white. If you took a side street down toward the river, all the places—pool halls, cafés, beer joints—would be run by and for niggers. If you went the other way, over towards Main street, everything would be white. One exception, though, was Washington street between Assembly and Main where there were some colored tailors and barbers who served white people. That was a holdover from slavery times when there were a lot of nigger tailors and barbers. Skilled trades like electrician and plumber—that came along 50 or 60 years ago, about the time the segregation laws were passed—were set aside for whites only. A nigger couldn't get a city license to be an electrician or a plumber.

As we walked down Assembly street we passed Emery-Hill ten-cent store, where Sandburg's mother was a sales clerk, and A. Berry's clothing store. A. Berry's sold these fake tailor-made pants for $8.95. I mean they were ready-made pants hanging on a rack that were made up in the tailored style. They'd be drapes all right, with 16-inch pegs and one-inch welt seams and tunnel loops and two-button up-flaps or down-flaps, but the cut and stitching would be so sorry that anybody could tell right away that they weren't really tailor-made—even if they did fit you perfectly, which they wouldn't. No real dude would be caught dead wearing a pair of A. Berry's fakes. You'd be a lot better off buying a pair of good quality slacks at Copeland's Men Store for $7 and taking them to Owen and Paul, the nigger tailors, and getting them pegged for two bucks.

The S & L Army-Navy Surplus Store, Uncle Lewie's place, was two doors down from A. Berry's, just before you got to the produce market. Sam Levine, Uncle Lewie's partner, was sitting up front at the cash register.

"Hey Mr. Levine. Is Uncle Lewie around?"

"Howdy Clarence. I believe he's in the back helping a customer with some pup tents."

Uncle Lewie had just sold a pup tent to a lady and her little boy. He was about ten years old—too young for the Scouts, too young to go camping. They were probably going to set up that tent in their backyard. Uncle Lewie was counting the stakes and folding an equal number of them into each of the two canvas halves of the tent along with the pieces of a collapsible pole and a rope. He handed one bundle to the lady and the other to the little boy.

"If you'll just take these to the gentleman up front," Uncle Lewie said with a sincere smile, "he'll ring it up. Thank you ma'am. And you have a good time camping, young fellow." Then he turned to me and Browder.

"Well if it ain't my favorite nephew, Clarence Palmerston, and his buddy..."

"Billy Brown," I said.

"Why shore. How you doing, Billy?"

"Fine, Mr. Evans."

"And what brings you two cool cats to our humble emporium?"

"I got something to show you. You know about the Mirador Club burning down?"

"Read about it in the paper, that's all. Whatcha got to show me?"

"This picture." I unbuttoned my shirt and pulled out the manila envelope. "Me and Billy found it up at the Mirador Club yesterday after the fire." I handed the photo to Uncle Lewie and he studied it for a few seconds.

"Looks like the work of Cindy, the Speed Graphic artist. She got a little too close with her flash. Faces kind of washed out..."

"Do you know her?"

"Why shore I know Cindy. We were good buddies when I was dealing cards out there."

"No, Uncle Lewie. The lady in the picture."

"Hmmm. She does look a mite familiar. Gimme a hint."

"No, I don't know her. Thought you might. Like maybe she worked there, or came out there regularly."

"Well you know, Clarence old buddy, I haven't set foot in that place in two years. Not since that state legislator from Charleston caught me dealing one off the bottom of the deck in a game of five-card stud." Uncle Lewie scooted himself up onto the top of the wooden counter and sat there with his legs dangling and lit up an Old Gold. We were getting off the subject but we could come back to it later I figured. I'd never heard the full story of why Uncle Lewie quit working at the Mirador Club.

"Yessir, I thought I was a goner. That geechee pulled his gat and would've drilled me for shore if Silas Hobart hadn't been watching the game and got in between us real quick. O' course old Si could've got killed hisself; the reason he jumped in wasn't to save me, though I'm mighty thankful he did. He ran the club—and probably owned the biggest piece of it—and he could handle almost any problem with the law: whether it had to do with liquor, gambling, cocaine, reefers, white slavery... you name it. But he couldn't handle a killing, especially not one involving a state legislator. That would've called for an investigation that would've closed him down for sure. Well, I made old Si a lot of money and he saved my life. He apologized up and down to that legislator; told him he had no idea that I'd do such a thing; yelled at me to get my ass outta there and never come back. And that's what I did."

Uncle Lewie looked real thoughtful as he exhaled a long stream of smoke.

"You know, Clarence, I was a good dealer, but I got sloppy. I didn't drink while I was dealing, but sometimes during a break I'd go over and share a reefer with the boys in the band. It was supposed to slow the tempo for you and maybe it did, but it took the edge off my judgment. I mean a musician's just got to play music, but a card dealer's got to play cards *and people*. I was playing that Charleston lawyer like he was some linthead from Greenville. You can't do that, Clarence. You gotta have judgment. You gotta keep your head clear. You gotta be able to discriminate."

"Yes sir. You said that woman in the picture looked familiar. You think she's from Columbia? You think you've seen her around town?"

He studied the picture some more. "You know, she might be one of them carhops at the Friendly drive-in, one of them German war brides they like to hire... Naw, she's not one of them; she's not a foreigner. And she's not as blonde as she looks like in this picture; it's the flash that makes her hair look so light. I tell you where I've seen this woman: out at the Backwoods Inn. She's a waitress at the Backwoods Inn. Name's Marilyn."

"Maryland?"

"Marilyn. Like in Marilyn Maxwell."

"You sure this is her?"

"Well not absolutely sure. The picture's not too good. But it looks like her... Hey, why you so fired up about this babe?"

"Why shouldn't I be, Uncle Lewie? She's good looking ain't she?"

"She's too old for you. You got plenty luscious young things your own age you can fiddle with. You boys don't know how lucky you are. When I was your age white girls didn't put out; we had to fuck nigger gals. Fact was, where I come from, up in north Georgia, there weren't many niggers and we'd have to hop a train across the river to South Carolina to get a piece of ass. You know, it never happened to me, but they say there was this old boy who was getting this nigger gal going real good and she said White boy, I know you can't kiss me: Pull my hair!"

"Uncle Lewie, that joke's as old as the one about Johnny Fuckerfaster."

"Yeah? I haven't heard that one. Tell it to me."

The three of us were giggling like ninnies. It was a good thing there weren't any customers in the store. Mr. Levine looked back at us and shook his head slowly like he thought we were all bound for the State Hospital on Bull Street.

"Mr. Evans," Browder said, "you oughta see what these white girls that put out look like. They ain't just ugly: they're oogly. You can't kiss *them* either."

"Do you pull their hair?"

"How you gonna pull their hair," I said, "when they got a paper sack over their head?"

Uncle Lewie thought that was real funny. When he'd stopped laughing he asked us where we were going now. I said maybe we'd go over to the Sports Center and get a hot dog and shoot some pool.

Browder thought that was a good idea. "You wanna come with us, Mr. Evans?"

"No thanks boys. I better stay here with Sam and help tend the store. We gotta start putting out a shipment of stuff we got in yesterday."

As we headed for the door I remembered that I'd taken my pool permit out of my wallet before I left for Jacksonville. I asked Browder if he had his.

"Naw, but we won't need one at the Sports Center. Brunswick's the only place that ever asks you for one."

You were supposed to have written permission from your mother or father to shoot pool in Columbia if you were under 18. Like Browder said, most pool halls didn't bother you about one: the North Columbia Recreation Center didn't; N & G at Five Points didn't. Sometimes the Brunswick Billiard Parlor did. The fellow who ran the Brunswick didn't much want his place to be a hangout for young boys. He catered to businessmen and traveling salesmen who stayed at the Jefferson Hotel across the street. But if business was slow, if several tables were empty, he'd let you play there. He still might ask to see your permit—just to let you know you weren't entirely welcome. He didn't seem to care if your permit was forged or not, just as long as you had one. If you didn't, you'd have to leave.

I didn't know too much about the Sports Center; I'd only shot pool there once and nobody asked me for a permit then. Browder had been in there two or three times. It was on Main street only a couple of blocks from Columbia High. During the school year a lot of Columbia High boys came in there at lunch time. The pool tables were way in the back; you could hardly see them from the street. Up front there were a lot of pinball machines and a lunch counter where they sold the only ten-cent hot dogs in Columbia. If your mother gave you 25 cents for lunch—which was what it cost in the Columbia High school cafeteria—you could get a hot dog and a Pepsi at the Sports Center for 17 cents and have eight cents left over. If you could scrounge up two more cents—by matching pennies maybe—you'd have enough for a game of nine ball, ten cents. Or if you were real hungry you could feed your three pennies into the peanut machine and get enough salted peanuts to fill your Pepsi bottle up to the top, and you could buy a Baby Ruth with the nickel you had left. I'd already decided to eat lunch everyday at the Sports Center when I got to Columbia High in the fall. *If* I got to Columbia High in the fall. A month from now, I thought, I could be eating raw vegetables in some school cafeteria up in New Jersey.

I was bound and determined to do everything possible to prevent such an outcome. I'd follow up Uncle Lewie's lead on Marilyn at the Backwoods Inn as soon as I could—maybe after talking things over with Momma that night. In the meantime, I'd go to the Sports Center with my buddy Browder and we'd eat hot dogs and drink Pepsis and shoot pool and listen to Calvin Boze sing "Safronia B" on the jukebox. Just in case, I borrowed a pen and some paper from Uncle Lewie and wrote out a couple of permits, one for me and one for Browder. Mine said

"To whom it may concern:

My son, Clarence Palmerston, has my permission to play pool.

Mrs. Gwyn Palmerston."

For Browder I left out the "To Whom it may concern" and wrote "Please allow Billy Brown, my son, to shoot pool wherever he wants" and signed his mother's name. I used two different styles of handwriting; both were female and mature. I was good at this. Sometimes I signed report cards for my friends or wrote out excuses for them when they were tardy or played hooky from school.

We weren't asked to show our permits at the Sports Center that afternoon. Things went real smooth until that night at supper when Momma laid all her cards on the table.

9

ON THE WAY BACK from the Sports Center I bought a tire-patching kit at Ruff Hardware and Browder helped me fix my bike tire before he went home for supper. He said he was going to listen to "David Harding, Counterspy" and sack out early that night. I told him I'd call him in the morning. He left just before Momma arrived, a little after five. I drove Agnes home and we sat down at the breakfast-room table for supper—Momma and me —at six o'clock.

Momma just sat and looked at me with a Mona Lisa smile while I helped myself to a pork chop and some peas and crackling bread. We'd say grace only if we had company.

"You like some applesauce, sugar?"

"Yes ma'am." I plopped a couple of spoonfuls on top of my pork chop.

"Clarence, you heard what Dr. Summerville and I were talking about last night..."

"Not everything. I had to take Agnes home."

"All right. Well what it amounts to is that I can get a job with a chance for advancement and a lot more money than I'm making now..."

"Do we need the money?"

"No, sugar. But I need a change."

"Momma, are you sure Dr. Summerville can get you this job?"

"It appears so. This morning he came by the health department and talked to Dr. Carrington. He wanted to make sure he would give me a good recommendation. He said he would. Then he—Dr. Summerville—called long distance to New Jersey and talked to his hospital administrator to find out if there were any other likely prospects for the job. There weren't."

"When did he tell you all this?"

"He told me on the phone just before he checked out of the Wade Hampton and left town—a little after eleven."

"So what are you supposed to do now?"

"Nothing now. He's going to arrange an interview for me with the hospital board sometime next week—probably Wednesday or Thursday. The hospital administrator is going to mail some forms for me to fill out and bring with me. I'll have to take the train up to New Jersey next week."

"Momma, are you sure Dr. Summerville is legit?" My voice cracked just a little when I said that. It didn't ruffle her at all. She seemed kind of amused.

"What do you mean by 'legit,' sugar?"

"I mean, is he on the level? Is he really what he says he is? What if he's an imposter? What if he isn't even really a doctor?"

"My goodness, Clarence. What ever would make you think that?"

"It's happened before, Momma. On 'Mr. District Attorney' there were these people who swindled war widows. One of them would go to some lady and claim that he'd been a close friend of her husband's in the army. He'd win her confidence and then persuade her to turn over all her savings to him, or to sell her house cheap to somebody he was in cahoots with..." I was improvising some on the plot to make it fit the present situation.

"Well, he hasn't asked me to do any of that. Clarence you must think I've got kitty brains." Now she did seem a little concerned—or at least annoyed.

"No, Momma, you're a smart lady. But these fellows are slick."

"Well, I'll tell you: he did know your poppa. No doubt about that. You heard him. Why he even knew about the governor of South Carolina and the governor..."

"No he didn't. You had to help him out. All he knew was that it had something to do with drinking. Y'all had been drinking; it was logical for him to guess that it had something to do with drinking."

"Sugar, you've got a wonderful imagination. But there were other things. And besides, he's obviously a very successful doctor. Why would ..."

"But he could be an imposter. Remember Dr. Bradford who was the doctor out at the YMCA camp? Who wasn't a doctor at all. How many years did he practice medicine in Columbia before they found out that he was a fake?"

"Sugar, believe me: Dr. Summerville is a real doctor. He knows his business. He knows all about antibiotics..."

"You could learn that by reading *Time* magazine."

"How you do go on!" She was smiling now. "But I appreciate it, sweetheart—appreciate your concern. But what ever would make you think..."

"Momma, let me ask you something: how long do you think Dr. Summerville had been in Columbia before he called you up yesterday morning?"

"Why I think he said he'd gotten in the day before."

"The night before?"

"I don't really know." Good, I thought: she didn't know about him going to the Mirador Club with that blonde venus.

"What if I could prove that he and another person were in Columbia for several days last week nosing around—checking on you, checking on your financial situation, on what property you had?"

"If you could prove that I'd call Chief Campbell and have him arrested. O.k., Mr. D. A., where's the proof?"

"I don't have it all yet, but I've got a... I've got a hunch." I almost told her about the photo, but I decided to check out that dame at the Backwoods Inn first.

"Look, sugar, you don't like Dr. Summerville, do you? And you don't like the idea of us moving to New Jersey. That's what this is all about, isn't it?"

"No ma'am. There's more to it than that. You'll see."

"Well I can't see it right now, so I'm just going to assume that's what it is. I'm going to level with you, Clarence. I've been feeling a little depressed the past few months—been wondering about what's going to become of us. I never used to worry about that because I thought everything was all set—all laid out for us by your poppa and your grandmomma. All we had to do was just go about our business everyday just as we did before your grandmomma died and everything would work out just fine. I had an important job and the respect of the people I worked with and the people I served, and you were bright and healthy and mature, an honor student in school who didn't need any supervision at all—least of all from me. You were going to whiz right through high school and college and go on to become a doctor or a lawyer and carry on the Palmerston tradition and honor the family name. All your grandmomma seemed to expect from me was that I not get in your way. And that's what I tried to do: stay out of your way. But..." She stopped and took a sip of iced tea; she hadn't touched her food.

"Momma, I'm sorry if—if last year..."

"Just a minute, sugar. Let me say what I've got to say, what I've never said to you before, You see, I'm your mother; without me you wouldn't have been born. That might sound simple, but it's really complicated. A mother's feelings for her child's never a simple matter, and our case is more complicated than some others, as you've probably figured out." Momma started cutting the meat from her pork chop into little pieces.

"I'm sure you've thought about the fact that you were born seven months after your poppa and I were married." No, I said to myself, I hadn't thought about it. In fact, I didn't think I'd even known when they got married—what day and month. Even when Poppa was alive I couldn't remember them celebrating any anniversaries. Of course I was pretty little then.

"You were too big a baby to be premature, sugar; ten pounds and four ounces. Even your grandmomma, bless her soul, didn't try to pretend that you were." All this was interesting, but came as no shock. I speared another pork chop. "You didn't have to be born. You were conceived by a bachelor doctor and an unmarried nurse. Your poppa could've done an abortion on me right there in an operating room in Central Hospital in Atlanta just as easy as pie. He left the choice up to me and I said no. We were going to get married anyway, sugar; I want you to know that. But we'd planned to do it after he'd finished his internship. Your poppa was still trying to figure out how to break the news to his mother—your grandmomma —that he was gonna marry me, when we found out you were on the way. Actually, you were already there: in my uterus. That was you, sugar. It wasn't anything or anybody else. And we did consider killing you."

"Momma, you don't have to feel guilty..."

"And I don't. Because we didn't kill you. Even if we'd done it, I might not've felt guilty, because I never would've known you. Later on I might've conceived and given birth to another baby like you. But it wouldn't have been you; you would've been dead. Well, I've known you now for more than 15 years—felt you grow in my abdomen; watched you develop as an infant, as a child, as a young man. I know now who that baby was—the one I thought about killing, but didn't. That's what makes you so special. Do you understand what I'm trying to say, sweetheart?"

"Sort of."

"Look, you know I'm not very religious—sometimes I wonder if I even believe in God—and I'm not all that opposed to killing. We kill animals to eat, or to get rid of them when they're troublesome or inconvenient; we kill other people in wars; we execute criminals. I often think we could do with a lot less of all that, but I'm not against it on principle. There're even times when I think killing somebody for personal reasons can be excused. I've seen it happen: when one person makes another person so miserable that that person feels her own life won't be worth living until that other person is removed from the face of the earth. When wives kill husbands, most of the time it's justifiable, or at least excusable. But a wife and a husband's not like a woman and her baby. Her husband's only an in-law, but her baby's her own flesh and blood."

Momma took a bite from her plate. I knew she wasn't finished talking so I didn't say anything.

"I said maybe I wouldn't 've felt guilty if I'd 've killed you in my uterus because I didn't know you then. But maybe I would've felt guilty. I knew that you were kin and I think I might've felt bad about that. The Bible says that the worst thing you can do is take the life of kinfolks. I don't know why I believe that—it's not because it's in the Bible—but I do believe it. You can't treat your blood relatives like you might treat other people. You have these special obligations to your kin, even though you never agreed to them. I mean, you choose your friends, you choose your husband or wife; whatever obligations you have to them you took on of your own free will. You don't choose your relatives but you're just as obligated to them—more obligated, in fact, than if you'd chosen them."

This was getting confusing, but I nodded to Momma that I was following her as I soaked up the pot liquor on my plate with a piece of crackling bread.

"Your grandmomma Palmerston and I weren't blood kin and we had to thrash out all sorts of agreements—some before your father died, some afterwards. Most of those agreements had to do with you, in one way or another. And sugar, I've done my level best to hold up my end of the bargain." Momma paused and took a sip of iced tea. She was always careful when she started talking about Grandmomma.

"Your grandmomma wanted you raised in Columbia, where your ancestors had lived since before the town was built. You know the story: Columbia was built on a plantation that the state bought from one of your ancestors back in the 1700's. It was like she thought you were the young Duke of Columbia and was afraid I might snatch you away from your ancestral lands and take you with me back to Georgia, where all those Scotch-Irish and Welsh and descendants of convicts lived. Well, I promised your grandmomma that we'd live in this house—you and I after she was gone—until you'd finished high school and decided where you wanted to go to college. And we agreed that I'd look after the house and her other property as trustee of her estate until you were 25, when everything would go to you. Of course, all the trust business is legal and recorded. My promise about you going to high school in Columbia wasn't put down in writing."

Now I knew what Momma was getting at. It was my turn to smile; I felt pretty safe. Even if Dr. Summerville turned out to be on the level, she couldn't take me up to New Jersey unless I was willing to go, unless I agreed it was o.k. for her to break her promise to Grandmomma. Of course, I'd rather not have to make a big stink and make Momma mad. All that would be unnecessary if I could prove that Dr. Summerville was a crook.

"I can understand why you'd smile, sugar. Your grandmomma was crazy about you. She'd do anything in the world for you if she felt it was in your best interests. And so would I. That's what it boils down to: what's in your best interests. Right now I think a change of scene might be good for you. We could go up to New Jersey and you could finish high school there; we'd keep the house, of course—rent it out—and you could come back and live in it if you decided to go to college at Carolina; or you could live in a dormitory if you liked. You'd only be gone three years. Don't you think the change might be good for you? You did get bogged down this past year..."

"Momma, that was at Wardlaw. Next month I'm supposed to start Columbia High..."

"That's not going to be any easier..."

"Do you think New Jersey would be easier?"

"Academically, yes, because you won't have all the distractions you have here, all the commitments to friends and activities. You'd make new friends and commitments up there, of course, but you'd be starting out fresh and you could put your schoolwork first in the beginning; you could get back into a pattern of achievement."

"Momma, I told you I was going to do my best to make a good record at Columbia High this year ..."

"And that's what worries me: you said that you would do your best, not that you would do it."

"But I can't do any better than my best."

"Sugar, I think you can do a lot better than what you think is your best."

"Momma, I thought we settled all this when you decided not to send me off to Christ School."

"I decided not to send you off to Christ School because I couldn't go with you. Because I wanted to be with you for at least another couple of years."

For the third time in my life that I can remember I saw tears in my mother's eyes. I looked down at my plate; it was clean as a hound's tooth.

"I think I'll get me some of that ice cream for dessert," I said as I got up from my chair, "unless you'd planned for us to have something else."

"No, go ahead and get yourself some ice cream. I'm gonna skip dessert tonight. I had a big dinner at the cafeteria today." She must have wiped her eyes while I was around the corner at the Frigidaire because when I sat back down at the table with my dish of vanilla ice cream they were as dry as they could be.

"Momma, you said you didn't have to do anything about that New Jersey job until next week. Why don't we wait a few days and talk about it then. Like I said, I'm doing some checking on Dr. Summerville. I'll let you know everything I've found out in a few days, by this weekend. I'll show you something that'll surprise you; I guarantee you that."

"I hope I can wait. The suspense is killing me!" She was smiling again now; her eyes were merry. I think she really enjoyed talking with me.

"Look Momma, if it's o.k. with you I'd like to take the car tonight and go see that new picture at the Carolina theater, 'Winchester '73.'"

"Sure it's o.k. I'm glad you're going to see a cowboy movie. I think you've been seeing too many mysteries lately."

We both laughed.

The Backwoods Inn was across the Congaree river in Lexington county. It attracted a lot of soldiers from Fort Jackson and National Guardsmen who trained there during the summer as well as white trash from the surrounding countryside. It was a hillbilly dance hall and beer joint, a pretty rough place. Bobby Skinner of the Eau Claire crew liked to brag about going to the Backwoods Inn and all the women he'd picked up and fights he'd seen or been in out there. I'd never before set foot in the place and I wasn't too keen on going out there by myself to try to find Marilyn, the woman Uncle Lewie said looked like the one in the picture with Dr. Summerville. In fact I didn't even know exactly how to get there. I decided to go first to the North Columbia Recreation Center, the pool hall where the Eau Claire crew hangs out, and see if I could get little Skinner and maybe some other boys to go out to the Backwoods Inn with me. I'd told Momma I was going to see "Winchester '73" at the Carolina theater.

I noticed Brewster Gannett's 1947 Ford in the parking lot of the North Columbia Recreation Center when I drove in. I parked my Plymouth next to Brewster's gray ghost and sauntered into the pool hall where I spied Brewster leaning against the wall next to a rack of cue sticks and drinking a Pepsi; he was watching Skinner and Dude Adolphus play a game of rotation. It was Skinner's shot and he was hunched down over the table concentrating real hard on running the eleven ball down the rail; the National Guard fatigue cap he always wore was pushed back on his head and the toothbrush he always carried was sticking out his back pocket. Skinner tried too much left english and miscued. "Shit!" he said.

"Awk," Brewster responded, "the cry of the doo doo bird: aaaww shit!"

It was Dude Adolphus's shot now and Skinner was chalking his cue—his own personal cue, a collapsible 16-ounce stick that he carried around in a leather case. Skinner took up the bird-call litany: "From the deepest jungles of darkest Africa comes the cry of..."

Dude Adolphus tuned him out and sank the eleven ball. He had good position on the twelve.

"...the queer tropical fruit bird!"

"Wanna blow!" Brewster responded.

Dude Adolphus started laughing and missed the twelve ball.

"You didn't think you was gonna run the rack on me did you, Dude?"

"Well I might if it wasn't for all them goddam birds squawking around here."

Dude Adolphus was only 13 but he looked and acted a lot older. True to his nickname he was always well dressed, usually in tailor-made pants. He turned his shirt collar up at the back and wore blue suede shoes in the winter and white bucks in the summer. His sandy blond hair was combed into a perfect ducktail. He was almost six feet tall and, as I said, didn't look young—except that there was something kind of fresh and innocent about his face. Even with a cigarette dangling from his lips he would have this angelic look.

Bobby Skinner was just the opposite. Skinner always had a bad-boy expression on his face; sometimes he looked downright mean. He was several inches shorter than Dude Adolphus but a lot older, probably 17. It was hard to be sure because he lied so much. He was in the National Guard; I knew that to be a fact because I'd seen him in his uniform. He could've lied about his age and joined when he was 16. His older brother was a yo-yo champion and went around the country—and Cuba and Canada too—giving exhibitions for the Duncan Yo-Yo Company. That was true too, because I'd seen him in his brother's Oldsmobile convertible with "Mac Skinner—Yo-Yo Champion" painted on the side. Mostly he lied about how many women he screwed.

Skinner acknowledged my presence by sticking the tip of his pool cue in my gut. "Hey you wanna play the winner between me and Dude? If you wanna, I'll shoot you nine ball for a quarter."

"Naw Skinner. I just came by to see if any of you cats wanna ride out to the Backwoods Inn."

"Why?" Brewster asked. "What's going on out there?"

"Well, I gotta check out this split-tail that works out there. I thought y'all might give me some pointers on how to handle her."

"You came to the right place," Skinner said. He'd just made the 15 ball and won the game.

Dude Adolphus tossed a dime and a nickel on the table and hollered, "Rack 'em, Lee!" The rack man, a short muscular nigger about 40 or 50 years old, took his time getting up out of his chair next to the men's room; he walked slowly towards us with his triangle rack in one hand and a Philip Morris trailing smoke in the other.

"We gotta go now, Lee," Skinner said. "We're going out to the Backwoods Inn and get us some nookie." Lee stuck the fag between his lips and didn't say anything. He dropped the 15 cents into his coin apron and began digging balls out of the table pockets. He never smiled and hardly ever talked except to chew somebody out for leaving a burning cigarette on a table or for trying a jump shot that might rip the felt. White people did what that nigger told them to do; they might kid around a little about it, but they did it. Old Lee's word was the law in that pool hall.

I went to the men's room to take a leak before we left for the Backwoods Inn. There was a rubber machine on the back of the door. I'd almost forgot that we were going to pick up Sandburg the next night. With all the talk I'd heard in the last couple of days about VD and getting pregnant, I figured I'd better buy some protection. The sign on the dispenser said "For the prevention of disease only." I put a quarter in the slot and turned the knob. A pack of two Green Light prophylactics dropped into the opening below. I put them in my wallet.

I met the others outside in the parking lot. They were talking about Stringbean. "You know he's cutting that stuff," Skinner said as he got into the front seat with me. Brewster and Dude Adolphus got into the back.

"Well it sure hasn't hurt his batting average," Dude Adolphus said. "Old Stringbean's batting over .400."

"And hitting a home run every night," Brewster added.

"Guess that's why we never see him anymore," I said as I gunned the Plymouth out of the parking lot and onto Main street. Stringbean was the star first baseman of the Eau Claire American Legion team, which had a good chance of winning the state championship. He'd been going steady with Mandy Jackson since around the first of the year.

"I'm worried about Stringbean," Brewster said. I glanced at him in the rearview mirror and he looked serious. "My sister says Mandy's telling people that Stringbean's gonna marry her."

"I hate to hear that," I said. "Nobody oughta have to go that far just to get a little pussy."

"You really think he said he'd marry her?" Dude Adolphus asked Brewster, who was Stringbean's best friend.

"Shit no. But you know how Stringbean is. He might've given her the wrong impression."

"On purpose," Skinner said. "Sometimes you gotta talk junk to 'em."

"Like to little Nancy Gray?" Dude Adolphus asked. He looked angelic.

"We ain't talking about her," Skinner snapped. He looked mean.

"Awk!" Brewster squawked. "Little Skinner's still got the sweet ass for Nancy Gray. Ooooo." I didn't see it but I could imagine Brewster rolling his eyes and nudging Dude Adolphus in the ribs.

"Reckon that's why he's so pissed at Calhoun?" Dude Adolphus said. "Thinks he's birddogging him?"

Skinner was having trouble with the car's cigarette lighter. Finally he got a red glow and lit his Chesterfield and then turned to the boys in the back. "Y'all wanna know what pisses me off about Calhoun? It's him acting like I oughta give him that shotgun. He dropped that shotgun in Crane creek during duck hunting season and I found it this spring when the water was down. He lost it and I found it. Finders keepers. It's the same as if you raise up a boat off the bottom of the ocean."

"You can't blame him, Skinner," Brewster said; "that's a high-quality moot blaster."

"It's a 16 gauge Fox-Savage double barrel. But it was in sorry shape when I found it, all rusted and pitted on the outside; parts corroded on the inside. I had to put in a new ejector. Refinished the stock. Then that fucker takes a look at it and says, 'Ooooh, that's mine.' Like hell it is."

Dude Adolphus was chuckling. "Calhoun drops Foxy Savage and Skinner picks her up. Skinner drops Nancy Gray and Calhoun picks her up. Sounds about even."

"Well, he better watch his ass." From the way Skinner said that I knew he and Calhoun were heading for a fight. I figured it to be a pretty good match-up. Calhoun was bigger and had a lot more reach than Skinner and probably was stronger. But Skinner was older and more experienced; he seemed harder and tougher than Calhoun, more compact; and he was probably faster too. Both of them were bullshitters—the two biggest ones in Eau Claire—but neither one was chicken. It ought to be a good fight, I thought. I hoped I'd be able to see it.

Skinner blew a stream of smoke out the window as we were crossing the Gervais street bridge. "Now the Backwoods Inn's a pretty good place to pick up women but it's better on Saturday than week nights. It's mostly working girls that hang out there and they gotta get their sleep during the week. Oooo-weee! Y'all shoulda seen that lovely thing I found out there a few weeks ago. One of the best pieces of ass I ever had..."

"Well why ain't you tapping it now?" Dude Adolphus asked.

"Because she's too embarrassed to go out with me again. You see, I was banging away at it real good and she cuts this tremendous fart. And she says 'Oh, excuse me Bobby.' And I says 'That's all right, baby; I usually makes 'em shit.' But she still felt too embarrassed to go out with me again."

"Aw, go on Skinner," I said.

"It happens sometimes. Women are funny. Now tell us, Cap: who's this cunt you got a line on?"

"She works out there; name's Marilyn. You know her? She's a blonde."

"That don't help much. Backwoods Inn's got more peroxides than Carter's got liver pills. I can't place her—but she probably knows me. What makes you think she'd be interested in you?"

"My Uncle Lewie at the surplus store says nobody else can satisfy her, not even him. She needs a young stud like me who can lay out twelve inches."

"Don't be so fucking modest, Cap," Skinner sneered.

"I can't help it. It's the crew I'm with."

"Well, you stick with us and I'll teach you something about bagging poontang... Hey, up there's where you turn off."

I swung a left where Skinner indicated and a couple minutes later we pulled up outside the Backwoods Inn. It was a long cement-block building set down on a sandy lot amongst a bunch of scraggly pines. The windows were open and gave off a mixture of incandescent light from weak bulbs and neon light from a variety of beer signs behind the bar and from the bubbly Wurlitzer on the dance floor. The sounds we heard came from live amplified guitars, not from the jukebox.

Skinner advised us to march into the Backwoods Inn like we owned the place, and that's what we did. "Have no fear," Skinner saluted the bald-headed fellow behind the cash register at the near end of the bar, "the Nasty Guard is here." Only about half the barstools and a third of the places at the tables were occupied. On the bandstand a cat in a cowboy suit was singing the "Cocaine Blues" to the accompaniment of a hillbilly trio. We filed into

four seats about halfway down the bar where a red-headed waitress was stationed; Skinner immediately started flirting with her.
I looked around for Marilyn, the woman in the picture, but
couldn't see anybody who resembled her.

While the waitress was hunting up our order—a Red Cap for
Skinner, Bud for Dude Adolphus, Pabst for Brewster, and Schlitz
for me—the vocalist and the trio folded up their act and somebody fed the Wurlitzer. The first number that came up was "I'll
Sail My Ship Alone" by Moon Mullican; pretty soon three or
four couples were on the floor slow dancing. When the waitress
handed me my Schlitz—with an inverted glass riding over the
long neck of the brown bottle—I asked her if Marilyn was around
that night.

"Marilyn? You know Marilyn, honey?"

"Well I know somebody who knows her. Told me to look her
up." I didn't touch the two dimes and a nickel that she'd put in
front of me as change from my half dollar.

"No kidding? Well that's her waiting on that table over by
the jukebox."

It was hard to make her out; she was standing way across the
room in a neon-tinted fog of cigarette smoke. I could tell she was
blonde but otherwise couldn't see much resemblance to the
woman in the photo. I had to get a closer look. I picked up my
beer bottle—leaving the unused glass and the change on the
bar—and moseyed on over toward where she was standing. I
could feel Skinner's eyes on me as I weaved nonchalantly
through the tables. I glugged most of my Schlitz on the way over
and almost ran slap into Marilyn when she turned around and
headed back to the bar with a tray of empties.

"Hey, watch it sonny..."

"Miss Marilyn, I'm so sorry... I-I was blinded by your beauty."

"Do tell." She flashed an indulgent smile. "Have we run into
each other before?" She resumed her march to the bar and I
tagged along.

"Sho nuff. Out at the Mirador Club. Don't you remember?"

"The Mirador Club? That place that burned down? Sweet-pea, I never been out there in my life." I believed her. She definitely was not the woman in the picture; her hair curled too much off her shoulder; her eyebrows came too close together; her chin was different.

"Well then it must've been at Lewie Evans's place up at the lake."

"Honey chile, I've never been there either. Never been invited." She looked at me with a crooked grin that I knew would impress the Eau Claire trio who were watching us now from only a few barstools away.

"Well let's go tonight. I'm inviting you." I knew how to get into Uncle Lewie's lake house—the key was hanging on a nail under the front porch—and if he happened to be there on a week night, which was unlikely, he wouldn't turn me and Marilyn away. I was amazed at how well I was thinking; the scent of pussy had reactivated brain cells that had lain dormant for over a year. I didn't get it that night, but I was proud of the effort I made. I'd never done that well on a Latin test.

"Sonny boy," Marilyn said as she laid the tray on the end of the bar, "that's mighty nice of you. But you see, the fellow I'm married to is getting off his shift at Olympia Mill right about now and he'll be out here to get me at closing time and I'm afraid he won't be in no mood to do any partying up at Lew Evans's place."

"That's too bad. Well, maybe some other time."

"Yeah, shore." She scooted behind the bar and began digging bottles of beer out of the cooler. I strolled backs to where I'd been sitting.

"What'd she say?" Brewster asked.

"She says she's gotta go home with her husband tonight."

"That's what they all say," Skinner said. "She don't mean it. I saw the way she was looking at you. Go back to her. Tell her you'll eat it; they like that."

"Naw, man. She means it."

"Well, you opes watch me. See that broad sitting at that table with those two dogfaces? I'm gonna ask her to dance."

You could tell the men at the table were soldiers by their short haircuts and the Hawaiian shirts they were wearing. The girl looked bored. Her friend, who had been sitting at the table when I went after Marilyn, was dancing with another serviceman.

"Skinner, you crazy as hell," Dude Adolphus said.

"Shit, they ain't but three of 'em. We can handle 'em."

"Man there dogfaces all over this place," I said. More than half the males looked like they were from the fort. There were only a few female customers, none unattached. Before Skinner made a move the couple who had been dancing came back to the table and two more military types joined them. That made five.

"I see what you mean," Skinner conceded. "Well, like I said, this place ain't worth a shit for picking up women during the week. Hey, let's go back to town and get us some telephone operators. They'll be getting off work pretty soon."

I was thinking about my next move in the Summerville case and didn't need the distraction of chasing after a bunch of telephone operators. Even if we could pick some up, I thought, there'd be no guarantee we'd get anywhere with them. Some other time I might've been game, but not then; the experience with Marilyn was enough for that night. It was the least painful rejection I'd ever received, but a rejection just the same. I told the boys that I'd had my heart set on that blonde waitress and just couldn't settle for some mousy telephone operator. But I said I was ready to wheel them back to the pool hall where Brewster's jet was parked; they could moan on over to the Southern Bell building in the gray ghost.

After a lot of discussion over another round of suds, that was what we agreed to do, more or less: I'd drop them off at Brewster's car and head on home; they'd go on to the telephone building or wherever they wanted. It wasn't easy to ditch the Eau Claire crew.

On the way back as we were coming up to Main street on Gervais, Skinner spotted Charleston, the newspaper man, standing on the corner selling the early edition of *The State*. "Let's holler quarter at Charleston," he said.

It was a tradition that began when some boys drove up to that corner one night acting like they wanted to buy a newspaper but when Charleston came over to the car the boy riding shotgun said to him "Suck my dick for a quarter?" That threw old Charleston into an eye-popping rage. He wore these black horn-rimmed glasses with lenses that looked like they'd been made out of the bottoms of Coca-Cola bottles. He'd really go wild when somebody'd say "Suck my dick for a quarter?" or just yell "Quarter!" or "Flush the toilets! Charleston needs water!" That was where he was from, Charleston, and he had this geechee accent that made him sound as weird as he looked.

"Quarter! Quarter!" Skinner and Dude Adolphus hollered from the right side of the Plymouth as I swung up Main street.

"Son-of-a-bitch! Bastards! Bastards!" Charleston responded. I watched in the rearview mirror as he ran halfway out into Main street. For a long time he stood there spread legged with his newspapers under his left arm and his right hand clenched above his head and his whole body jerking like a spastic Statue of Liberty. We could hear him screaming all the way to Lady street.

"Bastards! Bastards!"

10

THE ONLY THING for me to do after the Backwoods Inn expedition was to go back to Uncle Lewie and tell him the whole story. He'd agree we had to find that woman in the photo with Dr. Summerville, I thought, and he'd probably want to start out by talking to Cindy, the photographer who took the picture. I'd decided on that course of action before we left the Backwoods Inn. But the next morning I wasn't in any hurry to go and see Uncle Lewie. I was a little bit afraid of what his reaction might be—Uncle Lewie wasn't the most predictable person in the world—and also I was distracted by thoughts of other things. My mind was wandering again, though it wasn't as bad as before. Like I said, I'd already figured out what needed to be done and I was going to do it. But first I was going to mull over a few things.

Mandy Jackson was telling people that Stringbean was going to marry her. When? She was just barely 15 and Stringbean's birthday was still a few weeks off. It seemed pretty stupid to talk about getting married at that age. Was she doing it to justify herself to her friends and fellow Baptists—justify letting Stringbean screw her? It should've been funny but nothing Mandy did was funny to me. She'd been getting on my nerves ever since we were in the first grade at Logan school.

I hadn't known Stringbean that long, only since the seventh grade at Wardlaw. Stringbean actually lived inside the city limits of Eau Claire and should've gone to Eau Claire Junior-Senior High, but his mother taught at an elementary school in Columbia and used her pull as a schoolteacher to get him into Wardlaw. Stringbean was a good old boy; I really liked him. He was the only boy besides me in our eighth-grade homeroom who was in the honor society. We both fell out of the honor society in the ninth grade, but his fall wasn't as hard as mine. The main reason for that was he didn't take Latin; his mother told him not to. She knew how dangerous Latin was for a boy just going into the ninth grade—unless he was some genius who didn't have anything else to do except study, which wasn't Stringbean. So Stringbean's momma advised him to skip Latin in the ninth and tenth grades and wait and take French or Spanish in the eleventh and twelfth grades; that was all the foreign language you needed to get into college. My momma, not being a schoolteacher and never having taken Latin herself, and considering me to be Einstein the Second, thought it was a real high-class subject that I'd just sail through like I'd done everything else up to that time.

I signed up for Latin at the end of the eighth grade just when my mind was turning to mush. Plenty of people who'd taken Latin and flunked it tried to warn me about it, but I was too befuddled to get the message. Something that added to my confusion was the fact that Snake was passing Latin at Dreher High and I couldn't believe Snake was any smarter than me—although I knew he was shrewd as hell. Maybe the Latin teacher out at Dreher was a lot better—or a lot easier—than the one at Wardlaw.

Anyway, I signed up for Latin at Wardlaw and Stringbean didn't. Instead of Latin, Stringbean took Business Training, which was a real crip and gave him extra time to put into courses like biology and geometry and English. In my case, Latin didn't just take time away from other academic courses: it battered my already traumatized brain so bad that I couldn't 've gotten better than a C or D in those subjects no matter how much time I might've put in on them.

If my mind had been in tip-top shape I would've mastered Latin. When I was in my prime, in the seventh and eighth grades, I could learn anything. I knew the English language backwards and forwards; I could diagram the most complicated sentence you could think of. I could solve any equation in algebra. Back then I could work things out logically. And I had virtually unlimited capacity for memorizing stuff: elements in science, dates in history, poems, whatever. Memory, logic, concentration—that's what you needed to master Latin and that's what I had at one time, but not in the ninth grade. At the beginning it wasn't too bad; even in my debilitated mental state I could absorb most of the vocabulary. And I had some feeling for Latin verbs and tenses—from English grammar—although they were pretty strange. What short-circuited my overloaded brain were those declensions—all five of them. I just couldn't grasp the logic of all that; the ablative case left me totally mystified. If I made a lucky guess and got the case right, something else would be wrong. You had to keep too many balls in the air at the same time, and in my condition I just couldn't do it. After the first grading period I made straight F's in Latin until the last period when Momma went to see the teacher and I got a D- with the notation "This D- is given with the understanding that Clarence will not attempt second-year Latin." I didn't do a whole lot better in my other subjects.

Stringbean avoided all that and was able to get through the ninth grade with a low B average. The girlfriend he latched onto halfway through the school year, Mandy Jackson, had always been a B student and her grades didn't get much worse in the ninth grade (she didn't take Latin, either). Mandy probably never made an A in any hard subject in her life, but she hung around with smart girls like Kerry Higgins and Jane Slade and considered herself an intellectual. On top of that she was a fanatical Baptist—I mean she had this obsession about being a Baptist. To her, Baptists were God's chosen people; they were number one.

When her beloved Park Street Baptist Church was organized, according to Mandy, somebody wanted to name it the Second Baptist Church, but the congregation rose up and said no: Baptists were second to no one, not even to other Baptists. That's the kind of horseshit Mandy would bore you with, even in the ninth grade after she started smoking, drinking, necking like crazy and probably screwing.

I never took Mandy out myself, but once I went on a double date with her and Stringbean. That was after Christmas vacation in the ninth grade. Before Christmas I'd been dating this nice eighth-grade girl—not really good looking, but kind of cute, with a good personality. The trouble was, I didn't know what to do with her: I was that confused. She gave me a silk scarf with my initials on it for Christmas and that compounded my confusion. It was like I was paralyzed; I couldn't do anything. I mean, with all my fear of being rejected by a girl, here I was with this girl making overtures to me and what did I do? Nothing. I ignored her, never took her out again, never called her. I rejected *her* for Christ sake, before I'd even put a finger in her pussy—before I'd even tried. I was really messed up mentally. I didn't have sense enough to pour piss out of a boot, with the directions on the heel.

Anyway, I'd broken off with that eighth-grade girl when I went on that double date with Stringbean and Mandy. The girl I dated that night was one I'd never been out with before; she was in the tenth grade and already 16 years old. Her name was Jackie and she was right good looking; she had a pair of knockers that wouldn't quit. That was the main reason I wanted to take Jackie out that night: because her figure would drive Mandy crazy with jealousy. (In the disordered state of my mind, pissing off Mandy had become my main purpose in life.) Jackie was kind of dumb and she came from a poor family, but she was smart enough and rich enough to dress well and accentuate her best features. She was a knockout that night in a light blue cashmere sweater.

We went in my car to the Starlite Drive-in theater. I kissed Jackie a few times but mostly we just watched the flick while

Stringbean and Mandy went at it hot and heavy in the back seat. To tell the truth, I was actually intimidated by Jackie—with her being so old—although she was a real sweet girl. She said "Zowie!" the first time I kissed her, I guess to encourage me to do it again. I did, but we never got passionate. She was pretty passive; never gave me any physical encouragement.

After the movie we drove across Garners Ferry road to Henry's drive-in where they sold Champale malt liquor. That Champale is strong stuff and it didn't take much to get Mandy going—going against me. She ignored Stringbean and began lecturing me about my shortcomings. She was articulate; I'll hand her that. Poor Jackie—who had trouble speaking grammatically although she tried hard—had to just sit there while Mandy told me what a jerk I was to be dating somebody like her. Of course, Mandy didn't come right out and say that, but that's what she was inferring. My main problem, according to Mandy, was that I had an inferiority complex. I was afraid of people on my own social and intellectual level she said. She was telling me this for my own good she said; I needed to recognize my fear and overcome my subconscious feelings of inferiority so that I could make proper friends and learn how to behave in society. She'd switched to the gospel according to Dr. Freud, but it was the same goddam Baptist preaching.

While Mandy was carrying on I rolled my eyes at Jackie and she smiled faintly and looked like she didn't know what to make of it all. Stringbean seemed highly amused. When Mandy came to a stopping place he asked me to pass my cigarettes back to him. Stringbean didn't smoke regularly; he just did it sometimes to be sociable and never bought any fags of his own. Mandy said Have one of mine, and offered him a Pall Mall, but he said No, pass me those Luckies. He took the pack from me and held it up to show what was printed on the bottom and asked me if I knew what it meant: L.S./M.F.T.

"Sure, Stringbean," I answered but didn't say what it was because I didn't want to make Jackie mad. He kept insisting so I said "Lucky Strike means fine tobacco."

"Naw, man, you know what it means. Come on, tell us."

Well, I had a pretty good buzz on by then and anybody could tell by looking at Jackie that it didn't apply to her, so I went ahead and said it: "Loose straps mean floppy titties."

"Naw, that's not it either," Stringbean said as Mandy started giggling. "What it means is: Let's screw, my finger's tired." The expression on Mandy's face suddenly changed to serious and she drove her elbow into Stringbean's ribs and he doubled over and said, "Hey, I didn't mean for you to take it literally." The way she started laughing then practically confirmed that he'd been finger-fucking her during the movie. Back then Stringbean hadn't been dating her very long, but already he'd gotten that far. I really admired old Stringbean. Now he was probably getting pussy regularly.

The thought occurred to me that he might've gotten Mandy pregnant: maybe that was why she was talking about them getting married. No, I thought, Stringbean was smart enough to use a rubber. And I was too, I said to myself as I lay on the bed in my room after breakfast and looked over at my wallet lying on the top of the dresser with a pack of two Green Light prophylactics in it. I was prepared for that night's outing with Sandburg, my first piece of ass. I wondered if Browder had any rubbers. He was probably still sacked out after running his paper route. I decided I'd clean my pistol and then give him a call.

The reason I had to clean the Luger was because I'd shot up a lot of war surplus ammunition in it back in June. Uncle Lewie gave me the ammunition, which was really bad stuff, from the Romanian army or some such. About one out of every five rounds was a dud. And the ones that went off were corrosive as hell, almost as bad as black powder. Of course I cleaned the Luger right after I'd finished shooting, but when I checked it the next day the bore was all crudded up. Boy, that worried me, because that bore was just about perfect; I sure didn't want it to get pitted. So I started cleaning it every day using solvent. But the bore had absorbed so much fouling that it kept on coming out; even weeks later it'd leave traces when I'd run a clean patch through the bore. It seemed o.k., though, when I cleaned it right before I left for Jacksonville and gave it a light coat of oil. I needed to check the bore and wipe off some of the oil. From now on I was only going to use non-corrosive commercial ammunition. There was about half a box of Remington Kleanbore 9 mm next to the Luger in the top drawer of the dresser.

I got the Luger last summer at Kirkland's Gun Shop on Main street. I traded Mr. Kirkland my .32 nickel-plated Astra automatic plus $15 for the Luger and its German army holster and one extra magazine. I'd gotten the Astra from a boy named Frankie Lorrick—traded him my .410 and $5 for it. I didn't need the .410 since Momma gave me Poppa's 12 gauge Stevens double barrel on my twelfth birthday. I also had a single-shot .22 rifle and a Red Ryder B-B gun.

While I was field stripping the Luger I thought about what Momma had said the night before about me being an accident, only she didn't use the work "accident." But that's what most people would say I was—except Catholics. They'd say I was a gift from God: that's a big difference between Episcopalians and Catholics. Episcopalians have this organization called Planned Parenthood and they believe that people should plan their children. The trouble with that is, if somebody plans you they think they created you, that they own you, that you're their project. I've seen them: these project children of rich Episcopalian families. They raise you real carefully and you wind up like one of those steers you see at the State Fair, somebody's 4-H project: fat and well groomed, no balls, no shit in your stall—but pretty soon, after they give the person that raised you a blue ribbon, somebody hits you in the head with a hammer and it's all over.

I ran a clean Hoppe's patch through the bore of the Luger and wiped it around on the inside of the breech. Nothing but clean oil came off. So I reattached the bolt to the barrel flanges and slid it back onto the receiver, making sure the hook fell into place in front of the ramps inside the grip. That's a big difference between Lugers and other automatic pistols: the recoil spring in a Luger is in the handle instead of underneath the barrel. When you shoot it and the bolt is blown back, this round toggle rides up and compresses the spring which then drives everything back into place for the next shot. That way it grounds the recoil and lets you keep on target for the next shot. And the way the Luger's designed makes it the most beautiful automatic pistol in the world. Compare it with the U.S. Army .45 automatic for instance: that gun has about as much aesthetic appeal as a couple of two-by-fours nailed together at a right angle. The .45's ugly and it's hard to shoot, but it's a little more powerful and probably a lot cheaper to make than the Luger.

My Luger, I thought as I fondled it that morning, was a work of art. The handle was as elegantly curved and thrust forward as the neck of Queen Nefretiti of Egypt. The trigger guard was almost a perfect circle and formed a rounded triangle with the toggle on top and the circular magazine thumb grip on bottom; from that curvaceous base emerged three inches of exquisitely tapered barrel. And the Luger felt as good as it looked. It was perfectly balanced, not muzzle heavy like the American .45. I liked to hold the Luger in my hand—to curl my fingers and thumb around the contoured grip and feel the stimulating scratch of checkered wood on my palm. Of course it felt even better to shoot it.

I decided to go down by the canal for a little target practice that morning. I had to be ready, I told myself, in case I got into a showdown with Doc Summerville and his gun moll. Later—in the afternoon—I'd go see Uncle Lewie.

When I called Browder I invited him to go shooting with me—after I'd told him about what Momma said the night before and about my excursion to the Backwoods Inn with the Eau Claire crew. Browder liked to shoot although he didn't have a gun of his own except a B-B rifle; when we'd go hunting he'd borrow his grandfather's 12 gauge. He wanted to go down to the canal and shoot the Luger with me but he said he could only be gone about an hour because he'd promised to help his momma dig up some bushes around the house that afternoon. He said he'd hop right on his bike and meet me at the corner of Gadsden and Richland.

I slipped the Luger and holster and ammunition into my knapsack and put the knapsack in the handlebar basket of my bike and set out for Gadsden street. Browder was waiting when I got there, leaning up against the Jewish cemetery sign. Together we pedaled down Richland to Wayne street and then cut over to Elmwood avenue and followed Elmwood down to where it deadends at the C. N. & L. railroad tracks. Browder and I walked our bikes about 70 yards along the tracks to the beginning of the trestle where we eased them down the steep path to the left through the bushes to the edge of the canal.

We found three tin cans and a pint whiskey bottle down by the water and set them up as targets on top of an old poplar log that stuck out a little ways into the canal. I grabbed the gun and ammunition and we stepped off 20 yards along the bank upstream from the targets. We had to pull up some weeds and break some branches off a few bushes to get a clear view. I loaded seven rounds into each magazine and gave one to Browder along with the pistol. He remembered how to load the magazine into the Luger and work the safety. Browder's shooting style was about the same as mine except that he put his left hand on his hip and kind of leaned back on his heels, while I liked to bend my knees and lean forward a little and stick my left hand into my pocket.

Browder's first three shots were low and to the right and went into the log. Then he put a shot over the log and into the water between two of the tin cans. His next shot must have grazed the can on the end because it went spinning off into the canal. He was zeroed in now and he put his next shot right through the middle of the can on the left—drilled it so perfectly that it hardly moved when he hit it. He hit the other can near the top on his last shot and knocked it over.

Now it was my turn to shoot. I lost my first shot but hit the bottom of a can on the second—knocked it back against a knot on the log which made it go somersaulting up into the air. My next shot was in the log under the target; I tend to shoot low because I'm so safety conscious. I aimed a little higher at the whiskey bottle and hit it square on; it collapsed in a pile on top of the log with the neck and bottom intact but the rest reduced to little slivers of glass. I hit the tin cans in two of my last three shots. My average was a little better than Browder's—which figured, since it was my gun we were shooting.

There were ten cartridges left in the Remington box after we'd each shot a magazine of seven. Browder agreed that I'd better save them for an emergency. Besides, it was getting to be time for him to go home and help his momma. So we tossed the bullet-riddled tin cans into the canal and picked up our bicycles and began pushing them up the steep red-clay path to the railroad bed. It took a lot of huffing and puffing to get them up there. When we did we only stopped for a few seconds to catch our breath before we started walking the bikes up the tracks. We'd gone about 20 yards before I noticed a city of Columbia squad car parked at the end of the Elmwood extension. The policeman inside must have seen us about the same time; he got out of the car as we came toward him. I asked Browder if he recognized the cop and he said no. I didn't either. There were a lot of Columbia cops we didn't know.

"That you boys doing that shooting down there?" the policeman asked as we rolled our bicycles off the tracks and onto the dirt road near where he was leaning against his Ford cruiser.

"Yes sir," I answered.

"Whatcha got?"

"Nothing. We were just target practicing."

"Naw, I mean what kinda gun you got."

"I got a Luger." I reached into the knapsack in the basket and pulled out the German army holster with the Luger inside and handed it to the cop. He took out the pistol and removed the empty magazine and pointed the muzzle at the round and pulled back the bolt and let it go forward. He examined the markings on the breech.

"Yessir, it's a Luger all right," the cop said. "Nineteen eighteen. The last year they made 'em in Germany."

"You wanna shoot it? I got some bullets left."

"No thank you. I know it shoots real good, though. My brother was over in Germany in the war and he brought back one. Got him a P-38 too. Now that's a real advanced automatic, that P-38. It's got double action." He put the Luger back into the holster and handed it to me.

"I tell you boys," he paused to light up a Camel, "those automatics are mighty fine, but I'm gonna stick with my trusty old Smith & Wesson Police Special here." He patted the holstered revolver on his hip.

"And I'll tell you why. Lemme present y'all with a hypothetical case." He blew a stream of smoke out of both nostrils. "Suppose you was me and had to go into this nigger juke joint and arrest some buck nigger. You got him covered but before you can get the cuffs on him, three or four o' his buddies start coming at you—and they got guns. So whadda you do? You grab your prisoner around the neck—with your left arm of course, since your gun's in your right hand—and you use him as a shield. Suppose then one o' them other niggers tries to maneuver around you. If he don't stop when you tell him, you shoot him. Right?" Browder and I both nodded our heads.

"But suppose you're armed with one o' them automatics and you got a bad round in the chamber. You pull the trigger and it goes 'click.' Whatcha gonna do now? You can't fire a shot until you can pull that slide back and get that bad round out. And you need two hands to do that. You'll have to let go that nigger you got around the neck—and soon as you do, you gonna have him and all them other bucks on top o' you. Y'all see what I mean?"

"Yes sir," Browder and I answered in unison.

"Now if you got a revolver instead of an automatic, all you gotta do to start shooting after a misfire is pull the trigger again. Things like that can happen: you're gonna get a bad round every now and then. I don't care if you got the best ammunition money can buy, you're bound to get a few duds. I know. I've shot up thousands o' rounds on the police range. I tell you, ordinarily I don't take no stock in what a criminal says, but old John Dillinger got it right when he said never trust a woman or an automatic pistol."

I knew about John Dillinger. The FBI man who killed him, Melvin Purvis, was a friend of Grandmomma's. He came to our house for dinner one day; I shook the hand of that great South Carolinian. But I didn't mention it to that Columbia cop because I was afraid he'd think I was bragging. So I changed the subject.

"The other day we saw 'em digging a grave over there in Potter's Field. Was it for somebody they electrocuted at the penitentiary?"

"Naw. That was just for some hobo they found dead out at Andrews Yard. But they got a nigger they're gonna electrocute this Friday morning. Nigger that killed a white man up in Laurens county. Emptied both barrels of a 12 gauge into him while he was sleeping. Poor fellow ran a country store and was asleep on a cot in the store one night when this nigger broke in to rob him and saw him sleeping there and just blew him to kingdom come. Nigger killed him and took $60 outta the cash register. You boys know how they caught him?"

"Didn't they use a lie detector machine?" I remembered reading about it in the paper.

"They shore did. Sheriff Weir and his deputies rounded up all the likely suspects and hooked them up to this lie detector machine and the one that did it knew he couldn't lie out of it, so he confessed. He even took the sheriff to where he hid the money he stole. Yessir, old Sheriff Weir did a bang-up job solving that case. I was up there at the Laurens county courthouse back in June when they had the trial. That's gonna be a famous case in history: they say it's the first time a lie detector machine's been used to convict somebody of murder. That machine's gonna put the fear of God in niggers who think they can get away with robbing and killing white folks. We need all the help we can get in law enforcement these days."

"The niggers are getting pretty uppity," Browder said.

"They sure are," the cop agreed. "I was on duty at the Township Auditorium when they had that big campaign meeting for the election last month and, I tell you, I saw things there that night that I never thought I'd ever see in a Southern city. Niggers were hooting and booing the governor of the state and the U.S. senator like that was just the regular thing for them to do. 'Course Strom and Olin D. were getting at one another pretty good themselves and I guess that set a bad example for the niggers. In a way you can't blame 'em—can't blame the niggers for acting the way they did. We got some pretty educated niggers here in Columbia and them's the ones that was up in the balcony at the Township Auditorium that night, educated niggers, not your ordinary blue gums. These were niggers who seemed to think they were just as good as white people. There weren't too many of 'em—less than 150 in the section we roped off for 'em —and there were more than 4,000 whites in the auditorium that night. But that didn't stop them niggers from hooting and hollering and carrying on just like if they'd been white folks. Strom would accuse Olin D. of not stopping integration in the armed forces, and the niggers would boo Strom. Then Olin D. would accuse Strom of inviting a nigger to sleep in the Governor's Mansion, and the niggers would boo Olin D. They had no respect at all."

"Nobody tried to stop the niggers from carrying on like that?" I asked.

"Well, you gotta remember, the white folks were divided and they were whooping it up too: some pretty strong words were passed back and forth between Strom's people and Olin D.'s people. They just didn't pay that much attention to the niggers. Somebody'd say 'Shut up, nigger,' but wouldn't do anything. And we were there—the police were there—to make sure they didn't do anything. We gotta keep law and order. Niggers get a lot o' consideration these days. We even got a couple o' nigger patrolmen on the Columbia police force."

"Nigger police? I never seen any," Browder said.

"Well you wouldn't, 'less you went down to Washington street on Saturday night. They only patrol nigger areas and don't have any authority at all over white people. Mayor Owens, he hired them. First niggers on the Columbia police force in over 40 years. Now I have to admit they do a pretty good job handling nigger problems that you really don't wanna mess with yourself. So it's probably a good thing: it'll work out o.k. as long as those nigger patrolmen know their place and don't get the big head. They seem to be pretty good niggers. It's all politics, though. Now that niggers can vote a lot of politicians 're secretly catering to 'em."

"I think Olin D. was doing that," I said.

"Maybe. But old Olin's the best friend the white working-man's got. He's the one that's keeping niggers from taking jobs in the textile industry. Old Strom's a good friend of the mill owners; if they thought they could make more money for themselves by hiring niggers, I'm afraid Strom would let 'em do it."

I wasn't about to get into a political argument with a policeman, so I just said it was too bad white people couldn't decide these political questions themselves without niggers getting involved.

"That's the way it was until a couple years ago," the cop said; "until that federal judge down in Charleston said we gotta let niggers vote in the Democratic primary. I can't understand how that judge could do such a thing. He was born and raised right here in this state."

"But he's married to a Yankee," I said.

"Well, she oughta go back where she came from and take him with her. The way I look at it, Northerners in the South are like hemorrhoids: if they come down and go back up, they're no problem; but if they come down and stay down, they're a real pain in the ass."

That was a joke, so Browder and I both laughed. Grown-ups do a lot of worrying about hemorrhoids.

"Well," the cop said as he flicked his cigarette butt into the air and sent it arching toward the gravel railroad bed, "I guess I better get back to my rounds." He got into the squad car and as he started the engine he stuck his arm out the window and gave us a left-handed salute: "You boys be careful."

We waved as the cruiser spun around and headed up Elmwood avenue.

I went to the surplus store that afternoon and told Uncle Lewie all about Dr. Summerville and the job he said he had for Momma in New Jersey and how I recognized him in the picture we found at the Mirador Club. The woman in the photo definitely was not Marilyn at the Backwoods Inn: I explained how I'd checked her out the night before. I had the picture with me and Uncle Lewie took another look at it and agreed that it wasn't Marilyn. "You right, Clarence: that ain't her." He studied Dr. Summerville's image. "You sure that's him?"

"Ain't no doubt about it."

"Well I tell you: he looks like a doctor to me. And if your momma thinks he's one, then he's one. It's her business and she's a better judge of appearances and character than me. It ain't easy to fool your momma; I haven't been able to do it more'n two-three times myself. Your momma knows what goes on. I don't think she'd be much surprised to find out her doctor friend was out at the Mirador Club with some little chickadee. I swear half the doctors in Columbia 're diddling their nurse or receptionist or some other doctor's nurse or receptionist. Lots o' times they'd take 'em out to the Mirador Club. You wouldn't see any doctors' wives out there but you'd see plenty o' doctors and working girls."

"But don't you think it's suspicious that he'd be out there with that woman the night before he called up Momma acting like he just blew into town?"

"Clarence old buddy, there ain't much in this world that's not suspicious."

"But if me and Momma gonna pull up stakes and leave Columbia and move all the way up to New Jersey on account of this scutter—shouldn't we find out all we can about him first?"

Uncle Lewie didn't answer the question. He extracted the pack of Old Golds from his shirt pocket, tapped out a fag, packed it with a couple of licks on his wristwatch crystal, and lit it with one swipe of his Ronson lighter. He inhaled deeply and when he finally spoke the words came with the fog of thin blue smoke that drifted out his mouth and nostrils. "You know, I'd really hate to see y'all go. Y'all'd have to be gone by Labor Day, I suppose. I was gonna ask you if you wanted to go with me to that stock car race over in Darlington on Labor Day."

"I'll go with you. I sure will. We ain't going to New Jersey—not if I can help it."

"You gotta do what your momma says, Clarence."

"O.k., I will. But me and you gotta help her decide. We gotta give her all the information we can get on that Dr. Summerville. So she'll know what she'd be getting into. We gotta find Dr. Summerville's lady friend and talk to her. Look, how 'bout asking the photographer that took the picture—ask her if she knows where we can find that woman. Please do that for me, Uncle Lewie."

"Well I reckon I can do that. Gimme the picture and I'll run it by Cindy when I get a chance, in the next day or two."

Uncle Lewie didn't seem too enthusiastic about looking up Cindy the photographer. I got the idea that he had something else in mind that he wasn't going to tell me about. That was o.k. with me, but I hated to give up that picture. "Look, when you're ready to go see Cindy let me know and I'll give you the picture then. I wanna keep hold of it until then in case I run across somebody else who might know something about it. Really, time's running out: Momma's planning to leave for New Jersey early next week. What we need is two pictures, one for me and one for you... "

"You can get it copied. Take it around the corner to Carolina Camera Shop and they'll make you a duplicate. Cost four or five bucks. You got it?"

"Not on me. I could get it outta my savings account at the bank, but they're closed now; it's after two o'clock."

Uncle Lewie took a five-dollar bill from his wallet and handed it to me. "Actually, you won't have to pay 'em until tomorrow when you pick up the copy. They do that kind of work overnight. But take the money anyway. We can settle up next week."

"Thanks, Uncle Lewie; I sure appreciate it. Who you think's gonna win that race? Fireball Roberts?"

"Maybe. Depends on what he's driving."

"He's gonna qualify in a Cadillac, ain't he?"

"If he does, he'll be making a big mistake."

"You think he oughta go with an Olds 88?"

"Clarence, that track's one and a quarter miles long and banked like you never seen. Anybody who takes an 88 or a Caddy on that track'll have to fight like a fool just to keep the sumbitch on the road. Those GM gook wagons just ain't engineered for that kinda driving. Suspension's sorry, steering's mush. They got power all right, but it don't do you no good if you can't put it where you need it. And those overhead-valve V-8's ain't all that reliable anyway. You can't do anything to 'em for this race—can't even add another carburetor. They gotta be strictly stock."

"So you think one of them new Hudson Hornets gonna take it?"

"Hell no. Ain't no Hudson Hornets gonna finish that race. We're talking 500 miles. They'll all fall apart after a few laps. But they got the right kind of engine: an L-head six. I betcha the car than wins that race is gonna have an L-head six."

"Uncle Lewie, you don't mean..."

"You goddam right. Lee Petty's gonna qualify in a bug-backed Plymouth just like the one I got—and he ain't gonna be the only one that qualifies in a Plymouth. Somebody—maybe somebody you never heard of—somebody driving a bug-backed Plymouth is gonna grab the lead early and hold it and make a lot of money for me and anybody else who bets on him. I guaran-damn-tee you."

Uncle Lewie was a big Plymouth fan. He's the one who convinced Momma that that's what she ought to get. Of course, the model she bought was a four-door Deluxe sedan instead of a two-door 98 Junior like Uncle Lewie's. The engine and the transmission were the same, though. Uncle Lewie told Momma that dollar for dollar and pound for pound those Plymouth sixes were the best cars ever built in America.

"That bug-backed Plymouth's a running little sumbitch," Uncle Lewie said. "You just can't beat that Chrysler engineering. I know; I've put a lot of rough miles on a lot of different cars in my time. Back when I was running corn liquor from Jalapa to Atlanta I had me a '40 Ford coupe, and that was a good car for its time. Had a lot of pickup at slow speeds: could get 60 in 15 seconds. And had a pretty good top speed too—over a hundred on the speedometer. 'Course she was modified a little; had twin carburetors and hot heads—not real hot, just eight to one. And I had me a crackerjack mechanic, old boy who really knew how to keep her in tune. Ain't easy to keep a V-8 in tune, specially them flat-head Ford V-8's. But even when my old '40 Ford was running right, that Plymouth woulda took it on the road—not on the get-off, not around town, but on the road. Fact is, I never seen a Ford or Mercury strictly stock that wouldn't start cutting out at around 80 miles an hour. You don't have no problem like that with that little old Plymouth; she runs so smooth and steady and handles so fine. The other day I averaged 95 miles an hour coming back from Union. I ain't shitting you, Clarence. You know how there's all them straight up and down hills on state road 215 between here and Union? Well I floorboarded that scutter the whole way; she'd hit more'n a hundred going down them hills and wouldn't drop below 90 going up 'em. When that little Plymouth's wound up, she royally hauls ass."

"I believe you, Uncle Lewie. But the Darlington 500's supposed to be the top stock car race in the whole country. You really think a Plymouth can win it?"

"Sho as gun Zion. Me and you gonna watch it happen—I hope."

"I hope so too, Uncle Lewie."

11

As I GOT INTO THE CAR after supper I could faintly hear music coming from the jukebox at Arsenal Hill Community Center. It was Wednesday so it was teenage canteen night. When I drove across Lincoln street I looked over that way and saw a couple of early birds shagging under the lights on the patio. I wondered why the Baptists didn't try to get the teen canteen switched to some other night since it competed with their prayer meeting.

My first stop was to pick up Browder. He came out right after I blew the horn at the side of his house. He got into the front seat and we drove around the corner to Daniel Sellers's place. Sellers was waiting on the porch when we pulled up. I parked in front of the house and cut off the engine as Sellers ambled up to the car; we needed to go over our plans for the poontang expedition. He got into the back seat and we each lit up a teege. Sellers briefed us on the first phase of the operation.

"Awright," he said, "y'all let me off around the corner from Sandburg's house. Then y'all go on to Lincoln street; park about halfway up the block from Chester—that's the way we'd be walking if we was going to Park Street Baptist. I'll hustle her in the back seat and then let's get outta there real fast—just in case her momma takes a notion to follow us."

163

Sellers seemed a little nervous. He took a quick drag on his Lucky and asked, "Where we gonna take her?"

"Let's take her to Broad river," I said.

"To the locks?"

"Naw. To the rocks." The rocks were on the other side of the river from the locks. At the locks there was just this big open space where you parked. Taxi drivers sometimes brought whores and their customers there; the driver would sit down on the stone steps that went up to the top of the locks and smoke a cigarette while the people in his cab screwed. There wasn't much privacy there; other cars might pull up beside you with people who came to screw or neck or just to fish. The bluff on the other side of the river, where there were all these big boulders lying around, was a better place to fuck. There were lots of loops and side roads going through the woods up there and you could be pretty sure of finding a place where nobody would bother you.

"We might have to buy her something first," Sellers said, "like a milkshake."

"That ain't no problem," Browder said. "We'll just go on out 176 to the Dairy Queen. Ain't much danger of anybody seeing us there—Freddy Mercer maybe, if he's working there tonight. But we can park in the back and whoever goes in to get the stuff don't have to tell him we got Sandburg in the car."

"But what if Ashcan and the St. Andrews crew happen to drive by and see us," I said. "Boy, they'd give us a hard time; they'd try to horn in on us too."

"That's a possibility," Browder agreed, "but we're not as liable to run into people we know at that Dairy Queen than at any other place within a reasonable distance. I mean shit, we don't wanna drive her all the way to Lexington. We ain't got that much time. Those prayer meetings don't last all night."

"You right," I said. "We'll take her to the St. Andrews Dairy Queen and then double back to the rocks where we'll all get a good fuck. You can go first, Sellers."

"That's right," Browder said. "We always let the one with the littlest peter go first; that way the pussy don't get all stretched out the first thing."

Of course that wasn't the real reason Sellers was going to get the first turn. He had to be first because he was the one who was going to pick her up and sit with her in the back seat and take off her clothes and warm her up for everybody. He could handle her better than either of us because he knew her better than we did and he'd fucked her before. Browder and I were both a year older than Sellers but we'd never fucked anybody before. This was a case where age had to defer to experience. We wouldn't admit it but we didn't know how to get the gangbang started and he did.

"Everybody got a rubber?" I asked.

"Unh unh," Sellers said. "She won't let you use a rubber."

"She won't? How come?" Browder asked.

"She won't let you use a rubber on account of what her momma told her. Her momma told her about one time a rubber came off inside a girl and they had to take her to the hospital and operate on her to get it out. She's scared of rubbers."

"Well if that don't beat all," Browder said. "But I reckon we don't have a whole lot to worry about. If she gets knocked up she couldn't ever prove which one of us is the poppa."

"And if we get a dose o' clap," Sellers said with a grin, "all we gotta do is go see Cap's momma and get us some shots."

"Yeah, sure," I said, but I didn't think I'd ever go to Momma myself if I needed treatment for VD. Instead I'd probably ask Theron Velakis at the Waverly Drugstore to get me some penicillin and a hypodermic needle. But if somebody else got the clap from Sandburg and they took her down to the health department and she named me as one of her contacts... I didn't want to think about it. I turned the key and started the engine. "O.k., let's go."

We drove to the end of Wayne street where Sellers got out. Then I swung the car past Sandburg's house—she wasn't in sight but the lights were on inside—and hooked a right on Lincoln and parked about 30 yards from the corner. Then Browder and I began our wait. We both twisted around in the front seat and stared back at the corner where Sellers and Sandburg were supposed to appear. Though it was dark where we were parked, under a canopy of red oaks, the intersection and the sidewalk at the corner were washed in the pale glare of a fluorescent street-light.

The houses in this area north of Elmwood were built around 40 years ago, about 100 years after the oldest ones on the south side of the avenue where Momma and I lived. Our house and a lot of others in our neighborhood were bigger than any north of Elmwood, but some were a lot more rundown than your average place in this newer section—although some in this area were starting to get a little ratty too, especially down by the Seaboard railroad tracks. On both sides of the avenue, from Arsenal Hill to the Seaboard tracks, the people were about the same—pretty much all white-collar working class—no poor white trash, no niggers, but no real wealthy people either, though I guess you'd have to say that Mr. Milam who owns the electric company is pretty well-to-do. The Milams' house had two stories but wasn't by any means the biggest in the area: some had two and a half stories, with one or two gabled windows jutting out from the attic. But a whole lot more were smaller, only one or one-and-a-half stories—like Sandburg's. No matter what the size of the house though, the front porches there north of Elmwood were comparatively small; few of them extended for the entire width of the house and none had two-story columns like ours.

The really big difference was the size of the yards on the two sides of Elmwood. Where we lived the houses were set way back on big lots with flowering trees—magnolias and myrtles and dogwoods—all around them, and big bushes like azaleas and oleanders. But there north of Elmwood the houses were practically jammed up against one another on tiny lots with only space for a few small shrubs between them and maybe a couple of nandenas or camellias on each side of the front porch. There was no room for trees in the front yards, which were little and narrow like cemetery plots. But big trees—mostly oaks—were planted on the city right-of-way, on the strip of ground between the street and the sidewalk; so the area was well shaded. It was real dark there at night when you got away from the streetlights on the corners.

Browder and I'd been waiting less than five minutes when Sellers and Sandburg appeared under the streetlight on the corner of Lincoln and Chester. Seeing her walking with Sellers made me think how short she was. Sellers was only about five foot six and Sandburg was almost a head shorter than he was. She was little, I thought, but she sure was well built; she was wearing a light-colored blouse and dark skirt that clung to the impressive contours of her hips and breasts. I remembered that even Mandy Jackson once said that Sandburg had "a cute figure"—a damn sight cuter than hers, though she didn't say that.

"Here they come," Browder said. He reached over and opened the back door and the overhead light went on in the car. I started the engine. "'Lo Shirley," Browder said as she ducked in with Sellers quick behind her.

"Hi y'all," she responded.

I was concentrating on getting us out of there, but before I drove off—before Sellers closed the door and the overhead light went out—I turned around and got a good look at her. She was ugly, but I already knew that; I'd seen her plenty of times from a distance. It was no shock to see her up close; there were a lot of uglier girls in the world, I thought. In fact if you didn't know she was a whore you might not even think of her as ugly—just plain. Her face was kind of pushed in and her eyes were pretty far apart and she had a few small pimples—but no big hideous goobs. And, like I said, her body was something else. I knew I wouldn't mind fucking her. "Hi Shirley," I said.

"Shirley wants a milkshake," Sellers announced as we swung left on Park street away from the church. "Let's go to the Dairy Queen."

"Sounds good to me," I said and glanced at them in the rearview mirror. He had his hand up her blouse and she seemed to be enjoying it. I knew he wouldn't kiss her—not with Browder and me in the car. You weren't supposed to kiss whores. If you did and some other boy found out he'd say It must've tasted good because she sucked me off right before you picked her up. And he'd tell everybody and they'd call you a dicksucker by proxy. You only smooched girls who were pretty or cute, who were at least halfway respectable and didn't put out for everybody. Sellers knew the rules.

There weren't any other cars at the Dairy Queen when we pulled up. I parked in the back and Browder and I went inside; Sellers wanted us to bring him a double chocolate-dip cone. Browder and I decided we'd have the same. Luckily, Freddie Mercer wasn't on duty that night; his stepfather was running the place by himself and he didn't know us from Adam. He made Sandburg's shake first and then took three large cones and filled them one by one under the ice cream faucet, moving each down and around to shape the white goop into a spiral peak. With a flick of the wrist he dipped the tops of each into a vat of molten chocolate, giving them a smooth ebony crust. The chocolate coating tasted a lot better than the bland airy mixture it covered. The stuff you got at Dairy Queen wasn't rich and creamy like at Zesto.

Sellers had undone the side zipper on Sandburg's skirt and his hand was down the front when we got back to the car. He accepted his cone with his other hand and Sandburg reached for the milkshake with both hands. She held the big paper cup in one hand and fiddled with the straw with the other as she slurped the shake. Sellers kept finger-fucking her as he lapped his ice cream cone. Browder and I turned back around in the front seat and nobody said anything. There wasn't anything to say. As soon as I'd eaten the ice cream down to the top of my cone—I didn't want it dripping on me while I was driving—I started the car and we took off for the rocks.

We made the circle and passed one parked car—an old Chevy—on the bluff directly over the dam. I doubled back and pulled into a side road just across from the path that goes down to the sandbar.

"This looks pretty good," I said to Browder.

"It'll do." We parked about 20 yards down that side road. It was narrow and washed out and rattlesnake ferns scraped the car on both sides going in; there was a pile of trash a few yards in front of us and I don't think we could've gone much farther.

"Y'all take it easy," Browder said to the pair in the back seat as he and I got out of the car.

"We'll take it anyway we can," Sellers replied just before I closed the door and plunged the Plymouth into darkness.

It took awhile for our eyes to adjust to the dark; Browder and I both stumbled a few times as we made our way back to the main road. It was a normal dog-days night—warm but not ungodly hot—with the usual background music of chirping crickets and humming cicadas. The air was pretty still but from time to time a breeze rustled the sweetgum leaves overhead. Now and then you could hear the croak of a bullfrog from down by the river.

Browder and I crossed the rutted dirt road we'd come in on and climbed up on a boulder where we could keep an eye on the car and also look down on the river. The moon hadn't risen yet and the stars were only pinpoints of light in the black sky and didn't provide much illumination; we could barely make out the dam. We couldn't tell if any water was going over it. The back slope of the dam was so gradual that water going over it would hardly make a sound, even if the overflow was a foot deep. It was a real quiet river, wide and slow and mysterious. We each lit up a teege and waited.

Browder broke the silence: "You gonna go next, ain't you?" Since it was my car, the choice was mine.

"Yeah. Hope I don't make it too big for you."

"Don't worry." We liked to joke about who was better hung. Actually we were about the same.

I looked down the side road to where I'd parked the Plymouth. All I could see was a darkened hulk in the woods—there were no signs of activity and no sounds coming from it. But I knew that important business was being transacted inside and pretty soon I'd be in there getting my share. Perched up on that rock I felt the full force of the knowledge that I was finally about to get a piece of ass. My mind was locked in focus on that one thing. Physically I was fully aroused and leaking dogwater.

A few minutes after I'd finished my cigarette the overhead light came on in the car as Sellers opened the back door. When he got out he was buck naked except for the shoes and socks on his feet. His clothes were in his hand and his pecker was at halfmast, still semi-hard. He stood in the pumpkin-colored light next to the open door and hollered, "Hey, I need something to wipe with."

"Use your drawers," Browder yelled back.

"Hey you clowns pipe down," I said as I scrambled off the rock. "You want the whole fucking world to hear us? There's some Kleenexes in the glove compartment."

As I walked toward the car Sellers reached in over the front seat and got out the box of Kleenexes. I could see him hand some to Sandburg but I couldn't see her; she was lying down out of sight on the back seat. I stopped a few yards short of the car while Sellers wiped himself off and stepped into his pants. He closed the door and the light went out; he headed for where Browder was and I started again for the car. "Don't fall in," he said as we passed in the dark.

I grabbed the handle of the door and opened it with a resolute pull. For all my second-hand knowledge, all my imaginings, I wasn't prepared for what I saw in the back seat of the Plymouth. The light came on and revealed Sandburg stretched out completely naked on the seat with her legs slightly apart and one foot on the floorboard and her head and shoulders propped up against the opposite door; one elbow was on the armrest and the other arm was draped across the back of the seat. She was the first naked girl I'd ever seen in person and boy did she look good to me. My god, I thought: The Naked Maja. Sandburg's body could've come right out of that famous painting; it was just as good. I hadn't expected a work of art. "Son-of-a-bitch!" I exclaimed out loud.

Sandburg might've been smiling slightly—I got the impression she was—but I can't say for sure because my mind blanked out her face just like those art books blanked out the maja's pussy. There was no such deletion at the apex of Sandburg's fine thighs; it was there: the center of her attractiveness, the dark triangular bull's-eye. Of course I'd seen plenty of drawings of cunts—Dixie Dugan's, Blondie's, Tillie the Toiler's, even Little Orphan Annie's—in fuckbook comics; and I'd seen photos of ordinary looking naked ladies with their pussies showing in the nudist magazine *Sunshine and Health*. Those pictures always got a rise out of me so I figured I'd react even more strongly to the real thing. And I sure did. For the life of me I couldn't understand how any man or boy could come face to face with a real live pussy and not get a hard on. I'd heard that doctors who examined women wore specially made Jockstraps to hold their peckers down.

For a couple of seconds I stood there gaping at the naked Sandburg. Then I slid quickly into the back seat and closed the door and pulled off my clothes in the dark and threw them over the front seat. I hurried because I was all sexed up and afraid I might shoot off before I got it in. But that was no problem and neither was getting it in a problem. As I crawled on her Sandburg automatically opened her legs wide and I easily found the entrance to her snatch. I gave a little push and slipped in and, to my surprise, discovered that the tunnel turned up instead of going straight back. I adjusted my thrusts accordingly. Soon I was totally buried in her pussy. I'd wondered if I'd be able to do that, with her being so little. After I knew the answer I asked the question: "It's not too big for you, is it?"

"Unh unh," she replied, which was the extent of our conversation during the act.

It was the adventure, the exploration, the continuing revelations that kept me from going off prematurely. My satisfaction mounted as I discovered that in fucking—no less than in fighting and more than in drinking—I had staying power: I wasn't going to be knocked out in the first round. As my strokes became strong and regular she began to move with me—and that threw off my concentration. My control weakened as the realization of what I was doing overcame me: I was actually fucking and I was going to come and couldn't stop it and didn't want to stop it. The explosion rattled my teeth and curled my toes and liquified the rest of my body and sent it surging into Sandburg's pussy. I was free; I'd broken loose.

The sensation was far greater than anything I'd ever experienced before. And afterwards there was none of the disgust I usually felt after beating off. Instead there was a feeling of accomplishment—elation really. My body was a little wobbly but my mind was clear as a bell—sharper than it had ever been. Contrary to what Tommy had said at the green hole, fucking didn't make you weak; it made you strong—strong mentally and physically too, after the initial shakiness wore off. I felt strong and tough as a bear as I strolled back to the rock after screwing Sandburg.

While Browder took his turn in the back seat of the car Sellers and I sat on the rock and smoked cigarettes and talked about Sandburg and other whores including some out in Rosewood who didn't usually gangbang but were a sure thing if you took them out alone. There was no shortage of available pussy in Columbia. I knew I'd be getting my share in the weeks and months ahead—if Momma didn't drag me off to New Jersey. I told Sellers about that possibility but he didn't react much to it. When you're only 14 years old there's a lot you can't really comprehend, especially when it doesn't affect you directly.

"Boy," I said, returning to the subject of immediate concern, "Browder sure is taking a long time."

"Maybe he couldn't get a hard on," Sellers said. His old man used to tell him jokes about men who were impotent, like in the song "Too Old to Cut the Mustard"—Now I'm old, my balls are cold, can't raise a bone to save my soul—but that didn't apply to young boys like us.

The speculation ended when the light came on in the car and Browder emerged naked from the back seat. With his clothes in one hand and shoes in the other he raised his arms over his head like a matador showing off the ears of a dead bull and hollered, "I cut it twice!"

Sellers and I jumped down from the rock and ran for the car; we wanted another turn too. But Sandburg already had her skirt on and was stuffing her blouse down into it.

"Unh unh, y'all," she said. "I gotta get back. Prayer meeting'll be getting out any minute now."

So we called it quits and took her home.

After we dropped Sandburg off I asked Sellers and Browder if they wanted to go up to Arsenal Hill.

"Naw, not now," Browder said. "Let's go to Seawell's. After all that work I'm hungry as a motherfucker. Gotta get me one of them Seawell's hamburgers."

I was hungry too, so I headed the Plymouth up Main street toward Seawell's drive-in. Coming up on River Drive I slipped into the left lane to swing into Seawell's but the red light caught us at the intersection. A stationwagon pulled up on our right—a '50 Ford, maroon with yellow wood trim. It was Calhoun with Dude Adolphus riding shotgun. Calhoun grinned at us and kept gunning his engine and edging up like he wanted to dig.

"Dig him," Sellers said. "Ain't no cops around."

"Man I ain't got a chance against that Ford. It's geared for the get-off." But I raced my engine anyway and eased the clutch out to just a cunt hair from being in gear. I let it pop out as the light turned green and we lunged forward with a big roar of the engine. Calhoun's back tires screamed as they propelled the Ford ahead of us in one big jump. I almost caught him as my low gear was winding out, but then Calhoun grabbed second and jumped farther ahead with another squeal of his tires. I backed off as I shifted into second; we swung into Seawell's and left Calhoun and Dude Adolphus barreling off towards Eau Claire.

We'd just given our order to the carhop when Calhoun's Ford pulled into the space beside us. Dude Adolphus stuck his head out the window. "Ain't y'all embarrassed," he said, "riding in a car so slow?"

"You tell Calhoun to take it out on the road," I said, "and I'll show you who's slow."

"That's a good idea," Calhoun said as he got out of the Ford and waved for a carhop. "I'll race you over the roller coasters."

"Man you crazy as hell." I got out of the Plymouth and scooted up on the front fender. "That fucking stationwagon'll break in two going over the roller coasters."

It was fun going over the roller coasters, especially if you had girls in the car. Those hills were so close together and steep that you'd actually take off into the air at the top of them if you were going fast enough. You'd get this falling sensation—you *would* be falling—lots of screams and laughs. But you'd have to be out of your mind to race over the roller coasters. You couldn't see over the hills and the road wasn't even paved; no telling what you might run into—rocks or holes or whatever—which you wouldn't be able to dodge if you were moaning top speed and close together.

"Come on," Browder said to Calhoun, "be serious." Everybody was outside the cars now, sitting or leaning on the front fenders. "Take it out to the straightaway."

"The straightaway? Where's that?"

"Out past the Veterans Hospital," I answered. "It's this paved road that runs off Garners Ferry toward Bluff road. Never any traffic on it, no houses, and it's perfectly straight and level for a mile. The measured mile ends at some railroad tracks—which is the finish line; the crossing's real smooth. This old Plymouth's won a lot of races out there."

"Well we ain't talking Chevrolets and Pontiacs tonight, Cap. I got me a V-8 under that hood—a hundred hellacious horses."

The carhop brought our order of hamburgers and shakes and French fries and Calhoun ordered a couple of beers for him and Dude Adolphus. He lit up one of his cork-tipped fags. "Hell yes, I'll take you on out at that straightaway. You opes finish garbaging up and we'll be ready. You wanna make a bet?"

"Naw. I just race for funsies," I said.

"Hey Calhoun," Browder broke in, "where's your good old buddy Bobby Skinner?" Dude Adolphus and I looked at each other and rolled our eyes.

"How the hell should I know? I ain't studying him."

"I hear he might be studying you though," I said. "Might have something to say to you next time you go out with little Nancy Gray."

"Well we'll just have to see, 'cause I got a date with her tomorrow night."

"You ain't been out with her tonight?" Browder asked.

"Naw. Me and Dude been up at Arsenic Hill."

"What's going on up there?" I asked.

"Not much. Nobody interesting showed up."

"He means Sandburg," Dude Adolphus said with an impish grin. "She didn't show up tonight like she did last Wednesday. Said she would but she didn't."

"I'll tell you why she didn't show up," Browder said—Sellers and I were laughing—"She didn't show up because she was out with us tonight."

"That's no shit," Sellers said. "She was with us. We just now took her home."

Calhoun and Dude Adolphus just stood there not knowing whether to believe us or not.

"Yep," I said, "we all cut it at least twice and then she sucked us all off."

"And she told us all about y'all picking her up last week," Browder said. "She thinks Dude Adolphus is real cute and said he sure likes to smooch—said it's too bad though his peter's so little."

"You lying," Dude said. "I never kissed her."

"All I know is what she said. 'Nother thing she said was that Calhoun shot off all over his tailors."

"Now *that* was the truth," Dude Adolphus giggled.

"Come on you opes, let's hit the road," Calhoun said as he paid for the beers and handed the tray back to the carhop.

• • •

We lined up on the smooth two-lane blacktop with Calhoun's Ford in the right lane and my Plymouth on the left. Of course there wasn't any on-coming traffic; if there'd been any we could-'ve seen their headlights a mile away across the finish line. Browder rode shotgun with me and Dude Adolphus rode with Calhoun; both cars had their windows rolled up to cut down on air resistance. The starting signal was to be given by Sellers who was standing on the left shoulder of the road about ten yards in front of us and well illuminated in my headlights. Sellers raised his right hand above his head. He counted off three seconds —though we couldn't hear him with the motors revving and the windows closed—and then he lowered his hand in a swift downward motion like he as dropping a starting flag. "Go!" Browder shouted.

I didn't pay any attention to Calhoun's Ford as I concentrated on getting the most out of my low gear. At about 35 miles an hour I could feel it winding out. With the accelerator floored I stomped the clutch pedal and simultaneously slammed the gearshift lever into second; the clutch pedal bounced off the floor and the Plymouth charged into second gear. But second was the Plymouth's weakest gear; before it got to 50 it'd be wound out and time to shift to high. With the Ford it was just the opposite; second was the best gear. Calhoun ate me up in second; he shifted out of low long before I did—probably around 20 miles an hour —and held it in second until almost 60.

By the time I hit 60 Calhoun was three or four car lengths ahead. He lost a little momentum shifting into third and I gained about half a car length. Then the gap between us stabilized as we accelerated at the same rate: 65, 70, 75, 80. I was dogging him but not getting any closer. My speedometer needle moved on past 80 and then something amazing happened: old Calhoun's Ford just seemed to stop; I passed him like he was sitting still. Eighty-five, 90—the Plymouth kept accelerating as Calhoun's headlights receded in my rearview mirror. I crossed the railroad tracks with a rapid thump-thump at 95 miles an hour.

"Hoooo wee!" Browder hollered as he rolled down his window. "We ate that scutter up!"

I made a U-turn and blew the horn at Calhoun as we headed back to pick up Sellers. From where he was, looking down the straightaway a mile from the finish line, Sellers said he couldn't tell who'd won. He acted like he didn't believe it when we told him we did, but then Calhoun pulled up and confirmed it. His Ford wasn't running right, Calhoun said; he was going to have to get it tuned up. Yeah, that's what they all say, I told him; anytime he wanted to run it over again I'd be ready. We could put some money on it next time, I said.

Calhoun followed us to Belt Line boulevard where he peeled off and we continued on Devine street to Five Points. We'd decided we wanted to whip through Sox's. I hooked in the Harden street entrance and eased on back to Sox's main lot.

"Would you look at that," Browder pointed out the window, "the three fastest cars in Columbia!"

Sure enough, there they were, lined up next to the Greene street exit: Hamilton James's '49 Cadillac, Coy Starr's '50 Olds 88, and Adam Melton's new Hudson Hornet. The drivers and a few other boys were all standing around talking. Adam Melton was drinking Coca-Cola out of a Dixie cup. Jack Sox had stopped selling beer last March after he got religion at the Billy Graham crusade, but people still liked to hang out at his drive-in.

We waved at the fast-car crew but nobody paid us any attention and I didn't feel like stopping and talking to them anyway. I figured they were debating about who was going to win the Darlington 500—whether it'd be a Cadillac or an Olds or a Hudson. Wouldn't be any sense in me getting into it; they'd just laugh at my explanation of how a Plymouth was going to win. No, we wouldn't stop and talk, but I still wanted to make a statement because I felt pretty damn good that night.

The Plymouth wouldn't lay rubber on bare pavement, but Sox's exit on Greene street was at the bottom of a hill where sand accumulated and would give your wheels an extra spin. I gunned the motor and popped the clutch and the old Plymouth let out a soul-satisfying screech as we took off toward Harden street. Tomorrow, I thought, I'm going to find Dr. Summerville's lady friend.

12

WHEN I WOKE UP Thursday morning I thought of two things: that there was going to be a nigger dance at the Township Auditorium the next night and that I'd promised this girl—Jenny Lynch—that I'd call her this week. Jenny lived out in St. Andrews but she used to live in our neighborhood and I'd known her since the first grade at Logan school. But I'd never gone out with her until the week before I went to Jacksonville when she invited me to go on this Training Union hayride at the St. Andrews Baptist church. We had a good time together on that hayride and I thought about asking her to go with me and sit in the white observer section at the Tiny Bradshaw dance. I didn't see any need to curtail my social life during the search for Dr. Summerville's ladyfriend. In fact I figured the more I circulated the more likely it'd be that I might run into her or somebody who knew her. So I decided to ask Jenny Lynch for a date Friday night to go to that function at the Township Auditorium.

Jenny was a nice girl and right good looking—almost as pretty as Mandy Jackson who she used to run around with at Logan school before she moved to St. Andrews. Jenny and Mandy both went to Park Street Baptist church back then and were really devout, although Jenny never was as obnoxious about it as Mandy. Jenny would just stand around and nod her head sadly

179

when Mandy would tell some other little second- or third-grade child that they were going to hell because they coveted something or stole a piece of chalk or went to a movie on Sunday. Mandy used to pull that crap on me and I'll admit that she had me worried. I'd come home and go up to my room and cry about it; Mandy convinced me that I was going to burn forever in the fires of hell. Finally one day Grandmomma got tired of seeing me moping around the house and made me tell her what was bothering me. She told me I didn't need to worry about going to hell. We're Episcopalians, she said, and we believe in a merciful God; don't pay any attention to those Baptist children. God didn't like children misbehaving and He'd make sure they got punished if they did, Grandmomma said, but there wasn't anything a little child could do that was so bad that God would send them to hell for it.

Merciful or not, God could be pretty tough on children who misbehaved: I knew that from Episcopal Sunday school. If you were disrespectful to an adult, God might send some she-bears after you and they'd tear you limb from limb like they did those children who mocked the prophet Elisha. That was pretty terrible, though not as bad as burning forever in hell. Episcopalians just didn't talk a lot about hell—at least not to their children. There were plenty of things in the Bible they could scare you with without bringing up those everlasting fires. Episcopalians take a relatively reasonable approach and their children are still just as well behaved as Baptist children. After all, if you're only eight years old the prospect of going to hell really isn't going to do much more to stop you from sassing your teacher than the fear of a big black female bear jumping down from a magnolia tree and ripping you to shreds. But that wasn't good enough—or bad enough—for Mandy; she wanted you to burn in hell for all eternity.

When I told Mandy what Grandmomma had said, she admitted that God didn't actually send little children or anyone else to hell for breaking commandments or not loving your neighbor or drinking liquor or doing any other bad things: He sent people to hell for not being saved. But if you were saved you wouldn't do any of those things; if you did any of those things that was a sure sign that you weren't saved and were headed straight to hell. What's more, Mandy said—and Jenny solemnly confirmed it—you could be good and not misbehave, be honest and polite and charitable all you life, and still go to hell—because you weren't saved. You could only be saved by having a personal experience with Jesus, by taking Him into your heart. He was either in your heart or He wasn't; you were either saved or you weren't; you were either highballing it on the high road to heaven or hurtling to hell in a handcar. Baptists use a lot of alliteration when they talk about salvation.

Mandy was sure she was saved and Jenny was pretty sure *she* was, but I wasn't sure at all about me. I wasn't even sure it was necessary: I could see why you had to behave, but I couldn't see why you had to be saved. Mandy said it was because Eve ate that apple in the Garden of Eden. God told her not to eat any of those apples but she did anyway. She didn't eat a whole bushel of apples, just one—and gave one to her husband Adam to eat—but God got so mad He threw her and Adam out of the Garden of Eden and all of their children and grandchildren and great-grandchildren forevermore had to go through all this crap of getting themselves saved if they didn't want to roast in hell for all eternity. It didn't make much sense to me, but Mandy said that's the way it is because it's in the Bible.

Mandy and Jenny believed that everything in the Bible was true. I did too, until around the fifth or sixth grade when we began studying a lot of science. How can you believe the world was created in six days, I asked Mandy, when all the scientists say it took millions of years? Mandy said that maybe back then a day was a million years long, and Jenny endorsed that view. But I knew those verses about the creation; I'd memorized them for Episcopal Sunday school: "God divided the light from the darkness ... and the evening and the morning were the first day... and the evening and the morning were the second day..." If they thought it took a million years for the sun to rise and set, I told them, they were crazy. No scientist believed that.

Well then, Mandy said, the scientists were wrong—because God could make days a million years long if He wanted to; He could make a day go on forever; He could make the sun stand still; He could do anything; He was all powerful... But I knew something God couldn't do and I told her: He couldn't make a rock so big he couldn't lift it. Mandy didn't have any response to that except "Aw phooey!" That was when I realized she really wasn't so smart, and she realized I realized it.

The next day at recess I sauntered over to where she and Jenny and some other girls were playing hop-scotch. I'd just been to the boys' room and I'd forgotten to button my fly; three buttons were exposed on the front of my knickers. "Three o'clock in St. Petersburg!" Mandy pointed and screamed, "Yah! Yah! Yah!" Usually girls didn't do that; they'd giggle and wait for a boy to say it. But Mandy just had to get back at me.

Jenny Lynch, as I said, was never as obnoxious as Mandy and she remained true to Baptist teachings after Mandy started backsliding in junior high. By that time Jenny had moved out to St. Andrews and came in to Wardlaw on the schoolbus. She was in a section with a lot of other St. Andrews students and not in the homeroom with Mandy and me. Mandy started running around with honor society girls like Kerry Higgins and Jane Slade and didn't pay much attention to Jenny anymore. But I'd still see Jenny occasionally around the school and sometimes we'd talk about religion.

Like a good Baptist, Jenny thought it was a sin to drink alcoholic beverages. I took the Episcopal viewpoint. Jesus drank wine, I reminded her; in fact He *made* wine, for his first miracle... That was really grapejuice, Jenny said; in the Bible they had the same word for wine and grapejuice. The stuff Jesus made and drank was grapejuice... No they didn't have grapejuice back then, I said, except right after the harvest, because it wouldn't keep. It'd turn to wine, just like apple juice'll turn to hard cider if you don't pasteurize it; and they didn't know how to pasteurize stuff back then... But the stuff that Jesus made for the wedding, Jenny insisted, was grapejuice, because it was fresh—He'd just made it. But what about all the other wine Jesus drank, I said, like at the last supper? And all the wine other people in the Bible drank and got drunk on—like Lot? Did Lot get drunk on grapejuice?... No, Jenny said, that was wine. Sometimes when the Bible says wine it means wine and sometimes it means grapejuice. It depends on the context.

But I said the Bible's supposed to be God's word: you can't go changing it around—changing wine to grapejuice whenever you feel like it. If God had meant to say grapejuice He'd 've said grapejuice. What if people started changing other words around in the Bible? What if they said that Thou shalt not commit adultery really means Thou shalt not commit adulteration? That was what my Uncle Lewie said Baptists did to the corn whiskey they sold you... Jenny laughed because she knew some bootleggers who were big contributors to the Baptist church.

Jenny had a pretty good attitude for a sincere Baptist. I was willing to concede to her that Baptists had the right to interpret the Bible in their own way. I didn't mind Baptists preaching to their own people about the evils of drinking or anything else; what I did mind was for them to try to get the government to pass laws to keep other people from doing things that were perfectly o.k. according to *their* interpretation of the Bible. Jenny could see my point; she wasn't one of those people who'd try to push their religion on you every chance they got.

There were plenty of those people in Columbia. The YMCA on Sumter street was infested with them. I used to go there after school in the winter to swim and box and play basketball. It wasn't the coaches; it was these student preachers from Columbia Bible College who tried to pound Jesus into you. They were in charge of the devotionals that everybody had to go to before the start of the basketball period. These cats carried big Bibles with all kinds of markers sticking out of them and usually wore dark blue preacher's suits and pointy-toed black shoes. They'd march back and forth in front of us young boys sitting on the floor in

the devotional room at the Y swinging that big Bible in one hand
and pointing up to God in heaven with the other and talking
about how white it was of Him to send Jesus down to earth to
save us. John 3:16—that was their favorite Bible verse; they knew
it by heart but they always flipped open their Bible and pretended to be reading when they recited it to us. God was making
us this wonderful offer: all we had to do was get down on our
knees and accept Jesus as our personal savior and we'd be born
again and have everlasting life. If anybody was interested in being
born again, the student-preacher would be available in the
devotional room after basketball and the free-swim period to help
them or give them more information.

If they'd just left it at that, it would've been o.k. I mean the
YMCA program was pretty cheap and having to spend 15
minutes in the devotional room listening to these Bible-school
cats was an acceptable added cost. But they wouldn't leave it at
that. They'd pester you on the sidewalk outside the Y or at your
locker or even in the swimming pool—trying to strike up a conversation that would wind up with them asking you if you were
saved. It didn't do any good to say you were; that wouldn't get
rid of them: they'd ask you a lot of questions to raise doubts, to
make you think maybe you really weren't saved and that you'd
better get born again one more time just to be safe. That'd give
the student-preacher credit for another conversion on the Bible
College scoreboard.

Those cats were relentless in their pursuit of converts. Like I
said, they'd even chase you into the swimming pool, buck naked
like the rest of us. Nobody was allowed to wear bathing suits in
the Y pool, which was indoors and heated and reeked of chlorine
and ammonia. The water was clear as a crystal and the pool had
nice long racing lanes, but if the weather was right I'd much
rather swim at the green hole or even Crane creek. Those places
smelled better and out there you didn't have to put up with
Baptist preaching.

There weren't many places around Columbia where you'd be
safe from preachers after the Billy Graham crusade attacked early

this year. They even invaded Wardlaw Junior High School. Billy Graham was this famous evangelist who'd been written up in *Life* magazine. He and his crew held revival meetings at the Township Auditorium on week nights and during the days they went around visiting schools and work places to drum up attendance for the revivals. We had them for an assembly program at Wardlaw. Everybody had to go—Episcopalians, Catholics, Greek Orthodox, Jews—nobody was spared. I sat between Mandy and the boy we called Preacher, whose old man was the pastor at Epiphany Lutheran church; Stringbean sat on the other side of Mandy.

"Well," I said to Preacher as we waited for the program to begin, "I guess all you preachers are happy to have so many people corralled for these devotional services."

"Hunh unh," Preacher said, "not us Lutherans. We don't believe in all this emotionalism. We didn't have anything to do with it."

"Well then," I turned to Mandy, "it must be a great day for the Baptists."

"Not necessarily," she snipped. "Billy Graham's not a Baptist; he's a Presbyterian. I don't pay any attention to him." She tossed her blond head toward Stringbean who clapped his hands in approval.

I couldn't believe Billy Graham was a Presbyterian. I'd always thought of Presbyterians as civilized—almost as civilized as Episcopalians. Snake was a Presbyterian; he went to their Sunday school regularly. I couldn't imagine Snake or any member of his family at a revival meeting. Billy Graham wasn't like any Presbyterian I'd ever known, so I decided I'd keep on thinking of him as a Baptist. (And he really was, I found out later; although he started out as a Presbyterian, they wouldn't give him a job preaching so he switched to the Baptists and they were the ones who ordained him.) But the Presbyterian churches in Columbia did join with the Baptists and the Methodists and the holy rollers to sponsor the Billy Graham crusade. I was glad the Episcopalians stayed out of it.

Billy Graham wasn't much older than those Columbia Bible College students who hung around the YMCA, but compared with them he was a real dude. When he came out on the stage at Wardlaw he was wearing a light brown double-breasted suit with pants that were moderately draped, almost pegged. His hair was tousled in front and combed back on the sides—not quite into a ducktail, but close to it. He wore a gardenia in a buttonhole and had on a flashy black-white-and-red checkered tie. He went on about how some big businessman out in Los Angeles gave him that tie—because he was so grateful to old Billy for converting him to Christ. But it was that brown suit that struck me. It reminded me of the time I went to the Governor's Mansion with Momma and Grandmomma for Strom Thurmond's inauguration reception and there was some fellow in a brown suit talking to Strom over by the punchbowl; Momma asked Grandmomma Who is that gentleman in the brown suit? and Grandmomma said You must be mistaken: gentlemen don't wear brown suits... I don't think Grandmomma would've cared much for Billy Graham.

Billy talked about what a sorry state the world was in: how the English had voted for socialism and turned away from God; how the Russians were getting ready to blow us all up with their atom bombs; how the Communist fifth column in the United States was undermining our morals. He said one of the main goals of Communism was to destroy our homes; it was anti-God and anti-everything that America stood for. The Communists wanted us to worship science, he said, and that was what we were doing and it was bringing us to the brink of destruction. The Communists and the scientists have lured us away from God, he said, so we now find ourselves living in a sex-crazed age: the emphasis these days is on the beastly and the lower nature of man. Our magazine shelves, he said, are filled with such dirt that they must be a stench in the nostrils of God. Reverend Billy urged us young people to ignore all that and keep our minds and bodies clean; if we did, God would honor us in special and glorious ways.

Billy Graham didn't rant and rave like a lot of evangelists; actually, he was pretty calm. He was a good speaker, I'll hand him that. And he really didn't try to convert anybody right there in the Wardlaw auditorium. What he did was invite all of us to come to the regular nighttime revival meetings at the Township Auditorium and to a special session for high-school students that was going to be held there on Saturday afternoon. I didn't go to any of those revivals at the Township Auditorium but from what I heard and read in the newspaper they were really well organized.

The Billy Graham crusade went on for three weeks in February and March and drew a full house every night. They rigged up some speakers in the basement of the Township Auditorium so they could take in the overflow. Behind the stage they set aside a couple of rooms for people to go for prayer and counseling if they wanted to make a decision for Christ. A section in the balcony was reserved for colored people, just like when they have professional wrestling matches there. There'd be a big choir on the stage with Billy, and also a bunch of dignitaries: Governor Strom Thurmond was there on several occasions, and so was Senator Olin D. Johnston when he could tear himself away from important business in Washington. This was a few weeks before Strom formally announced that he was going to run against Olin D. for the senate, but everybody knew he was going to. The two of them were falling all over themselves to get the Baptist vote. Both of them jumped up when Billy asked for people to come forward and be saved and they went to the backroom and met with counselors and came out and gave separate statements to the press calling on everybody to accept Jesus; later Strom proclaimed an official day of religious revival in the state and Olin D. introduced some kind of bill in congress.

Now Strom and Olin D. didn't exactly claim that they'd been saved at the Township Auditorium. After all, they were both hard-shelled Baptists who supposedly had been born again before they even got into politics; they weren't about to admit that they'd been backsliding all this time they'd been in office—they weren't going to admit it right before an election anyway. They didn't need to be saved; they just got a little booster shot for their faith in that backroom. But some other celebrities got the full treatment: they were completely reborn in the backrooms at the Columbia Township Auditorium and came out with their lives totally rededicated to Christ. One of them was Kirby Higbe, the star pitcher for the New York Giants. Another was Jack Sox, who owns Sox's drive-in.

The grand finale for the Billy Graham crusade was out at Carolina stadium and they packed the place with more than 40,000 people. Some seats under the scoreboard in the north endzone were set aside for niggers. They had the prayer and counseling sessions in the locker rooms. Olin D. couldn't make it for the big outdoor revival but Strom was there on the podium and so was Jimmy Byrnes—despite the fact that he was an Episcopalian and used to be a Catholic. He was going to run for governor and he had to court the Baptist vote like everybody else. At least he didn't stand up in front of everybody and make a decision for Christ.

Jenny Lynch didn't either. She went to the revival at the stadium and also to the special one for high-school students at the Township Auditorium. That one was real emotional, Jenny said, but she didn't accept the invitation to come forward and be saved because she'd had her personal experience with Jesus at the time she was baptized when she was twelve and didn't need to be born again again. Still she said that she felt the urge to get up and go stand in front of the pulpit, but she didn't. According to her, Billy Graham started off talking about morals like he did at Wardlaw, and gradually worked up to the really important question: Where will you spend eternity? It didn't matter if you were a Baptist or a Methodist or a Presbyterian or a member of no church, he said; if you were washed with the blood of the lamb you'd be saved, but if you didn't have Jesus Christ you were going to spend eternity in a lake of fire that burns forever. Then he issued the invitation for people to come forward and accept Jesus. Everybody who remained seated was supposed to bow their heads and close their eyes, but Jenny said she couldn't help sneaking a look at the ones who were going forward to accept the invitation. Many of them, boys as well as girls, had tears streaming down their cheeks. The choir was singing softly accompanying the baritone soloist, George Beverly Shea, in a rendition of "Almost Persuaded." Jenny said she got goose bumps all over her body.

The music went on and on as nearly 800 teenagers—about a quarter of the audience—left their seats and crowded around the stage. Even a few niggers came down from the colored balcony and stood there with the white boys and girls. It took a long time to process all of them through the prayer rooms behind the stage. The ones who were serious about making a decision for Christ —and almost all of them were—signed pledge cards which were turned over to the church of their choice, which was supposed to give them follow-up attention. Jenny said she knew that her church, St. Andrews Baptist, got at least three pledge cards from that revival meeting.

I liked talking with Jenny about religion at school, but I never thought about going out with her until a couple of weeks ago when I ran into her at Belk's department store and we got to talking and she said her Training Union—that's the Baptist Sunday school—was going to have a hayride and wiener roast and asked me if I'd like to go as her guest. I said o.k. as long as you all don't try to convert me, and she said that nobody would and that the only prayer I'd hear would be the blessing right before we ate the wieners. And that was true.

We left the St. Andrews Baptist church about sundown on a bed of hay—actually it was oat straw—on a big flat-body International truck and headed for Lake Murray at about 30 miles an hour. There were a couple dozen of us teenagers and three chaperons, including the driver, who all rode in the cab. Most of the boys and girls in the back were paired off in the hay, like Jenny and me. The excursion took us across the Lake Murray dam—the largest earthen dam in the world—to the park on the other side where we stopped and built a fire and roasted and ate wieners and marshmallows and drank Pepsis. But the main attraction of the evening, of course, was the hayride up there and back.

The night was warm but the steady stream of air across the back of the moving truck cooled things off considerably and caused some people to huddle up against the back of the cab and others to bury themselves deep in the hay and snuggle up to the person they were with. That's what Jenny and I did. The sunny fragrance of the oat straw was nice and it wasn't long before I got up the nerve to kiss her. We did a little light tasting and nibbling but no heavy petting or deep probing. When I tried to French kiss her she didn't pull away like some girls would've done but blocked my tongue with her teeth. When I tried it again on the return trip she did the same thing, so I gave up on that and we stuck to the approved smooching for the rest of the hayride.

The bunch up against the cab began singing songs on the ride back to the church and sometimes Jenny would join in. I enjoyed putting my face against her throat and feeling the vibrations. They sang popular songs like "Now Is the Hour" and "Forever and Ever" and hymns like "Shall We Gather at the River" and "Bringing in the Sheaves." I had to admit the Baptists were right about one thing: you didn't have to smoke and drink to have a good time; lying in the hay and singing hymns and necking with a pretty Baptist girl was an acceptable substitute.

I'd have had more fun that night if I hadn't been so preoccupied with going to Jacksonville the next week. I told Jenny I'd call her after I got back and maybe we could go to a movie or something. So I called her on Thursday morning of this week—the day before yesterday—to ask her to go with me to that nigger dance at the Township Auditorium. But she wasn't home. Her mother said she'd gone to spend the day with this other girl whose mother was going to take them out to Sesqui —Sesquicentennial State Park. So I told Jenny's momma Thank you, I'll call her back later.

After I hung up I got to thinking that maybe Browder and I ought to hitch-hike out to Sesqui and see if we could find those girls out there. He might like the girl Jenny was with and maybe we could get up a double date for Friday night. But first I had to go downtown to the Carolina Camera Shop and get those pictures of Dr. Summerville and his ladyfriend and drop off Uncle Lewie's copy at the surplus store.

13

SESQUICENTENNIAL State Park—Sesqui for short—is where there's this sandy-bottomed lake northeast of Columbia off U.S. Number One. That highway almost exactly follows the fall line in South Carolina—I mean it runs parallel to the coast and crosses the rivers at the points where the red clay of the piedmont changes to the sandy soil of the lowcountry. Lake Murray's upcountry from Columbia and Sesqui's downcountry. They have real good facilities at Sesqui: a big swimming area, a high dive, bathhouses, and a pavilion.

Browder liked the idea of hitch-hiking out to Sesqui. We couldn't leave right away though, I said when I called him Thursday morning—not until I got back from downtown with that picture of Doc Summerville and Blondie. I didn't want to take it out to Sesqui and risk losing it or getting it messed up; you never can tell what might happen when you're hitch-hiking. I couldn't wait and pick it up after we got back from Sesqui because it'd be too late, the stores would be closed. And I needed it that night: I wanted to bring it to the Scout meeting and show it to Snake.

So I took the bus in front of the Governor's Mansion and got off on Main street and went directly to the Carolina Camera Shop. When the fellow showed me the photos I was amazed how good the copy was; you couldn't tell it from the original. He put the two pictures together in a brown photo envelope with a string fastener on it and cardboard stiffeners inside. I paid him $3.50 and he handed me the envelope and I headed for Uncle Lewie's surplus store.

As I was crossing Lady street at Assembly I saw somebody familiar leaving the surplus store and coming in my direction. It was Gordon the mulatto.

"Howdy Gordon," I said as we met on the sidewalk.

"'Lo Clarence," Gordon responded. He was carrying a paper bag and seemed to be in as big a hurry as I was, so we didn't stop to talk. I was kind of surprised he remembered my name, because he probably hadn't seen me more than two or three times in his life, and it was funny that he'd call me Clarence, which is what mostly only teachers and kinfolks call me.

Uncle Lewie was standing in the door to the surplus store. "Hey Uncle Lewie," I greeted him and explained: "That was Gordon the brass ankle that works for Dr. MacNab the veterinarian."

"Yeah I know, Clarence. He trades with me. I sold him a McClellan saddle the other day but the bellyband was too big for that little old horse he's got. So we exchanged the bellyband for a shorter one." Uncle Lewie flipped his cigarette butt out into Assembly street. "So it looks like you got some pictures there..."

"Yes sir. The copy came out real good. Why don't you take it and I'll keep the original. You can't hardly tell 'em apart."

"'At's a fact," he said as he looked them over. He put the original back into the Carolina Camera Shop envelope and handed it to me. He drew his index finger across the other photo—across Dr. Summerville's ladyfriend's tits—and said, "I tell you something, Clarence: I'm gonna find us this luscious thing if she's still in Columbia. If she ain't, at least I'll find out who she is. I'll know before the weekend's over. I guarantee you."

• • •

Browder and I took the bus out to Two Notch road and began hitch-hiking a little before one o'clock on Thursday afternoon. We were carrying our bathing suits rolled up in towels so just about anybody who came along would know we were headed for Sesqui. We hadn't been standing there five minutes before this old pre-war Dodge pulled up and this boy who was riding shotgun stuck his head out the window and said, "Y'all going to Sesqui? Get in."

The boy's name was Elton Brayboy. Browder and I knew him but not the boy who was driving. Nobody else was in the car. We got into the back seat.

Elton Brayboy was about 17 or 18 years old and didn't go to school. He worked out at the fairgrounds as an exercise boy at the racehorse stables. He'd ridden Assault, the Triple-Crown winner. Brayboy was pretty small but he was still a little too big to be a jockey. He had a humpback and a long face like a horse's. He said he and his buddy were going over to Camden to see about getting a job in the stables there until the Max Hirsch horses came back to Columbia from up North for the winter.

As usual when three or four boys get together, the topic of conversation eventually turned to pussy. "Pussy is good," Brayboy said, "but ten-year-old boys are better. There ain't no piece of ass better'n one of them ten-year-old boys."

I didn't argue with him but I couldn't see how anybody would think that. There's just no accounting for some people's tastes, as Grandmomma used to say. Anyway, we didn't have time to pursue that subject because we were almost at Sesqui when it came up. Brayboy's buddy pulled the car over and they let us out at the main entrance to the park. Then we had to hoof it almost half a mile down the park road through the scrubby sand hills between the highway and the lake.

The swimming area was pretty crowded. After we'd changed into our bathing suits Browder and I moved through the people towards the water keeping an eye out for Jenny Lynch. We didn't see her, but I spotted Jane Slade stretched out on a beach towel on the grass; she was with some girls I didn't know. We went over to say hello to Jane and I stayed to talk with her while Browder plunged into the water and swam out to the high dive. Jane looked as good as ever—if not better. She'd matured a whole lot in the last year; she wasn't near as silly as she used to be. Of course, I'd always liked her—to one degree or another —and it occurred to me out there on the grass at Sesqui that one of these days I ought to ask her for a date. The trouble was, her mother probably still thought I was wild and wouldn't let her go out with me. I was always scared when the time came to ask a girl for a date and usually I could find some excuse not to.

We talked about old times at Wardlaw, Jane and I, and about Kerry Higgins moving away. Everybody was going to miss Kerry. I didn't say it to Jane because I didn't want her to think I was disrespectful to my elders, but I thought Kerry's old man was a real bastard to take his family away from Columbia. There was no call for him doing that just because the TB sanitorium where he worked was shutting down; he was a doctor and there were plenty of other jobs and opportunities for doctors in Columbia. I couldn't get over how some people just didn't seem to mind in the least ripping their children away from all their friends and everything they held dear. When I get married and have children, I said to myself, I sure as hell wasn't going to do that. I thought about telling Jane that I might be moving away too, but didn't. Instead I told her See you at C.H.S. and went off looking for Jenny Lynch.

I looked all over but couldn't find her. I waded through the shallow water and swam out to where Browder was doing half-gainers off the high dive, but didn't see hide nor hair of Jenny Lynch. She wasn't in the pavilion either: I walked through there twice. I figured she and her friend must've left early in the afternoon, maybe before we even got there. It was after four now and getting to be time for Browder and me to leave. We didn't have to hitch-hike back though, because we ran into Radar and Jimmy McCrew out there at Sesqui and got a ride home in Radar's Buick. I was back in time to drive Agnes home at 5:15.

• • •

I pulled into the parking lot next to the Sunday school building at Covenant Presbyterian church a few minutes before Scout meeting was supposed to begin. Just as I was starting to get out of the Plymouth these headlights suddenly flashed up behind and this '47 Mercury slithered in next to me so close—about two inches—that I couldn't open the door on the driver's side. Snake extracted his gangly frame from the Mercury and raised his hand in the Roman salute: "Hail Cappus Maximus." He'd started calling me that—Cappus, or Cappus Maximus—last year when I began taking Latin. By then Snake already had a year of it at Dreher and was pretty good at it. He didn't teach me much, though—much Latin, that is.

One thing he did teach me was to drink beer. That was right after we got back from Camp Kanuga when I was twelve and he was 13. His voice had already changed by then and he could talk just like a grown-up. I was spending the night at his house and we were fooling around downstairs after his parents and sisters had gone up to bed, and Snake said he was going to call Community Drugstore at Five Points and order some beer for us to drink. And that's what he did, only he couldn't let it go at that: just call up and ask them to send so many bottles of such-and-such beer to such-and-such address. Not Snake—he had to elaborate on everything, go through all this rigmarole. I thought I'd go berserk listening to Snake talk on the phone to the man at Community Drugstore.

"Well how you do? It sho is a nice night, idinit? Real warm. You know, I was just talking to my friend here who lives up in north Columbia in the Elmwood area and I said it sho is warm and wouldn't it be nice to have some nice cold beer, and he said it sho would and I said I'm just gonna call up Community Drugstore and ask them if they'd be so kind as to deliver some cold beer to us. Now I suppose y'all have Budweiser... Well that's good. Now is that in bottles or cans?... That's good because I always like to drink Budweiser from a bottle because you get a tinny taste from a can that sort of counteracts the beechwood aging. Now my friend here likes Schlitz and it dudn't much matter whether it's in a can or a bottle. Fact is, I think Schlitz is better in a can; it brings out the flavor of the hops. So why don't you send us two cold cans of Schlitz and two cold bottles of Budweiser. Send it up to the McBane residence on Monroe street—2419 Monroe... No, don't charge it; I'll just pay cash tonight. I always like to do that whenever it's convenient, and give the delivery boy a little tip. I'll be looking out for him; the porch light'll be on. I'm much obliged... You're welcome, and goodnight to you too, cap'n. Goodbye."

Boy, that was some performance; it inspired me to sign up for the Junior Theater when I started to Wardlaw that fall. Snake met that delivery boy on the front porch before he could ring the doorbell and paid for the beer and gave him a big tip. We laughed and cut up and drank that beer in the den while the rest of the family was upstairs asleep and then I got so woozy that I almost passed out and Snake practically had to carry me up to his room and throw me onto one of the twin beds. The next day I was still pretty shaky but Snake was fine and we went out riding bicycles.

We did that a lot—rode bicycles around town—until the next year when Snake got his driver's license and we began cruising around on weekends in his old man's Mercury. When we rode bikes we often went out to Owens Field and watched the airplanes take off and land. Also, we liked to go to this store out there near the airfield where they sold fireworks—including torpedoes and cherry bombs. One of those cherry bombs would blow a mailbox to smithereens. Actually, I never did that—blow up a mailbox—because it's a federal offense, but I did ride around with Snake throwing torpedoes at people, first from bicycles then from cars.

Snake and these other boys who went to Hand Junior High—and later to Dreher—liked to run this obstacle course at Bowers Beach. Bowers Beach is a stretch of open pine woods that runs down to Lake Katherine; there isn't any underbrush to speak of and the trees are usually far enough apart for a car to go between them. The boys would drive into these woods from Kilbourne road and race down to the water and back. Snake always won. He didn't win because he was more reckless than anybody else or just because he faked people out; he won because he could judge distances better than anybody else and always knew where he was and knew the best way to get to the next place he was going before he got to the first place. That boy has a phenomenal ability to calculate distances. He won every time he raced at Bowers Beach and never put a scratch on his old man's Mercury.

Snake's ability to judge distances and position himself also made him a natural pool player. He taught me the games but he never could teach me to be as good as he was at shooting pool. I don't have his judgment or his manual dexterity either. Anyway, Snake taught me the basics one Saturday afternoon in Nick the Greek's pool hall at Five Points. That was last winter, a couple months before we went to this state Latin conference at Rock Hill.

That Latin conference was held in the Winthrop College auditorium in Rock Hill. All the schools in South Carolina that taught Latin sent delegations; they put on skits and made speeches in Latin and had contests. Most people signed up for one event or another, or two or three—but not Snake and me: we just went along for the ride and to get out of school that day. All the Latin students from the various schools in Columbia who were going met at Columbia High early in the morning and rode up to Rock Hill together on the same schoolbus. When we got there we all filed into the auditorium for the welcoming ceremonies. Then they had a break for people to go to the restroom and get their acts lined up; that's when Snake and I sneaked out. We were supposed to stay there in the audience but instead we spent the day in a pool hall.

Rock Hill is this grubby little overgrown town in the piedmont where practically everybody works in a textile mill. Winthrop Training College for Women is right in the middle of town and Snake and I found this pool hall only a couple blocks down the street from the college auditorium. It was definitely a hangout for lintheads but there was only one game going on and a couple of cats watching when we walked in. We got a table and starting playing eight-ball and I'll have to admit that I was shooting pretty good for somebody who'd only been playing for a couple of months. Snake started off good—made a hell of a break—but then his game steadily went to pot. I would've beat him that first game in Rock Hill if I hadn't scratched on the eight-ball. I *did* beat him the second game, the first time I'd ever done that. Though I was happy to be shooting so well myself, I was puzzled about Snake doing so poorly. He was missing shots that I'd never seen him miss before. He seemed to do the worst when people were watching him—like when the fellow at the next table had to stand aside and wait for Snake to finish a shot so he wouldn't bump into him. It was like Snake was self-conscious that people were watching him, although I'd never known him to be self-conscious before. I figured it must be because of us being in a strange place in a strange town.

Right after we'd finished our third game—which Snake won, but not too impressively—this cat who had been playing at the next table came over and asked if either one of us wanted to play nine-ball for a quarter. I said right off that I didn't but Snake hesitated.

"Well I don't know..." he drawled as he tapped out a Chesterfield. He took a few seconds to light it and take a drag. "Well maybe just one or two games." I thought Snake was crazy because he was shooting so bad that day and we didn't have much money to lose. But Snake did a lot better playing that linthead than he did playing me. At first I figured it was the stiffer competition that stimulated him to do better.

Snake lost the first game to that Rock Hillbilly but won the next three in a row. He dropped the fourth one and then got onto another winning streak. When he was a dollar ahead I went up front to the grill and bought us a couple grilled-cheese sandwiches and Pepsis.

When the fellow who was playing Snake had to leave, this other local cat who had been watching came over and challenged Snake. Again Snake hesitated and said we really ought to be going

... but wound up playing him. This cat was better than the first one, but Snake still beat him—took $1.50 off him. Of course it didn't take me too long to figure out that Snake was hustling those hicks, and I did have a few worrisome moments when I was afraid they were going to catch on and gang up on us and beat our asses to a pulp. Those lintheads can be as mean as they are stupid. But Snake always seemed to know what to do to keep everything on an even keel—when to miss a shot, when to lose a game.

After the second linthead quit nobody else wanted to play Snake. So we went and sat down at the lunch counter and ate pickled pigs feet and drank beer until it was time to go back to the Latin conference. We returned to the Winthrop auditorium in time to catch the last act and take the schoolbus back to Columbia. Nobody had missed us.

It's a wonder that Snake and I didn't get caught and kicked out of school for that Latin-conference caper. But the strange thing is, I never got into trouble doing anything with Snake. What's really ironic is that only one week later I did get expelled from school for misbehaving on another excursion: a biology-class field trip to the state forestry experiment station on Broad River road. What happened was that Browder and I and a couple other boys just dropped back from the group as we were walking down this path and lit up teeges. Of course we weren't supposed to do that and when our teacher looked back and saw us she got all excited and said she was going to report us to the principal. She was pretty young and didn't know how to handle people. When we got back to Wardlaw she took us to the principal and he said we were all expelled and couldn't come back until we brought our parents with us and got ourselves reinstated.

Momma was pretty upset when I told her about it that night, but she brought me back to Wardlaw the next morning. The principal kind of apologized to her for expelling me, since I used to be an honor student and all that; he said I'd gotten into some bad company and he couldn't kick them out without expelling me too. He and Momma and I all agreed that I should stay out of bad company. For a little while after that Momma thought about getting me transferred to Dreher so I could go to school with people like Snake. But even without me saying anything she soon realized that that might not be such a good idea.

One thing about Snake is he's unpredictable. I was totally unprepared for what he had to say to me before the Scout meeting on Thursday night—the night before last. I was eager to show him the Summerville photo but he came directly over to the Plymouth as I was getting out on the passenger side and asked me right off: "Whatcha gonna do tomorrow night, Cappus?"

"Think I'm gonna go to that nigger dance at the Township Auditorium."

"Naw man, you don't wanna go to any jigaboo dance. Whatcha oughta do is come with me. Some of us are going over to this girl's house and play bridge. We need another hand."

"Snake you crazy as hell. Anyway I don't even know how to play bridge."

"You can learn, Cappus. We'll teach you tomorrow night. You gotta know how to play bridge to be a social success."

"Well I got plenty of time to learn..."

"So whatcha do tomorrow night is pay a buncha money and sit up in the balcony at the Township Auditorium and watch a buncha coons jumping and jiving..."

"I'm gonna take this girl..."

"Looka here, Cappus, you gotta stop running around with those sluts up in north Columbia. You may be getting a lot of nookie, but you gotta start thinking about who you gonna marry; you gotta start dating girls with background."

One reason Snake thought the girls on this side of town were sluts was because I'd lied to him so much about all the pussy I was getting. In fact he'd been pestering me about getting him a date with a Wardlaw girl because he thought any of them would be a sure piece of ass. I had to keep making excuses and putting him off. Now that I could line up Sandburg for him and his Dreher crew, he wanted me to do just the opposite.

"Snake, the girl I'm gonna take out tomorrow night is respectable."

"Naw Cappus. No respectable girl'd go to a jigaboo dance. You gotta come away from that stuff man. You gotta think about your future—think about going to college. You can't take those Elmwood floozies to a college fraternity party..."

"Snake, I'm not studying college now. I got three more years of high school and you got two."

"That's where you're wrong, Cappus. Next year at this time I'll be a freshman at Carolina. And you could be the year after that. You don't hafta go to high school for the twelfth grade. When they added on the twelfth grade last year they passed a law that said you could still go to any state college—to Carolina or The Citadel or Clemson—after you finished the eleventh grade. You just hafta pass the entrance examination. I'm gonna get in The Ozman's fraternity, Kappa Alpha. I can get you in the year after next."

That's what Snake called his old man: The Ozman. "Well I didn't know about that law," I said and then thought of something. "Tell me something, Snake: what if you just finished the eleventh grade in some other state—could you still get in Carolina?"

"Naw man. That law's just for citizens of South Carolina, for people who go to South Carolina high schools. If you come from outta state you gotta have a high-school diploma. Why the hell you ask that?"

I thought about telling him but decided that I wouldn't right then. Snake was too unpredictable. You never knew how he might react to something.

"'Cause I like to know things, Snake; that's all. Looka here, I got something I wanna show you. Take a look at this picture." I took the photo out of the envelope and held it under the overhead light in the Plymouth and Snake stuck his head in and studied it.

"That looks like it was taken out at Forest Lake Club," he said. "Those people relatives of yours?"

"Naw Snake. That picture was taken at the Mirador Club. I found it out there right after it burned down. I don't know who those people are—but I sho would like to know who that woman is."

"What fur?"

"Cat fur to make kitten britches. So I can ask her to go out jiving with me at jigaboo dances."

"She's too classy for that, Cappus. And what about this cat she's with? I bet he won't let her outta his sight. He's probably her daddy."

"Naw, he's not old enough to be her old man."

"I said her daddy, not her old man. Hey let's go ask Master Elrod if he knows her."

Mr. Elrod the Scoutmaster was already upstairs in the meeting room. We knew that because his DeSoto was in the parking lot when we got there. Several boys had come and gone through the door of the Sunday-school building while Snake and I were talking in the parking lot. It was almost time for the Scout meeting to begin.

Snake took charge of the photograph and led the way up the stairs to the Sunday-school classroom where the Scouts were meeting. They were all sitting around a big table and the air was pretty dense because Mr. Elrod and most of the boys were smoking cigarettes.

"Hey, whatcha got there Snake?" Roy Beverly asked.

"Cap wants to know if any of y'all know who this lady is," Snake said as he handed the picture to Roy. Roy examined it for a few seconds and said she looked like the girl he used to go steady with in the seventh grade but that he'd forgotten her name. He passed it to Sonny Dodd who made some wisecrack that made Mr. Elrod laugh but I couldn't hear it.

Then Scott Batey took a look at the photo and said, "Well I know this girl. She works in my father's office. She doesn't usually wear her hair that way, but I've seen her with her hair down before. No kidding. She works for the South Carolina Progressive League. Her name's Amy Kuhn."

Oh boy, I thought, if that's true I've hit the jackpot. And I believed it was, because you could tell Scott was serious. Scott's old man, the Reverend Scott Batey, was the biggest integrationist in South Carolina next to Judge Waring down in Charleston. If she worked for him she had to be one too, and probably a Communist to boot. And if Dr. Summerville was associating with her, then he must be one: an integrationist and a Communist. That was just as good as being a crook as far as I was concerned. Momma definitely wouldn't want to get mixed up in the Communist fifth column.

"Sounds like you been cutting that stuff," Snake said to Scott.

Scott smiled and took a deep drag off his Philip Morris. "All I said is I know her."

Scott was a regular good old boy despite the fact that his old man was an integrationist and a Baptist preacher. (Actually the Reverend Batey belonged to the Northern Baptist church which is a lot different from the Southern Baptists.) Scott smoked cigarettes and drank beer and shot pool and chased girls just like the rest of us. Nobody held it against him what his old man did. In fact he's pretty popular out at Dreher. He's big and well built and right good looking, with dark curly hair.

"Well if she doesn't mean all that much to you," I said to Scott, "how about giving me her phone number."

"I don't know what it is."

"Go on and give it to him, Scott," Mr. Elrod said, "so we can get on with our business."

"No really, I don't have it."

"Well I'll just look it up in the phone book," I said. "You say her name's Amy Koon?"

"Yeah. Amy Kuhn. Only she spells it K-u-h-n, like they do up North. But I don't think she's in the phone book; she hasn't been here that long. Look, you can call her at the office. She should be there in the morning. Number's 5-1624." He handed the picture to me and I wrote the phone number on the back.

Then we got into the main order of business which was planning a camping and fishing trip to the Santee-Cooper reservoir before school started. I can't remember much about it because I was all wrapped up in thinking about how I was going to approach Amy Kuhn the next morning.

14

I WAS PRETTY EXCITED but not the least bit nervous when I dialed the number that Scott Batey had given me the night before. It was only a couple of minutes after nine but Momma had left for work over an hour before because it was Friday and she had to drive down to Eastover for a well-baby clinic. I'd known she'd need the car that day so I hadn't asked her for it.

After three rings a female voice answered the phone: "Progressive League. May I help you?"

"Could I speak to Miss Amy Kuhn, please?"

"This is she."

It sure was: Yankee and businesslike, but not unfriendly. I imagined her sitting serenely at a big mahogany desk behind a vase of flowers like some bigshot's secretary in the movies.

"Uh, Miss Kuhn, I'm a friend of Dr. Gregory Summerville's. He gave me something to deliver to you..."

"Really? What is it?"

"Uh, it must be a photograph—some photographs. It's in a photo envelope. He gave it to me just before he left town."

"No kidding?" She was sizing me up. God how I wished I had an adult voice like Snake's.

"No ma'am—I mean I could bring it to you this morning if that's o.k. with you."

"Why sure. I'll be in the office until noon; come on by."

"Ah, I'm not exactly sure where your office is at..."

"It's at 1533 Harden street"—she was amused, I could tell —"across from Allen University, next to the Carver theater. We're on the first floor."

"O.k. I'll be over in a little while."

"Swell. Say, what's your name?"

"Uh, they call me Cap. Cap Palmerston."

"Greg Summerville's friend Cap Palmerston. Great. I'm looking forward to meeting you."

"Me too. See you. Goodbye."

"'Bye Cap."

That was easy I thought. She seemed to be in a real good mood. I'd never thought of nigger-loving Communists being in a good mood—not with all the agitating they did. *I* certainly was in a good mood; now I could prove to Momma that Dr. Summerville ran around with dangerous integrationists. That'd be enough to give her second thoughts about going up to New Jersey to work with him. But I needed more evidence to clinch the case—evidence that Dr. Summerville might be up to even worse things—and I aimed to get that evidence by questioning Miss Amy Kuhn at the headquarters of the South Carolina Progressive League.

The Progressive League office was around the corner from the Waverly drugstore where Theron Velakis worked. I decided to ride my bike over there and leave it in the rack in front of the drugstore, then go on into niggertown on foot. The drugstore was on the edge of the colored district, on the corner of Hampton and Harden streets, and faced Columbia Hospital across Hampton street. It was a great location for selling medicine, not to mention magazines and other reading material. Across Harden street from the Waverly drugstore was Allen University, the biggest nigger college in Columbia, and behind the drugstore was a colored movie theater. To make the best of the location they served both races at the Waverly drugstore; even the soda fountain was integrated. There were a couple of nigger customers in the drugstore when I parked my bike and walked inside. One was standing in the back waiting for a prescription and the other was browsing at the magazine rack and sipping a fountain Coke. The Coke was in a Dixie cup; if the fellow had been white Theron would've given it to him in a Coke glass. Theron was sitting on a stool behind the cash register reading a Plastic Man comic. He looked up as I strolled through the open front door under the overhead fan that was supposed to keep the flies out.

"Well if it ain't old Cap Palmerston. What brings you here, old buddy? Your momma got business over at the hospital?"

"Naw man. I gotta deliver something to an office back there on Harden street. Zit o.k. if I leave my bike here?"

"Why shore. I'll keep an eye on it."

The colored fellow who'd been standing at the magazine rack came over to the counter with a copy of the *Chicago Defender.* Theron took his dime and two pennies and said Thank you. Theron got along real well with niggers—and white folks, too. Right after he rang up that nigger's twelve cents a pair of middle-aged white nurses came in and Theron hopped down off his stool to serve them. They ordered cherry Cokes and I watched Theron fix them; he pumped generous squirts of Coke syrup and cherry syrup into real Coke glasses. The nurses had to drink their Cokes standing up, though, because there weren't any stools at the soda fountain or any kind of seats for customers in the Waverly drugstore. That way there wasn't any danger of a nigger sitting down next to a white person. What they had at the Waverly drugstore was stand-up integration, which people didn't seem to mind too much. But there was no question that the Waverly drugstore catered to niggers. They carried all sorts of nigger newspapers and magazines, like *Ebony* and the *Afro-American* and the *Lighthouse and Informer*—which was printed right here in Columbia. I often wondered how they got away with publishing the *Lighthouse and Informer* in Columbia; it was filled with the most rabid integrationist propaganda I'd ever seen. Of course, you wouldn't see the *Lighthouse and Informer* except in nigger areas; they didn't sell it in the newsstands uptown and schools and libraries didn't get it. The only place I'd ever seen it was at the Waverly drugstore. They never mentioned it in the white newspapers and nobody talked about it on the radio. Most people didn't even know it existed.

I left Theron chatting with the nurses and walked out the front door onto Hampton street and swung around the corner of the drugstore to Harden street. There the sidewalk turned to dirt, indicating that I was entering niggertown (the street was paved though, because it was a main thoroughfare). I passed under the marquee of the Carver theater, which was playing some movie I'd never heard of, scooted across an alley made muddy by the runoff from the theater's cooling system, and found myself at the doorstep of 1533 Harden street. It was a dirty three-story brick building with peeling and rotting woodwork trim. The front door was propped open and led into a dingy hall with a staircase in the back and a row of doors on the right side. As I stepped inside I could hear the sound of a radio coming from the first door on the right which was half open. I pushed it all the way open and nonchalantly walked in.

The room was big with a high ceiling of flaky plaster and walls that were covered with faded striped wallpaper. A big water stain ran down from the ceiling on the wall to the left, and straight ahead and to the right were two sets of curtainless windows laced with crinkled and disheveled venetian blinds. Sunlight streamed in from the east revealing zillions of dust particles floating in the air. The floor was covered with scuffed linoleum that looked like it'd never been polished. There were a bunch of pasteboard boxes scattered around on the floor, and a couple of olive-drab war-surplus file cabinets stood against the wall next to the door. A mimeograph machine sat on an enameled metal table in the corner between the windows and was hemmed in by boxes and overflowing waste-paper baskets. Centered on the wall to the left, next to the water stain, was a picture of Abraham Lincoln. There were several rickety-looking chairs of various types and two desks in the room. Both of the desks were made of light-colored wood and were pretty scarred and beat up and both faced the door. The one on the right had a fan and a big typewriter on it; Amy Kuhn was sitting at the one on the left. She was by herself in the room.

She'd smiled for the camera at the Mirador Club and I'd imagined her smiling when she talked to me on the phone, but she wasn't smiling now. She was the lady in the picture all right, but she looked different. Her blond hair was pulled back off her face into a tight bun, accentuating her high cheekbones. She seemed annoyed at the sight of me.

"Miss K-Kuhn..." I stammered.

She held up her hand signaling me to be quiet. She was listening to the local news coming from the Emerson radio on her desk.

"Larry Elmore, 43-year-old Negro from Laurens," the announcer said, "paid with his life this morning for the murder of a storekeeper in Laurens county. When he was strapped into the electric chair at the South Carolina state penitentiary, Elmore was asked if he had any last words. The condemned Negro mumbled a bit and rolled his eyes as he blamed his troubles on liquor and advised the nearly 30 witnesses against its use. Elmore was pronounced dead three minutes and 32 seconds after the switch was thrown. It is believed that Elmore is the first electric-chair victim convicted through the use of a lie detector. Sheriff C. W. Weir of Laurens county and his deputies used the detector on Elmore in the case..."

She snapped off the radio. "Mumbled and rolled his eyes! How insensitive can you get?" She glared at me as I stood before her desk holding the photo envelope with both hands in front of my crotch. I had to say something.

"I-I don't know..."

"Used a lie detector on him! That's psychological torture. Do they think this is the Middle Ages?"

"Uh, he was guilty though, wasn't he? I mean he confessed..."

"That's not the point. They might just as well have gotten the confession by stretching him on the rack or breaking him on the wheel. Torture is torture. You can't do that in this day and age.

The Constitution forbids it; it's unreasonable search and seizure, cruel and unusual punishment."

"But why didn't somebody object?" I had to call her on that; she was spouting Communist nonsense.

"Plenty of people objected," she said fiercely. "The problem was we simply didn't have the resources to make ourselves heard—not in this case. We had to throw everything we had into the fight to save those seven boys in Virginia."

"I read about them. They... attacked a white lady..."

"They were convicted and sentenced to death for *rape*." She spat the word out.

"Ah, have they been executed yet?"

"Don't you read the papers? Last week a federal judge stayed the executions and ordered a new trial."

"Oh yeah." I really hadn't known about it because I'd been in Jacksonville all last week at a Scout encampment and didn't get to see any newspapers or hear any news broadcasts down there. I didn't try to explain that to Miss Amy Kuhn who kept prancing around on her high horse.

"Do you realize that no white person has ever been sent to the electric chair for rape? Not a single one—anywhere in this country. But the state of Virginia was just hours away from snuffing out the lives of seven Negro boys before that federal judge granted our petition for a new trial." She pronounced Negro knee-grow. She talked fast with a thick Yankee accent but I could understand her o.k.

"Does the South Carolina Progressive League operate in Virginia?" I asked when she stopped to take a breath.

"Of course not. When I say 'we' I'm talking about the ACLU—the American Civil Liberties Union. That's the organization I belong to. The South Carolina Progressive League is an umbrella structure—a clearinghouse—set up to support and coordinate the efforts in this state of the various equal-rights organizations, like the ACLU and the NAACP and the Progressive Democratic Party. Reverend Batey is the director of the Progressive League. He's doing a tremendous job. He wanted us to try to save that poor man who was electrocuted this morning, but that case was hopeless. The ACLU has to employ its limited resources where it has a reasonable chance of success, where it can do the most good. Saving those boys in Virginia—the Martinsville Seven—took precedence over everything else. It's unfortunate—tragic—that we have to make these choices."

She sighed and sank back in her swivel chair. Then she blinked her eyes like she was waking up and realized for the first time that somebody was in the room with her.

"So you're Cap Palmerston?" Her thin soft eyebrows arched upward and she almost smiled.

"Yes ma'am."

"Don't say ma'am to me; I'm not your mother. I'm Amy. Pleased to meet you." She *was* smiling now; her icy blue eyes had warmed up considerably. "Pull up a chair and sit down."

I removed some papers from the seat of a ladder-back chair and put them on Amy's desk and sat down.

"Nice place you've got here," I said.

"It's a dump, but this is a low-budget operation. What have you got for me?"

I handed her the envelope.

"Well, well," she said as she ran her eyes over the picture, "here we have café society Carolina style." She laughed as she held the photo up for me to see.

"You... you look real pretty," I said.

"Thank you. When Greg came to town he said he wanted to taste the best of the local nightlife. I'd never been to this place, the Mirador Club, but my roommate—she's a nurse at Columbia Hospital—said that was where the doctors liked to go, so that was where we went. Then the damned place burned down a few hours after we left... Which makes me think: how did Greg—how did you—get this photo? I told Greg I didn't want one when the girl took it, and he didn't have it when we left the club..."

"Ah, well you see... Amy... it's a long story."

"Then suppose you start by telling me how you know Greg Summerville." She leaned forward and looked at me quizzi-

cally—not hostilely, just quizzically. That reassured me, because
I have a hard time handling female hostility. I began to feel
confident; I knew I was thinking clearly.

"I really don't know Dr. Summerville very well, but he's been
courting my mother and I'd like to know more about him."

"A-hah," she said, not really surprised, "your mother must be
the army buddy's widow he was going to visit."

"Right. My mother's Mrs. Gwyn Palmerston."

"Hmmm. I didn't know he was serious about anybody, but
why *should* I know? There's nothing going on between me and
Greg, I can assure you of that, Cap. Never has been, really. I
didn't have anything to do with his divorce..."

"Oh, I didn't think that..."

"I was just the babysitter. We—my family—lived next door to
the Summervilles in Plattville, New Jersey. I used to take care of
Tod when he was a baby, when I was in high school in Plattville.
About the time Greg went away to the war I went away to
college. When the war ended I was going into my senior year at
Columbia..."

"In Eau Claire?"

"God no! Not Columbia College—Columbia University in
New York." She acted indignant, like Columbia College people
do when you get their school mixed up with Columbia Bible
College. The fact is, there're just too many Columbias in the
world: colleges, cities, rivers—even a country in South America.
No wonder people get mixed up. When I was little I was
hopelessly confused by that song "Hail Columbia" that goes
"Columbia! The gem of the ocean..." I knew Columbia wasn't
on any ocean—and who the hell was Jim? Eventually Grandmomma straightened me out: Jim was a jewel and Columbia was
the whole country, all of America.

"I didn't mean to make you mad."

She smiled. "You didn't. How old are you, Cap?"

"I'm 15."

"And you're the man of the family—looking after Momma."

"I guess so."

"Well I can vouch for Greg Summerville's character. He's a real gentleman—a Southern gentleman. It wasn't his fault his marriage broke up. His problem was he married the first girlfriend he ever had. And he didn't acquire her until he was in medical school in Richmond. She was only a teenager, a student at Sweet Briar College. For some reason the New Jersey bourgeoisie like to send their daughters to school in Virginia—to expose them to high Southern culture I guess. Denise's father was—is—a prominent surgeon in Plattville.

"Little old Denise just went native down in the Old Dominion"—Amy was trying to imitate Southern speech the way Yankees do without realizing how stupid they sound. "All that Southern chivalry and tradition just addled her little old brain. She was absolutely mesmerized by Greg's family. From what I hear they're really old school, authentic New World aristocracy, one of the Famous Families of Virginia. And Greg was authentic. Lordy was he authentic! He was—is—the genuine article: the archetypical idealistic, bookish, sensitive Southern boy..."

"Sissy boy," I interjected.

"Yeah, you might say so. Denise's problem was that she didn't get around to sorting out the various Southern types until after she'd married Greg. She'd hooked an Ashley Wilkes—the guy played by Leslie Howard—but what she really was after was a Rhett Butler. Just the opposite from the movie. She confused Virginia with Georgia—Richmond with Atlanta—life with a movie." A fly dove at Amy's head but ran into the stream of air coming from the fan on the other desk and was deflected toward the ceiling.

"During the war Denise turned into Scarlett O'Hara and when Greg came marching home she decided he wasn't what she wanted. Greg came back from England doubly sensitized. All the wartime suffering made a deep impression on him, and he was appalled by the plight of the British working class. He said he almost joined the Communist party in London. He came home all fired up and ready to jump into the struggle for social justice in America.

"But he had those family obligations—and Greg's not someone to ignore any kind of obligation. It wasn't just the wife and kid: he was also obligated to his father-in-law who'd set him up in medical practice and treated him like the son he never had. Denise was bored by—and jealous of—Greg's newfound social and political interests. Daddy-in-law was more understanding. He was a pretty liberal guy himself: did a lot of charity work, contributed to progressive organizations. He convinced Greg that he could do more to help the oppressed by practicing medicine in Plattville than by running off to New York City to take part in rallies and demonstrations—which Greg used to do on weekends when he wasn't on call. The funny thing was, it was when he gave up all this activity—about halfway through the Wallace campaign—that Denise left him. It turned out that she could stand his absences better than his presence. So she took little Tod and moved into Daddy's house at the beach, leaving Greg to establish himself as a pillar of the medical community in Plattville—with her broad-minded daddy's continued patronage. She deals in real estate now on the Jersey shore; has her own company..."

"'Scuse me," I broke in, "you say Dr. Summerville campaigned for Wallace?"

"Yeah, for awhile. He was chairman of the Progressive Party county committee in Plattville. But he became disillusioned about the way the campaign was being run on the national level. Too many Communists."

"He didn't like the Communists?"

"It wasn't that, exactly—although he didn't have much rapport with them. With American Communists, I mean. They weren't like the Communists he'd met in England, who were well mannered, refined—his kind of people. He found American Communists to be pretty crude, always trying to impress people with how tough and ruthless they were. But the main thing was that they weren't smart. They did a lot of thinking but they weren't smart. They dreamed up all these complex and elaborate schemes that had absolutely no basis in reality and they pushed their fantasies on the campaign and really fouled things up.

"Greg resigned as Progressive Party chairman in Plattville right after the Communist rally for Wallace in Madison Square Garden. He was at that rally and so was I. That was the first summer I worked for the ACLU in the city. We compared notes on the rally a few weeks later in Plattville. We both agreed it didn't make sense—what the Communists were doing. There were better ways to fight poverty and oppression in America ..."

"Like buying yourself the latest model Cadillac?"

"Don't be absurd; that's got nothing to do with it. Anybody who really hates poverty is not going to live in it if he can help it. Quite the contrary. Anyway, the money to buy that car didn't come from the poor; it came from bourgeois hypochondriacs, mostly. And besides, Greg's a generous contributor to the ACLU and the NAACP and many other worthy causes. He has every right to spend a little money on himself and try to get some enjoyment out of life. He had his share of suffering and deprivation during the war—and in his marriage. And he missed out on a lot of things growing up..."

"Yeah. That's what he told my mother."

"He did, hunh? Well every guy's got to have a line. Look Cap, I know you want to know about me and him. Well here it is: we were neighbors in Plattville; he was interested in my graduate studies at Columbia, in anthropology; I was interested in his experiences in England; he was interested in my work with the ACLU; we had similar social and political views; we corresponded; he'd look me up when he came to New York City —before and after his divorce. We'd talk, that's all; our relationship was—is—strictly platonic. That's the truth. Now you level with me. He didn't give you that picture; where'd you get it?"

I told her the truth, told her how I'd found it in the ruins of the Mirador Club.

"Well how about that," she said and looked right past me. Then I heard this deep nigger voice coming from behind me.

"Morning Amy. Is the Reverend around?"

"No, Mike, he's in Charleston for the day. But come on in. There's somebody I want you to meet."

"Mike," she said as he shuffled over, "this is Cap Palmerston."

Instinctively I stood up and stuck out my hand. He was a real dark nigger in a seersucker suit. For a split second he hesitated, but then he grabbed my hand and pumped it three or four times.

"I'm mighty proud to meetcha," he said, grinning like a Cheshire cat.

"Likewise," I responded. It was the first time I ever shook hands with a nigger. When he turned to Amy and they started talking about the state NAACP convention in Orangeburg, I began to edge toward the door.

"Hold on, Cap," Amy said. "I still want to talk with you. Sit down."

So I sat down.

15

BOY DID I WANT A TEEGE. I fingered the pack of Luckies in my shirt pocket as Amy and the colored fellow in the seersucker suit were gabbing. When they'd finished and he was leaving I got up and told him So long but we didn't shake hands again.

"You want a cigarette?" I held the pack out to Amy.

"No thanks, I don't smoke; but you go ahead. There's an ashtray on the other desk."

I picked up a big clamshell astray half full of week-old butts and brought it over and set it down on Amy's desk.

"You say you studied anthropology?" I said as I sat back down and prepared to light up.

"Still do; I'm working on a Ph.D. at Columbia University. You know about anthropology?"

"Of course; you study all those native tribes in Africa." I leaned back in the chair and took a satisfying first drag off my Lucky.

"And in the United States, too. I did my master's thesis on African survivals in non-verbal communication patterns in the Negro community of upper Manhattan."

"No kidding?" I had no idea of what she was talking about. "Well once I read an article by a famous anthropologist in our encyclopedia that said that the reason colored people... ah... have

219

such a hard time learning things, is because their heads are shaped wrong."

"You must have an old encyclopedia. No anthropologist believes that today. We don't go around measuring skulls anymore, and we don't believe that any race is inherently inferior intellectually to any other race. Do you believe that Negroes are intellectually inferior to whites?"

"Well not necessarily. There're some pretty intelligent colored people, like Ralph Bunche. He sure seems smarter than a lot of white people."

"But you believe Negroes in general are not as intelligent as white people?"

"Well—down here at least—you'd have to say that's the way it is."

"No I wouldn't say that's the way it is. It might appear that way because you white Southerners have systematically denied Negroes the opportunities to get an adequate education and develop intellectually. Negro public schools in this state are a joke."

"But you got to realize that a lot of colored children really don't want to go to school and if you spent a lot of money on schools for them it would just be wasted."

"Is that so? And how did you come to be such an expert on Negro aspirations? Tell me, Cap, how many Negroes do you know personally?"

"I know a lot. I've lived here all my life."

"You know them by name? And they know your name?"

"Of course..."

"Well tell me who they are. Name them."

"O.k. There's Agnes, our cook. And Gonzales, who comes by to trim our bushes and mow the grass. And there's Lee, the rack man at the North Columbia Recreation Center—that's a pool hall."

"These are all servants—older people, I take it. Is there no Negro teenager—boy or girl—in all this vast Southland who can call you by name?"

"Yeah there is. There's this colored boy named Gordon who works for Dr. MacNab the veterinarian. He spoke to me just yesterday on Assembly street."

"This is a person who will talk freely with you, joke with you, share intimacies, discuss his ambitions, his plans for the future..."

"Yeah, some of that. But look, you're right: we don't associate much with colored people. That doesn't mean we have anything against them. We just choose to associate with white people instead. And if you don't mind me saying so, I don't think people up North or the federal government's got any right to tell us who we can associate with."

"Tell you who you can associate with? On the contrary: we're trying to tell you that you should have the right to associate with anyone you choose—associate in public—at a dance, at a movie, at a ball game, on the bus, in a restaurant. It's the law of the state of South Carolina that forbids you to do this with anyone who's not white. It's your state government, not the federal government, that denies you a choice."

She got me there. Actually, I should've known better than pull out the old they-can't-tell-us-who-to-associate-with routine. Miss Amick had demolished that argument in the eighth grade. But it was one of those things you believed even when you knew it wasn't true.

"Unlike you, Cap, I have many Negro friends and acquaintances—in the North and down here—and Negro students here at Allen University; I teach half-time in the sociology department. I can assure you that they aspire to the same things white people aspire to—a good education, decent employment, a rewarding career—and they're quite willing to work hard for it. But they are severely handicapped by the pitifully inadequate schooling they receive in this state."

"Well, it'll soon get better. Jimmy Byrnes won the election for governor last month on a platform of improving the colored schools."

"That's because Mr. Justice Byrnes knows what his ex-colleagues on the Supreme Court are up to. They've already ruled that segregation in graduate education is unconstitutional because of its inevitable inequality. Next they're going to rule that segregated undergraduate education is unconstitutional; then secondary education; then primary. No matter how much money Mr. Byrnes spends on the Negro schools, he'll never be able to convince the Supreme Court that they're equal to the white schools—or ever can be equal. Yes, Cap, in a few years I believe the Supreme Court will declare segregation in all public schools to be unconstitutional. And the president—Truman or Taft or Stassen or whoever it happens to be at the time—will enforce the ruling."

"That'd be a terrible blow to our constitutional form of government—to states' rights. It might even start another civil war."

"I doubt that. But you're right about it being a blow to states' rights—the peculiar regional fascism of the United States of America. And that's why I wanted to talk with you: to find out why you believe so strongly in the authority of the state over the individual. I've talked with only a few white youngsters since I arrived here in June, but practically all of them believe as you do. Your're so damned conservative! It goes against human nature: young people aren't supposed to be conservative. Aren't you just a little bit put off by the unfairness of the regime you live under?"

"I don't see where it's so unfair."

"You don't think it's unfair for the state of South Carolina to enact a law forbidding Negroes to hold production-line jobs in the textile industry?"

"Well, it may seem unfair to a few colored people, but it's best for everybody as a whole. You see, those people who work in textile mills are pretty rough people; they'd never work side-by-side with colored folks; there'd be fights all the time—riots. Nobody'd get any work done. The textile mills wouldn't come down here in the first place if that was the situation. We wouldn't have any textile industry."

"That's the argument for all segregation: keep the races apart to avoid friction..."

"Well it makes sense. You need law and order and that's what we've got. We're pretty peaceful down here compared with up North. Look at the race riots in Detroit..."

"Yet Southern Negroes are still migrating to Detroit..."

"That's their privilege. If they don't like the way things are down here and think they can do better somewhere else, they can leave. This isn't Russia."

"No, it's more like Nazi Germany. Like the Nazis you're paranoid about a supposed threat to the purity of your race and culture; you deliberately employ the police power of the state to perpetuate blatant injustice; you're all of one mind—if you can call it that. There's no dissent among the master race, no evidence of freedom of speech or freedom of the press. You have only one political party and your elections are nothing more than personality contests because all the people you allow to vote share the same warped ideology. There's total conformity everywhere. You place no value whatsoever on individual rights or civil liberties. If that's not Naziism, I don't know what is."

"Well, it might seem that way to you," I said slowly—she was looking at me intensely, almost smirking—"but we see it differently. The rights of the individual sometimes have to be set aside for the common good. And that's one thing you've got to admire about the Germans: their willingness to sacrifice for the common good—as they see it—their devotion to their way of life..."

"Cap, you would've made a fine squad leader in the Hitler Youth. Really, this is something that transcends politics and it baffles me. Why are you like this? Why are all Southern white boys like this? You call yourselves rebels but there's not one ounce of rebellion in you. Your attitude is the same as the Hitler Youth's: you want to be exactly like your fathers. That can't be; you can't become an adult until you've established your own identity—and this requires at least some conflict with the older generation." It was hard to tell when she was talking about me personally and when she meant Southern boys in general because, like all Yankees, she refused to use the plural "you all." It kept me from getting mad—trying to figure out who she was referring to.

"Well I can't quarrel with my father because he's dead. And I don't have anything against my mother..."

"No, no; I don't mean that. Isn't there anything in adult society that you object to? How about all the hypocrisy, all the phonies..."

"We don't have much of that down here..."

"Oh come off it! Yesterday I was in the checkout line at the Piggly Wiggly and the woman in front of me was carrying a baby and the cashier said 'Oh that's the most precious baby I've ever seen.' And the woman behind me had a baby too, and when she got to the cash register the cashier said the same thing: 'Oh that's the most precious baby I've ever seen.' You don't call that phony?"

"No. That's just the way we talk. We don't mean everything literally and everybody knows what we mean. That cashier wasn't trying to deceive those ladies; she was just being polite..."

"What you call politeness would be called hypocrisy anywhere else. Down here I've seen men who I knew hated each other's guts act like best friends when they run into each other in a public place. And a stranger on the street can literally run into somebody—do something careless or thoughtless that in the North would get him cursed out royally—but here everybody will just smile polite little smiles and say polite little words they don't mean. To me that's hypocrisy. Unwillingness to express one's true feelings. Cowardice..."

"No it's not. Just because we're not rude and loud-mouthed doesn't mean we're cowards. Just the opposite. When we're polite to strangers or somebody we know and don't like, all that means is 'I don't feel like fighting you now'—not 'I'm afraid to fight you.' When we feel like fighting we're just as rude as Northerners. The difference is, down here when you're rude you expect to fight."

"The old Southern code of honor, eh? It's a wonder dueling's not still legal in this state."

"The last duel in the country was fought in South Carolina. That was with pistols. Now we just duel with our fists—young boys anyway."

"Well if you're such tough brave fighters, why do you so meekly submit to the authority of the state?"

"What do you mean?"

"I mean if an officer of the law walked in here you'd be out of that chair in a flash, bowing and scraping and yassuh-ing and nahsuh-ing just like any cotton-field Negro."

"I respect the law..."

"You don't resent the police for wielding authority over you?" She pronounced it the Yankee way: puh-LEASE instead of PO-lease.

"Why should I? The cops won't do anything to me if I'm not doing anything wrong."

"And what if you *are* doing something wrong? Then you say Here I am officer, I surrender, I confess..."

"Of course not. You try not to get caught. If you do get caught, you try to lie out of it. If they catch you in the lie, then you admit it and say you're sorry. That might help; if not, then all you can do is take your punishment..."

"Even if that means the electric chair?"

"I guess so—if you can't figure out a way to escape. Crying sure won't do you any good. If they're going to electrocute you, they're going to electrocute you. Besides, I wouldn't want anybody feeling sorry for me. But it'd never come to that; I'd never do anything that they'd want to electrocute me for."

"Just what might you do that could get you into trouble with the law?"

"Well, I might... speed. They might get me for speeding..."

"For drinking alcoholic beverages maybe?"

"Well... yeah... I mean no. The cops never bother you for that—unless you get drunk and rowdy and cause people trouble and they report you."

"But it's against the law for you to drink. The legal age is 21 and you're only 15..."

"The police know you can't enforce a law like that. After all, they were boys once themselves ..."

"White boys."

"Of course. And besides, they've got more important things to do—like catching robbers and murderers..."

"And keeping the Negro in his place. They do enforce the segregation laws don't they? I'll tell you something, Cap: Cops need a defenseless class of people to push around; if they ever stop picking on Negroes they'll have to find somebody else to bother and it'll probably be young people; that's the way it is in the North. You may not need the ACLU, but your children might."

"I'll teach my children to respect the law..."

"Will you teach them that Southern nursery rhyme about the police? Or rather the PO-lease. How does it go...?"

I was surprised that she'd heard it. I laughed and recited it for her—with a few theatrical flourishes:

> "Police, police,
> Don't git me,
> Git that man behind that tree,
> He stole money and I stole none,
> Put him in the calaboose
> Just for fun."

She must've thought I was funny; she laughed—giggled—for the first time. "Amy," I said before she could recover, "you think all of us Southerners are just awful."

"No I don't, really. Southern Negroes are wonderful. And you Southern whites aren't all bad. Except for the racism this isn't a bad town, Columbia. There's a lot of diversity in the white population—I mean in terms of national origins. It's fascinating from an anthropological standpoint. The degree of assimilation is amazing, far more than in any Northern city of comparable size. It's just too bad that the newcomers have adopted the worst prejudices of the original English and Scotch-Irish. You've made Southern bigots of Greeks and Jews and Irish Catholics and Italians and Syrians and Lebanese and Armenians and Japanese and Portuguese..."

"And Germans. Don't forget the Germans. There're a lot of Koons in Columbia..."

"You're telling me. And Oehmigs and Doerichts and Kaufmanns too—only they spell their names A-m-i-c-k and D-e-r-r-i-c-k and C-a-u-g-h-m-a-n. Talk about assimilation! I wonder why the Carolina Koons didn't change the K to C like the Caughmans? "

Before I could say anything she said, "No, don't tell me. I suppose you'd consider it entirely appropriate if I spelled my name with a C. You don't approve of niggerlovers." Her saying that jolted me as much as if she'd said fuck—maybe more.

"No... I mean I don't blame you for the way you feel. You were brought up different from us..."

"So it's all in the upbringing?"

"Well not entirely," I said, thinking back to something she'd said earlier. "All the things we do—all the things we like—we didn't learn from our parents. For example, a lot of my friends like... colored music. I like it..."

"You like the blues?"

"Well, *rhythm* and blues..."

"That's interesting, because the Negro families I know here in Columbia despise rhythm and blues—won't allow their children to listen to it—think it degrades the Negro race. Of course, these are very conventional middle-class families. If their children are musically inclined they want them to become concert pianists or opera singers like Marian Anderson. For some of them even jazz or swing is beyond the pale—certainly bebop, despite its popularity with the white avant garde."

"I don't know much about bebop..."

"It's being taken over by whites, like swing before it. But I don't think it'll ever be really popular. I used to go to Birdland—in New York—and listen to the boppers, with friends from the university. But I never became a bop fanatic like some of them. The show could be exciting, but I could never really grasp the sounds. To me bop seemed to have no purpose other than the gratification of the musicians who played it; it's musicians' music. They don't care about the audience. It's not people's music. It's not danceable."

"Well rhythm and blues sure is danceable. I'm going to a colored dance tonight at the Township Auditorium—as a white observer, of course."

"Do you have a date?"

"Well I'm gonna call this girl..."

"Take me."

"Hunh?" To say I was flabbergasted would be an understatement. I don't know how long I sat there with my mouth hanging open like a blooming idiot.

"Look," she went on, "I've never been to a live rhythm and blues performance. I'd really like to go and I don't know anyone else to go with. I wouldn't embarrass you in front of your friends, I promise. I'll respect the native customs; I won't make you ashamed of me..."

"No, I wouldn't be ashamed—just the opposite ..."

"Then why not? Unless that other girl is special..."

"No, it's not that... It's... It's nothing. O.k. Where do you want me to pick you up?"

We made a date. But if we'd had any inkling of what was in store for us that night, we would've said goodbye forever that morning in the Progressive League office.

16

AS SOON AS I GOT BACK from the Progressive League office and got me something to eat, I called Browder. But his phone was busy. I couldn't wait to tell him about what had happened so I hopped on my bike and peddled over to his house. I spotted him across the street sitting on the curb in front of the Elmwood Pharmacy talking to Jimmy McCrew. As I pulled over to where they were, McCrew was getting up; he said he had to get back to helping his old man at the grocery store.

"What did old McCrew have to say?" I asked Browder after he'd left.

"Oh he was just talking about how fast them Ford products are." That was McCrew's favorite subject; his old man had a Mercury.

"He's worse than Calhoun about that," I said as I extracted the pack of Luckies from my shirt pocket. "You want a fag?"

We both lit up and I proceeded to tell Browder all about my encounter with Amy Kuhn. When I finished he kind of shook his head not like he thought I was lying but just that it was something that was hard to believe. "And you really gonna take her to that nigger dance tonight?" he said.

"Yeah man. Why don't you come on too. You gotta see this chick; she's as good looking as her picture."

He said he'd like to but that he'd been talking to this girl named Barbara that morning and told her that he'd meet her up at Arsenal Hill that night. It was Friday—the night they always have a live square-dance band at the community center—and Barbara was going there with a bunch of her girlfriends. Browder had been chasing her—in a half-assed sort of way—all summer.

"Look," I said, "why don't you just call her up and ask her to go with you to the nigger dance?"

"Naw man. Her momma wouldn't let her go. Even if she lied to her about where she's going, she couldn't stay out past eleven."

"That's when them niggers'd just be getting warmed up... Hey, you could come by the Township Auditorium after Barbara goes home. Maybe they'd let you in free that late..."

"Naw, they don't ever let you in free."

"Well after it's over I'm gonna spin Amy through Sox's. If you can catch a ride down there I'll let you talk to her—maybe even touch her."

"That's mighty white of you, old buddy. I'll sho nuff take you up on it if I run into y'all tonight. Right now I feel like shooting some pool. You wanna go over to the Brunswick?"

I said o.k. and we spent the rest of the afternoon at the Brunswick Billiard Parlor, shooting a few games ourselves but mostly watching the sharks play.

After supper I picked up Amy at her place which was a garage apartment in the white section next to Columbia Hospital. She looked good—not as glamorous as in the picture, but plenty good. She had on a cotton print dress with a modest V neck and a gold-chain necklace and locket and diamond-stud earrings. Her gorgeous blond hair flowed to her shoulders; it draped a little over her forehead but was held back from the rest of her face by silver barrettes. She wore Cuban-heel shoes without socks or stockings. She was appropriately dressed for the Township

Auditorium. I told her she looked good and she said I did too. No girl had ever told me that before.

The Township Auditorium was only a few blocks away and I drove straight there. It was a little early but I explained to Amy that I wanted us to be there in time to get seats in the balcony near the rail where we'd have a good view of the action on the dance floor. I pulled into a parking space on the street near the auditorium and Amy got out of the car before I could go around and open the door for her. That pissed me off a little. Then she offered to pay for her ticket—since she'd invited herself. I said Absolutely not, and reminded her that she'd promised to respect the native customs, which called for the boy to pay for both tickets. I had plenty of larsh: Momma had given me $10 before I went out and, as usual, hadn't asked me where I was going or who I was going with, and I hadn't volunteered the information.

Amy didn't give me any argument. I got the impression then that she was really going to behave the way I wanted her to, and that made me feel good. The fact that she was ten years older than me didn't matter anymore. She didn't look ten years older—I felt pretty sure of that as I maneuvered her through the sweaty black multitudes to the stairs at the side of the Township Auditorium that went up to the white balcony. She was just a mature girl, good looking as hell, who did what I told her to. I couldn't wait for somebody I knew to see me with her.

"Hey Cap," the voice came from behind us as we were going up the steps, "you going the wrong way: your people're downstairs."

"Stringbean!" I exclaimed—ignoring both his joke and his girlfriend, Mandy Jackson. "Haven't seen you in many moons. Got somebody I want you to meet. Ah, Amy Kuhn, this is Ron Stark... and Mandy Jackson." Everybody smiled radiantly and mouthed one- or two-syllable greetings: Hi... H'lo... Howdy...

Before Mandy could say anything more I looked straight at her and said, "Amy goes to Columbia University in New York." Then I turned to Stringbean. "Sorry about Eau Claire getting knocked out of the play-offs."

"Yeah but we had a good season," Stringbean said as the four of us started up the stairs. "We oughta do even better next year; we got a young ball club. Ackbo and Burnt were really connecting with the ball there at the end."

Mandy pretended to be listening to us talk baseball, but I could see her eyeballing Amy. She was as jealous as I'd hoped she'd be. She looked good—Mandy did—but she paled in comparison with Amy. Her straw-colored hair seemed positively dull next to the platinum brilliance of Amy's. Mandy knew Amy outshone her in every way, physically and mentally. She wouldn't be giving me any jive that night about inferiority complexes and me dating below my social and intellectual level.

I spotted four vacant seats in the second row and led the way to them with Amy dutifully behind me and Stringbean and Mandy following her. After we sat down Stringbean and I continued talking with Amy between us and Mandy left out on the end. She didn't like that and turned around in her seat to watch who was coming in. She nudged Stringbean and pointed out somebody and he nodded his head and grinned but I didn't know who it was. Then we saw Bobby Skinner come in with Nancy Gray.

"Uh oh," I said, "look who's got Nancy Gray. I wonder what he did to Calhoun..."

"Not much," Stringbean said. "Me and Brewster saw the fight last night. Skinner was waiting at Nancy's house when Calhoun brought her home. Skinner'd told us what he was gonna do so naturally we went along to watch. Well, Nancy ran inside her house when she saw Skinner, and Calhoun said they oughta go around the corner if he wanted to fight. Skinner agreed and that's what they did. It was a pretty good fight. Skinner seemed to land some hard blows at first, but Calhoun shook 'em off and rassled Skinner to the ground. He got him in a scissors and neck hold and Skinner about wore himself out breaking it—but he did. Actually, both of 'em were pretty winded when they got back up and started trading punches again. Skinner did manage to bloody Calhoun's nose, though, and when he saw it he said You're bleeding Calhoun—I ain't gonna fight you no more. And Calhoun said Don't let that stop you Skinner, but if you wanna shake that's o.k. with me. They both just stood there for about a minute, breathing hard and staring at one other. Then Calhoun said that Skinner oughta know that he wasn't birddogging him; Calhoun said everybody thought Skinner'd dropped Nancy Gray. She didn't mean anything to him, Calhoun said, and since Skinner felt the way he did about her, he wasn't gonna date her anymore. That's when Skinner stuck out his hand and they shook on it."

Amy was intrigued by Stringbean's account of the fight. The way she was listening you never would've thought she didn't know any of the people he was talking about. When he finished she was the first to speak up: "These are fifteen-year-old boys fighting over this girl?"

Stringbean seemed startled by the sound of her voice. Maybe it was her Yankee accent that threw him off.

"Calhoun's 15," I answered for him, "but Skinner's 17."

"Here comes Calhoun now," Mandy announced, pointing to the side entrance to the balcony. "Who's that with him?"

"Well I'll be dipped," Stringbean said. "It's Nancy Frohman, Nancy Gray's best friend."

She's a nice-looking girl I thought, prettier than Nancy Gray; looks a little like Gloria Grahame. Calhoun did all right. He grinned and waved at us as he and Nancy Frohman sat down in the back row.

Then the music started and drew everybody's attention to the stage. The first number had a South American beat; it was called the "Rhumba Blues," I think. Tiny Bradshaw, the bandleader, was standing out in front of his combo shaking a pair of maracas next to Dorena Deane, the vocalist. She had a smooth slurpy voice. Some niggers on the floor were dancing but more were just milling about; a lot of them were crowded up against the stage gaping at Dorena and Tiny and his boys who were decked out in plumb-colored jackets and black bow ties and two-tone shoes. That first song was pretty low key—no great instrumentals or anything—and there was only scattered applause when it was over.

Dorena barely had time to take a little bow before Tiny grabbed the microphone and shouted, "I heard the news... there's good rockin' tonight!"

The band kicked in like a motorboat taking off—trumpet and saxophones, piano and drums and bass—all together. But Tiny's voice was louder than them all. He got the joint jumping all right. All the niggers on the floor were dancing, or at least jiving to the music.

"Now this is real rhythm and blues," I said to Amy.

"I know. I have the Wynonie Harris record. But this is different: they're doing it without the boogie beat." We had to talk loud over the roar of the music. "Boogie's going out of style," she added; "this is more up to date—a jump beat."

"You sure know a lot."

"It's my business; I'm a cultural anthropologist."

"This is culture?"

"You bet it is."

"... Gonna hold my baby tight as I can,
Tonight she'll know I'm a mighty man..."

Amy was smiling and gazing at Tiny and nodding her head to the music. He wasn't bad looking for a nigger: not too dark, with real short hair and a neat thin mustache.

"You know," Amy said when the song was over, "Tiny Bradshaw has a college education. He studied psychology at Wilberforce University."

I said That's interesting.

After "Good Rockin' Tonight" Tiny played some of the songs he'd recorded—that he was famous for—like "Breaking Up the House" and "Boodie Green." Tiny really hammed up "Boodie Green": he and Dorena started dancing on the stage while the band laid down this throbbing beat.

"Makes you want to dance, doesn't it?" Amy said.

"I can't dance."

"Sure you can..."

"No I can't. I can feel the rhythm but I can't keep time. Metabolism's all messed up. And I got two left feet."

"You can overcome that. I'll teach you... Hey look!" She pointed over to the aisle where Dorn Dell was shagging with a girl from Dreher.

"They're not supposed to be doing that," I said. "The cops'll get 'em." And sure enough, a policeman who'd been standing in the doorway went after them; they stopped dancing all of a sudden when they saw him coming. The Dreher girl turned and smiled nervously at her friends while Dorn faced the law. You could tell he was acting real respectful; whatever he said must've satisfied that cop because instead of throwing them out he let them go back to their seats.

Meanwhile, down on the stage, Tiny and Dorena stepped to the side and the tenor sax player came forward for a solo. The tenorman had done some honking in earlier numbers but this time he pulled out all the stops. He blew that sax so low it sounded like it was farting; then he made it scream so high you thought it'd bust your eardrums. All the time he was gyrating like a maniac. He arched his back and stuck his instrument so far up into the air that it looked like he was going to fall over backwards. Then he dropped to his knees and kept on honking. By this time a lot of niggers on the floor had quit dancing and crowded around the stage to watch the tenorman. They stomped their feet and clapped their hands as that crazy sax went on quacking and quivering.

The people in the white balcony had a better view of the tenorman's antics than anybody else. The white people started stomping and clapping too, and the tenorman flipped onto his back—where he could look straight up at us—and began blowing this screeching high note and kicking his feet up in the air like a little child throwing a tantrum.

"He's razzing us," Amy said.

Nobody else thought that, including me. The white balcony gave the tenorman a big hand when he took a bow at the end of the number.

The next song was what everybody was waiting for: Tiny Bradshaw's latest hit, "Well-Oh-Well." The tempo was about twice as fast as anything else they'd played that night and it sent the niggers on the dance floor into a weaving bobbing frenzy. While Tiny shouted the lyrics the bassman went wild plucking that bass: whoomp-whoomp-whoomp. The piano player and the drummer were going to town too. The dancing niggers looked like one big swarm of bees, they were so packed together. You couldn't make them out individually—except for one couple.

Out in the middle of the floor there was this pair of light-skinned niggers whose dancing was so good that the others began stepping back to admire them and give them more room. The space around them grew bigger and bigger as the nigger boy kept slinging his partner out farther and farther. He'd keep her at arms length while his hips were churning like a Bendix washer and his feet were moving twice as fast in the opposite direction without breaking contact with the floor; you'd think his knees were made of rubber. Then he'd pull that high-yellow girl in towards him and spin her like a top. When he threw her over his head, that got the attention of everybody who wasn't already watching them.

"Did you see that?" Amy exclaimed.

"Yeah," I said, "I know that colored boy." Just to make sure I turned around and looked at Calhoun who was standing up on his seat in the back row and pantomimed Zat Gordon? He grinned and shook his head up and down. I reached over and poked Stringbean and he nodded, because he knew Gordon too.

Amy was so captivated by the show on the dance floor that what I'd said didn't register on her at first. Then it did. "You say you know that boy?"

"Yeah. That's Gordon, the colored boy I told you I know who works for Dr. MacNab the veterinarian."

"You *must* introduce me to him." She was leaning forward in her seat with her eyes glued on Gordon and shaking her right hand in time to the music.

"Yeah, sure," I said, but she wasn't paying any attention to me and I didn't think she'd heard me.

I noticed Gordon wasn't smiling. In that respect he was dancing like a white boy. Niggers do a lot of laughing and clowning when they dance, but white boys don't even smile —girls don't either, usually. For white people dancing is serious business, and that's how it seemed to be with Gordon.

The crowd closed in on Gordon and his high-yellow partner when that number was over. I spotted him later slow-dancing with a darker girl while Dorena was singing a torch song. For a long time after that I didn't see him again and I don't think Amy did either, although I could tell she was looking for him. "I really want to meet your friend Gordon," she reminded me when the dance was about over.

"Well, o.k.... if we can find him. Maybe he's already gone home." The crowd was starting to thin out.

"No he hasn't," she pointed to the dance floor; "there he is." Gordon was doing an easy shag with the high yellow we'd seen him with the first time.

Stringbean had noticed Amy's interest in Gordon and seemed amused. "Amy's an expert in African dances," I explained to him. "She wants to talk to Gordon because he's so good at it. We're gonna try to find him when this thing lets out..."

"Well be careful. There's a mess of niggers down there."

Amy shot Stringbean a dirty look and I poked her pretty hard in the ribs for it. Dammit, I thought, she was really pissing me off now—after all that promising to respect the native customs and not make me ashamed of her.

Stringbean saw me poke her and chuckled. "Hey," he said, "maybe you oughta try to catch Calhoun before he gets outta here. He could help y'all run down Gordon."

"Calhoun?" Amy said—if she was mad at me for poking her she didn't let on—"the boy who was in the fight?"

"Yeah," I said, "Angus Calhoun MacNab, Dr. MacNab's son. That's a good idea, Stringbean. Come on Amy, let's go."

She got up and said goodbye to Stringbean and Mandy—very pleasant and mature like, telling them how glad she was to have met them—and then followed me into the aisle and up to the last row in the balcony where Calhoun and Nancy Frohman were. They got up as we approached—the band had stopped playing now and most people were moving toward the exits—and we went through a quick round of introductions before we headed for the stairs ourselves. I'd never met Nancy Frohman before; I really liked her Gloria Grahame smile. I explained that Amy was studying African culture and wanted to talk to Gordon because he could dance so well. I don't think Calhoun could quite grasp that, but he said he knew where Gordon's car was in the parking lot and would take us to it. Calhoun's left eye was a little puffy but wasn't black; I suspected he'd covered up some bruises with Clearasil pimple cream.

We made our way to the parking lot through the nigger hordes streaming out of the Township Auditorium and found Dr. MacNab's 1942 Packard Clipper. "Gordon musta drove in right before we did. I'm parked over there." Calhoun pointed to the '50 Ford Country Squire in the next row. "Here he comes now." Gordon was walking between the two colored girls we'd seen him dancing with.

"Howdy Gordon," Calhoun said.

"'Lo Bud," Gordon replied. "I didn't know you was here."

"Gordon you remember Cap..."

"Sho nuff. How you doing Clarence?"

"Fine," I said and glanced at Amy who was smiling sweetly at Gordon. The two nigger girls were standing behind Gordon now, looking nervous. Nancy Frohman was standing behind Calhoun looking enigmatic. After an awkward silence I said, "Ah... Gordon, this is... Miss Amy Kuhn. She was admiring your dancing..."

"Pleased to meet you, ma'am."

"The pleasure is all mine, I assure you." Her saying that let all the niggers know she was from the North. I was relieved she didn't try to shake hands with Gordon. "I work for the Reverend

Scott Batey," she said and paused like she expected him to say something, but he didn't. "Do you know the Reverend Batey?" "Uh... no ma'am."Gordon acted like he thought she was trying to catch him in something. "Well, I also work for the NAACP. You know about the NAACP don't you?" "Yes'm." Gordon didn't bat an eye, but Calhoun about swallowed the Herbert Tareyton he was smoking. He gave me a what-the-hell-is-this look and then glanced back at his date who raised her eyebrows slightly but otherwise didn't appear phased at all.

"You people certainly seemed to be having a good time in the auditorium. Where're you going now?"

"We just going to somebody's house and listen to records" —Gordon was more relaxed now—"and dance."

"May we join you?"

I knew damn well she was leading up to that, so it didn't come as a surprise to me when she said it. Calhoun and Nancy didn't look like they were shocked either, but there was pure consternation on the faces of those two colored girls. We all knew Gordon had to say yes; he couldn't refuse a white person. What mattered was how he said it.

"Shore, come on." He sounded sincere—even enthusiastic. "Y'all folly me; I'll lead y'all to where the party's at. You coming, Bud?"

"Naw, 'fraid not," Calhoun said; "I gotta take Nancy here home. It's past her bedtime."

I thought about making some excuse too, but I was afraid Amy'd go without me. If she left me standing there in that parking lot and took off with those niggers I'd really look like a chump to Calhoun and Nancy. I didn't have any choice—but the fact was, I was kind of curious about what those niggers did. It was an opportunity I might never have again, I thought.

Gordon opened the front door of the Packard and the colored girls scooted in under the steering wheel as Calhoun and Nancy Frohman walked away. He asked me where my car was and I told him it was parked on the street. He said he'd take me to it and motioned for me and Amy to get into the back seat. As I was crawling in after her Gordon tried to crank the Packard: row-r-r-r-o-w... r. The engine stopped turning over. "Goddoggit!" he swore. "I told Mr. Doc this here battery was all used up." Nobody else said anything. After a few seconds Gordon pushed the starter button again and it sounded more feeble than before but this time the engine caught: Room! Room! Room! Gordon kept pumping the accelerator to keep it going. "I was afraid we'd hafta push," he said.

As we waited in line to get out of the parking lot Gordon turned around and said to me: "You got any juice, man?" He acted different now that Calhoun was gone.

"Liquor? Naw I ain't got any."

"Well a fellow ought not traipse into a colored folks party without him bringing something to drink."

"I can get some whiskey at Tuck Booker's..."

"Where zat?"

"Up on Blanding street—other side o' Seaboard Park."

"Naw, we ain't going that way. I'll show you where you can get some that's close to where we going." He pulled up on the street in front of where the Plymouth was parked. "Y'all just folly me."

As soon as we'd transferred to my car Amy said, "Cap, I really appreciate your going along with this. I hope I haven't offended you. If I have, I apologize—and you can take me home right now if you want to. I certainly understand how you'd be apprehensive about being around Negroes. You've been swell..."

"I'm not apprehensive."

"Great! The experience will be as good for you as for me. I've never before had a chance to mix socially with working-class Negroes." She seemed real happy.

"Your friend Gordon's an interesting guy," she said as I eased the Plymouth out into the street behind the Packard. "Why does he call you 'Clarence'?"

"That's my real name. I guess colored people just like to be formal when they're talking to white people."

"But he calls Calhoun 'Bud'."

"Well that's what they call him at home. Gordon works for the MacNabs and hears them calling him that all the time, so he does too. That's Dr. MacNab's car he's driving."

Gordon was driving slow and cautious, the way niggers usually do in a white area. It was easy to follow him. We went down the Pickens street hill by the University of South Carolina and after we'd crossed Blossom street Gordon stuck out his arm and signaled a right-hand turn. I followed him onto a dirt road lined with nigger shacks. He stopped in front of one place and turned off his lights but kept his motor running. As I pulled in behind him he motioned for me to get out. I did, but I left my motor running and told Amy to roll up her window and keep the doors locked.

"This here's Momma Lola's place," Gordon said when I went over to where he was sitting in the Packard. "She's used to selling to white boys. Just knock on the door and tell her you want a pint."

That's what I did. The house was dark except for a light on in the kitchen. When I walked up on the front porch I could see through the screen door all the way back to the kitchen where this fat nigger woman was sitting down and sleeping or resting with her head on the table. She raised her head slowly when I rapped on the screen door and then she got up and waddled toward me.

"I like a pint, please," I said.

"Hit'll take me jest a minute to git it. Come on in." She unlatched the screen door and I stepped inside the front room and waited while she went back to the kitchen. It was pretty dark in that room but I could see that the walls to the outside were covered with newspapers and the inside wall was decorated with what probably were family photographs and a picture of Jesus like the one in the Presbyterian Sunday school. The place smelled like scorched cloth.

She was back in a couple of minutes holding a regular brown-glass pint flask with no label on it. "Hit's two dollar," she said. That was pretty steep for white lightning but it was late at night. I handed her the bills and took the bottle. "Thank you kindly, suh," she said.

I hustled back to the Plymouth and Amy opened the door for me. She was enjoying herself; you could tell. Gordon turned on his lights and led us around the block back to Pickens street; we headed up the hill toward Rosewood but only went a short distance before Gordon signaled for a left turn. I put on my blinker and looked in the rearview mirror and saw this car zooming through the Blossom street intersection on a yellow light and heading towards us like a bat out of hell. The driver blew his horn and he and his passenger waved as they swerved around us on the right.

"Jerks!" Amy yelled.

"That's a friend of mine"—I laughed—"a boy we call Radar because he's got these ears that stick out like radar antennas. That's his old man's Buick Super. It's got this automatic transmission called Dynaflow that so slow—we call it Dynaslow—that it'll hardly even move around town. He had to get up all that speed coming down Pickens street hill to pass us like that."

I'd noticed that Browder was riding shotgun with Radar. They were probably on their way to the Friendly drive-in, I thought as I made the left turn behind Gordon; the Friendly was one of Radar's favorite hangouts.

We followed Gordon into this nigger district on Wheeler Hill which is right next to Wales Garden, a ritzy white area where a lot of the colored women from Wheeler Hill work as maids. Gordon made two left turns and parallel parked on this steep stretch of dirt road pointing straight down at Maxcy Gregg park. I pulled in front of him.

"Naw, Clarence," Gordon said as I was getting out of the Plymouth, "don't block me off. Reason I parked here was so's I could roll-start this booger case the battery's dead—which it probably is. The party's in that house back yonder round the corner where all the lights on. Y'all go on back there and park in the front. We'll meet y'all there."

So I started the Plymouth up again and made a U-turn and went back and angled it into the front yard of this one-story nigger house where several other cars were parked—mostly pre-war rattletraps. All the other houses in the neighborhood were dark but this one had lights burning on the porch and in the front room and in the back. You could hear the sound of music and talking coming from inside, but it wasn't as loud as at some white parties I'd been to. The place didn't look too bad for a nigger house—for one thing, it was painted. There were some hickory trees in the yard and one of them was about smothered by honeysuckle vines—which also ran up one side of the house. The dew had formed and the air was sweet with damp honeysuckle. It counteracted the nigger smell.

Gordon and the two colored girls walked up just as I was helping Amy out of the Plymouth. We locked her purse in the car. Before we went into the house Amy asked Gordon to introduce us to his girlfriends.

"Well," Gordon said as he put his arm around the high yellow, "this here's Ida, and that there's Laura." Both of them smiled; they were much more at ease now than they'd been in the parking lot at the Township Auditorium.

Amy said "I'm Amy" and Gordon all of a sudden turned on his heel and stalked off toward the front door of the house. The rest of us followed him inside. Later I would consider myself extremely fortunate to get out of that place alive.

17

"BRE'REN AND SIST'REN," Gordon announced as Amy and I walked into that house full of niggers last night, "this here's Miss Kuhn and my... friend... Clarence. They here on my invitation." But everybody was so glad to see Gordon that they didn't pay any attention to us. Nigger boys ran up to Gordon and shook his hand or squeezed his arm and black wenches hugged his neck; they hugged and kissed Ida and Laura too. It was like we weren't even there. They were all jabbering at the same time and I could hardly make out a word they were saying. The Victrola was playing a blues record—by Lightning Hopkins, I think—and all the furniture had been pushed up against the wall to clear the floor for dancing, but nobody was dancing when we came in.

The niggers at the party were all my age or a few years older; some might've been considerably older, though; it was hard for me to tell. The one who looked the oldest was sprawled out on the sofa dead to the world. When Gordon finally turned away from his fans and spoke to me and Amy he pointed to the body on the sofa. "That there's Curtis, the man o' the house. He been juiced ever since his old woman left on the Silver Mete'r to Baltimore last night. They got a tub o' purple Jesus in the kitchen. Y'all want some?"

"No thanks," I said, "that stuff gives me a bad headache. I'll just stick to this." I held up my pint of corn whiskey. By then several niggers had taken their eyes off Gordon and now were studying Amy and me the way the natives look at Jungle Jim in the movies. The only one who looked hostile was this big mahogany-colored buck who was standing in the kitchen door eating a barbecue sandwich. He looked away when I stared back at him.

"Well I'm gonna get me a beer," Gordon said. "They's some out on the porch. You want one?" He looked at Amy.

"Why yes, thank you. I *would* like a beer if it's cold."

"Well they oughta be. I brung 'em a 50-pound block o' ice before the dance. Let's go see."

Amy and I followed Gordon through the hall past a half-opened bedroom door to the back porch. Ida and Laura had merged with the crowd in the front room and only one of Gordon's admirers tagged along with us to the porch—a coconut-headed little coon that Gordon called Pigmeat. He might've been 14 or 15 years old but you couldn't tell. It was obvious though that Gordon was his idol.

The porch was screened in and next to the screen door that opened onto the back steps there was a big galvanized tub half full of water with beer bottles in it and a chunk of ice floating around. A swing was suspended from the ceiling and there was a dinette chair and some drink crates on the porch floor near the tub. Gordon squatted down and fished out an Atlantic ale and popped the top off with the church key that was on a sting tied to one of the handles of the tub and handed the bottle to Amy. She said Thank you and sat down in the swing. I moved quick and sat down next to her while Gordon was opening himself a beer.

I pulled out my fags and held the pack out to Gordon. He waved them away but his buddy Pigmeat reached out and took one. I had to give him a light too. Amy leaned back in the swing and started it rocking and Pigmeat backed away to keep from getting hit by it.

"It certainly is pleasant out here," she said. A slight breeze was blowing but not enough to disturb the lightning bugs that blinked and darted about on the other side of the screen. The lopsided moon was white and high over Rosewood now, throwing shadows off the trees in the backyard; it was a pretty bright night. You could see the pale buildings of the University of South Carolina on the hill across the valley that Rocky Branch runs through.

I took my first swig of the corn liquor and it wasn't too bad—about the same as the stuff I'd drunk in Georgia. Gordon had a beer in his hand but his buddy Pigmeat didn't have anything to drink and just stood there smoking the Lucky I'd given him and staring at me and Amy. I held out my pint bottle to him and he took it without saying a word and glugged down a couple of mouthfuls.

"You musta got it from Momma Lola," he said as he handed the flask back to me; "she done cut it down to white-boy stren'th."

Amy laughed. She was shaking her foot to the music coming from the front room. The Victrola was playing "Pink Champagne" and there must've been a lot of jigs dancing in there because you could feel the vibrations all the way out on the back porch.

"Y'all don't wanna dance?" Gordon said.

"No, not just now," Amy replied.

Gordon knew better than ask her to dance with him. I could tell he wanted to, though. "Me neither," he said; "I'm about wore out."

"I can understand why," she said and took a little sip from her Atlantic ale. "Too bad your friend Calhoun couldn't come. Have you known him for very long?"

Gordon just stood there for a few seconds looking real serious like he was trying to make up his mind whether to run away or stay and talk to us. Finally he said "Buddy?... Knowed him since I come to live with my grampa after the war." He picked up the dinette chair and set it down in front of the swing—only with the back of the chair in front of the swing. Gordon straddled it and faced us like he was riding a horse. Pigmeat took his cue from his hero and mounted a Jax beer crate that he'd flipped on its side.

"My grampa and his wife live on Buddy's poppa's place. She ain't my grandmomma but I call her that. Doc MacNab, Buddy's poppa, he's a veterinarian; Grampa farms for him. I do odd jobs when I ain't going to school. When Buddy was little I used to look after him."

"They paid you to take care of him?" Amy asked.

"Naw, I didn't git no pay. I didn't take care of him; just looked after him—played with him when we'd be home from school. Buddy, he didn't have nobody else to play with out there on Doc MacNab's place and he couldn't go nowhere by hisself because he was too little. He was ten years old and I was twelve when I started living on the place."

"What did you do when you played together—I mean what kind of games did you play?"

"Games? Well we played checkers... and Chinese checkers... and marbles. We'd play Monopoly too. We'd set up this old card table under the chinaberry tree in front of my grampa's house and play Monopoly. I liked that game—liked the idea o' me gitting rich—liked beating Buddy in Monopoly. It was his game, o' course."

Gordon took a big swallow from his Jax beer as Amy looked at him half smiling, her red lips slightly parted. She'd barely touched her Atlantic ale. I lifted my pint of white lightning and—for the first time in my life—drank after a nigger. Calhoun did it and survived, I said to myself, so I ought to make it too. The trouble was, he drank after Gordon who was at least half white and I was drinking after Pigmeat who was a total spook. It was kind of funny though, how people were afraid of drinking after a nigger when so many white babies were raised on some black mammy's milk—me for instance. Momma told me that when I was born Grandmomma didn't think she had enough milk for me so she hired a nigger wet nurse to make sure I'd get plenty. It's o.k. to suck milk out of their tits but you don't want to swallow any of their spit. It's the same way with cows, I guess: you drink their milk but you don't kiss them. I hoped there was enough alcohol in that moonshine to kill Pigmeat's germs. He refused my offer of another swig—which was a relief—and got himself a beer out of the galvanized tub.

"Yeah," Gordon said, "near 'bout everything we played with belonged to Buddy or his poppa: them games, the magazines Buddy'd bring out for us to read—*Boy's Life*, *National Geographic*—the horses we rode, the dogs—everything 'cept my grampa's .22 rifle. I taught Buddy how to shoot with Grampa's rifle; taught him to hunt squirrels. Couple years later when Buddy was twelve his poppa gave him a brand-new double barrel 16 gauge shotgun and he'd take that when we'd go squirrel hunting together. But I could still git more squirrels with Grampa's single-shot .22 than Buddy could kill with that double-barrel shotgun. You can only teach a white boy up to a certain point; you can't never teach him to be as good as you."

"Did he teach *you* anything?" Amy asked.

"Naw—taught me a few things about white folks, that's all."

Pigmeat had glugged down his beer and started blowing into the empty bottle making a sound like a foghorn. Gordon told him to hush.

"I'd never lived with white folks before I moved in with my grampa on Doc MacNab's place," Gordon said as Pigmeat opened himself another beer. "Never lived next to a big city, either. Never'd been to a picture show. My grampa'd only seen one picture show, 'Birth of a Nation.' It was about the Ku Klux Klan. He said they showed it on the side of a building up in Oconee county where we come from—brung in all the colored people to see it. After that Grampa said he didn't care to see no more picture shows. He said I could go if I wanted to, and I did. Every Saturday afternoon I used to walk over to Mr. Hinnant's filling station and catch the bus to town and go to the cowboy movie at the Ritz theater. That's a white folks theater but they got a colored balcony. Then the next day, Sunday afternoon, I'd tell Buddy all about it—tell him the whole story—how Don Red

Barry rode his horse off that cliff, how Johnny Mack Brown killed all them Indians.

"Well, Buddy sho wished he could go see one of them cowboy picture shows. Sometimes his momma and poppa'd take him to some high-class movie at the Palmetto theater, or the Carolina, but not to one of them shoot-'em-up westerns at the Ritz. Miz MacNab wouldn't be caught dead at the Ritz—she called it the Rats, according to Buddy. Only good thing about the Ritz, Buddy's momma said, was the free shoeshine you got from all them rats running across your feet.

"But Buddy wanted to go real bad. One Saturday afternoon when I was fixing to take off for the Ritz theater, Buddy came running up to me and axed me if I'd let him go with me. I said Sho, but you gotta ax your poppa first. So the both of us went over to where Doc MacNab was working on his tractor and Buddy axed him, Poppa kin I go to the picture show with Gordon?

"Mr. Doc, he looked kinda painful and he said Son I wish you could but you can't; they won't let you and Gordon sit together in the theater and you can't even sit together on the bus gitting there; you can't go nowhere with somebody under them conditions. And Buddy 'lowed as how his poppa was right and I went off to the picture show and Buddy had to stay home till he was big enough to go by hisself. I reckon Mr. Doc 'splained to him all about Jim Crow after I left that afternoon, though Buddy never said nothing to me about it. Mr. Doc knowed Jim Crow was wrong—I could tell—but he never done nothing about it 'cept pass it on to his boy. But Mr. Doc's old—like my grampa's old—and you can't spec much from old folks..."

Gordon was talking the kind of bullshit Amy'd been waiting to hear. "You're absolutely right," she said. "We've got to look to the younger generation..."

But Gordon just took a swig of beer and went on like he hadn't heard her. "One thing I'll say about old Doc MacNab though: he's a pretty fair minded fellow for a white man. Couple-three years back—when Buddy was twelve and I was

14—Mr. Doc set us up to make a crop o' cotton. Me and Buddy was supposed to split the money even shares after we'd paid off all his poppa's advances. 'Course if you ever seen a white boy chopping cotton you know who done the work. Mr. Doc knowed. After we settled with him they was $150 left and Mr. Doc took that money and handed me $100 and gave Buddy $50. That was the first time since the beginning of the world that a colored boy got paid twice as much as a white boy for only doing four times as much work."

Gordon laughed but he sounded bitter; he seemed to harbor a lot of resentment against Calhoun. The swing creaked and Gordon reached for another beer. Amy studied him a few seconds and then asked him if he knew many other white boys.

"I know some o' Buddy's friends... like Clarence here. I used to play with 'em when they'd come out to the place to see Buddy when they was in the fifth or sixth grade at that school in Camp Fornance..."

I interrupted to explain to Amy that the children Gordon was talking about didn't include me—that I didn't know Calhoun back then because I went to another grammar school: Logan on Elmwood. Gordon looked at me like you look at somebody who's lying but who you're going to let get by with it for the time being. Pigmeat was staring at me too, like an evil moron. About that time an even nastier looking nigger—a big prune-colored, blunt-nosed jig with washboard waves of pomaded hair the same color as his skin—came in and fished a couple of beers out of the tub and laid a hand on Gordon's thigh and flashed him a toothy grin. Gordon smiled back and gave him a friendly punch in the ribs. I was relieved when he took the beers and went back to the front room.

"Yeah," Gordon said looking at Amy again, "I used to play with them children who came out to Doc MacNab's place to see Buddy. They'd come out on wheels—bicycles—and they'd let me ride 'em. I had me a wheel too—but not near as nice as them boys from Camp Fornance had. Same with Buddy: his wheel weren't much better'n mine. Me and Buddy didn't ride wheels much on them dirt roads out there; we'd ride Mr. Doc's horses instead. But them white children from Camp Fornance had some fine bicycles and they let me ride 'em... Shore, I played with them white children lots of times—chucked baseballs with 'em and shot basketballs. 'Course lots of times I had work to do and didn't have no time to play when they came out.

"One thing Buddy and them young white boys started doing on Saturdays was going on hikes. Each of 'em would bring a lunch—like you take to school—and they'd walk a few miles up the river and find a nice place and eat they lunches there. Well, one Friday after school Buddy told me some o' his friends were coming out the next morning to go on a hike and he axed me if I wanted to go and I said Shore. Usually I had to holp my grampa on Saturday mornings but I knowed he'd let me off if I axed him. I'd get Grandmomma to fix me a lunch just like on schooldays.

"Well I got pretty excited about going on a hike with them white children. On Saturday morning when I seen Buddy standing out on his porch I grabbed the paper sack with my lunch in it and went over to where he was at. Buddy said he'd talked to some o' the boys on the phone and they'd be there directly. Then he said Look here Gordon, you know I don't mind you going, but some o' the other boys don't want a colored boy going on the hike with us... He didn't need to say another blessed thing; I just turned around and walked away. I felt like stomping his butt into the ground though—because I didn't believe any o' them boys'd said they didn't want me along. I figured Buddy was just afraid they *might* say that. Someday I *am* gonna stomp his butt into the ground."

"B-but," Amy sputtered, "you seemed to get along so well tonight... and..."

"We gits along because we *has* to git along. We live on the same place and take orders from the same fellow: Doc MacNab. It's like we brothers—neither one kin git shed o' the other—so we just make the best of it. Sho, we go out riding horses together"—he was looking at me—"them horses gotta be exercised and they like being together. And with me riding with Buddy I

git to go places I couldn't go by myself—couldn't go without a
white boy—like through Eau Claire. Lots o' po' buckras live over
there—white trash. Them white children see a colored boy riding
a horse down they street they gonna start hollering nigger and
throwing rocks at him. But they see me riding with Buddy they
don't think I'm a nigger—think I'm an Indian, Lone Ranger's
faithful Indian companion Tonto.

"Old Tonto—that scoundrel never had to put up with what I
done had to put up with. Le'me tell y'all something happened last
winter..."

Amy leaned forward in the swing, making the chains jangle
overhead; she was all ears. I fortified myself with another swig of
white lightning. Pigmeat was drooling in his beer bottle.

"One cold Saturday morning Buddy came stomping up on our
porch with that fancy shotgun o' his. He hollered for me to come
out and go hunting with him. Well I was fixing to split some
firewood for my grampa but he said to never mind and told me
to take his rifle and go on hunting with young massa. I told
Grampa I'd try to bring him back a squirrel or two.

"But Buddy said he'd seen some ducks flying over and wanted
to go down to Crane creek and hunt ducks. Hid been raining a
lot last winter and the creek was up. I seen this boat that was
floating upside down and tied to a willow branch that was under
water. That boat'd been hid in the willows but'd floated up out
o'em when the water riz over the bank. Le's git it, Buddy said,
and he give me his shotgun to hold and crawled out on a limb
over where that boat was and grabbed the rope and pulled it in
to the land. When we flipped the boat over we found a paddle
stuck under the seat. Buddy handed it to me and said You paddle
and I'll look for ducks.

"We didn't see no ducks. After awhile Buddy got to clowning
up in the front o' the boat; we was on Crane creek a little ways
above the railroad trestle. Buddy was leaning out over the water
and aiming his shotgun up in the sky and saying Pow! Pow!
Pretending like he was shooting ducks. He started tossing that
shotgun around—switching from shooting right handed to shoot-

ing left handed—and kept on blasting away with his mouth at them make-believe ducks. But one time he missed—I mean he missed the shotgun. Hit fell in the water and went straight to the bottom.

"Buddy cussed and then he about cried. Oh what is we gonna do now? Poppa'll beat the tar outta me if I lose that shotgun. We gotta dive down and git it. Only you know I can't dive under water Gordon... on account o' my weak eardrums; they can't stand the pressure. You gotta do it, Gordon—dive down and git that shotgun. I sho will appreciate it.

"Le'me tell you that water was cold, hardly above freezing, and it was deep, near 'bout ten feet. And you couldn't see nothing—not after you got the mud all stirred up on the bottom. I musta dove down there five or six times; kept feeling around on the bottom till my lungs like to busted. My whole body started getting numb from the cold; I reckon I was turning blue. Just before I was about to freeze to death Buddy said Tha's o.k., Gordon; come on git out and putcha clothes back on and le's go home. I appreciate you trying, he said.

"I still don't know why I done it. Maybe just to be doing something Buddy couldn't do. And once I got started I didn't wanna stop till I found that John Brown shotgun. But I didn't find it. A white boy from Eau Claire did after the water went down in the spring..."

"Buddy must have been grateful for your efforts," Amy said. "You must be a strong swimmer ..."

"I do all right. Lotta colored boys can't swim 'cause they ain't got no place white folks'll let 'em swim. At least they 'low me to swim in Crane creek in the middle o' the winter," he laughed. "Matter o' fact I swim there in the summer too. Both colored and white swim in Crane creek—and they dogs. Buddy takes his setter dog Mutt swimming at Crane creek; likes to throw him off the train trestle. He goes down deep—old Mutt does—but he always comes back up..."

"Yeah," I said, "I've seen them swimming at the green hole—Calhoun and Mutt. That dog sure likes to swim. Calhoun'll chase him in the water and try to pull him under, but most of the time he gets away. Mutt can swim almost as fast under the water as on top of it. I never saw a dog swim that good..."

"He's talking 'bout swimming at the green hole," Gordon said to Amy. "Colored people can't go there; just white folks and dogs—white folks dogs. Old Mutt's about as white folks as any dog can git. Yes-suh, he's white folks all right: thinks he owns the world and all the other critters better git off his proppity or least git outta his way when he comes sashaying along. I seen him stop and bark for five minutes at an old box terrapin in the woods. 'Course that old terrapin's all closed up and he don't move. Finally old Mutt he quit barking and stuck his nose up in the air and pranced around that terrapin. You dumb nigger—I knowed that's what old Mutt was thinking.

"One time, though, old Mutt liked to made a bad misjudgment. He was running ahead o' me and Buddy and peeing on the daisies alongside the Southern Railway tracks when we heard a train a'coming. Buddy called for Mutt to come over to the other side o' the tracks where we was at. Old Mutt picked up his ears and started loping 'cross the tracks but then he stopped right smack in the middle and commenced barking at that train that was coming straight at him. He didn't like that big black steam locomotive making all that racket blowing off smoke and steam and clanging his bell and blowing his whistle. He didn't think it was something white folks oughta have to put up with. Me and Buddy was yelling at him Mutt! Mutt! Come on boy! Git off that track! And he did—'bout half a second before that locomotive would've shredded him like a barbecue pig. Yeah, that dog's white folks; he'll jump off the train track when he has to, to save his butt, but he ain't gonna do it a second before he has to."

"That's a good analogy, Gordon," Amy said. "You're very perceptive. But there must be some white people in the South who don't believe in standing in the way of progress—who might even welcome it—who're just afraid to come out and say so.

We've got to appeal to them to stand up for what they know is right..."

Gordon gave me a this-lady's-crazy-as-hell-ain't-she smile and reached for another beer. Pigmeat opened one for him and one for himself.

"White folks set in they ways," Gordon said; "young ones same as old ones. Young ones might do something for devilment or to show off, but they ain't no different from the old ones when it comes right down to it.

"One time when his whole family was gone Buddy took me inside his house. Not just to the kitchen but to the dining room and the setting room and this here room that had all these swords and old-timey guns hanging up on the wall. They was a bunch o' pitchers on the wall too, and one o'em was o' this old fellow with a lot of whiskers on his chin, and I axed Buddy if that were Abraham Lincoln and he said No, man, that's Jeff Davis; we wouldn't have no pitcher o' Abraham Lincoln in this house. And I said Abraham Lincoln freed the colored people; how come you don't like Abraham Lincoln? And he said 'Cause he was against the South..."

Pigmeat had been beating out a rhythm on the beer crate in front of him and now he began reciting this jive:

"Abraham Lincoln was
King o' the Jews,
He wore Lee Rider britches and
Brogan shoes,
He jumped on the train
With his dick in his hand,
Said 'scuse me folks,
I'm a railroad man."

"Hey man," I said, "there's a lady present."

"That's all right," Amy said—she didn't act offended, just a little perplexed—"I've heard that word before. In the North, though, they usually say cock."

I knew they did because I'd seen it in fuckbook comics. It just goes to show you how screwed up Yankees are about even the most basic things. Somebody ought to tell them that dick means pecker and cock means pussy.

Amy didn't want to get off the subject of Abraham Lincoln. "But Gordon, not all white people in Columbia feel that way about Abraham Lincoln. Isn't there a street named for him?"

I answered the question. "No, that's named for General Benjamin Lincoln—from the Revolution."

"That's right," Gordon said. "White folks don't have no truck with Abraham Lincoln. Try to act like he never lived—like this here's still slavery times. Only thing is they don't call you slave no more—just nigger—same difference. Well I ain't no slave and I ain't gonna have no white folks calling me nigger. I done told that to Doc MacNab—I sho did." He sat there a couple seconds nodding his head like he was congratulating himself and then he went on and told us all about it—though nobody asked him to.

"Doc MacNab had this short-haired bitch—a Doberman Pinscher—what kept running away. One day I was talking with Doc outside his back door when Miz MacNab hollered out the kitchen window and told him that Mr. Heathcliff was on the phone and that Robin was at his house and he had her tied up. Doc hollered back to Miz MacNab, said Tell him I'll send my nigger after her. Doc took his car keys outta his pocket but before he could say anything to me I said Mr. Doc, I ain't your nigger and I be obliged if you don't call me that. Doc, he looked sorta surprised and he said Well all right, Gordon. And I said I'll go git that dog.

"Doc MacNab like all white folks: when they see you they don't think *people*—they think *nigger*. And they *say* nigger when you ain't around—even when you *is* around if they talking to other white folks—'cause they don't see you then. You just disappear when white folks talk to one another—like you invisible."

Gordon was drinking too much and getting himself all worked up. I could tell he was going to be a mean drunk and I started getting concerned—especially when I noticed a couple other big niggers standing in the doorway glaring at us. I had to figure how to get me and Amy out of there before the party got too rough. I shook out a Lucky and stuck it in my mouth and as I was putting the pack back in my pocket, Pigmeat grabbed my arm; I shook out another fag which he snatched away real quick; I gave him a light before I lit my own teege. He never said a word. He was the most ungrateful and disrespectful nigger I'd ever met.

"Some white folks think they got a license to call you nigger to your face," Gordon went on. "The police do. One time me and Buddy was up at Mr. Hinnant's putting gas in the Packard and this depitty sheriff was cussing out this colored fellow, calling him a shiftless no 'count nigger; saying You better straighten out nigger; saying Next time I gonna put you *under* the jail nigger; saying You hear what I say nigger? Well I heard what that depitty said and so did Buddy. I told him when we was driving back to the place—told Buddy—Ain't no motherfucker ever gonna talk to me like that; anybody ever calls me nigger's gonna get his goddam head busted open."

Amy didn't flinch. "And what did Buddy say?" she asked after she took a little sip from her warm Atlantic ale.

"He didn't say nothing. But he acted like he was thinking Why you telling me this? I never call you nigger—he never said it, just acted like he was thinking it. Naw, he don't call me nigger, but he thinks it. He don't call nobody nigger to they face; he's just as nice as pie when he's around colored people. He even calls Mr. Miles—old colored fellow lives next to the place—calls him Mister, Buddy does. 'Cept when he's talking about him to another buckra—then he ain't Mister a'tall, just that nigger. That's who he was last week when Buddy was talking about him to the cracker that works for Mr. Hinnant; Buddy clean forgot I was in the car. They shoulda gone inside the filling station if they was gonna talk about niggers. Colored people ain't allowed inside.

"White folks rub your nose in Jim Crow's shit every day. I swear I can't take it no more. I gotta find me a place where a colored man kin be a man. I'm gonna be like old Muddy Waters—just a Rollin' Stone. I'm gonna roll right out of this here Dixieland..."

Boy was he agitated. It was time for a little levity, I thought. I was kind of light headed from that corn whiskey. "So you gonna pull a Hank," I said and blew a stream of smoke straight up at the ceiling.

"Hunh?"

"You gonna pull a Hank Snow and be Movin' On."

"I ain't studying none o' that peckerwood music." The driving beat of "Safronia B" was coming from the Victrola in the front room. Gordon jumped up and kicked the dinette chair over towards the screen door and looked at Amy and said, "Let's dance."

"I-I'm sorry," she said. "We have to leave now. It's late..."

"You don't wanna dance with a colored person ..."

"No, it's not that..."

Just as I stood up Laura rushed in and grabbed Gordon by the arm. She and Ida must've been standing in the doorway watching us. "Gordon, we gotta go," Laura said; "take us home."

"I gotta dance," Gordon said. "Roscoe'll take y'all home. Go on..."

"Come on Gordon," Ida said; "please let's go. You gonna get in bad trouble, honey."

She was right about that.

18

I SOBERED UP real quick last night—actually it was early this morning—when Gordon asked Amy to dance and she said no. He acted like he wasn't going to take no for an answer and several other bucks had come out on the porch where we were and were leering at Amy. A couple of nigger girls were there too, but they were scared. Other niggers were looking at us from the kitchen and the hall. I figured we'd better make our exit through the screen door and down the stairs to the backyard. We had to move fast, I thought, before one of those bucks made a grab for Amy.

I put my hand on her shoulder to guide her in that direction but she turned the other way and smiled at Gordon and said, "Well, o.k. Just one dance. But really, it's getting late; I must go home after that." Before he could say anything she took him by the hand and began leading him through the house to the front room. I followed right behind Gordon as the niggers on the porch stood aside to let us pass. The ones in the hall ducked into the kitchen to get out of our way or backed into the front room ahead of us.

All the niggers who were dancing stopped when Amy and Gordon came into the front room. Some stepped aside to watch, but a lot of them headed straight out the front door. Almost all the nigger girls left. A couple of bucks were sitting down; one was Curtis, whose house it was. Curtis was now sitting on the sofa, bent over with his head in his hands like he wasn't feeling well. I went over and stood next to where Curtis was sitting while Gordon and Amy danced.

Amy led him into a shag and she danced just like a Southern girl. Gordon didn't try anything fancy. Amy kept him at arm's length and seemed to have him under control. The record was half over when they started, so they only danced for about a minute. When it was over she dropped his hand and smiled and said Thank you, Gordon, and headed towards me.

Then that ugly prune-colored nigger grabbed her around the waist. "May I have the next dance?" he said nasty and sarcastic.

"No!" Amy said firmly and tried to pull away.

Somebody grabbed my arm as I started towards her. It was Pigmeat. I slammed that little shit against an empty armchair. Then two big niggers jumped me: one grabbed my right forearm and spun me around and the other one wrapped both his arms around my neck and kneed me in the small of the back.

"Put on 'So Long'," I heard Prune Head say; "we gonna slow dance." But the Victrola was silent. I could hear cars cranking up outside; headlights shone through the windows. Most of the niggers were getting the hell out of there.

"Please," I heard Amy say, "some brave man help me!"

"Gordon!" I yelled as I struggled with the two bucks holding me. I could see him standing by himself in the middle of the room. I knew everybody else was watching him.

"I'm gonna get me a beer," he said and walked out of the room. As he did, Prune Head stuck his leg behind Amy's knees and put both his hands on her shoulder and pushed her down on the wood floor. She rolled over onto her stomach and Prune Head and another nigger grabbed her ankles.

"You black bastards!" I hollered as I kicked at the niggers holding me and swung out wildly with my one free arm. "They gonna electrocute every one of you fucking niggers!" Tears of anger and hate filled my eyes and my head jerked to the side as one of the niggers landed a terrific blow to my right cheek. The salty taste of blood was in my mouth. The next blow was even harder and must've caught me higher up, on the temple. It set off a blinding explosion in my head; for a split second I thought my eyes had popped out. Then I stopped thinking. Everything went blank.

When I came to I was lying on the floor in front of the sofa. The sounds I heard came from Curtis: "Oh what has you boys done," he moaned. "Y'all gonna put us all in the 'lectric chair." I slowly opened my eyes and made out four or five niggers sitting cross-legged or squatting in a semi-circle around me and facing Curtis who was still on the sofa.

"Well, well. Look like young Mr. Charlie done come to," Prune Head said.

I bolted up into a sitting position. "Where's Miss Kuhn?" I demanded.

"Miss Coon?" A red-haired freckle-faced nigger sneered, "All the Miss Coons done gone home. All we got lef' is Miss Ann; she in the bedroom fucking Gordon." All the niggers laughed except Curtis.

"I already got mine," Prune Head said, "and le' me tell you, soda cracker, never in all my borned days has I ever stuck my black dick in a pussy that was so pink and so silky."

The worst thing that could happen, I thought, had happened—except me and Amy getting killed. To avoid that I knew I'd have to use my head. Considering the blows it had taken, my head wasn't in too bad a condition. I was a little groggy but I wasn't in pain—maybe the alcohol in my system had anesthetized me—and I could still think. Actually I was thinking better than I was before I got hit. Self-preservation instincts were regulating my thinking now.

"Did you ever see such pretty silk drawers, white boy?" Prune Head waved a pair of pink panties in front of my nose. Then he stretched them across his face and looked through the waist into

the crotch. "Well I do believe: I believe they's a silk hair in here."
He made smacking noises with his lips. I just sat there and tried
to act nonchalant with my feet stretched out in front of me and
my arms extended behind me with my palms flat on the floor.

"Maybe you like to sniff these here," Pigmeat said to me and
dangled Amy's Cuban-heel shoes in my face. "That lady's got the
pinkest pink toes you ever did see. I sho do like white ladies."

"Me too," Freckle Face said. "I like big fat white ladies the
best, 'cause they go mo' white on 'em."

"Naw," Prune Head said, "skinny white ladies better, 'cause
the white's closer to the bone."

"Now me," this pecan-colored jig chimed in, "I likes old white
ladies—'cause they been white fo' so long."

"Young white ladies is good too," Prune Head said, "'cause
they got so long to be white—if they corporate with colored
mens... Like Miss Ann in there."

"They corporate with me, I corporate with them," Pecan
Head said. "I gonna be the next one to fuck Miss Ann. What
chew think about that, white motherfucker?"

I just gave him a blank look. I couldn't believe Amy was
cooperating with those apes.

"Lordy, lordy," Curtis wailed, "we going to the 'lectric chair
for shore."

"You right," Prune Head said, "but hit'll be worth it. You kin
fuck Miss Ann after Lonzo. After you done did it you'll know
hit's worth gitting your black ass fried for. And for extra
enjoyment we kin hogbutcher young Mr. Charlie here. They
can't burn you but one time."

"Let's do it!" Pigmeat squealed.

Prune Head held the back of his hand in front of my face; his
thumb and fingers were slightly curled. Sprack! A shiny four-
inch blade popped up. It was thin and pointed, the deadliest nig-
gerjigger I'd ever seen. I rolled away from him intending to jump
over Pigmeat and run for the backdoor. But some other nigger
caught my leg and pulled me back. Within seconds those bucks

had me spread eagled, pinned to the floor. Prune Head straddled me and touched the point of his shiv to my throat.

"Now we gonna see if young Mr. Charlie got any o' that white blood they's always talking about," he said. I felt a prick just above and to the left of my adam's apple as I was looking over his shoulder at this body flying through the screen in the window on the front porch.

It was Browder. He came through with his head down and somersaulted into Freckle Face. Browder's feet caught Freckle Face in the chest and slammed him into Prune Head, knocking him off me and causing him to drop the knife which clattered on the wood floor. I scrambled out from under Freckle Face and gave him a rabbit punch that stunned him but didn't knock him out. I felt a trickle of blood running down my neck.

Browder jumped on Prune Head and the two of them fought for the shiv—which in the course of the struggle got knocked under the sofa. When I got to my feet I faced off Pigmeat and two bucks. I could tell they were shook up by Browder flying in there like Captain Marvel.

"You niggers better run," I said. "The rest of the Ku Klux'll be here in two minutes."

"Oh lord, the Ku Klux," Curtis moaned. He was still sitting on the sofa; I don't think he'd gotten off it all night.

Pecan Head looked like he was about to spring at me when the siren went off. Whee-oo! Whee-oo! Whee-oo! A spotlight beam plunged through the tattered screen in the front window and hit Pigmeat square in the face. I think he was the first to run for the back door.

While the niggers scurried about I just stood there feeling greatly relieved. I felt my throat: it had about stopped bleeding. It was only a nick—no worse than what you might get shaving. I looked down at my feet and saw Amy's shoes and panties lying on the floor. I'd forgotten all about her. I kicked her panties under the sofa.

Just about then a policeman busted through the front door— breaking the lock as he popped it open—like in the movies. He

had a revolver in one hand and a slapjack in the other. "Freeze!"
he yelled over the screeching of the siren. "Don't nobody move!"
By then all the niggers except Curtis were hightailing it for the
back door. Curtis stood up in front of the sofa and froze.
Browder was standing a few feet from me breathing hard. We
knew the cop didn't mean us, but we froze too.

Pigmeat stopped dead in his tracks in the hall and the other
niggers piled into him. It wasn't because the cop with the pistol
had told them to stop, but because another cop was coming
straight at them across the back porch with a sawed-off pump
shotgun leveled at them. He made them turn around and
marched them back into the front room.

"All you niggers put your hands on your head and get up
against that wall," the first cop said. It was hard to hear him with
that siren going. He looked around and located this figure
standing in the front door and said, "Ray, you go turn off that
spotlight and the sireen like I showed you how." It was Radar.

As the cop with the shotgun was lining up Pigmeat and Curtis
and the other four bucks against the wall, the policeman with the
revolver took a look at Browder and then me. "Well I be
doggone," he said, "if it ain't them boys that was shooting that
Luger down by the canal. Now how in the *hell* did y'all get in a
mess like this?"

Before we could say anything Amy walked in from the
bedroom with Gordon following her at a respectful distance.
You'd think nothing had happened to her. Her dress was on
straight; her hair was combed and the barrettes were in place; the
gold chain and locket were around her neck. Except for her being
barefooted she looked the same as she did when we first walked
into that house.

"Officer," she addressed the cop with the pistol, "what is the
meaning of this?"

"Ma'am, we got a complaint that there's been a ... an assault
in this house."

"Well I assure you that no one here has been assaulted. I demand that you put away your weapons immediately. These people are my friends..."

"Ma'am," the cop interrupted, "that boy there's got blood on his neck." He pointed to me and for a second she looked like she might lose her composure.

"I'm o.k.," I said bravely.

"He's o.k.," she said. "Obviously it's just a scratch. He must have gotten it when he was wrestling with the other boys. There's broken glass on the floor. I cut my foot on it when I was dancing... with Cap."

Boy could she lie! At first I couldn't figure out why she was doing it, but pretty soon it dawned on me that even a Yankee girl wouldn't want it known that she'd been fucked by niggers—even if it *was* forcible rape. The poor lady was trying to protect her reputation and I decided to help her. Browder was standing there dumbfounded—I didn't know how much he'd seen or heard—and I tried to signal him to go along with us.

"I reckon I better take a look at that foot," the policeman said as he holstered his pistol and stuck the slapjack in his belt.

"I beg your pardon," Amy said indignantly. "I have no intention of exhibiting myself to every bozo who charges in here off the street." Then she turned to me and said, "Cap, please hand me my shoes."

As I brought them over to her I caught Browder's eye. He got the message.

"O.k., Cap," the policeman said, "you tell me: did them niggers attack you?"

"No sir, not really. We were just having a friendly wrestling match ..."

"Ain't it against the law for niggers to rassle with white people?" the cop with the shotgun said.

"It most certainly is not," Amy said. "One may wrestle with whomever one chooses to wrestle with in the privacy of one's home..."

"Now wait a dadgum minute!" The first cop acted exasperated. His partner lowered his shotgun and the niggers up against the wall gradually dropped their hands—except Curtis who kept his on top of his head. The first cop pointed his thumb over his shoulder at Radar and said to Amy, "That boy there flagged us down on Blossom street and said his buddy looked in the window o' this house and seen their friend lying on the floor like he was dead—with a passel o' niggers sitting around him and talking about... assaulting a white lady."

"Well I assure you I have not been *assaulted*—and I doubt that word was used if these boys were engaged in ribald conversation—which they might well have been. Cap was merely resting as he lay on the floor. His friend simply misread the situation. One can understand his error, however..."

"That's right, officer," I said. "I was just resting. And nobody meant to do anything bad to Miss Kuhn—not really. Browder just made an honest mistake." The cop turned and looked at Browder.

Browder still seemed a little confused. He had to say something and he was smart to start off with the truth. "Well, the way it was," he said, "was me and Radar—Ray—passed Cap and this lady on Pickens street as they were turning off to here. We went on to the Friendly drive-in for a little while and then went down to Sox's where we were supposed to meet Cap. But he never showed up. People down there told us he hadn't been there before we got there, either. Well I knew he was out with... uh ... a lady who knew a lot of colored people. And I got kind of worried. And I said to Ray, Let's go back to where we saw Cap turn off and see if we can find him and see if he's o.k. Well we turned down this road and saw Cap's Plymouth parked in front of this house. I told Ray to wait in the car and I'd sneak up on the porch and look in the window and see what was going on.

"Well, like they said, I saw Cap stretched out there like he was dead, and those colored boys were talking... you know... like boys do, and I guess I just jumped to the conclusion. I ran back to Ray and told him to go get the police and I'd stay here and watch. When I saw this colored boy and Cap start rassling again I thought they were fighting and I jumped in to help Cap. I made a mistake. I sho am sorry..."

"Well if that don't beat all," the cop said and turned to his partner. "O.k., Shep, go out to the car and radio headquarters to cancel that backup. Now don't none of you niggers leave yet; I gotta get all y'all's names for my report."

"Uh, officer," Browder said, "me and Ray gotta get home..."

"All right, go ahead," the cop said. "I already got y'all's names."

I waved and grinned at Browder as he left with Radar. I didn't blame him for wanting to get out of there before he got caught in a lie. We'd have a lot to talk about later.

The first cop took out his pocket notebook and started to take names while his partner was out front in the squad car talking to police headquarters. All the niggers were still standing next to the wall—except Gordon, who was standing on the other side of Amy. The cop looked at him and said, "O.k., nigger, what's your name?"

Gordon just stood there with this blank look on his face.

"I said what's your name, nigger."

Gordon reached in his back pocket and pulled out his wallet and started toward the cop holding it out in his left hand.

"I didn't ask for no identification," the policeman said. "Just tell me your name, nigger. What is it?"

I didn't notice Gordon's right fist was cocked until he let that cop have it in the stomach. As the cop doubled over, Gordon hit him with a left to the jaw. The lawman crumpled to the floor unconscious and Gordon leaned over and picked up the wallet he'd dropped. He glanced around at the people in the room who were all staring at him in stunned amazement and said, "Don't nobody tell 'em who I am." Then he turned on his heel and sprinted towards the back door.

Some of the other niggers wanted to do likewise, but Amy blocked their way. "Don't any of you leave," she said looking square at Prune Head. "Anyone who does will be in big trouble.

I'll see to it." They all backed up against the wall again, trying to get as far away from Amy and the fallen policeman as they could. Amy looked at me. I knew she was thinking How long's it going to take Gordon to get to the Packard and start it rolling down that hill?

"We better do something to help this officer," I said. I walked slowly to where he was lying and bent over and unbuttoned his collar and loosened his tie. He seemed to be breathing o.k. I stretched out his legs and laid him flat on his back and reached over and picked up an *Ebony* magazine off the sofa and began fanning him with it.

"I'd better go outside and tell his partner," Amy said to me. Then she looked at the niggers. "Don't any of you leave," she repeated. "Curtis, don't you let anybody leave."

"N-no ma'am, I won't," he said. They must've come to their senses because nobody tried anything.

The fallen cop began to stir just as his partner came bounding through the front door. "My god, Zeke," he said. "What they done to you?"

"It was that yellow son-of-a-bitch," Zeke the cop said as he sat up blinking his eyes. I knew how he felt.

"I'm gonna call an ambulance," his partner said.

"Like hell you are. Ain't no nigger gonna put me in the horsepital. I'm all right. Gimme a hand." Zeke grabbed Shep's arm and pulled himself up.

"Would you like a glass of water?" Amy asked.

"Now look here, little lady," Zeke said ignoring the question, "I done had enough of your Northern ways. A crime's been committed here tonight: an officer of the law's been assaulted and battery'd. Now there ain't no doubt about that. You and your little boyfriend and all your nigger friends're material witnesses and I aim to ask y'all some questions and y'all're gonna answer 'em..."

"I'm perfectly willing to cooperate," Amy said.

"Then tell me who that nigger was?"

"The young man who hit you? I don't know."

"What d'ya mean you don't know? You was cavorting with him all night..."

"I most certainly was not. Officer, I'm an anthropologist. I came here tonight on scientific business."

"Dancing barefoot—that's scientific bidness?"

"Yes. I must learn the steps myself in order to describe them correctly. It may surprise you, officer, but in Africa where these dances originated all the women dance barefooted."

"Was you dancing barefoot when you was in that room alone with that brass ankle?"

"Of course not. I was conducting an interview. It was so noisy out here with the music blaring and the boys wrestling and horsing around that we had to go somewhere else—where it was quiet—to talk. So we went in there..."

"So you was conducting uh interview? Le'me see ya notes."

"I haven't any. It's all in my head. I shall write it down when I return home tonight. Taking notes during an interview can inhibit the flow of information—it can have an intimidating effect on the subject..."

"But you don't even remember the name of the suspect..."

"The subject? I didn't ask his name. We anthropologists are not concerned with individual identity; we seek general scientific truth. Furthermore, we guarantee the anonymity of our subjects. I didn't want to know his name and I didn't ask it."

"O.k., o.k.," Zeke the cop said; he was really exasperated now. "We wasting time. Cap, who was that nigger? Tell me the truth, boy."

"I-I don't know sir." I was glad he didn't press me. He was in a hurry and went on to the niggers. His partner Shep was standing glaring at them with his hands on his hips. He must've left his shotgun in the squad car. Shep's pistol holster was unsnapped for a fast draw.

"Whose house is this here?" Zeke demanded.

"It's Curtis's," Amy answered and Curtis meekly raised his hand to identify himself. "It's quite possible," she went on, "that Curtis doesn't know..."

"Will you hush up! Who was that nigger Curtis?"

"Uh... uh..." The cat got his tongue.

"It's traditional in the Negro community to receive uninvited guests..."

"I told you to be quiet!"

"... even strangers..."

"Shut up!... ma'am."

Amy stopped talking then but she kept her eyes on Curtis. Finally he got some words out. "Ossifer, I don't know who that yellow nigger was. That's the truth. When you has a party the word gits around and people you don't even know... They musta been a hundred people here tonight... I never seen that nigger what hit you before in my life..."

"You, boy!" Officer Zeke pointed at Pigmeat. "Who was that nigger?"

"Naw suh... I don't know suh."

One after another Zeke questioned the bucks lined up against the wall. I really enjoyed seeing those niggers squirm. Each one had to decide what was the best bet for staying out of the electric chair: lying or telling the truth. If they told the truth and the police caught Gordon and hooked him up to a lie detector and he told them what had really happened that night—they'd all fry. So they all lied. They said they didn't know who Gordon was. He just appeared a little after midnight with some other colored people they didn't know. They all noticed that he was a good dancer.

Amy volunteered the information that the suspect told her he'd learned the boogie shuffle in Charleston county. He was definitely from the lowcountry; there were unmistakable traces of Gullah dialect in his speech, she said.

"Well, one thing's for certain," officer Zeke said to her; "that nigger sho didn't wanna give me his name. I bet there's a bulletin out on him. We'll get him. And when we do I'm gonna make sure he gets ten extra years on the chain gang for what he done here tonight." Then he turned to his partner. "Shep, I reckon we

better call the paddy wagon and take all these niggers down to
the station house for further questioning..."

"In that case," Amy broke in, "I'm going to use Curtis's phone
to call my lawyer. He'll be here in a minute. I won't have you
violating the civil rights of my friends." She turned and started
toward the kitchen.

"Hold it lady," Zeke said, "no need to do that. I think we'll
just take down all the names and addresses of the witnesses. We'll
summons y'all when the time comes."

"That's sensible," she said. "My name is Professor Amy Kuhn
and I live at..."

He interrupted her to ask how to spell her first name but not
her last. After he'd taken down her name and address, I gave him
mine. While he was writing it down, Amy turned to the niggers
and said, "I think it would be a good idea if you boys would leave
as soon as you give the officer your name and address. Curtis
needs some rest. We all do; let's all go home."

But Amy and I stayed until after the last buck had walked out
the front door. Amy pointed to the door as officer Zeke was
putting away his notebook. "I trust the city of Columbia will do
something to fix that door..."

"Oh they ain't no need for y'all to worry 'bout that," Curtis
spoke up; "I kin fix that door. Hit's been broke before."

Both cops gave the busted lock a sideways glance as they
walked through the doorway but neither said a word. Amy and
I followed them out after saying goodnight to Curtis.

"Cap," officer Zeke called to me from the front passenger seat
of the squad car.

"Yessir?"

"There's something fishy going on here..." He paused for me
to say something but I didn't. "If you think of anything you
wanna tell me, call me at the station."

"Yessir, I will—if I think of anything."

"Be careful, boy. You done got in bad company. I hate to see
it."

"Goodnight, gentlemen," Amy said to them over my shoulder. Officer Shep gunned the squad car and spun it around in Curtis's yard and headed for Pickens street.

"I don't know what to say, Cap." Amy seemed to collapse when she got into the front seat of the Plymouth.

"You don't have to say anything." I started the engine and backed out of Curtis's yard. For several blocks neither one of us spoke.

"It's a nice night." She broke the silence. "It'll be dawn soon."

"You gonna be o.k.?" I asked.

"Sure."

"Well I just want you to know that if there's anything you want me to do, I'll do it." I really felt sorry for her even though she'd brought it all on herself. I hated those niggers and I wanted them all to fry—including Gordon. As I was pulling up to her garage apartment I suddenly realized she didn't have on any underpants.

I walked her to the door and she fumbled in her purse for the key. Finally she found it and opened the door. "Cap, you're a jewel," she said, her voice quivering slightly, "a diamond in the rough." She hugged me and gave me a wet kiss on the side of the face in front of the ear the way Momma does. Then she stepped inside and closed the door.

Amy Kuhn sure has long hair, I thought as I drove home, but she's like that Short Haired Woman that Lightning Hopkins sings about—nothing but trouble.

19

THERE WAS A CAR parked on the street in front of our house. I saw it as I crossed Park street intersection after taking Amy home. Oh shit! I said to myself and jerked my foot off the accelerator; it was Dr. MacNab's Packard. How the hell did Gordon know where I lived? And what did he want? He sure as hell couldn't expect me to help him after he'd abandoned me to those bloodthirsty bucks—not to mention what he did to Amy. I wanted to kill the bastard. As the Plymouth coasted in behind the Packard I wished I had my Luger; then I'd just get out and walk over to the Packard and pump his high-yellow hide full of nine-millimeter holes. Dead men tell no tales. I could see the headline in *The State*: Local Lad Bags Fugitive Negro.

But I didn't have the Luger and I had to be careful. I made sure all the windows were up and the doors locked as the Plymouth rolled to a stop about three car-lengths behind the Packard. I kept the headlights on and the motor running. Maybe I'd run over him as soon as he got out of the Packard; it'd depend on how he looked, I decided. The funny thing was, the fellow who got out of Dr. MacNab's Packard didn't look much like Gordon. It was Uncle Lewie.

Uncle Lewie had a piece of paper in his hand as he walked toward me. I rolled down the window.

"Clarence, old buddy," he said, "I need you to help me return this car to Doc MacNab's place."

"Where's Gordon?"I asked.

"He's got my car. I sent him up to my place at the lake..."

All of this should've surprised me—and I guess it did, a little—but somewhere in the back of my mind it was starting to make sense. "Did he tell you what he did tonight?" I asked.

"Yeah. He said he cold-cocked a police."

"That ain't all, Uncle Lewie."

"He had some trouble with that woman me and you been looking for. Here, I wanna return your picture." He handed me the copy of the photo of Amy and Dr. Summerville. "I never thought we'd find her this way..."

"He raped her," I said.

"Did you see it?"

"No, but..."

"Even if he did, Clarence, I gotta help him..."

"I think I know why..."

"That's good. Then I don't have to explain—'cause we ain't got much time. We gotta get this car back to Doc MacNab's place before people start getting up out there. They get up early —before daybreak—to milk the cows..."

"Will it start?"

"Naw, battery's dead. You gotta push me... On second thought, lemme push *you*; you drive the Packard and I'll follow in your car. You been out to Doc's place, ain't you? You know his dogs..."

"I know one of his dogs, Mutt..."

"You can drive the Packard into Doc's garage and walk outta there without raising a ruckus. I'll wait for you at his gate. Come on, boy, let's go. Get in the Packard... Oh yeah: leave the keys over the sunvisor when you park it in the garage. Gordon says he always does that."

• • •

I did as Uncle Lewie told me and everything went off without a hitch. I parked the Packard in Calhoun's garage next to the Ford stationwagon and patted Mutt on the head when he came over to investigate. A couple other dogs appeared, but none of them bothered me as I took off walking for the gate on the county road where Uncle Lewie was waiting. I got into the front passenger seat of the Plymouth and let Uncle Lewie drive back to his house.

"In a little while," he said, "I'm gonna send a colored fellow out to tell Gordon's grandpaw that he went to Blythewood to pick squash..."

"But he's really up at the lake?"

"Yeah. Sunday I'm gonna drive him up to Oconee county where he was born and we gonna be at the army recruiting office there when it opens on Monday morning and sign him up..."

"But you gotta be 17, and Gordon's got a couple of months to go. You gotta have a birth certificate..."

"All that's easy to fix, Clarence. By the time that cop finds out who it was that hit him, Gordon'll be a soldier in the U. S. Army. There's a war on now; the army ain't particular about minor offenses—especially if the charges get dropped. I can slip that police some money and Gordon can pay me back with an allotment. We'll work it out."

"You got it all figured, Uncle Lewie," I said as he stopped the car in front of his house. He smiled and clapped me on the shoulder. Then he got out and I slipped over into the driver's seat.

"Now don't forget," he said as I was about to drive off, "you and me's going to that stock-car race in Darlington on Labor Day."

"I won't forget," I said. "Right now I'm going home and get me some sleep." And that's what I did.

It was around noon when I woke up but I didn't get out of bed until I heard Momma come in from work at 12:15. My back ached a little and I was pretty sore in the shoulders and chest; the muscles in my arms and legs felt strung out and the inside of my cheek was raw. There was a bump on my temple at the hairline but it wasn't too noticeable. The cut on my throat wasn't noticeable at all with the blood cleaned away. All in all, I wasn't in too bad a shape considering I almost got killed.

The aroma of fried chicken drifted into my room as I washed up and got dressed. I wasn't very hungry. I didn't go downstairs until after I heard Momma come back from driving Agnes home. Then I picked up the photo of Amy and Dr. Summerville and went down to the breakfast room

Momma was sitting at the table looking over the mail. The food was still in the kitchen.

"Hey sugar," she said.

"Morning Momma—or I reckon it's afternoon..."

"What've you got there?"

I handed her the photo. As soon as she looked at it she said, "Why that's Dr. Summerville. Isn't that an attractive young woman he's with... Speaking of Dr. Summerville, I got some things from him in the mail today: employment application, sample contract, job description, fringe benefits... He has an appointment set up for me with his hospital board on Wednesday morning—in Plattville, New Jersey. Let's you and me talk about it over dinner. You want to help me get it?"

We went into the kitchen where Momma got the chicken out of the frying pan and I got the biscuits from the oven and the corn-on-the-cob out of the steamer. We brought that stuff to the table and then Momma went back to the kitchen for the rice and gravy. A pitcher of tea was already on the table and ice was in the glasses; I poured us each a glass of iced tea and sat down.

Momma sat down and helped her plate. I did too, but I didn't take much and Momma noticed it. "I'm not so hungry," I said. "Besides, I got a lot to tell you."

I told her everything—only I didn't tell her about what Uncle Lewie and I did this morning and I didn't mention the wild-goose chase to the Backwoods Inn, which was an idea I got from Uncle

Lewie. I just left Uncle Lewie out of the story entirely. I told
Momma all about Dr. Summerville's Communist background
and all the details of my date with Amy and the terrible experiences we had last night.

Momma stopped eating about halfway through the story. She
got up and examined my neck when I told her about Prune Head
trying to cut my throat. She was relieved to see that I wasn't hurt
bad, but she was truly horrified by what I told her—especially
how I'd lied to the police.

"Clarence," she said with fear written all over her face,
"you've got to go to the police and tell them all you know about
Gordon..."

"Momma, I promised Amy I wouldn't. It's to protect her
reputation. If they catch him and hook him up to a lie detector..."

"You *know* they're going to catch him, Clarence..."

"If they do, it won't be because of me. Actually I hope they
do. If it wasn't for Amy's reputation I'd be glad to help them
catch him. I'd like to testify in court against Gordon and all those
other niggers..."

"Please don't use that word."

"...but she wants to keep it a secret. She doesn't want people
to know what happened to her..."

"Too many women feel that way," Momma said sadly. "They
won't report sexual abuse; they're too ashamed. Sometimes they
blame themselves... It's very chivalrous of you, though, to try to
help her keep her secret. I'm proud of you for that, sugar, but I
don't think it's wise and I'm not sure she's worth it."

She let out an audible sigh and took a sip of iced tea. "You're
really in trouble now, Clarence: you're in trouble with the law.
I've got to take you away from this place—so you can make a
new start. Maybe New Jersey would be..."

"Momma, excuse me, but you're not thinking too clearly. I
know you're upset, but don't you remember it was New Jersey
people that got me into this mess? If it hadn't been for Dr. Summerville and Amy, I never would've wound up in that nig...

colored house with a knife to my throat. What happened there happens all the time in New Jersey. All the parties up there are integrated. Boys and girls run around in gangs and cut one another up with knives all the time. They're always in trouble with the law. They kill schoolteachers. Don't you remember that movie we saw—'City Across the River'? Momma, you wouldn't want to take me up there and expose me to all that..."

"Oh Clarence, you're exaggerating..."

"Maybe a little bit—but you know it's the truth. They don't have segregation up there so what they have is race riots. You throw white and colored people together and you get a situation like last night. That's normal for up North. Things like that don't happen down here unless some Yankee lady comes along and ignores our customs and tries to change them and influences an unsuspecting young boy to go along with her. Well Momma, I promise you I've learned my lesson. I'm never gonna see Amy Kuhn again as long as I live if I can help it. I don't wanna see any more New Jersey girls—white or colored—or New Jersey boys either. I don't wanna be mixed up with them in high school. I wanna stay in Columbia where it's safe and segregated. I swear I'll never go to another colored party..."

"I believe you, sugar. But I also believe that you could get into trouble no matter where you happened to be..."

"Momma, if you wanna talk about getting into trouble, think about what could happen with you and Dr. Summerville..."

"Clarence!"

"N-no, I don't mean that. I mean with his background and you being associated with him. What if you took that job and one of those congressional committees started investigating him. They'd find out about those Communist meetings he used to go to, and they'd get him kicked off the hospital staff. Then they'd find out that he was the one who recommended you, and they'd get you fired too—for being Un-American. You'd be a lot better off just staying here in Columbia until I start to college. Then you could go on off to California without depending on Communist connections. It won't be so long—only two more years."

"You mean three more years—you're just going into the tenth grade."

"Yes ma'am, but I plan to go to Carolina after the eleventh grade. You don't have to graduate from high school to get in; you just have to finish the eleventh grade. Zack McBain's going next year..."

"But sugar, you'd really have to be mature to do that. And you'd have to pass the university entrance exam, which probably isn't as easy as you think. Remember, you almost failed the ninth grade..."

"I can do it, Momma. Forget about the ninth grade. I'm gonna burn up the tenth and eleventh grades—I guarantee you. I'll do so well next year, they'll let me take extra courses in the eleventh grade. And I've decided to go to summer school next year; I'm not gonna piddle away next summer like I did this one. With all the extra credits I'll get, I might even have enough to graduate from high school year after next. But no matter what, I'm going to Carolina year after next—unless of course you take me to New Jersey. Then I don't know what I'll do."

"Are you really serious, sugar? You do sound determined."

"I sure am Momma."

"You know, Clarence, for some reason I believe you. I've noticed a change in you this week—even before today. Since you came back from Jacksonville you've seemed more capable, more confident. That Boy Scout trip seems to have done you a world of good. Of course, I'm distressed about the events of last night, but maybe even that awful experience will turn out to have been for the best... Anyway, sugar, I think we can forget about moving to New Jersey..."

"Thank you, Momma."

She smiled at me in a way I'd never seen her smile at me before. "Sugar, please step in the kitchen and get me the pencil that's next to the grocery list. I want to compose a telegram to Dr. Summerville to tell him to cancel the appointment on Wednesday. I'll need to call it in to Western Union today. I'll write him a letter later."

When I handed her the pencil she said, "Oh, I almost forgot: a letter for you came in the mail today." She handed me a small white envelope that was neatly addressed in blue ink; it was postmarked Atlanta, Georgia. I sat back down at my place and opened the envelope; the letter was written in ink on onion-skin paper—the kind you make carbon copies on.

Aug. 2, Wed.
5 P.M. (got to be formal, you know!)

Howdy boy!

Well, was I ever surprised when I looked over my letters that I got today to find one from you! You could have actually knocked me over with a feather. You were the last person in this whole wide world I would have expected to hear from.

Wish I had been in Jax. on July 23 to 29th only there is the little detail that we moved to Atlanta, Georgia on the first! Glad you liked Jax! But then of course you'd have to cause just look who's home town it is!!! (Laugh—the jokes over!!!) I love the beach too! If I had been there you probably would have seen me there cause all the kids get together and go down about everyday! See, Pops had been transferred to Atlanta last summer when we moved from Ft. Jackson. We didn't come to Atlanta with him; we went back to good ole Jacksonville and stayed every bit of a year & one extra month! Oh, I had so, so much fun that one year & a month! I could write a book!!!! There was never a dull second the whole time! Well, anyway we had to move up here (blast it!) and no sooner we get here and get settled they say for us to pack up our duds and go to—guess where! Knew you couldn't! Ft. Jackson!!!! Yes, sir, I is acoming back (you poor people, you!) Thought you had finally gotten rid of me, huh?? I'll probably be there at the end of the month! Dad's already there now! Start shining up the old brass band, boy!

Yeah, I managed to pass (don't understand it myself though) and I'll be in the 10th grade, but the only trouble is, is that Pops wants me to go to Dreher and I want to go to Columbia High!! Parents are a problem, I'll clue ya.

Gad, I just got through eating a hard ole green apple—do I ever feel sick!

You'll just have to put up with this stationery of mine but after the rest of the family digs in "my" box of stationery there's not a speck left or any to be found! Finding things in this house is as bad as finding a needle in a haystack!

Anita was telling me the other day how the old crowd has "split"! Kerry's gone, Mandy about to get married (rather old for that, what say!) and everything! Hope everyone's the same cause I surely haven't changed a speck! Still same ole Gunter!!! No hope, I guess!!!

Hey, guess what! Pops was gonna get a T.V. set the other day but they said Columbia doesn't have T.V. yet! I say, still an ole hick town!! Seems as though you all would have it cause Jax. has had it for over a year and a half now, for sure!!!

Well, man (25 cents charge here!) that apple is getting me down! (I'll learn someday not to eat green apples, maybe!) Besides that the page is coming to an end!

I'll see ya in a while — Till then

Just me,
Juanita

P.S. Be good, if that's possible!

I folded up the letter and put it back in the envelope. Momma was counting the words she'd written for the telegram. When she finished I said, "Momma, I'm gonna need your Belks charger-plate. I gotta buy me some clothes for school."

I will open my mouth in a parable:
I will utter dark sayings of old:
Which we have heard and known,
And our fathers have told us.

PSALM 78: 2-3